D0810843

"PUT YOUR ARMS AROUND ME," HE WHISPERED.

Her eyes were huge, staring up at him, her face pale. Her lips trembled, and Sam knew with a sinking feeling that he'd stepped over an invisible line. He'd never tasted a woman like Emma. . . .

Her hands fluttered at his sides, then, impatient with her slow, untutored movements, Sam wrapped her arms around him and held her.

Hungry for her mouth, he bent his head and brushed his lips against hers, feeling the silky warmth enfold him. The soft rush of her breath stopped. . . .

"Open for me, Emma," he whispered, desperate for more than a taste.

She breathed unsteadily, her body taut against his, and Sam found her legs with his thigh, inserting it slowly, slowly, until she rested upon him. He nudged her gently, wanting more, and then Emma's tongue touched his. . . .

Be Mine

Cait Logan

A Dell Book

Published by
Dell Publishing
a division of
Bantam Doubleday Dell Publishing Group, Inc.
1540 Broadway
New York, New York 10036

ISBN: 0-440-22242-7

Printed in the United States of America

Published simultaneously in Canada

July 1997

10   9   8   7   6   5   4   3   2   1

OPM

Author's Foreword

This book is dedicated to those immigrant women who entered a new life in the American West yet were bound by Old World traditions. They brought with them that which had been passed down to them from their mothers and gave those traditions to their children. They met husbands from different heritages or, like Emma's Sam, men who sprang from the wilderness. With love, these immigrant women handcrafted lives and traditions together as painstakingly as they would stitch a fine quilt filled with hand-carded wool.

Each time I look at my mother's artistic starched crocheting or my grandmother's intricately stitched quilt, I remember my grandparents' story—they began with sixty cents and a cow and created a legacy. When he had lived his life, my grandfather remembered my grandmother on their wedding day. She was just sixteen, and he recalled, "She was the most beautiful woman I had ever seen."

My thank you to the Germans from the Russia Historical Society and to the Montana Historical Society and the Rivers and Plains Historical Society of Fort Benton, Montana, and the Powell County, Montana, Historical Society.

Prologue

Seattle 1875

"I will not provide your father with his desired grandchildren. I will never sire a child," Sam stated firmly to his wealthy spoiled fiancée. Delphinia had been pushing him to begin the children her father required as soon as possible. An expert at business contracts, Sam wanted the matter of children settled before their marriage. Long ago he had decided that no child would share his blood—Sam was the bastard son of a Blackfoot woman named Feather, and a big rough *mountain man*—Harry Taggart.

His fiancée volleyed more threats, and the door slammed behind her, leaving Sam alone with his thoughts. The profitable alliance with her logger-baron father was over. In the background Seattle's late-afternoon waterfront noises filtered into the back room Sam used as an office. February rain drizzled against the window, shrouding the harbor from him. Over the waves crashing against the wharf, a chowder vendor hawked soup from the street, calling out that sourdough rolls were included in the price.

Sam braced a well-polished expensive boot on a crate. At twenty-eight he had tucked away a tidy amount to start his own business, and he knew what he wanted— power, money, and respect. He studied his handcrafted boot, the mark of a successful man, and reached to dust away a fleck of sawdust from the mills. He took good care of his boots because at one time he had been a young boy in the Union Army, shaking as Civil War cannons and balls blasted over his head. Then, Sam had worn rags. He'd taught himself to read from a bloody Bible and had promised that one day he would wear fine boots, that he would be powerful and rich, and that nothing would stop him.

Yet along the way to surviving cattle drives, the war, bloody whaling decks in hellish storms, and more recently the life of the logger-baron's top man, he'd seen what he was inside. He didn't want to pass his inheritance to a child. The old label came to taunt him: *"Harry Taggart's half-blood bastard."*

He had begun to wonder if he could escape what burned inside him—the knowledge that he could be as savage as his father. Through the years, he'd pasted himself together with dreams of going back to Montana Territory and wiping his success into the faces of those who had shown him what he was—Harry Taggart's bastard.

The image of Feather, his mother—raped, scalped, and dead in Montana Territory—ripped across his mind. Another image tore into him—his father had lived up to his *mountain-man* legends, savagely killing the murderers.

Sam expertly flipped the knife that Harry had tossed to him with the order, *"Make your mark, boy."*

"No more," twelve-year-old Sam had said. Harry's slap had knocked him to the ground, and from that day Harry could not bear to look at Sam.

Sam had survived without love; he didn't need it. He needed a woman as cold-blooded as himself, educated to be the perfect business wife. With a woman wanting money and power at his side, he intended to make his mark; he'd had enough of poverty. He took his comb and carefully parted his mussed hair, the mark of a gentleman with breeding.

But every time Sam looked in the mirror, he saw Harry Taggart's features stamped on him—the same jutting cheekbones and fierce eyebrows, the same come-and-get-me jaw.

Sam tossed away the comb, dismissing his office on the waterfront and the subtle scent of sex with his ex-fiancée. At times, he could smell the lodgepole pines in the Bitterroot Mountains and the scent of wild roses and feel the fresh mountain wind tugging at his bare skin. At times, he hungered for the taste of roast camas root and cowcatcher cakes and the scent of sweetgrass clinging to his buckskins. He shifted again, uneasy with the premonition that running from Montana and his past would haunt him forever—unless he returned to clear it.

Chapter One

May 1881

Sam Taggart hated playing a dead man, flat on his back in Montana Territory's cold mud. Caught out in the open without the protection of trees or rocks, he had faked injury at the first glint of a rifle barrel and the hiss of a bullet slicing by his head. Now, stretched out in early May's mud and snow, he waited for the bushwhacker to approach.

A meadowlark trilled, the first sound to break the early morning silence after the rifle shots. The chinook, the warm wind that had melted the snow quickly, swept across the rolling hills of the valley, surrounded by mountains. The valley used to be peaceful—the name *Deer Lodge* derived from a word in the Shoshone Indian language that meant "white-tailed deer's lodge."

With the mining boom in full gear and mountain towns springing up and dying just as quickly, a lone rider would be like "easy picking." Sam had never been easy, and on his way to finish the past with Harry, he wasn't exactly in a good mood.

Sam lay still, cursed the bushwhacker, and wondered how much money it would cost to clean and repair his greatcoat and suit. Whoever had sent those small-caliber rifle bullets peppering at him was going to pay for his clothing repairs and a good shine on his boots. Partially covering his face, the straight brim of his spotless western hat slid into the mud. Through the bullet hole, he saw May sunshine skimming the rolling hills to the south. Just past the stand of lodgepole pines and fir trees, the Big T—Harry Taggart's spread—lay at the base of the mountains, fed water by the Dancing Miranda stream.

The valley was sacred to the Indians, hot springs bubbling up out of the ground, and for years white man and Indian had lived in peace. No one fought in the valley, though the countryside was torn by wars.

Sam's money belt nudged his stomach, and he forced his snarl back down in his throat. He spat away a drop of mud clinging to his lip. Against his back, he felt the familiar weight of the big knife his father had tossed to him years ago; the bushwhacker was going to pay.

Sam tried not to shiver as cold mud seeped into the clothing on his back and slid down the collar of his immaculate shirt. He inched his hand toward the coiled whip that had slid from his shoulder during the ambush. The whip was a gift from a Spanish don, and Sam preferred the quiet, deadly hiss of it and his knife for protection. He lay still as Tenkiller nudged his face. The black stallion's nudges could throw men yards from where they were standing, but at the moment he was playful. "Go away," Sam ordered.

Tenkiller lifted his head and stared toward the sound

of approaching footsteps. Trained by Sam's mother's people, the Blackfeet, and his father, a reformed mountain man, Sam noted the noisy careless approach. Judging from the sound of the bushwhacker's stride and the branches breaking beneath his feet, he was small and light.

Tenkiller nickered and began high-stepping toward the fast-moving footsteps. The stallion had always picked the wrong times to show off his fancy training as a racing trotter.

The hat was lifted away from his face, and Sam reached up to grab a fistful of shirt. With his other hand, he jerked away her scarred small rifle. The girl's battered hat slid from her head to her back, tethered by the thong around her neck.

The girl scowled down at him with stormy blue eyes, her thin hands clawing at his wrist. "Too bad you're not buzzard bait," she stated levelly.

Sam eased to his feet, cold mud sucking at his backside. He held the girl at arm's length and scooped up his hat by pushing a fingertip through the bullet hole. He studied the hole and brooded on the hat's good price. "Missy, you are about to learn it isn't polite to bushwhack. I'm paddling your backside until you can't sit down."

She scrunched her pale face into a frown and flopped back a black frizzy braid over her ragged coat. "I'd rather be a good bushwhacker than a low-down skunk of a rustler. You come sniffing around my dad's ranch, and you'll be on the other end of my rifle sights every time."

Sam hauled her along to where Tenkiller stood. He

placed his hat on the ornate silver-tipped saddle horn, grimaced, then flipped open his saddlebags and extracted a neatly folded towel. He wiped mud from his head and down his backside, then shoved the towel into her hands. "My boots are expensive, custom made, and I don't like having mud on them, little girl—"

She drew herself to her full height, glaring at him. She wiped her sleeve across her nose and spat. "I ain't no little girl, mister. I'm twelve—that's almost a woman full grown."

The thin angular girl had a long stretch ahead of her before she came close to anything feminine. The wind washed her odor against Sam. "Fine. Take that towel and wipe off my boots."

She eyed him shrewdly. "How much?"

"How much for what?" The cold sweeping Montana wind sliced through Sam's wet clothing. He ripped off his woolen greatcoat and grimaced at the mud clinging to it. He refused to wear Montana's favorite yellow slicker because he wanted to give the people he dealt with the image of a businessman. He was impatient, ready to be on his way, to complete a task that had interferred with his life too long—that of meeting his father, man to man now, and walking away.

The girl eyed his boots, Tenkiller's ornate saddle, and the etching on his Sharps rifle and squinted up at Sam. "Polishing boots costs, you know. I can't just go around wasting my time without getting paid."

She should have been frightened; she wasn't. Sam hauled her closer. He'd take her to her parents and get the cost of a new hat from them. "What's your name?"

The girl's chin went out. "Mary Taggart. My dad is

Harry Taggart, the roughest, toughest mountain man ever bred. He's a cross between a grizzly and a mountain lion, eats more than ten men put together, and scalps men like you and eats them for breakfast. One or two a day at least. He fought Paul Bunyan once and won. Why, he'll take some Nancy-boy, sissified city dandy like you and skin you and roll you up into a ball and toss you up on the highest tree in Montana. He's so big, he can step from mountaintop to mountaintop—"

"Harry Taggart?" Sam repeated carefully. Sam thought he'd be prepared for the first mention of his father; he wasn't. For years Harry Taggart had haunted Sam in his lonely hours—images skipping through his mind, like the way Harry showed him how to throw a knife or a tomahawk, calculating the correct number of rotations before impact.

"Harry Taggart," the girl stated proudly. "Part grizzly, part mountain lion, and mean clear through. He's big as a mountain, mean as a rattler, and—" Mary's eyes widened as Sam tossed her onto Tenkiller's ornately carved saddle.

For the first time she looked frightened. "You look like my dad, mister. Except he's got curly hair and a beard. You're big and strong like him, only thinner," she whispered softly. "Except younger and maybe meaner."

"Harry Taggart is my father." Sam slammed the words into the cold air and swung up behind her. Pain sliced through him before he pushed it away—once he'd said the same things about big tough Harry Taggart. If the girl was Harry's, she'd be tough. Sam saw no reason to spare her now. He'd learned that from Harry—life was cruel, and sparing harsh realities didn't help a child grow strong.

Mary stared at him, her blue eyes rounded and huge. Freckles danced across her nose, stark against her pale skin. *"Are you Sam?"* she whispered unevenly.

Sam moved Tenkiller toward the ranch, the girl staring at him all the time. "Close your mouth," he ordered curtly as she studied each feature of his face that marked him as Harry's son.

"Where've you been, Sam?" The freezing wind almost swept away Mary's childish voice.

"Lots of places, and none of them sweet." From mopping up swill on barroom floors to sucking dust behind a cattle herd, Sam had done it all and learned.

He slowly took in the Big T Taggart spread, twelve-hundred-acre ranch where he had been born. Marked on the boundaries by short jackleg fences—a series of three poles braced against each other and topped by a longer pole—Harry's valley nestled on the slope of a pine-studded mountain and spread out into rich grasslands. The Dancing Miranda—the stream tumbling down from the snowy mountains—cut down into Harry's land, feeding a number of smaller streams. The corral that once held wild mustangs was empty, the sprawling log house missing wooden shingles, the board porch that had been Harry's gift to Sam's Blackfoot mother broken in places. The open door of the log barn banged on its hinges; pigeons wandered in and out of the hole in the roof, covered by broken limbs and moss. Winter wood lay in an uncut mountain—Harry had always precisely stacked and sized it.

The garden fence, once stacked into a neat zigzag,

was broken and covered with brush and vines. Dead weeds and small trees stood where beans and cabbages once grew. Nothing remained of the big cornfield Harry used to plow with his fine team of mules. Feather had buried fish from the Dancing Miranda beside the stalks to feed and make them strong—her prayers for the summer corn whispered on the spring wind.

Sam inhaled sharply, memories smashing against him. He saw his mother, her braids gleaming in the sun, laughing as Harry tossed her into the air. He saw her smiling at him as they hoed the corn. He could almost smell the fresh scent of her hair, the sweetgrass fragrance that clung to the doeskin dress she wore for special occasions. *Harry should have married her; he didn't.*

Sam straightened in the saddle, his body tense. He glanced at the spot where he'd found his mother, sprawled lifeless upon the ground, her everyday calico dress torn at her breasts, her skirt pushed high, her legs spread open. The girl riding in front of him was the same age as Sam had been when he followed Harry, tracking the killers.

Sam inhaled sharply. The big house sprawled before him, laden with memories.

The girl twisted free of Sam's light hold and agilely dropped to the ground, running long-legged and free toward the house. She snatched up a kitten and cuddled it to her for comfort. "Pa! Help! Some stranger here is saying he's Sam. But he ain't! Sam wouldn't be no duded-up sissified dandy."

From the shadows of the house moved a bear of a man, about Sam's six-foot-four height but heavier.

There was no mistaking the breadth of Harry's shoulders, nor the killing look in his slate-colored eyes as his girl-cub ran toward him. Gray hair shot through his long black curls and the full beard that sat upon his chest. The buffalo rifle in his arm could tear a man in two, but the cane in his other hand and the lumpy wrapping around his foot said age had come to visit.

Sam slowly dismounted his horse, leading him toward the house. He had to look into Harry's eyes, let him know that there was nothing between them, and walk away— A sparrow of a man moved quickly from the shadows, squinting at the brilliant daylight. "Sam!"

"Monty. Good to see you looking well." Sam kept his eyes on his father while he shook Monty's scrawny hand.

"Sam. You've grown a mite. I remember holding you as a baby, and now that doesn't seem possible. I always stopped here when I was a drover, just to play with you." Monty looked anxiously at Harry, then at Sam. "Your pa is just going through a rough time, boy," Monty said. "He'll come around. It ain't that he don't love you . . . it's that he hurts."

Sam found what he remembered in Harry's eyes, the cold distance. It shouldn't have hurt after twenty years, yet a knife twisted slowly, effectively within him, reminding him not to care.

Monty hurried on, "I came down from Butte a few years after he lost that last woman—Mary's ma, Juliet. Juliet took the childbirth fever. Harry gave the baby girl a *sugar tit* just as good as any woman whose milk hadn't come in. He paid my IOUs so they wouldn't kill me or worse," Monty said.

Mary stood close to Harry and glared at Sam. "Say he

ain't my brother, Pa. Say he ain't. He's mean clear through. Wanted to paddle my backside. He's a nonbeliever, Pa. Didn't blink when I told him that you'd fought Paul Bunyan and won."

Harry lowered the buffalo rifle. Sam stood, legs spread, body tense. The old man hadn't softened, and Sam met his level stare as heartbeats stretched into minutes. Sam wanted Harry to know that his half-blood son was alive, evidence that Harry had taken a Blackfoot woman to his bed.

Harry's scowl deepened, his body rigid. Sam braced his legs and waited as Harry's cold gray eyes ripped down his son. Then they locked with Sam's. This time Harry would have to look away.

"Oh, hell, Harry. The boy is wet—covered in mud— and it's freezing. I'll put your horse up, Sam," Monty said finally. "You just get your bones in where the fire is going."

Monty leaned closer and whispered sadly, "Dog died. Wouldn't eat after you ran off. Just looked at Harry as though waiting for him to track you. Harry said if you went, it was because the spirit called you. He wouldn't have another dog, no matter if Mary did pester him."

Sam didn't move. "Dog" had been his only friend after Feather died; he'd tied Dog to the porch when he left, because wolves were shot on sight.

He didn't want to go back into the shadows of his life. "I've got holdings nearby. I'll check on my mother's grave, and then I'll be going."

Something dark and intense flickered in Harry's eyes. "She hasn't moved. Feather is up on the hill."

"So's my ma," Mary stated, as if all the women were related to her. "And my aunt Evie."

Sam should have known his father wouldn't be without a woman. After two years of drinking, Harry had married Evie and had no time for his half-blood son. "That's three women. You've been busy. When I left, it was Evie."

"Evie got the plague carrying food to sickly Indians. The women and children were camped up on the mountain where the army couldn't get to them. Juliet was Mary's ma and Evie's sister. I got bad luck with women." Harry tried to straighten away from the cane; an expression of pain shot through his face as a cat bounded across his foot.

Damn. The old man was hurting from losing his wives and from his injury, and Sam didn't want to care. He owed Harry nothing. . . .

"I'll be going to Mother's grave." Sam inhaled a blast of cold air and tried to stop remembering.

"You do that." Harry nodded and continued to stare at Sam with an unreadable expression. Then something flickered in his gray eyes, and it wasn't shame but pride. Then he looked away to the mountains.

Monty tossed Sam's saddlebags to him. "Oh, hell and fiddlesticks. Get into the house, boy. Have a cup of coffee first. I just made some. Change those wet clothes."

"I'll be going," Sam returned. The pit of his stomach felt as cold as the piercing wind. His father still couldn't bear to look at him—Big Harry Taggart's half-blood bastard.

"You're scared, boy." Harry's booming voice cut through the cold wind that lifted his full beard and riffled through his tangled long hair. Then he turned and, with an arm around the scowling girl, lumbered painfully into the cabin. He rubbed the top of her head affectionately, and Sam knew Harry had never touched him like that. But then his mother had been a Blackfoot and not white-skinned.

Sam pressed his lips together, fighting a retort. After twenty years the old man still knew how to toss a challenge at him. Fine, he thought darkly. He'd go in the house, and for a few more minutes Harry would have to look at his half-blood son; Harry would have to share the same air. Sam slapped the reins of Tenkiller into Monty's waiting hand. The bowlegged old man grinned when Sam followed Harry into the house.

Sam passed Harry and Mary on his way to change clothes. In a room filled with litter, he quickly changed into his remaining suit. When he stepped free of the curtain that served for a door, Harry was sitting on a chair, his injured foot propped on another. Mary glared at Sam, her thin arm curled around Harry, staking her possession.

Sam glanced at his old room, littered with crudely made toys, paper, and the girl's clothing. He remembered how his mother had insisted on neatness.

Cats were everywhere, and the sprawling room smelled of bad food and filth. Sam met Harry's shuttered gaze, then opened the front door. He looked at Mary and touched the whip coiled over his shoulder. "Cats. Out."

Her eyes widened. Sam knew she recognized the terse tone that Harry used when he meant business. "Pa, tell him to go away. He ain't my brother, and he's got no right to tell me—"

"Go along now, pretty girl. Take your kitties out to the barn." Harry's voice was tender, low, and almost melodic, the voice Sam remembered using talking to his mother, cajoling her—

Mary smirked. "Can't. Fritzi's pigeons are in the barn. He gave me four pair last spring, and they've got young 'uns. I was supposed to send 'em back by January, but I been holding them hostage until he sweetens up to me. Last time we talked in October, he was plain mean— dreaming of females when he woke up in the morning— and that just made him plain crotchety. . . . You know, Pa, cats and pigeons don't get along."

Harry lifted one thick bristling black brow, and Mary's eyes widened. "Okay, Pa. I'll take them outside. Just for you. Not for him. I'd never do anything for him."

The girl skillfully corralled her five cats and put them into a wooden box. She covered the box lovingly with an old blanket. Her glare accused Sam as the pitiful sound of mewing began. "Wish I'd have shot just a mite lower."

When the door was shut, Sam poured a cup of coffee from the old charred granite pot. Then he poured a second for Harry and placed it in front of the older man. He shouldn't care what happened to Harry— maybe it was perversity, or maybe it was some forgotten memory of how well Harry had treated his mother. "What happened?"

"When?" Harry stared at the fire and ignored the mug, making it clear that he didn't want anything from his son, not even coffee.

Sam's inheritance from Harry was enough sheer stubbornness to press on. The ranch had once been neat and thriving; he had to know what happened. Maybe he wanted Harry to admit his failure. None of it should matter. The fact that it did, grated on his nerves.

Just five minutes after Mary left, she and Monty entered in a blast of freezing wind. Out of breath from hurrying, Mary went to Harry and hung her arm around his neck. A thin girl dressed in a battered jacket and trousers, she leaned close to him, clearly protective and possessive. Her thin hand smoothed Harry's grizzled beard as if he were her pet.

Sam stood, hardening himself against the memories. The house had once been neat, filled with the scent of herbs and fresh bread. Clothing would be hung to dry near the hearth. Now the two men were almost as filthy as the girl, their clothing tattered. "Your . . . daughter needs a bath," Sam said, not wanting to care about any of them.

"My Mary doesn't like baths. She swims in the summer, that's good enough." Harry stared at the flames, and Mary grinned evilly, triumphantly at Sam.

The coffee tasted as bitter as Sam's memories. His mother had always insisted on clean hands at her well-stocked table. Sam glanced at Mary, who glared at him. Beneath the grime, her skin was white, and she was his half-sister. She should be drinking fresh milk and eating better. Feather had always wanted a daughter— Sam pushed away the pain and said, "I'd better go."

"You do that." Harry didn't move.

"Ouch!" Mary's thin hands reached up to press

against her flat chest. "I hurt. Bosom growing hurts. Fritzi said his sisters' used to, too."

Harry's skin, once dark from the sun, changed to an odd shade of red. His jaw, square set like Sam's, sank lower into his shoulders. Monty flushed brightly and looked cornered. Clearly both men were unnerved by Mary's approaching womanhood.

"Well, they do. I got two," Mary objected, glaring at both older men as if they didn't believe her. Monty whistled under his breath and found an interesting spot on the rafter above him. Harry seemed to draw into himself, a huge man avoiding a topic that clearly embarrassed him. Sam found the situation almost humorous. Almost. He wasn't a man to find anything amusing.

He didn't owe Harry anything. It shouldn't matter that the house was filthy, that Harry's foot was injured, and that hard times had settled on the ranch. Maybe it was because he'd grown up here, and memories of his mother lurked in every corner. He should walk out the door and—

"Why did you come back?" Harry asked suddenly, as though he'd latched on to an escape from the bosom problem.

"Montana is wide open—cattle, mining, and logging. Up north, wheat farming is coming in, and the Northern Pacific will soon tie it all up in a nice big bow. I'm a partner in two mines now and own three stores, one in Beartown, one in Garnet, and one in Coloma. I'm a partner in two more. You'd better get used to the idea that I'll be around."

Sam omitted how he'd slaved to save for his dream, how he'd sunk every penny into buying goods, how he'd packed them on half-broken mules and was his own "freighter" from Fort Benton down to Beartown, Garnet, and Coloma. He hadn't had money to spare for a hired man. He'd moved fast, just after the Missouri River thawed to allow shipping, and in two hard weeks he'd made his mark. "I'm just getting started, but I intend to make my name, Harry—Sam Taggart Enterprises. I'm setting up business just thirty miles from here in Deer Lodge City. Get used to it."

"You think the kings of the country are going to let you in their pack? Con Kohrs and the like? Your name is the same as mine." Harry studied Sam's neatly combed, clipped, and parted hair. "You can part the hair, boy, but the blood remains true."

"I'm your half-blood bastard, Harry. Is that what you're saying?" Sam shot back, the old rage boiling in him.

Harry's eyes locked with Sam's, and Monty shifted restlessly. Mary watched the men curiously and hooked her arm around Harry's neck as though to protect him. Sire and cub, Sam thought furiously, remembering how he had worshiped big tough Harry Taggart.

He glanced at Mary. As a girl, she'd have a tougher time when the dream shattered for her. Sam didn't want to think about his half-sister's future. He rolled the word *half-sister* around in his thoughts and discarded it like extra baggage.

"Go clean up your room," Sam found himself saying as he moved into the small room littered with bird's nests, pretty rocks, and dirty clothing. He wanted to see the room that had once been his mother's favorite. A woman's tintype picture was crudely tacked to the wall;

she wasn't Evie but had the same big, strong Nordic blond look.

Mary scurried past him and jerked closed the tattered cloth that served to separate the room. Sam jerked it open, allowing him to see the girl in her room and Harry's reaction. Sam wanted to see how much his interference would stir Harry. "Pa! He's going to kill me," Mary screamed. "Help! Help!"

But her father remained quiet, and Sam said very quietly, "Clean it up. Now."

"Can't. Don't know how," she answered, and from the look of the room, she was telling the truth.

"That's all right, little dearie, old Monty will help you, Monty said, moving toward the room. The small man stopped in midstride as Sam's look pinned him. The girl should respect the house where she was born; his mother had taught him to be neat and clean.

Monty remembered, too. "Maybe you could try just this once, honey."

"Pa!" The girl's yell was an outraged demand. But Harry kept staring at his coffee, his powerful hands gripping the chipped cup tightly.

The man Sam remembered wouldn't have let anyone interfere with his home or his life and didn't take advice. Sam expected Harry to order him out of the house any minute, and that would have made his leaving easy. But Harry didn't say anything, his chin locked down on his chest.

Sam cursed himself silently for not walking out the door that minute.

"Come out when you're done. Not before," Sam murmured, expecting his father to defend his precious girl-cub. If Harry said one word, Sam promised himself he'd walk out the door.

Damn. Harry's lips remained clamped together.

The girl's screams ranged from enraged to pitiful, and Monty whipped out a handkerchief in a practiced manner. He looped it around his jaw and tied it on top of his head, covering his ears. When she was out of breath, Mary hunched her shoulders, kicked the crude bed that had once been Sam's, and began to stamp and scream again. Sam reached in his pocket, slowly extracted a neatly ironed, starched white handkerchief, and looked at her. "I'd hate to waste this by stuffing it in your mouth."

"Pa! He's breaking my arm!" Mary tried to peer around Sam, who was looking at two coins that had just rolled across the floor, dislodged by her stamping. Caught with the damning evidence, Mary closed her mouth and blinked as the coins rolled, circling the floor.

Sam bent to retrieve the big brass coins, studying them. They were tokens purchased from a bartender and advertised the accommodating women in the upstairs rooms. He ran his finger over the bent rim of one advertising "Screw. Bath. Beans. Whiskey. Three dollars."

"Don't say nothing. Pa would kill me if he knew," Mary whispered after hurriedly closing the curtains. "Please?" she begged, her blue eyes huge.

"What are you going to do with them?" Sam slid the coins into his vest pocket and pushed away the grubby thin hand that snatched at them.

"Shh. You want Pa to hear? Them coins is for whores

for Fritzi. Once he gets all that steam worked off, he'll be my friend again."

"How did you get them?" Sam watched with interest as the sulking girl began to slowly pick up her clothing.

"Sold a few things," she muttered.

Sam didn't want to know what Harry might be missing. "I'll just keep these for that hole in my hat. Come out when you're done."

"You won't tell, will you?"

"I'd clean real hard if I were you," Sam returned levelly, and left her to draw her own conclusions. He stepped out into the main room of the house and found that Harry hadn't moved. The girl started banging things in the room and muttering.

Harry's head sank lower into his beefy shoulders, and he glared at Monty, who said, "Anyone can see you two are of the same blood. One just as stubborn as the other. Harry, the boy came back. Twenty long years you've been aching for him. Now tell him you're glad to see him. Tell him what happened. Tell him how you been holding on, hoping to save this ranch for him—what's left of it."

"I don't want this ranch." Sam wanted to leave—instead he said, "You need a woman to clean up in here."

"We're doing just fine," Harry returned bullishly.

"No, we ain't," Monty interrupted. "We're nearly out of grub. That's the last of the coffee."

"Women stink," Mary added from her room, clearly listening as she hurried to finish her task.

Harry held up a big hand for silence. He looked at Sam. "We're doing just fine," he repeated.

Sam glanced around the dirty rubble of the house, the

childish drawings on the log walls, and wondered why he was still there. He eased into a chair. Whatever he felt about Harry, he couldn't leave them here, down on their luck. He hooked his thumbs into his belt because they were shaking.

"Rustlers got the cattle," Monty stated. "The Murdocks' New Alamo was moving in, putting the squeeze on us. Stopped the credit at the store. Tex Murdock has over seventy thousand acres, and he wants—"

"You talk a lot," Harry noted too quietly.

"Tex wants to dam up the stream and charge the valley people for the water they use. Harry won't let that happen to his friends," Monty continued. "Though he's a sour old dog, and the runt of the litter with under two thousand acres, some folks still like him."

"We don't need help," Harry stated again. Then he glared at Sam. "Go away."

"You'd like that, wouldn't you?" Sam realized that he spoke in the same too-quiet tone as Harry. He'd be damned if Harry would get rid of him that easily.

Monty clucked over the beans he was stirring in the pot. "Pride. Both of you, filled with pride. Two peas in a pod, just the same—"

"Shut up," Harry ordered tersely.

Mary came out of her room, warily eyeing Sam. "All done cleaning."

"Where are the nearest women?" Sam asked her.

"Those Recht women," Mary answered after a long wary moment. "They're cross-eyed and got warts on their noses. Bowlegged. Dumb clear through. Those Recht women can't speak American. They're German. They're too mean to come near civilized folk like me and Pa and Monty. I heard they're so fat that once they ate a buffalo herd and was still hungry—"

"That's enough," Harry stated, and Mary gaped at him as though she wasn't used to his reprimands.

Monty moved into the silence. "She and the Recht boy, Fritzi, send pigeons back and forth. They been sending messages for three—maybe four years. Old man Recht came over to offer for Harry's pasture land, and that was how they met."

The question crawled out of Sam, despite his will, "What happened to your foot?"

Harry didn't answer, glowering at him.

Monty moved restlessly. "All them winters fishing for beaver traps in ice water came to call on Harry's foot—"

"Get out," Harry told Sam in his quiet deadly tone.

Sam didn't think, his anger ruling him. He reached for the knife at his back. Then the big knife Harry had given him that day stood quivering on the table, the point deep in the scarred wood. "You gave me this once. I'm giving it back."

For a moment a pale tint crossed beneath Harry's dark weathered skin as though he'd seen a ghost. "You kept it then. I wondered."

Harry's big scarred hand slid from the table, and he looked out into the May sunshine as if distancing himself from the knife and the past.

Monty looked sadly at Sam. "You'd better take it. The girl has begun selling things. It ain't right, but she does that sometimes."

Impatient with his uncertain emotions, Sam jerked the knife free of the wood and jammed it back into the sheath at his back. He stood slowly, adjusted the whip coiled over his shoulder, and collected his dirty clothes. He nodded and walked out the door into the freezing wind, the blinding sunshine. In less than an hour he had aged years, the past weighing on him.

He breathed deeply and tried to push away his emotions, the shock that the ranch was no longer well kept. And that the man he remembered as twice as big as any other man was ailing and aged. Sam straightened his shoulders. He wanted his mind on business, on trading shares in mines and building an empire of money and respect. He looked up on the hill where his mother was buried, then to the road leading away from the ranch and his pain. Every protective sense he'd learned in twenty years away from Harry told him to stay away, to ride out and not to come back.

A crash sounded in the cabin, and Sam smiled grimly. He wasn't the only one with unsettled emotions. In a few minutes Monty was standing on the front porch, and Sam stopped Tenkiller to ask him, "Which way to the Rechts'?"

The grizzled old cowhand pointed toward the east and wiped away a tear. "Just a hop over that way, eighty or so miles. If you push that big fine fellow, you can catch some shut-eye and be there for tomorrow's lunch. They're too close. Old man Recht built his ranch house close to the edge of the Big T. He's got over fifty thousand acres and wanting to buy part of Harry's land. It's a squeeze either way—the New Alamo to the west and Rechts' to the east."

"And don't ever come back!" Mary's indignant scream carried on the freezing spring wind.

Sam stopped Tenkiller and turned him. He walked the

horse back to the porch and looked at Mary. "You have that room clean when I do."

Her small pinched face paled, and her eyes widened.

Monty began to chuckle. "You're Harry's boy, all right. Cut from the same cloth."

"No. You're dead wrong," Sam snapped, tension humming through him. Sam locked his body to the saddle, preparing for the long ride. He was too tired, raw to the bone after working the last frantic two weeks—and that was why seeing Harry again, and in bad shape, had gotten to him. *It was not because he cared.*

Chapter Two

Tonight I am almost too excited to write in my journal. A man is coming, and Papa does not let us visit often. It was almost dark, and a pigeon came from Mary at the Big T. She says an outlaw will be coming to rob us. Papa does not believe Mary's messages and says we will see what the man wants. I suppose he's another man who wants Greta. She is angry that I have not married. This is not my fault. I am plain, but I am useful and work hard and do what is expected. Papa says that the older sister must marry first, and that is why Greta is angry with me. Papa has promised that I must wed Gilbert, who works for us, if I am not married in a year and a half. I am twenty-six already, but I do not want to marry Gilbert. I do not want him to have the dowry that belongs to the oldest daughter in the family. The dowry is important to my family and to me. I came to this country when I was six, but still my family keeps close to tradition and custom. Papa does not think

*women should have business heads, but I do. I want
to be a businesswoman and travel. I can't wait until
tomorrow to see the man. Mama is excited, and she
is planning a big meal for the stranger. I will wear
Grandmother's brooch to keep me from trouble and
talking too much. Grandmother gave it to me for
luck, because she thought I was a little "berserker." I
think she is right. I like excitement and challenge. E.*

"Only one year and a half to escape Gilbert and save
Grandmother's dowry." The next morning Emma was
perched on a low tree branch near the road to the Recht
ranch. She'd hurried milking and doing her chores and
raced for the tree just as dawn became full morning. She
tucked her brown homespun skirts up under her and
readjusted her small brightly knitted cap, tied beneath
her chin. She had knitted the cap, making it extra large
to more comfortably confine her coronet of tightly
braided brown hair. Hoping that none of her clothing
touched the sticky pitch of the pine tree, she inspected
the old blanket she had wrapped around her thick winter coat.

Emma leaned forward, skimming the rolling hills,
searching for the man who would come from the Big T.
She should be making butter now and feeding the chickens and— She strained to see the horizon, shadowy in
the gray dawn.

She searched the hazy gray and shivered. In another
week, June would arrive, and time was slipping by too
fast. Sometimes she felt as though she would burst if she
didn't do something exciting, if she didn't find a challenge and conquer it. She wanted to wear trousers like

the woman who had stopped at the ranch and who spoke with a thin dark cigarillo dangling from her lips.

Joseph expected the rider to arrive in the early afternoon, but he had told Magda to have the midday meal ready early. There would be smoked duck and ham, sliced headcheese, freshly baked potato bread, whole potatoes in cream, and dried-apple pies with flaky crusts. Magda couldn't decide whether to place her dill pickles on the table in slices or whole—or to serve the pork roast in kraut and add the boiled potatoes to it.

Emma leaned comfortably back against the tree and waited. A flock of Fritzi's homing pigeons circled the ranch, cutting, dipping, changing directions. The earth smelled of spring, of new life. With a sense of accomplishment she looked at the men's knitted stockings she had just hung on the clothesline. They were all very large, to accommodate several pairs of stockings beneath them. Miners and loggers usually wore layers of stockings, but Emma's were so well knitted that she was certain only one pair of her stockings would serve for warmth.

Gilbert had worked for her father for six months, and an agreement had been made between the men concerning her. In another year and a half Gilbert would claim her grandmother's dowry—and Emma.

Emma shivered from distaste. She did not want her grandmother's prized dowry—ancient gold coins from the old country, a large velvet sack of gems and jewelry, a tiny leather book filled with perfume recipes, and a collection of tiny ornate jade and ivory animals—in Gilbert's sausagelike fingers. The money, gold coins of this country, did not matter as much . . . still, they were what her father had repaid to the dowry. He had borrowed money from the dowry to come to this country and to buy the ranch. With his good fortune and crops, he had replaced what he had borrowed.

Emma frowned, plagued by the thought of Gilbert possessing her dowry. *Somehow she would become a businesswoman and repay him for working at her father's. She would be independent and respected for her business talent. She would collect her grandmother's dowry and keep it safe.*

She straightened and narrowed her eyes at the man riding over the crest of the hill, the heavy gray sky outlining his western hat and the set of his square shoulders. A man with a purpose, she thought, as a deer leaped from the pines and crossed the road in front of him. The man, apparently used to wildlife, didn't trace the deer but kept his eyes on the road before him.

Emma pressed one hand to her lips. The man was all dressed in a black suit, a whip looped around his saddle horn. The horse was no common cowboy's but rather a sleek, big powerful stallion that suited the man—like those of King Arthur's knights. The horse was unusual—not a heavy draft horse or a spotted Appaloosa or a fancy Arabian—but there was a fancy fast look to him as he stepped high.

Beneath his black western hat, the man's expression was grim, deadly, determined, as if nothing could stop him. He stopped the horse a distance away from her and sat very still. Emma noted the ornate tooled saddle and the man's expensive boots. He didn't wear a coat, though the icy wind cut through the old blanket and her own layers of clothing. He removed his hat carefully and placed it on his saddle horn. He adjusted it meticulously, as though he were considering a great matter. He reached to his rifle, sheathed beneath his long legs, and touched it. He was a huge dark giant of a man and grim as death.

The angle of his head was arrogant, proud, as though he knew exactly who he was and where he was going. Emma held a branch tightly as he nudged the horse, and it moved directly beneath her tree. Emma held very still, aware that a slight movement would reveal her.

Fritzi's pigeons soared overhead, and she prayed that the man would not shoot them. Her brother loved his birds and they returned that love, but to some men, it was an irresistible challenge to try to shoot them, requiring a high skill because of their movements.

The man's dark face lifted slowly, and his black eyes riveted hers. The coldness in his eyes caused her to shiver, a flat black shade that revealed nothing, like a curtain drawn down over his soul. His hair was raven and glossy, cut short and neatly parted. His cheekbones pressed against his taut dark skin, and a muscle moved rhythmically in the square cut of his jaw. Emma had never seen such a beautiful man.

Then to her horror she realized that no matter how much she shifted, her black-stocking-clad legs were exposed to his view. "You must not look," she admonished in a whisper. "Shame."

"I like the view." He had a voice like velvet, washing over her, soft and low.

Suddenly the man's hand moved, curled around her ankle, and tugged her from the tree. She plummeted into his arms.

"Damn. Tenkiller, stand." The man's voice lashed through the air like the whip. But the giant black horse reared, spilling Emma—tightly held by the giant—onto layers of pine needles covering mud.

They rolled a short distance, the man grunting as her hand reached for a branch and hit his eye. They rolled into a thicket with new buds, frightening away a rabbit.

The impact of his huge body covering her, sent the breath out of Emma. Before she could recover, the man's large hand had claimed both her wrists, holding them over her head. He wasn't happy, the scowl on his face drawing his black brows almost together. She'd never seen eyes so black and glowing; they seemed to see right down to her bones.

He looked so tired, so haunted, that she ached for him.

Never at a loss for words, Emma said, "You look most fierce and angry. There is a horrible cut on your forehead."

His long hard mouth barely moved. "This is the second time in two days that a female has sent me into the mud."

He stared at her so long that Emma was obliged to speak. "Truly I am sorry. Forgive me. I was only studying my inventory of stockings on the clothesline. I am going into business—when Papa lets me. It is difficult to become a businesswoman when he will not let me sell my stockings."

"Stockings?" The man shifted slightly, looking at her more closely, studying every feature of her face.

Emma blushed. She had never been so close to any man, having escaped Gilbert's crude advances. "Someday, I hope to open a stocking business for all the bachelors in the region. There is always a need for well-made stockings, you know. Especially with so many unmarried men in the area."

She blinked, aware that the man's body was very warm and not at all uncomfortable over hers. She knew from experience why men circled the Recht property. "Have you come for Greta?"

He seemed oddly distracted, his thumb stroking the fine inner skin of her wrist. He studied the fast-racing pulse in her throat. "Greta?"

"My younger sister. Of course you have come to see her. . . . I have to tell you that my father won't let her go until I am married. I am already twenty-six years old and the obstacle to her happiness, although I am promised to a hired man—if he works another year and one half for my father. After I am married, perhaps you would like to try for Greta again."

She rushed on to another thought nudging her. "If you murder me here, please let my family know, so they can bury me properly and pray for me."

"I see." One of the man's hands molded her waist beneath her coat. His thumb seemed very near her breast. Emma barely breathed. Surely he did not realize exactly where his hand lay upon her.

Her heart raced as he studied her mouth, and his gaze slowly lowered to her throat. Her heart almost leaped out of her body when his eyes darkened and softened, locked upon her breasts. When he looked again into her eyes, there was amusement in his. "The next time you play lookout, don't wear white petticoats."

"Oh." She inhaled, wondering if the man knew that

his thumb had just brushed across the tip of her breast. Layers of clothing probably prevented him from noting the taut bud that was not caused by the cold weather.

He continued to stare at her, into her eyes, taking away her breath. The thicket seemed very intimate, and Emma was quite warm under the man's body, his eyes glowing in the shadows. "You must not look at me like that."

"Like what?" Again his thumb slowly crossed her breast, tightening the nerves in her body.

She blushed furiously and looked away. He was injured, and she excused the movements of his hands, seeking how to remove him from herself. "You're hurt. The wound on your head needs attention. Please let me see to it."

He seemed reluctant to move, this heavy giant of a man. She realized how badly he must be dazed. The muscles of his thighs surged once, heavily upon hers, and he groaned, a dark red color coming into his cheeks. His heat and pounding pulse raced against her body. His long hard body shuddered against her. She stared at him closely. "You are not well. Please. Let me take you to our home and tend you."

"I'd like tending now." The statement was flat and harsh, as if he resented his needs.

Emma realized that the man was having problems breathing. His broad chest pressed down on her softness several times, an erratic motion as he tried to breathe. His forehead had developed a fine sheen, and the spear of hair arcing over it trembled. She had caused him injury and felt immediately guilty. "You could have a broken rib. I have heard that sometimes broken ribs puncture lungs. Since you took the brunt of the fall, no doubt you are bruised and aching."

"I'm aching all right." There was wry humor in his tone that Emma did not understand.

The man's large hand moved slowly lower to find the curve of her hip and grip her firmly. Emma supposed that he was trying to find a place to brace himself, preparing to move away from her. "You may release my hands. I will help."

Again that quick flash of hunger—or was it humor? He glanced down their bodies, locked together. "Help? Do what?"

"We are caught in a thicket, are we not? I will help free us and take you home to tend your wound."

"What is your name?" The man's thumb caressed her wrists, not releasing her.

"Emma Recht. What is yours?" She looked at the thicket surrounding them. "I think we can work our way out easily. I will take care of you. Please lie still, or your wound will open more." She realized that he was looking down at her body, probably planning how best to untangle her skirts from his legs and the thicket. "You should not look at my legs or my personal clothing," she admonished him when she could speak. "Again, your name, please?"

"Sam. Sam Taggart." He seemed oddly distracted, and from his heat and flushed skin, she feared he was taking a fever. His hips jerked down on her, a fierce quick, demanding pressure, and she knew his back was probably injured.

"I cannot bear the guilt of causing you harm," she whispered quietly as his lips came close to hers. Perhaps he was injured so badly that he could not hold his head properly, and it was her fault. "Please let me take you home and care for you."

"You could do that here." His uneven husky whisper warmed her lips.

She frowned. "But I have no thread. You need the wound washed, and I fear you may have other injuries."

From the way his hips pressed down upon her, she was certain that he had hurt his back.

His nose brushed hers, and she jerked back, peering up at him closely. If he fainted upon her body, she would be trapped by his great weight. "Do not faint," she whispered firmly. "I will take care of you."

He closed his eyes, and his lashes were sleek and black and glossy as a raven's wing; Emma longed to touch them with the tip of her finger. He was pretty, lean and dark, the perfect mate for Greta's fair statuesque beauty. The thought angered Emma, though she didn't understand why. Legions of men trailed after Greta, who knew how to entice them with leisurely graceful movements, while Emma darted here and there and was much shorter. Emma pushed away the slight fury; if she took the stranger home to tend him, she would lose him soon enough to Greta's charms, and yet another man would be begging her to marry quickly.

He smelled of soap and leather and the clean fresh air of Montana. Yet there was a headier, darker scent beneath the rest, a scent she did not recognize. His body trembled upon hers, and his head sank down to rest upon her shoulder. She wanted to gather him closer and protect him. "Can you move?" she asked cautiously as his warm lips brushed her throat.

"I am trying not to. I need to rest a minute." His deep voice had an odd strangled tone, as though he were a man in desperate need, a hungry man needing food—

"You have a fever," she whispered back, fiercely wanting to take care of him. "Were you sick before falling?" she asked urgently.

"It's . . . ah . . . very new development." Again the man's tone was laced with humor that Emma did not understand.

She had never been so close to a man. The stranger's long muscled legs seemed to be logs of steel against her, taut and trembling. She was much smaller than he. She began to squirm, to ease out from under him.

"Hold very still," he said harshly. His lips moved against her throat. He released her wrists and sighed once, unevenly. "Emma, take me home and take care of me."

An injured man, tired and haunted, he needed comfort, and Emma would give him that. "Yes, I will take care of you, Sam Taggart."

Chapter Three

"**E**mma!" a man yelled, outraged. He tromped through the bushes and tore open the thicket. Sam felt himself being lifted from Emma and hurled against a tree. He cursed, because the pine's pitch and bark stuck to his dress coat.

The man was built like a bear, a small head, no neck, and heavily muscled through his shoulders and chest. He smelled like onions and sweat, and it was no loving look in his eye as he advanced on Sam, ham-sized fists raised.

"Gilbert!" Emma cried, scrambling to her feet.

"Shame. Lying with a man when you are promised to me. You are promised to me, Emma Recht."

Emma's small lush body snapped into a taut line, her face reddening with anger. She only reached Sam's chest and reminded him of a red hen, ready to defend herself and her nest. The dizzying thought flew by Sam that he was probably the chick in her nest and the one she was currently defending. He considered the notion and decided that since she'd fallen from the tree onto him, he'd stopped thinking rationally.

"I was not lying with Sam Taggart. You will not talk that way about a man I have injured, nor will you hurt him."

"Take it easy." Sam noted that Gilbert was a good four inches taller than his own six-foot-four height. As he advanced on Sam, Gilbert broke a sapling in the way, snapped it like a toothpick.

Emma wasn't to be ignored, clearly outraged by Gilbert's remark, her pride injured. "You—you—you think I was lying with him, Gilbert Schaffer? That he touched me? That I touched him in ways that are for married people?"

Sam watched, fascinated as Emma ignited beautifully. The color returned to her cheeks, and May sunshine caught the red in her brown hair. Her greenish-brown eyes changed to livid emerald, slashing at Gilbert.

"Nice married ladies do not lie in thickets with their underwear up to their necks. *He was touching your udder!*" Gilbert yelled, outraged.

Sam sidestepped the swinging blow of Gilbert's huge fist, jabbed into the man's side, and found it like stone.

"Stop this. You will hurt this poor man!" Emma ran to Gilbert's side and clung to his arm. He raised it, and her. She refused to let go, and her feet dangled above the ground.

Sam almost smiled, surprising himself.

"Shame, Emma," Gilbert repeated darkly as he lowered her to the ground and brushed her away. She landed against a small pine tree and clung to it as it wobbled with the impact.

"Gilbert, I have no udders. You are thinking of cows. *I am not a cow,*" she stated indignantly as she fought her way free of the pine tree.

"You have a milk-giving place. Men should not touch there. What kind of man is this, who will not fight?" Gilbert swung at Sam again.

With one punch Sam discovered that Gilbert's jowls were like steel. He rubbed his fist and glanced at Emma, who was hitching up her skirts.

"There. You see how defenseless he is," she said. "Not all men are animals, ready to fight and rut, Gilbert. Don't—" She leaped upon Gilbert's back and clung to him as he approached Sam.

The girl looked too fragile against the giant's rage and bulk. "Let her down, Gilbert. Then you can have at me," Sam said.

"Animals! Animals rutting in the bushes!" Gilbert yelled.

Emma pulled his ear. "Rutting? Me rutting? You are the one who pushes me into stalls and wants to rut. It is not poor, nice Sam Taggart. It is clear he is not a fighting man."

Emma's knitted cap slid awry, dangling by its ties, and her braids, wound over her head, shone in the bright sunlight. She grabbed a small branch of pine needles and swished them on Gilbert's head. "Stop this!"

Emma's comments about Sam's lack of fighting ability were beginning to snag at him. He glanced at his scarred knuckles to remind himself that he'd been a champion in a few bare-knuckle bouts.

"I'm mad," Gilbert replied stubbornly as Sam continued to back away. If he threw a punch, he could hit the girl.

Emma sighed wearily. "Gilbert is emotional. Please do not hurt him."

"Emotional. Hell! He's the size of a bear. Get away from him."

Over Gilbert's beefy shoulder Emma frowned at Sam. "Do not curse. If you curse, I shall have to punish you. Mama washes Fritzi's mouth out with soap when he uses bad words."

"Who's going to do it for you?" Sam asked, and fought a grin. Despite his fatigue and the unpleasant knowledge that he could be aroused instantly by a woman wearing a knitted cap and dropping from a tree, he was beginning to enjoy the humorous scenario.

"Emma can be evil," Gilbert muttered. "I did not like the taste of soap that time."

Sam ducked a ham-sized fist. "So you two are getting married? Congratulations."

"Not yet." Emma swished the pine branch at Gilbert's ears. "Only six months have passed of the two years he is to work for Papa."

Gilbert shoved aside a sizable young aspen on his way to Sam. "If I can rut with her and make a baby, then Herr Recht will make her marry me. I will have the dowry and be rich, and my bed will be warm with a woman. Emma is a good cook. I like her *hasenpfeffer* rabbit, but not her soap in my mouth."

Emma's face turned red, and she glared at Sam, who realized he had just chuckled. "Stop laughing," she said. "Gilbert is a good man. He is a wonderful carpenter and a good farmer, but no one has taught him better. I am trying."

"Any luck?" Sam asked, and from the flush on her cheeks and her scowl, he knew that Gilbert would rather rut with her than listen. Sam didn't blame the farmhand; a few moments ago with Emma under him, he'd been thinking the same thing.

"Hush, Sam Taggart." Emma spoke to Gilbert. "Now, Gilbert. Listen to me closely. I will never cook *hasenpfeffer* rabbit for you again."

The big man slowed his advance on Sam, and Emma dropped lightly to the ground. She hurried around to place both hands on Gilbert's chest, bracing against his bulk. Then she said very clearly, "And I will never give you the best apple dumpling with the most butter sauce again. I will give the best one to Fritzi and give you the worst, tiniest crumbled apple dumpling in the pan—one that is dry, because it has no sauce."

Gilbert's small eyes almost widened in fear. "I like big apple dumplings with much sauce," he stated worriedly, and stopped completely, staring down at her.

"Well, then. You are a smart man. Do you want to hurt this man, or do you want to have nice big juicy apple dumplings?"

"You must not lie with him again," Gilbert said doggedly, glancing at Sam over the cap that Emma had neatly replaced.

"That was an accident. He was trying to save me from Indians. We were hiding because he doesn't wear a gun. You can see he is not a fighter. Didn't he back away from you? He acknowledges that you are stronger and a better fighter than he is."

Sam glared at her. While she apparently soothed Gilbert, the woman had just nipped at Sam's pride.

"He is dark like an Indian," Gilbert persisted.

Emma waved her hand in a blithe explanation. "Sun. He does not dress like an Indian. And if he is of an Indian heritage, he is my Indian—I claim the right to tend his cut and take care of him. You can see, Gilbert, that he is a defenseless man—not a fighter."

While Sam reeled with Emma's claim on him, Gilbert nodded, accepting her wisdom. Emma smiled and brushed her hands together. "There. Now we are all friends. You go back to plowing, Gilbert. I must take Sam Taggart home to Papa. He is expected."

Sam tensed uneasily as the giant wavered.

Emma patted Gilbert's beefy arm and moved around him, brushing away the pine needles clinging to him. She plucked away a good-sized branch that he hadn't noticed from his chest. "You will not say anything about today, Gilbert, will you? Because from now on you'll get the biggest dumpling made just for you, with extra butter."

Cushioned by the layers of material separating them, Sam leaned back against Emma's soft breasts. Her arms tightened around him for better support as they rode to the Recht farmhouse. He wrapped his hand around hers to better rein Tenkiller. Beneath her mittens her hand was small and flexible and yet strong. He inhaled and wondered when he'd last had a woman, when a woman's hands had last been upon him. Emma had raised his dormant need to sink deep into a soft, willing woman and forget his cold life, if only for a moment. He realized he was running "thin," too tired, and that his emotions were riding too close to the surface. He should have slept last night, but after a few restless hours tossing on his bedroll, he was back in the saddle.

Emma Recht was soft and small and had eyes a man could fall into. They were a greenish brown, luminous and expressive. The darker flecks reminded Sam of golden autumn leaves upon still clear water. Her small hand fluttered in front of him, patting his chest. "There, there, Sam Taggart. Soon you will feel better."

Sam doubted that statement. In two days he'd been shot at by a half-sister he hadn't known existed, discovered his father had married yet again, and walked straight into Harry's hard times. Sam had discovered that he couldn't walk out and leave Harry, not with a good conscience. He'd had this small woman defend him and wound his pride. And he wasn't too happy about Gilbert getting the best apple dumpling either. *For a man used to being alone, laying out his life neatly, he'd acquired enough problems for one day.*

He glanced down at the petticoats bunched over Emma's practical black stockings, followed the shape of her knees and slender calves and ankles, and knew just what would make him feel better. Emma smelled like flowers, a light clean scent that went straight to his head—and a few feet lower to make him rock hard. He ached, just sitting in the saddle, her breasts pressed against him, her soft thighs clenched behind his long ones. Sam wondered if the fall hadn't really hurt him, because just then he had a quick thought to ride off with the woman.

The Recht house was sprawling and neat, dairy cattle

waiting in the barn lot. Smoke rose from the chimney, and the spring breeze fluttered the stockings neatly hung on the line. "What did you say you wanted to do with the stockings?" Sam asked.

"Sell them to all the bachelors in the area and become an independent businesswoman. The store ones aren't warm enough. I make fine stockings, Sam Taggart. I will give you a pair, but you must tell other men how fine they are, and you must not tell my father that I was sitting in a tree. He said that I'm supposed to be ladylike and quiet, or I will never be married."

Sam tensed, his survival instincts alert. "You were expecting me?"

Her small hand patted his chest comfortingly. "Yes. Do not be so alarmed. Mary Taggart sent back one of the pigeons she's been holding because my little brother behaves badly sometimes. Taggart—are you related to her?"

Sam didn't answer. He saw no reason to explain his relationship to his white half-sister, or to Harry.

Emma hurried on, filling the silence Sam found comfortable. "You look like Harry Taggart. Don't forget to give my father a place where you can be reached. You are not wearing a wedding band, and he is keeping a list of Greta's suitors. I am certain he would like a marriage arrangement with the son of Taggart lands. He has often said that Taggart land isn't used as it should be. I saw Harry Taggart when my father told him that and offered to buy the land. Harry looked thunderous, just like you. I am certain that he is not like you, however. Because it is said that Harry Taggart is a fighter when pushed. I will ask that you be placed at the top of Greta's marrying

list. Yes, I can see that he would like you to marry
Greta. I am sorry that I stand in your way."

If Emma was any indication of the Recht family, Sam
braced himself for the rest.

A huge bear of a man, neatly dressed with mut-
tonchop sideburns, came running from the barn. Two
women, an older one with a neat gray bonnet and a
younger taller one with neat blond braids crowning her
head and a lace collar upon her blue homespun dress,
came to stand on the porch.

"Shh. Don't tell my father that I was in the tree. And
don't tell him that you fought with Gilbert. And don't
tell him that we . . . I—you—me . . . under the
brush," Emma whispered as a young teenage boy eased
his crutches onto the front porch.

The boy was angular, his wrists jutting from his long
sleeves and his legs dragging uselessly on the boards. He
glared at Sam.

Emma lifted her lips to Sam's ear again and whispered, "We had a barn fire, and Fritzi rescued the
horses. He was ten and magnificent, caring for the
horses even when he was badly injured. I am certain he
will walk again someday."

"You have come just in time for our noon meal. I am
Joseph Recht," Emma's father stated in a proud, booming voice. "This is my wife Frau Recht, my daughter
Fräulein Greta, and my son, Fritzi. We would be hon-
ored if you would eat with us."

The Recht family stared at Joseph; from their expressions Sam knew that the man did not extend invitations
easily.

Joseph took Tenkiller's reins and stepped closer as

Emma slid down. She stood with her hands pressed together; Sam could only see the top of her red-and-yellow-knitted hat. "This is Sam Taggart, Papa."

Joseph stood and stared as if seeing into Sam as he dismounted. The older man noted Sam's mixed heritage and dismissed it, and his gaze ran down Sam's clothing and over the tooled saddle. Sam released the breath he'd been holding while Joseph looked at him. The two men's gazes locked and held, and finally Joseph nodded, as if he had seen what he wanted. He glanced down to where Sam had latched his hand protectively around Emma's upper arm. "He is bleeding," Joseph stated harshly. "Again you have hurt a man, Emma. Soon there will be no men in the territory that you have not wounded or shamed."

Joseph's eyes narrowed, but Sam did not remove his hand. He wasn't ready to release her just yet. He'd found the woman who just might be able to handle Harry's gang and ease Sam's conscience.

Everything was neat about Emma, despite her topple into the briars. She smelled like soap and flowers.

Sam pushed that thought away. From the way Emma handled Gilbert, she was a determined woman, and Harry—soft where women were concerned—didn't have a chance. She'd make Harry's life hell. Sam turned the idea in his mind and liked it.

Sam didn't want anything happening to Emma Recht, and once she was installed on the Big T spread, he would be free to check on his investments. "She rescued me, Mr. Recht. My horse tossed me."

Joseph plucked a piece of dried grass from Emma's bright cap and met Sam's level gaze. "So, Emma, you

have finally found a man who does not fear you . . .
yet. Take him in the house and take care of him. This is
a fine horse. I will give him grain in the barn. Welcome
to our home, Sam Taggart."

Again the Recht family stared after Joseph, who was
walking Tenkiller to the barn.

"Yes, Papa," Emma whispered meekly. But she
dipped her head to shield her smile, and Sam stopped
thinking, fascinated by the curve of her lips.

Then he hauled himself back to the people looking at
him. "Ladies . . . Fritzi. Pleased to meet you." Sam
touched his hat; they stared at the hole in it. Magda's
hand rose to cover her chest, her eyes wide and fearful.

As Emma tugged him toward the porch, Greta
crossed her arms over her chest and frowned at him.
"What have you brought home this time, Emma?"

What, not *who,* Sam noted. Greta had easily recognized his mixed blood heritage. Then Emma looked at
her sister, and there was no mistaking the steel in her
tone. "You will not be rude, Greta. Papa has made him
welcome. Sam Taggart has come a long way, perhaps for
you."

"No." Greta's voice was hard and flat. "But perhaps
he knows someone for you, and then, I can finally be
free to marry. You are a weight around my life."

"Ma'am," he said, stooping to enter the doorway as
Emma hurried him to the table.

She lifted a chair from those hanging on the wall and
placed it at the table. "Sit down."

Sam had seen chairs hanging from walls before—in
the homes of men who thought that sitting led to idle-
ness. The kitchen was spotless and brimming with food.

On a small corner table starched doilies were stretched and pinned neatly to a board to shape them.

A man used to sparse living, Sam noted the smell of women—clean good women. He'd lived in places where women smelled of sex and opium and sweat. Past the kitchen was a room with a fireplace and nicely made rocking chairs circling it. On the mantel was a small wooden chest, obviously revered, a lacy doily covering it. A quilt rack was tethered to the ceiling rafters, and a basket of clothing, obviously waiting to be mended, sat by one chair.

Everything in the Recht home was as neat and thrifty as the ranch. This was how Sam wanted his mother's home to look, just once more, before he left Harry for the last time. If anyone came calling on Harry and asking about Sam, he wanted them to see that though he was a bastard, he came from clean people.

Emma tore away her knitted cap and pushed her small efficient hands upward to smooth her hair. Sam found himself wondering just how much hair she had tightly confined in those two braids wound over her head. The tiny willful coppery tendrils dancing beside her forehead fascinated him.

He watched Emma quickly unbutton her coat. He traced the line of her full breasts and forced a swallow down his drying throat, grinding his teeth. He dragged his gaze away from Emma's body and tried to forget the lush, supple feel of her beneath him.

Magda and Emma hurried to fill a basin, and Emma cleaned his wound as he sat, enfolding him in the scent of her body. For a moment he went light-headed as though he were rolling in a field of fragrant flowers—

At his side, she angled his head higher to the light. Her hand braced his head, while the other patted at his forehead. He studied her frown of concentration and the way she bit her lip. "I am so sorry to hurt you. But the wound must be sewn," she said.

Sam nodded curtly, aware of her soft breast resting upon his shoulder. He realized that he'd begun to sweat, aware of each scent, each touch of this woman he'd just met. Emma's sharp needle and thread passed through his skin two times, and she efficiently tied the knots. Sam tried not to stare at the way her tongue touched her upper lip as she concentrated.

With her arms still crossed, Greta sat and faced Sam. "Do you know someone to marry my sister, Sam Taggart?"

"Greta!" both Magda and Emma exclaimed.

"If one does not ask, one will never find answers," Greta stated loftily. "Why have you come?"

Fritzi placed his crutches against the wall and eased into a chair, glaring at Sam. "Mary says he is an outlaw. When are you robbing us? Please take my sisters."

Emma looked steadily at him. "I will tell Papa about the things you wrote to Mary."

The firm statement confirmed Sam's belief that Emma could stand her own ground when threatened. She'd be perfect for Harry's growling mood and Mary's savagery. Sam wallowed in the perversity of installing Emma at Harry's—a minor but thorough revenge.

She took the comb from Sam's vest pocket and studied his hair part as though approaching delicate surgery. Her bosom was on a level with Sam's eyes as she reached to draw the comb down his part and neatly separate the sections. She smoothed his hair with her hands, and Sam closed his eyes, luxuriating in the moment. No one had ever tended him with such a light touch, like petting. She gave his hair one last pat as though satisfied with her work and slipped the comb into his vest pocket.

Sam stared at her, his body telling him that he should have had her in the bushes.

His mind told him that nothing made sense since the moment Emma fell from the tree.

The door clicked shut, and Joseph stated firmly, "The man has come to share our food. He needs his strength. Eat, Sam Taggart."

While Emma quickly cleared away the basin and thread, Magda began to serve huge bowls of food from the polished black stove. Emma helped her, hurriedly arranging the heavy forks and knives over neatly pressed and embroidered napkins. She poured coffee into the blue granite cups, which matched the dinner plates. Greta carried a dish of dill pickles to the table and sat down. She fluttered her lashes at Sam, and he briefly noted the sly flirtatious look. Greta liked to play at enticing men, but she didn't want him—a half-blood and a bastard.

When they were seated, Joseph began a German prayer, and when it was finished, the family all said "Amen" together. After the meal Emma and Magda cleared away the dishes and began washing them. Greta carried the dish of pickles back to the crock and dumped them into it. She hurried to another room, and Sam noted that the door did not close completely. He glanced at Emma, who was already up to her elbows in sudsy water. She seemed always in constant movement, ready to help.

He admired the sway of her backside as she worked and her skirts dancing around her ankles.

Joseph leaned back in his chair and lit his pipe. "Now we talk. Go, Fritzi. Tend your pigeons."

The boy's face turned red. "I am a man. I should stay at the table and talk with the men."

"Go." Joseph dismissed his son, who noisily exited the house. "So. Sam Taggart. You do not wear a gun. You have a good horse and a costly saddle. You dress well. Why have you come? Have you come to ask for one of my daughters?"

Sam leveled a cool look at him. "No."

Joseph puffed on his clay pipe, clearly enjoying the flavor. "I have two. The eldest must marry first. Emma would make a fine wife. She is smart and works hard."

"I didn't come after Emma. I—"

"Greta cannot marry until Emma is a wife. You cannot change my mind on this. What do you think about Emma's idea of selling stockings to cowmen and miners? It's foolish, isn't it?"

Sam had the feeling he was being pushed into a corral, and he didn't like it. "The stockings might make money. She wants to be independent, and that would be a way to do it. But getting married isn't why I'm here—"

Joseph persisted. "Emma comes with her grandmother's dowry. It is no small thing, enough to start a ranch. I did so with the money and then replaced it as is the custom. Custom is important to our family, the traditions and ways passed down to us. You say you are a Taggart?"

Sam had enough. "Harry Taggart is my . . . father. He needs a woman at his place, to tend the house and keep care of his daughter. I thought one of your daughters might want to work there. I'd pay well."

Emma turned, her expressions dancing rapidly across her face. She looked at Sam as if he'd presented a golden opportunity and then quickly veiled her reaction. She turned to slowly wash dishes, apparently intent upon the men's conversation.

Joseph nodded thoughtfully. "The Big T ranch is too far to come and go every day."

"She'd have to live there. The house is big. She'd have her own room and what she needs to tend the house. She could come home when you needed her. I don't want it said that I come from unkept people. I'm willing to pay well for better appearances at the Big T."

"Mmm. Tell me what you think of this, Sam Taggart." Joseph placed handbills advertising the sale of a ranch, notices of cattle sales, and years of farm records in front of Sam. Sam, realizing he was being tested, took out his glasses and began inspecting the neat handwritten ledgers. It was a woman's handwriting, and from the way Emma was peering curiously at him over her shoulder, Sam sensed she had noted the figures.

Joseph looked pleased as Sam skimmed the papers. "As I thought. You are a man accustomed to business," he murmured around his pipe. "Tell me your thoughts on these matters."

Sam asked direct questions, made notes on a paper placed at his side, and added sums. When he was finished, he folded his glasses and tucked them back into his pocket. He explained in rapid-fire order how Joseph needed to expand—acquire a new bull, grow chickens for miners' fare, and purchase more land for crops.

Joseph nodded. "How much will you pay me for one of my daughters to work at Harry Taggart's?"

"No!" Greta wailed from the other room.

Emma turned, a woman with a purpose. She wiped her hands on her large apron and clasped them together in front of her. "I will work for Harry Taggart, Papa. *If* you will agree that Sam Taggart has just agreed with me, and that I have a business mind."

Joseph's bristling thick brows lowered at her. "You are a woman. Women should not handle money or business matters. You will go with Sam Taggart and work for him."

Greta screamed and rushed into the room. "Papa! Who will make butter and mend clothes—make my dresses—and scrub the floors and—"

"You will. It is time you learned," Emma stated firmly.

Visibly shaken, Greta stared at her smooth well-tended hands. "But . . . but—who will wash my hair? You know it must be done at least three times a week."

Magda clasped her hands together and looked worriedly at her daughters, then at Joseph, who clearly made the decisions in the Recht family.

Emma stood on tiptoe to kiss Greta's cheek and Sam heard her whisper, "I'll come home to help, and while I am away, I will search for a husband to marry me right away and also a rich husband for you. Rich enough to afford a maid to tend you."

Sam met Emma's hazel eyes and recognized her desperate expression—she wanted him to remain quiet.

She wanted to escape the Recht ranch and Gilbert, and Sam was the door to her independence.

"You will search for me a rich husband?" Greta asked uncertainly, her hand wiping away the kiss.

"You know that I am very skilled at getting what I want. I want you to be happy, so I am willing to do this for you. If *you* go, you will have to deal with Mary and a house that has not been cleaned in a hundred years. Your hands would be rough the first day of sweeping and washing clothes and scrubbing dirty pots and floors. I have heard that men living without a woman, forget to empty the chamber pots beneath the beds. Probably the men live with rats as big as beavers."

Sam admired Emma's handling of her spoiled sister; Mary was in for a fight, because Emma knew how to manage difficult people.

Greta swallowed and smiled uncertainly at Joseph. "I think Emma should go. She is much more valuable as a hired woman than I am."

"How much?" Sam asked softly, convinced that Emma could manage the Taggart gang.

Not to be pushed, Joseph stacked the business papers neatly. He considered Sam. "I want to know what holdings you have. So that I know you can pay for hiring my Emma. And it would not be seemly for an unmarried young man to live under the same roof with my daughter—you *are* unmarried, Herr Taggart?"

"I'm not married, but I won't be at the ranch. I'll be traveling, seeing to my business interests. I'll be taking up residence in Deer Lodge City before snowfall—she'll be staying at Harry's. I'll see that she's paid the first of every month. You have my word." Sam placed forty silver dollars on the table—Tenkiller's winnings from the last race. "Payment in advance."

"Ah, a businessman. I thought so. And a successful one. I knew it when I saw the glasses and the way you studied my papers. You may take Emma." Joseph scooped up the coins and hefted them, and from his look Sam knew that Joseph Recht had a plan brewing behind his thick brows.

"You did not tell Papa what he asked," Emma said as Joseph talked quietly with Magda. "What do you do, Sam Taggart?"

"Catch women who fall from trees and roll with them in the bushes, once a day at least," he heard himself saying quietly, the urge to shock her overpowering him.

Then he wondered when he had last teased a woman who blushed so wildly.

Chapter Four

*E*mma sat very straight on her small pony, following Sam Taggart away from her family and to
the ranch near the mountains. She smoothed
her grandmother's brooch at her throat, a small comfort
reminding her of her family. When Sam had come out
to the Rechts, he had ridden the entire eighty miles in
one day and night, and he'd had time to camp and sleep.

If Sam wanted to ride throughout this night, Emma
prayed she would be able to match him, because she
didn't want him to think he had hired a weakling. Woden, her pony, trotted after Tenkiller at a sturdy pace
that Emma wasn't certain the pony could maintain.

Sam sat straight in his saddle, his broad back unre-
lenting. He was a determined man, and she wondered if
they would camp— Emma sucked in the cold evening
air, her body already aching from riding since eight
o'clock that morning. Sam rode very fast; he would not
complain, and she wouldn't ask him to stop . . . because he was unmarried, and she wouldn't shame her

father by sleeping beside a man who was not her husband.

Still—Emma stood high in the stirrups, relieving her aching bottom—she had never ridden so far on horseback. She'd heard all her life about the fierce Harry Taggart, a mountain man who held his land in an iron fist. Emma wore her best gray dress, her work boots, and her gray bonnet. The mule tethered to Sam's big horse was laden with her things, recipes from her grandmother, a quilt to remind her of home, her favorite sewing things and her crocheting, and her grandmother's hand iron and kraut cutting board. Tied to Emma's saddle was a bundle with the precious pot from her mother's kitchen.

The pot had been her father's mother's, and she thought she saw a tear in her father's eyes as he handed it to her. He stuffed her grandmother's tatting shuttles inside with soap and an apron, and a ball of delicate thread to make tatted lace. She'd hurled herself at her father, hugging him until slowly his arms had closed around her. "You take care of my Emma, Sam Taggart," he'd warned over her head. More tenderly, Joseph had added for Emma's ears alone, "My little berserker who takes chances. You will have to behave."

"I will take care of her," Sam's voice had returned, and Emma knew that once Sam had given his word, nothing could stop him from keeping it.

She glanced back at the open country that was the Rechts' and then turned forward to the mountains that stood behind the Big T. She'd always thought that when she left her family, it would be as a bride. If she was clever enough, she would escape Gilbert and find a proper husband—or even more exciting, she would become a businesswoman. In business she could take challenges and not be considered "a little berserker."

Emma lifted her chin. The label had always nagged at her. Part of her clung to the old ways, to what her grandmother's dowry represented. Yet within her, wild blood churned, ready for excitement and adventure.

Emma watched Fritzi's pigeons soar and dip through the clear blue Montana sky until they could not be seen. The pigeons would not leave the Recht land, circling within a twenty-mile radius of the farmhouse. Fritzi had sent four birds to act as messengers, flying back to the Rechts', and he had given her four paired pigeons with four-week-old chicks to raise on the Taggart land. Once handled by a loving trainer and raised in one place, the chicks would soon grow to birds who would always return to Taggart land, no matter how far away. The birds' cages were tied behind her, and they blinked at her with red trusting eyes while tending their chicks. An expert at pigeons, Fritzi had chosen them because of their eye markings, revealing them to have the best sight.

Emma missed Fritzi already. Her mother babied him, fearing he would hurt himself or cry when he was in pain. Though Emma felt these things, too, she knew that Fritzi needed challenges, just as she did. She glanced up, hoping to see Fritzi's pigeons circling her one last time, a farewell. But the sky was wide and empty, the light dying.

Her mother had sent a bundle of food for the trip, with a small crock of her yeast starter. Tucked into Emma's bundles were precious seeds from the Recht garden.

On top of her bundles on the pony were two setting hens, not at all happy about moving from their coop. Their eggs were carefully packed in sand and straw in a box beneath them.

The largest bundle contained all her stockings, her knitting needles, and her wool. Emma intended to sell every one of her stockings before she returned to the Rechts', with enough money to buy off Gilbert.

Emma inhaled the chilly evening air and wallowed in her happiness. While she loved her family, Sam Taggart had presented an opportunity she wanted with utmost greed. When he'd made the offer to her father, only her fear of losing this opportunity to go out into the world had kept her from begging him to accept it.

If she had seemed too eager, her father wouldn't have let her go. He was perverse that way, withholding what she wanted most, like his recognition of her business ability. When she returned with her stocking money, her father would be forced to admit that she was a true businesswoman.

Her grandmother's dowry shouldn't be wasted on Gilbert. Perhaps living at the Taggarts would change her father's mind about marrying her before Greta could get married.

Then, when she had proved that she could be independent and a businesswoman, and if she met a man who would not annoy her too much, perhaps she would marry him—because in her heart, she longed to hold a baby just like any other woman. With all the marriage candidates looking at Greta, Emma had pushed back her dreams of being a mother and now settled for what she was—a plain woman with a talent for making socks and bargains. She wanted to prove that she was a woman who could think, actually think and plan for herself.

She rested her hand on the pigeons' cages, crafted lovingly from supple branches by Fritzi. The pigeons' red eyes seemed to understand, and she stroked their smooth heads to reassure them. In return they "made milk," both parents spewing a nurturing white substance onto their hungry chicks.

Sam Taggart glanced back over his shoulder at her, and Emma's sense of well-being fled. There was nothing warm or happy about Sam Taggart. He was merely an impatient man, anxious to get her back to the Taggart ranch and to be on his way.

He rode back to her. The whip coiled on his saddle horn gleamed wickedly. "Is that all the faster that pony moves?"

She was used to men's impatience with her, but she would not allow Woden to be insulted. "Woden is—"

Sam reached to scoop Emma into the saddle in front of him. "I want to get there before the week is over. Your pony has enough to carry without you."

Shaken by being handled like a child, Emma sat very still. She held the bundle with her grandmother's cooking pot and her tatting shuttles. She pushed away the small flick of her temper, not wanting to insult her employer before she had begun work.

The pot clanged against his rifle. Startled, Tenkiller sidestepped. "What's in that sack?" Sam asked sharply.

Emma clutched the bundle tightly, fearing that he would want to take it away from her. "It stays with me.

It is my grandmother's cooking pot, and pictures of my family, and—"

"Enough."

He made an impatient noise that settled into her, nagged at her until she decided that Sam Taggart must learn that she had rules, too, and that handling her like a child wasn't to be permitted. "Mr. Sam Taggart."

She shivered, feeling small and feminine within the easy loop of his arms. She remembered his hard body covering hers in the thicket and his expression—impatient, hard, and disturbed by something she couldn't define.

"What?"

"If you wished me to ride faster, you had only to say so."

"You talk too much. You've been chattering away to those pigeons every minute or so."

She sat very straight, not wanting him to think that he had hired a complaining woman. Sam was a businessman and not a fighter; perhaps the whip was in his possession because he wanted to barter it.

"Fritzi's pigeons need reassurance, Sam Taggart." Emma pressed her lips together. This was the first time she had been away from her family; she was not far from crying. She would not reply to his rudeness. She wouldn't— "And you do not. You say little and expect me to know how—"

She wouldn't cry. She wouldn't reveal her irritation to her employer. She regretted the sniff she'd just made and sat very straight. She was tired, having gotten up early to see to the new foal and to help harness the horses for Gilbert—to say nothing of skipping out of his reach when he caught her between the workhorses.

In the evening light she could see for miles and forced herself not to look back toward the Recht ranch. The least Sam Taggart could do was to offer an encouraging word, or tell her how grateful he was that she would take care of his father and sister. She wasn't used to silence— She realized with horror that tears were dripping from her cheeks onto her freshly pressed blouse.

She squeezed her lids shut to get out the last of the hated tears, yet more burned in their place.

A jackrabbit sprinted between the serviceberry bushes. "I hope Greta makes the biggest apple dumpling for Gilbert. He was not happy with me."

Seated behind her, Sam was too quiet. She allowed herself to settle against his hard frame, because in another moment she'd be fast asleep, giving herself to the smooth fast rhythm of the horse. "I will work hard for you, Sam Taggart. You will be proud of your home."

"It's not mine, and I won't be around." His voice sounded like the closing of a door.

"You are angry." She looked up at him, her tears returning despite her efforts to stop them. "You didn't pay too much for me. I am a hard worker. I am only worried about my family and who will tend to Gilbert. I gave Greta my grandmother's ruby ring to take care of Gilbert."

His look down at her wasn't kind. "Wasn't that the man who was interested in your 'milk-giving place'?"

She flushed and straightened away from him. "I am teaching him manners."

"Stop crying." His voice was impatient, harsh, when she needed just a bit of understanding.

"You!" she wailed, startling his horse into rearing. She waited for Sam to control the beast, and then she stated precisely, "Today I have left my family for the first time. You trust me to care for your family—that is a great honor. I am"—she fought the trembling of her bottom lip—"I am a modern woman on an adventure. I will earn money for my father, and I will build my stocking business."

She sniffed, then continued, "You have good points, Sam Taggart. You do not wear a revolver, and you are not a fighter, but a man who wears glasses and who understands business. You should understand that I am worried about my family, and my heart is sad at the same time it is joyous, Sam Taggart—"

Sam shook his head wearily. He drew out a neatly folded handkerchief, shook it out, and mopped her face with it. "Blow. Could you manage to save that until you meet Monty?"

She blew into the handkerchief and watched as Sam tried to decide where to place the damp cloth. He obviously didn't want to place it into the pocket of his meticulous jacket. She took the handkerchief from him; when he got it back, it would be washed and ironed. "Tell me about Monty. And who is the woman who shot your hat?"

She wanted to wallow in details, to love the old men and the girl. Sam cared for them enough to seek a hired woman to tend to them.

Sam shifted her against him and tucked her skirts under his leg. "Tenkiller isn't used to talk or to skirts."

She allowed him that; the horse was just as black and evil-tempered as the man. They rode in silence through the moonlight, and Emma awoke as the horse stopped.

She realized that Sam was holding her very closely, his chin tucked over her bonnet, his body tense. He enfolded her with his heat, despite the chilling three o'clock air.

In the moonlight lines cut deeply in Sam's face. He looked tired and grim and wary, almost haunted. Emma firmed her lips; she would make a nice home for Sam Taggart, a comfort to which he would want to return.

The Big T ranch house lay in the dying moonlight, and the mountains jutted up behind it. Sam's arms tightened around her, as if he regretted bringing her to this place. She placed her hand on his tense arm and looked up to find his face rigid in the moonlight. "I will make it better, Sam Taggart," she whispered. "I will take care of your family."

"I don't have a family," he returned sharply, and leaped from the horse, lifting her down. Then he urged her up the steps of the house.

The front door of the Taggart house jerked open, and Emma found herself looking into the deadly barrel of a buffalo gun. She reeled back against Sam's hard body, colliding against his chin.

He grunted, and she looked up the barrel of the gun to the coldest eyes she'd ever seen, steam shooting from the man's nostrils. His full beard and long curling hair caused the man to seem larger than Sam. Her scream froze in her throat. Before cold fear could entirely enfold her, Sam's hand closed on her nape and jerked her away like a kitten that needed protection. "Emma, this is Harry Taggart. This is Emma Recht. I've hired her. You need help."

"A hired woman. Nobody asked you for anything," Harry growled.

Sam's fingers tightened on Emma's nape, and she could feel the tension quivering between him and the older man. "This was my mother's home. It needs care. This is for her, not you."

"No business of yours now," Harry returned. "You're a man, full-growed. Git. Be on your way. Won't no one here mourn your leaving, boy."

"I'd like to see my mother's house clean." Sam placed the words into the air like bullets.

The undercurrents running between the two big men frightened Emma—not for herself, but for them.

Sam's voice slid into a quiet dangerous tone, as though he were slicing at the heart of the problem between them. "I'm not like you, Harry. You'd like me to ride off, and you'd like to forget that I was raised here, that my mother was your woman. But that's not how it's going to be. I want you to remember me a bit longer."

"You're mighty full of yourself, boy, dropping a hired woman on me and then skedatling. That's a good hard ride to the Rechts', and you hurried some, I'd say, to drag this little thing back in short time." Harry's tone shifted to a darker ominous one. "What makes you think you got any rights here? You ran off and left. What makes you think I won't eat this little chickie for breakfast?"

The older man wanted a fight, and Emma wondered how she'd protect Sam this time. From the older man's fierce look, she saw that a bribe of an apple dumpling might not work.

Emma stepped between the two towering men; Sam's big hand remained firmly on her nape. Adept at diverting her family's arguments, Emma said, "Sam Taggart, go take care of my chickens and the pigeons. Fritzi said to feed and water them immediately. Do you have a place for them?"

"There's not a place for anything here." Sam's hand tightened on her nape, as though he wanted to keep her close to him.

A twelve-year-old girl dressed in a man's dirty shirt pressed up against Harry, who was standing in his long johns. Emma noted they needed patching and washing. A small, thin man who was peering around Harry also wore dirty worn long johns. All of them needed bathing and good food and care. She saw why Sam was so eager to get back to them, wanting them to have care. They were precious.

Emma loved them all immediately. Despite her fatigue, she grinned up at Harry. "You love fresh baked bread and apple dumplings, don't you? Do you have a cow?"

"We'll get a cow, a real pretty one for you, missy. If that's what you want," Monty said happily as he licked his fingers to smooth the peaks in his thinning gray hair. "Sam, we don't have anything to feed her."

Emma silently thanked her mother, who knew that men were always hungry and had packed a bundle of food. "I brought food, enough to make a few meals. There is bread and butter, headcheese, blood sausage, and wheat and dried fruit for breakfast. We cannot use the eggs. My hens are setting. We cannot eat my hens either. They are my friends."

"I love you," Monty said in an openly adoring tone.

"Ah, hell, Monty. Tomorrow we'll shoot a few birds for the lady," Harry rumbled.

"No bullets, Harry," Monty said worriedly.

"Hell, we'll snare 'em like we used to. Mary is right good at it."

"Oh, no, I ain't. Not for her," Mary stated.

"Hush!" Monty ordered, with an unusually sharp note to his voice. Mary looked up at him in surprise.

Sam made an impatient noise behind Emma, and she smiled up at him and patted his arm. "Go along now, Sam Taggart. Please take good care of Fritzi's birds and my hens. You may bring my things into the house in the morning."

She held her grandmother's cooking pot close to her, containing her shuttles and the soap. Her mother had tucked her best big apron inside, and from the stench coming from within the house, Emma knew she would need that apron and the soap.

And from Sam's expression, she knew he didn't like being dismissed. One hand was still on her neck, as though any minute he'd pluck her back from the family inside the cabin. She ignored their stench and turned to Sam, who looked wary. "My father will not mind if you sleep on the porch."

Monty snickered, and Sam seemed to grow two feet taller, his nostrils flaring and a muscle ticking along his cheek. Something like a smile curled around Harry Taggart's mouth, while Mary glared at Emma, defending her territory. "You ain't sleeping in here, lady." She leveled an evil look up at Sam. "My cats like to eat birds."

Emma was used to dealing with Greta and Fritzi's evil tendencies. "Sam won't let the cats get near them. Because if he sleeps on the porch or in the barn, the cats will probably sleep with him. There's enough of Sam to keep several cats warm. In the morning we can all plan the pigeon coop. You can hold the new babies when they hatch, chickens and pigeons. Sam, you may place my bundles on the porch for now."

A vein throbbed in his temple, and his narrowed look down at her said he didn't like taking orders.

Emma smiled slowly. As the eldest Recht daughter, she'd been giving orders for a long time. "You have hired me, have you not? Shoo. Now go along, so that I may start my work."

He hovered in the shadows over her, the moonlight shooting through the hole in his hat. She decided to adopt him as well as the old man and the girl.

She smiled and gently pushed on Harry Taggart's chest with her mitten. He moved aside, drawing Monty and Mary with him. Emma stepped into the dark stench happily. They needed her. They were her current adventure and her challenge.

Sam pushed the hind end of a cat away from his face. He came slowly awake, pushing away the nightmare of cannons and the sticky feel of blood on his hands. He lay listening, heart racing, pushing away the fear that often caused him to awaken with a cry on his lips; he focused on the cooing of the pigeons, their cages hanging from the rafters with the chickens.

The barn where he had slept was just as filthy as the house; Tenkiller had refused to spend what remained of the night in it. The horse was a crossbreed like Sam. Sam had wanted to make a statement when he returned to Montana Territory and chose Tenkiller to help that image. The big, black durable racing trotter was loyal only to Sam, a helpful trait in some of the wild towns Sam would visit.

Sam touched his chest pocket, checking the safety of his glasses. He quickly inventoried the money belt he wore beneath his shirt, the small knife in his boot, and Harry's big hunting knife strapped to his back. The familiar handle of the whip leaped into his hand, and he forced himself to relax.

Four hours of sleep in two days caused Sam to groan. He'd learned that he needed sleep to manage business, that his best deals were made when he was rested. He had the gold mine deal ahead of him, and a tough miner who didn't want to sell yet couldn't keep the mine running until it paid his bills.

The chickens began to move restlessly, signaling dawn, and Sam's mind swung to the woman in the house.

He was too tired, riding on nerves from seeing old Harry again and from knowing that he had a conscience where his father was concerned. He did not like that discovery.

Sam shifted restlessly as he remembered holding Emma as they rode to the Big T. She had slept in his arms, her bonnet holding all that hair. He hadn't allowed a woman to sleep in his arms in his lifetime. He was afraid that he'd awaken to lovemaking and forget to withhold his seed.

Yet he'd held Emma and fought the need to slip his hand over her soft breast. Her eyes were the color of rich dark green velvet, filled with innocence and too damn trusting. As she slept, her face pressed to the warmth of his throat hadn't helped.

Sam stretched his aching legs and studied the dust on his boots. His remaining suit was covered with cat hair from jacket to cuffs. He dusted at it impatiently and stuck his finger through the hole in his hat, lifting it. He'd get away from the ranch as quickly as possible and stay away. He'd sleep, clean up, and turn his mind to business—

Sam listened to Mary enter the barn; he opened an eyelid to see the girl standing in the dawn, her hands on her hips as she glared at him. "Why'd you have to bring *her* here? Couldn't you just have brought a plague to kill us in a natural way?"

Harry hopped by the barn's open doorway, his arms filled with firewood. Monty scurried after him with more wood.

Mary plopped down on a board and glared at Sam as he began dusting his boots with his last clean handkerchief. He thought of his handkerchief balled in Emma's fists as she fought crying. He didn't like feeling guilty, but he did.

"She's got them fetching for her. I won't. See if I will. No, sir. I won't," Mary persisted. "You brought this plague on us, worse than grasshoppers or a fire, and you just take her back where you got her, Sam."

She leveled a glare at the house. "She's in there scrubbing and singing and hauling things around where we'll never find them. She said to tell you that breakfast was in a bit and that you'll find wash water, soap, and a towel on the front porch. . . . I'm not washing. No, I ain't. Not me." She scowled at him. "You're going, ain't you? Going to use my whore tokens in some fleabag house. Here I been saving every penny I could find—"

"Find?" Sam asked with a lifted eyebrow.

Mary hunched down. "Fritzi has them morning dreams. You ought to know, if you were ever young, Sam."

"The Rechts live a good eighty miles away. Just where did you meet Fritzi?"

"Fritzi was with Joseph Recht that day he came to make an offer for some land. The next thing I know there's some cowpoke bringing me these pigeons and a note to meet Fritzi at the creek—that was three years ago, when I was a kid. Pa doesn't mind when I take off a day—says it makes me strong and I can learn things better on my own. I sure did that day with Fritzi. We spent a day there, just talking. That was one fine day. Then last fall Fritzi told me about his needing a whore to set things right and make him walk—like medicine, fixing him. There ain't no right for him, the way his pa is—always telling him to stay out of the way and not to bother about man things."

That information was more than Sam wanted; he lurched to his feet, shook his bedroll, and tied it neatly. He whistled for Tenkiller and began to saddle him. The stallion stomped and, eyeing Sam, nudged him hard. Sam looked Tenkiller in the eye. Tenkiller wanted more of the lush grazing out in the field; Sam wanted to shed this place and his past. In two days his life had lost its neatness, cluttered with the lives and needs of other people; he wanted his life back. Tenkiller stomped toward him, doing a fancy dance that would have scared most men. He nudged Sam hard, this time putting more muscle in it, but Sam continued to saddle him.

Perched on top of a stall, out of harm's way, Mary's eyes widened. "You're leaving? You're leaving us with *her*?" she demanded indignantly.

Sam tightened the cinch and swung up onto the saddle. "I've got business to tend. Tell the woman I'll send food back today, from the first ranch house I come to. There will be more from a store later. You tell Harry that he'll have a small amount of credit at the store."

"Don't you spend Fritzi's whore tokens!" Mary's yell was hushed so her father wouldn't hear.

"What did you sell?" Sam eased Tenkiller to the stall, eye to eye with Mary, who sat on the top board.

She looked away. "Nothing. Just some things hanging around that weren't no good to nobody."

Sam skimmed the barn and found the place where his father's beaver traps used to hang, oiled and waiting. Harry hadn't noticed or cared enough to keep them oiled and ready as he had years ago, waiting for a prime pelt. Sam had learned how to set those traps at too young an age, just barely strong enough to set the jaws. He'd feared failure then, sweating to do a task far beyond his years, and Harry always wanted more.

"It's been hard keeping up with you, Sam," Mary said quietly.

"What do you mean?"

Mary spat into the dirt. "You're Pa's firstborn, and a

boy to boot. Sam, didn't you know that? You're the yardstick he measures me against. 'Sam did this when he was six,' and 'Sam did that before he was eight,' and 'Sam—' "

Sam straightened; he'd done what Harry wanted of him, and it wasn't easy. He knew how Mary felt.

She eyed Sam. "I know you for what you are. Mean and cold clear through. You're an imposter—a charlatan like the play Monty took me to once. But I won't wither away and moan and groan and die like that stage woman. I got my ways to get rid of you and that woman you infested us with."

Sam dismissed what Mary had said about Harry, because he didn't want to remember those times with his father. He rode past the ranch house, subtracting the amount of money he'd have to pay for the food from the money he wanted to invest in Fletcher's gold mine.

Emma stood on the porch, dressed in her gray dress, now wrinkled, and the vast apron covering it was almost gray from dirt. She tightened her lips as Tenkiller pranced by, showing off for the woman.

Sam nodded and touched his hat, a small courtesy. He tossed a package of mixed shells and gunpowder onto the porch at her feet. Harry and Monty could make do; Sam carried the package of mixed-caliber rounds and balls because he'd found it useful more than once. A man who carried only a knife and a rifle had to be resourceful. Damning himself once more, he reached into his saddlebags and extracted Tenkiller's bag of grain, also tossing it at her feet.

He might not like Harry, but he wouldn't be responsible for pigeons and chickens starving on Taggart land.

Emma's clear hazel eyes showed no emotion as they locked with his. The morning sunlight glinted off her hair, catching red sparks in the braids wound on top of her head. A cobweb draped down her nape to the top button of her dress. The circles beneath her eyes shouldn't have bothered him; he'd seen tired women before.

Sam braced himself for her condemnation. But she stood very straight and alone, her hands in the folds of her skirts.

He wasn't taking her back to the Rechts', even if she asked. Sam waited for her to yell at him as Tenkiller pranced onto the road leading from the Big T.

He straightened his back and waited for her to run after him; he promised he wouldn't look back.

Emma never yelled, and Sam didn't look back.

Chapter Five

It is now the middle of June, and Sam Taggart has been gone two weeks. New green beans are sprouting in the garden, and I have started flowers on the graves of the three women that Mary calls "the sisters." One is Sam's mother, and not related, but it is a lovely thought that the women Harry loved would be sisters. Sam Taggart cares more for his horse and his fine boots than he does for sweet Harry. Sam did not say good-bye the day he left. He just stared at me. I have my pride. I would not ask him to stay. I would not tell him how his father needs him. Instead I worked very hard and fixed the chimney. I was so angry with Sam Taggart, I could have cleaned two dirty houses and three chimneys that morning. Monty has cleaned the chicken coop and put the droppings on the garden. The pigeons like their new coop and are setting on new eggs. When the chicks circle the ranch, I will feel more at home. Mary cannot read, and she does not like me or soap. I like

*Harry, and with my goose grease salve and clean
wrappings, his foot is much better now. At first his
hugs frightened me, but now I like them. He calls me
Buttercup. I like that. Monty teases Harry. I am starting a rug from rags. My stockings are selling well to
passing miners and cowboys. I like to trade, to barter. It is a game that I am skilled at playing, and now
I can do it without Papa scolding me. I love playing
this game.*

*I would not rut with Sam Taggart like Gilbert says,
but I would tell him that he should have said good-
bye to Harry, who loves him. Some kind word to me
would have been good manners. Or even a smile. He
is beautiful when he smiles, as he did when I was
scolding Gilbert for saying I had udders. Sam Taggart is the only man who can make me so angry that
I would like to thump him with my wooden spoon—
this to put some sense in his beautiful head. E.*

Seated on the front porch at dusk, Emma glanced at
Harry, who reminded her immediately of Sam with his
arrogant, sleek looks and neatly parted hair. There was
no mistaking the chiseled high cheekbones, deeply set
eyes, and jaw, though Harry's jowls and weathered look
had softened him. Beside Harry, Sam had looked like a
young hawk, poised to swoop. She could see Sam,
dressed as Harry once had been, striding through the
mountains, dressed in buckskins.

Monty came out, a thick slice of bread in his hand,
and sat on the porch beside Emma. "I wonder how Sam
is going to stop the rustlers."

"Dammit, man, I told you there aren't rustlers, not on

my land. The horses and those five scrub cattle just wandered away," Harry muttered.

"Uh-huh. Wonder how Sam is going to fix our credit at the store."

"Doesn't need fixing," Harry shot back.

"Does, too."

Harry was quiet, then he said, "If the boy says he'll do something, he'll do it. And nobody makes him do anything he doesn't want to do. I know that for a fact—he always did choose his own path, and it's been a better one than mine."

"I'd say the boy is wearing a few times that he did something he didn't want to do, and it's still stuck in his craw." Monty chewed on the bread, and Harry looked up at the graves.

Monty swallowed and nodded. "You're going to let the boy do what he wants on the place, aren't you?"

Harry pivoted to Monty. "You talk too much."

Monty grinned. "You didn't want this little filly afore you saw her, but you didn't fight the boy on the matter."

"The boy respects his ma and what she was, a fine woman who didn't hold with dirt. I wouldn't have it any other way."

Emma didn't want to think about "the boy." She sat in the dying light with friendly men who needed her and respected her. Each of them wore her stockings and marveled about them every hour or so. Harry was able to wear only one, but he tucked the other in his pocket as though fearing it would escape him. He allowed it to dangle on display, like a ribbon from a lady from King Arthur's knights. When passersby stopped at the ranch,

Harry always took out that stocking and advertised for her.

Emma inhaled; she was a businesswoman now, but she also needed a family around her. She thought of Sam, alone, doing his business without his family to care.

The three of them sat quietly, ignoring Mary, who was sulking after her first bath. Emma thought Mary looked pretty, but she didn't want to start the aching-bosom conversation again.

Emma turned to Harry and found the strong cheekbones, the hard jaw he had passed on to his son. "Why is it that Sam is so angry with you, Harry? You are such a nice man."

Monty snickered. "Nobody ever called him nice before. He's sweet on you, that's why. But you're my girl, for sure."

Harry glowered at Monty, his expression as fierce as Sam's when Emma had knocked him to the ground. She worried about the cut on Sam's forehead and wondered if it was healing.

Harry cleared his throat, and Monty stopped grinning. Both men stared off into the rolling plains. Harry inhaled harshly, and Emma waited. She suspected he was about to relate something close to his heart, like a locked door slowly creaking open.

"I made mistakes with the boy," Harry admitted harshly.

Monty slid a handkerchief from his pocket and wiped his eyes stealthily.

Emma patted Harry's rough hand and allowed him to

hold hers, because at times he seemed to need comforting. "You love him. That is not a mistake."

Harry grimaced as if remembering something unpleasant. "I never married his ma. Not rightly, with a preacher. That's one thing he's holding against me."

He looked up at the knoll as though he could see Feather waving to him. "She was the prettiest little bird I ever saw."

Softness laid on Harry's newly shaved, craggy face. "Feather was special. I knew it the minute I saw her, gathering serviceberries. I'd just come down from the mountains, headed into town to spend my money in a rip-roaring toot with the fancy ladies, when I saw her standing there in that leather shift, all decorated with blue beaded flowers. . . . I lost my heart that day. Decided I wanted a house for her and land to put down roots. I wanted to give her babies. Back then, my friends laughed at me. I'd cut too many Indians by that time, killed 'em, took their scalps. I used to be proud of that, back when I was a pup. Reckon they got some back at the Little Bighorn."

Harry's gaze searched the mountains behind the house and the sprawling countryside. "I brought her here to this little valley, where the Indians won't fight because of their legends. I thought Feather and our cubs would be safe. After she had Sam—" Harry swallowed and his eyes dimmed. "She had a hard time of it, and I wouldn't hold with no more babies after that, no matter that she wanted more."

The old mountain man clamped his lips shut and stared at the three women's graves on the small knoll. "She was my first love. I promised her if anything happened to her, I'd find another woman to take care of Sam—so he'd know how to be soft with women, not like I was raised. But he wasn't here long for Evie—only a week or so after we married. He wasn't here at all to meet Juliet. I loved them in different ways. They were good women, my wives."

His mouth open, Monty stared at his old friend. "Harry, that's the most I've heard you say ever. You dying?"

Harry glared at Monty and released Emma's hand. "Sam brought her here. You saying she shouldn't know what's wrong between me and my boy, when she's landed smack dab in the middle of the pile?"

Monty blinked owlishly. "Go right ahead."

Harry settled back down, looking at the mule in the corral, and a muscle worked in his cheek as though he was thinking about the past, how to say it. "Feather was . . . I got warm just thinking about her. She ran off with me when her folks wouldn't let me marry her. Her brother, Many Horses, came after her with five of his men. They had blood in their eye. They were the first Indians I fought that I didn't want to kill. I took special care not to, just knocked them around a bit to show Feather that I wasn't a weakling."

Emma patted his hand. "I'm glad Sam is not a fighter."

"Uh-huh." Though his tone was disbelieving, Harry grinned almost boyishly. "I let them knock me around so Feather would think I was hurt and would make a fuss over me. Then Feather lit into them with her broom. She was something, all het up. . . ."

Harry chewed on another thought, shaping it until he

spoke. "Traveling preachers came by, asking for hand-outs. Feather always treated them fine, but not one of them would marry us. There was bad trouble back in those days, killing on both sides. Then Sam came along, and the marriage paper didn't seem to matter. Pretty soon he was twelve and Feather was gone, killed."

Monty let out a sob and scrambled to his feet. "God, Christ almighty, Harry. I can't take no more."

When Monty closed the house door behind him, Harry began rocking gently, as though sealing in the pain. "I didn't do right by my woman or my boy. I should have married Feather. Taken her somewhere where they would marry us, but there always seemed to be crops, or mustangs to bring in and break—they paid more for them back then. I never killed buffalo for hides after I married Feather. We got along."

Emma rested her hand on Harry's, and he seemed to ease as he continued, "I didn't know how bad my boy was hurting. I'd been raised hard, my pa's back hand the only way he talked to me. I should have told the boy how much I loved her and him—I didn't. Instead I went on a two-year toot and ended up marrying Evie, a good woman. Sam needed me after Feather . . . left. I should have told him how I saw his mother in him and how it hurt just to look at him."

Emma ached for Harry. She wrapped her arm around his broad shoulder and hugged him.

"About fourteen or so he ran off to his ma's people and found they were just as tough. But back then, they were having bad days with the whites, and there he was, half white."

Emma kept her arm around Harry until he rose, cleared his throat, and entered the house.

She remained on the porch, and the door creaked open behind her. Monty brought her a cup of tea and her crocheted shawl. He patted her head and left her alone with her thoughts.

Emma wrapped her shawl around her and hoped they hadn't seen Gilbert sitting on his mule in the distance.

In the middle of June, Tenkiller pranced into Sleigh Bell City, a bustling frontier town filled with the roughest of men. Sam had just returned from checking on his northern stores in Beartown, Garnet, and Coloma. Sleigh Bell was like them, perched between the sharp inclines of rugged mountains; the small towns sprang up like weeds and died as quickly, leaving a few weathered board stores. The single street was filled with farmers' wagons and men living by their guns. Sam ignored the women calling from beer halls and calculated just how much he would spend on new equipment for the Fletcher mine and how much the new cook house and draft teams would cost for Jensen and Taggart Lumber.

Big Bo Jensen had been a hard businessman, his temper ruling him. He hadn't liked a fancy half-blood strolling into his camp, holding newly purchased partnership papers. Bo had knocked his partner around one too many times, and Rufus Pickford was headed to Anaconda to an easy life in the copper smelters.

Sam skimmed his hand over the bruise on his leg where Jensen had hit him with a chair. When Jensen was sprawled across the rough-cut board floor of his tiny shack, Sam had treated himself to a good cigar and tossed one to Jensen, who began to listen to Sam's plans to put the operation on a paying scale.

Sam was investing everything in building his new companies. He had profitable assets, and making them grow would be hard work. The two mines he'd acquired would take time to bring in a payload. Lumber was quick money, shipped down to Butte and to Fort Benton. He'd bought the store that had stopped Harry's credit; the former owner continued to run it. Sam sent a letter to Tex Murdock, asking him to return any stock with a Big T brand. The letter was brief and let the owner of the neighboring ranch know that a new player was in the game.

Sam flexed his fingers, wrapped in his handkerchief. The hide hunters he'd met didn't like fancy half-bloods, and he'd returned the favor. The scratches on his face were from Venus, an English earl's woman who didn't like losing her jewelry on a bet. Sam had traded the jewelry for cash, except for one ring on his little finger. He wanted Venus to remember who she had played and that she had lost to a half-blood.

When he left Sleigh Bell, two men followed him down the mountain passage to the rolling road leading toward the Big T. After hours of keeping track of them, Sam expected their bullets and let Tenkiller enjoy the hour-long race. Their bullets were no danger, out of range, and Sam knew the stallion needed the challenge. Tiring of the game, Sam pulled into a stand of aspens.

When the thugs topped a hill, Sam was waiting for them. "Looking for me?"

Twenty minutes later Sam bent by the stream and washed his face. He stripped his ruined clothes—one of the thugs had ungraciously bled upon his jacket—stuffed them into his saddlebag, and drew on fresh clothing. He checked the dust rising in the distance—the men were riding out of the country, as he had ordered.

In the other direction a short jackleg fence marked the beginning of Big T land.

Sam shook his head. He shouldn't have spent tight money on that big red cow and sent her to Harry's by way of a cowboy.

Tenkiller nickered as a small herd came down to water at the creek. The *Hutterite* man—a branch of the German Mennonite religion—walking beside the cattle, nodded at Sam.

The small cow, reddish brown and white, had small, neat circular horns. Sam shook his head again, because that cow reminded him of Emma and how she could ignite, all shimmering and red-haired and emerald-fire eyes.

Sam closed his eyes, feeling every mile of the last two weeks. He wondered briefly how the sweet full curve of Emma's breasts would feel, pillowing his head.

Every night I pray that I will not become Gilbert's wife and that my grandmother's dowry will not be his. I work hard, but life is easier when I do not have to run from Gilbert. I knit socks every night, so that I can make money to repay Gilbert's time. After I have proven myself as a businesswoman, I would like to marry one day, and have children. Many town women are married and work, too, I have learned. It is a good dream. Because I am plain, I do not expect

*a grand love, but I think a partnership can be worked
out, if the right man—a gentle man who respects my
intelligence—comes into my life. I do not expect a
man as beautiful as Sam Taggart, but one that respects me as I am. I wonder if a businesswoman can
work and be a good wife. I miss my family, but soon I
will have a rug like Mama's near my bed. Harry and
Monty built a smokehouse, and this fall we will make
sausages. In all this time Sam Taggart has not sent
word to his father, and I wish to tell him that he is
bad. How Harry loves him. Why is Sam so blind? E.*

Emma took the big round loaves of bread from the
tiny oven in the old black stove. She longed for her
mother's immense outside oven, which usually baked
ten to sixteen loaves on baking day. While her mother
used a bread tray about four feet long and a foot and a
half deep, Emma had only a small bread bowl.

She had traded a set of her stockings for the cream-
colored pottery bowl, and it was lovely, a part of her
that she had given to this home. Emma dipped her fingers in lard, smoothed them over the two freshly baked
loaves, then removed them from the flat baking pan.
She smoothed lard on the pan and placed two more
silky yeast loaves upon it and shoved it into the oven.

By Wednesday, her little family had already devoured
the bread she'd baked on Monday. When Frieda, the big
red cow, came fresh with a calf, the men would love
butter on the bread.

She loved her new routine and the way Harry didn't
mind if she sat at the kitchen table while she chopped or
cleaned. On Sundays she insisted on a day of rest—

except for knitting one sock. Then Monday was baking-bread and wash day, and Tuesday was cleaning day. Wednesdays she baked again and cooked a huge dinner from whatever game Monty and Harry brought to her. Thursdays were for gardening and mending and— She glanced at the big pile of clean clothing resting out on the front porch. The best pieces would go into her quilting scrap basket, but a good amount would be torn into strips for a new braided rug.

The door crashed back against the wall as Monty entered, breathless after running. "Sam's back. He's riding in."

Emma dusted her hands and smoothed her hair. She didn't want to look untidy for Sam. She placed her open hand over her heart to feel the leaping that just hearing his name brought.

She pressed her lips together and narrowed her eyes. How like Sam not to send notice that he was coming. He chose to arrive on baking day, with all the rags on the front porch waiting to be torn. He would arrive just after she'd finished hoeing the new garden and feeding the little pigs. Racer, Harry's favorite piglet, had scrambled between her legs, almost upsetting her. Emma quickly scanned the ranch yard, finding everything in its place. She wanted Sam to see how well the Taggart land looked now, with its newly plowed fields and— She jumped up and hurried to the back of the house, grabbing her damp petticoats from the bushes and hurrying into the house with them. Harry and Monty had promised not to look at them while they were drying and had meticulously avoided going into the back. Sam might not be as gracious, and she didn't want him looking at her petticoats. She tossed them upon her neatly made bed and hurried back to the porch.

Emma touched her grandmother's brooch and prayed her heart would stop leaping with excitement. Sam looked just as big and fierce and cold as before, riding Tenkiller, who immediately began prancing. Sam looked glued to the saddle, and thinner, worn by the two weeks. He jerked the reins impatiently as Tenkiller began high-stepping. From Sam's grim expression, she knew there was nothing he could do about Tenkiller.

Harry had tossed down his hammer and stood braced, his legs wide spread as he watched his son approach. Monty was hurtling down the road with daylight and dust between his bowed legs; Mary had gathered up all of her cats, clearly protecting them.

Sam came closer, and from behind Tenkiller a little cow hurried to keep up, her round udder swaying from side to side.

Because she could not stop herself, Emma flew off the porch and ran toward Sam. The sight of the running woman, her petticoats flashing around her boots, set off Tenkiller, who sidestepped warily, dragging the little cow behind him. Sam scowled at Emma, his mouth a hard line.

"I am sorry your horse is frightened, Sam Taggart," she said, not meaning it. She smiled up at him; she was happy to see him—

He tossed the rope to the little cow to her, and she saw the two deep scratches on his cheek. She had placed scratches just like that on Gilbert's cheek. She straightened, and her smile died. She had been glad to see Sam, to know that he cared enough to return to his father.

But another woman's marks on his face did not please her.

Monty grinned up at Sam. "How you been, Sam?"

"Fine." Sam swung down, because Tenkiller wouldn't stop sidestepping. He led the horse while Monty walked at his side. Emma thought Sam could spare Monty a smile. She eyed the marks on his face, and Sam glanced at her. "What's got your dander up?"

"Who's the cow for, boy?" Monty pressed, still grinning. He winked at Emma.

Emma wrapped her arm around the small cow's neck and petted her. If Sam meant to sell the little cow, she wouldn't let him. "She is a rich milk giver," she stated. "Cows like this are kept in the barn in the hard wintertime."

"The cow is yours. From the looks of Harry and Monty, you've done a good job," Sam said, his hair shining raven in the morning sun as he noted the flock of goslings scurrying across the yard. The two hens clucked for their chicks, tiny puffy yellow babies, hurrying behind their mothers. In the pen, the piglets began squealing.

Though he was neatly dressed in a black suit and clean white shirt, Sam looked as if he hadn't slept or eaten a decent meal. But his gentleman's hair part was as meticulous as ever. Emma ached to feed him. "Thank you for the cow. I will see that she is happy."

Sam looked at her blankly. "A happy cow," he repeated, as if he'd never heard the words.

Emma hugged the cow, her new friend. She whispered to her in German, and the cow seemed to understand, looking at Emma with beautiful big eyes. "She's beautiful."

Sam looked at her strangely, as though he'd like to devour her, but Emma didn't care. She continued petting and talking and hugging the cow. "Her name is *Hilda*."

Harry still stood by the new smoke shed, his arms folded across his chest and his legs braced wide. Sam studied Harry's clean-shaven image closely. Sam's lean body locked tensely as though he'd taken a blow . . . as though he might leave at any moment, rather than stay near Harry. The few yards between them could have been miles as they stared at each other.

Emma ached for both men. "I've just baked bread, and there's food and fresh coffee. Would you like to come in?"

"Maybe." Sam continued to stare at Harry as Monty took the little cow out to the pasture.

Emma touched Sam's arm, and a hard muscle leaped beneath her fingers. She lifted her hand away quickly. "Come inside, Sam Taggart. Rest."

He looked down at her, and his expression warmed before turning flat and unreadable. "I'm not staying."

Emma frowned up at him. "It would be rude of you to leave when I have offered to feed you."

She didn't like arguing with her employer, yet neither could she let him ignore the manners she was carefully building into the Taggart family.

"I'm rude?" he asked, as if the word held a huge humorous secret.

Emma looked up at him and did not retract her words. When he looked at her like that, a smile tugging

at his hard mouth, she felt as if she could ignite and
fling herself at him. Perhaps the woman who gave him
the scratches had felt that way too. Emma firmed her
lips. She would not discuss the women in Sam's life or
how he lay upon them as he had lain upon her. She
narrowed her eyes and tried to push away the image of
Sam rutting with a woman in such heat that she
scratched him. . . .

"You've got a temper, don't you, Red?" he asked in a
drawl that sent a ripple of heat up her nape.

She scowled at him. "I have the best of natures. Will
you come eat now, Sam Taggart?"

"If I have to," he returned wearily, as though it were a
burden to eat her food. But the sparkle in his eyes said
he wanted her to become angry.

She would not allow him to torment her. Before she
said more, Emma marched up the porch steps and into
the house. She turned just once to see if he was following and found him staring at her backside as though
he'd like to grab her.

The thought set her off, and her hand shook as she
removed the other loaves from the oven and sliced the
new bread. She hurried to place a mug on the table for
him and looked at her mug already on the table, where
she had been making lists of the new clothes she needed
to start sewing for Harry's family. "I sit at the table
during the day sometimes. It is what other women in
Montana Territory do. Harry and Monty said so," she
admitted as she stood on tiptoe to remove Sam's hat
from his head. "In this house you will remove your hat,
please. Your new hat is beautiful."

Sam looked at her warily as she hung his hat on a wall

peg. When she hurried to remove his jacket, he tensed, then let her ease it from him. Emma noted that his collar and cuffs were frayed and needed turning to last longer. She noted how delightful he smelled, like fresh clean sweetgrass, as though he'd been lying upon it.

The thought of Sam lying anywhere sent a flush through her, and she drew away his jacket, folded it neatly, and— She saw the huge sheath strapped to his back, the knife handle wrapped in leather coils. It was evil, lying upon his white shirt.

He lowered himself into the chair she had indicated, his long fingers wrapping around the mug she quickly filled. Harry filled the doorway, and Sam's gaze slid to him, instantly cold, locked shutters in place. Harry looked at Emma, who nodded and frowned, silently urging him to welcome Sam home. "Boy," Harry managed grimly.

Emma shook her head and hurried to place plates on the table. She cut thick slices of antelope roast and placed the whole platter on the table. "We have eaten all the soda cheese. Here—there is jam from dried berries, if you wish."

Eaten? Harry and Monty and Mary had devoured the cheese she had been given by a passing family of Hutterites in return for her fresh bread. Emma placed a pie, made of the last of the dried apples, on the table. "I would like this food to be eaten by men with gentle hearts, please," she stated quietly.

Harry sat down, and father and son frowned at her, nothing gentle in their eyes. Emma sat, poured cream into her coffee, and added four teaspoons of sugar. Sam and Harry now looked at each other, gauging, circling. . . . She held her breath.

"Is Mary still happy with me?" Sam asked finally as he began to eat a thick slice of bread.

She beamed at him, proud that he was trying to talk with his father. He stopped eating and scowled at Emma, who had just dabbed his lip with her napkin. He continued to look at her as he chewed slowly. Whatever he was thinking, the look of him sent waves of heat rushing through her body.

"Mary will come around," Harry returned. "Emma gets to people."

Emma shot him a brief approving smile to show that she recognized his compliment, and also because he was trying to talk with Sam.

"Is that so?" Sam asked, turning to Emma, who bent her head, her cheeks flushing. "Where did all this come from—the nails and tools, that new two-man saw on the porch, and the livestock?" He skimmed the neat home she'd tended. "You've been busy. I want to know where you got the money to pay for everything."

"We needed lard for pies and bread and—"

"She sold her stockings. She's a damn fine business-woman, she is," Harry stated proudly, and eyed Sam, who looked thunderous. "Ah, hell, Sam," Harry said finally as the room swirled with tension rolling off Sam. "The girl can bargain. Reminds me of the old days, when people didn't use coin, but traded what they had. She makes damn fine socks—"

Sam's expression chilled Emma as Harry yanked away his well-polished boot to expose one of her stockings.

He flopped the sock tucked in his pocket affectionately. "She's healing my foot," he stated proudly.

Sam turned slowly to Emma. "I didn't hire you to make a living for them," he stated in a voice that lifted the hair on the back of her neck.

"I am advertising. I had to start somewhere, and soon I will have a fine reputation for stocking making. I am only temporarily involved in the bread-bargaining business. Do you like apple pie, Sam Taggart?"

"I like women who—" he began, and then stopped, his gaze lowering to her mouth.

She swallowed the bite of pie she'd taken to calm herself. Sam's gaze continued slowly down her throat and lower, to the flaky bit of crust that had tumbled to her chest. He seemed fascinated by it, and the air in Emma's lungs rushed out. She hastily brushed at the crumb; but it stubbornly remained. Sam looked at the crumb as if he could devour it. She delicately dusted it away again and sipped her coffee, adding another teaspoon of sugar.

"Is that sweet enough for you?" Sam asked in a nasty tone.

She hated him then, and glared at him. He was counting the sugar she'd used, deducting it from his inventory.

"Hello, Red," he drawled in a low soft tone, and she knew that he'd found her evil place again—her temper.

Nothing had ever drawn it out from her. But Sam managed to find her weakest flaw and fire her temper. "I will never give you one sock, Sam Taggart," she said finally, meaning it.

"Ah, hell, Sam, don't make the girl mad," Harry pleaded, looking worried.

Sam turned to Harry, his tone deadly. "You got your eye on her, Harry? You won't get this one. I told her folks I'd take good care of her."

Harry leaned forward, meeting Sam's scowl just as fiercely. "She's a sweet little kitten, she is, boy. You just keep your paws off and what's in your pants buttoned up nice and safe."

Emma sucked in air, unused to men snarling at each other. Monty chose that moment to hurry into the house. "I just unsaddled Tenkiller and brought in your saddlebags—"

The smaller man stopped in midstride, glancing at the three people seated at the table. Monty struggled courageously to smooth the tense silence and finally settled for "Ah . . . is there any pie left?"

"Oh, hell," Sam and Harry said at the same time in the same disgusted tone.

Emma fought her smile and then couldn't stop laughing. Monty scratched his head, wondering what he'd said, and then he began to laugh, too. Harry's stern face slowly softened, and he smiled.

Sam looked at all of them as though they had eaten locoweed.

Chapter Six

"I am not certain what you like, Sam Taggart, and you will not offend me, if you change the home to suit you." Emma did not like how Sam chewed her best doughnuts, the muscles taut in his jaw as he studied the changes in the Taggart home.

"Offend you?" he asked very softly, that small vein pulsing in his temple.

"I wish to be worth the money you have paid my father. I see that you have scratches on your cheek. Please let me care for them."

Sam scowled at her and bit off another hunk of her doughnut as though he were tearing away flesh—hers . . . as though he'd like to tear her from his life. A wary prickle ran up her nape.

Unwilling to be intimidated, Emma straightened but kept her hands folded on her lap, resisting the urge to protect her doughnuts from Sam's unappreciative grasp. "You may speak freely," she offered finally, when he continued to scowl at her.

"I may speak?" The words were soft and spaced with deadly impact.

Emma detected male outrage in them. Who was he to be outraged, this man who did not say thank you? "When a meal is cooked, doughnuts are sprinkled with sugar, and a home is cleaned, sometimes men say kind things," she prompted, refusing to look away from his frown. "Perhaps your digestion is not the best."

The next instant Sam's big hand wrapped around her wrist. He smiled, rather like a wolf showing his teeth. "My digestion is just fine."

Sam released her wrist when Mary ran by, entering her room with the one cat she was permitted to keep there. She slammed the new door and yelled, "I hate you all!"

Harry's face went still as stone, and Monty winced.

"She just does that," Emma stated to soften the harsh moment. The skin on her wrist tingled, her heart leaping wildly at his touch. Her hands began to sweat, aching from gripping each other; she tried to appear calm, as if what Sam thought about her housekeeping did not matter.

"How much do I owe you?" he asked finally.

"You have paid in advance."

"The stocking money, woman. How much did you get?" He was impatient now, anger flicking behind his straight black lashes.

"I did not take money," she informed him very tightly. "Two bachelors from the mountains came, needing a drink of water. I gave them doughnuts and coffee and just happened to be laying out my socks on the porch, counting and folding them. I make fine socks, you know, Sam Taggart—"

"You ought to seen her," Monty interrupted, snatching a doughnut. Around a mouthful of it he stated, "It was something, all right. There she was, pretending not to be interested as she went about her business, hanging up her socks on the line, and the two bachelors—gold miners, they were—upping the price right along."

Emma liked Monty—*he* appreciated her talents. She passed the plate of doughnuts to him.

"She's smart," Harry stated slowly. "She's been setting up books for her business."

"You have nice manners, Harry. You are not rude." Emma looked directly at Sam.

"How . . . much . . . do . . . I owe you?" Sam ground out, glaring at her. She noticed that though the vein was throbbing madly on his temple, the cut she had inflicted upon him had healed nicely.

"Do you like my doughnuts?" she asked politely, trying to distract him. He might bully the others, but he needed to be reminded of his manners—if he had any. Emma inhaled slowly, calming the temper Sam could arouse in her. She was determined to teach him manners, too.

Harry lurched to his feet and tromped out the door. Monty looked helplessly from Sam to Emma, and then he joined Harry outside. Emma carefully placed a clean cloth over her doughnuts. "I will not run from you and your evil temper, Sam Taggart."

"I won't owe you— Get your books and see what I owe you. I just bought a store. How do you think it looks for you to be trading doughnuts?" His voice raised slightly, the tone indignant, arrogantly male. Emma was used to that tone, yet didn't like it.

She was beginning a new life as a businesswoman; she could not allow herself to be spoken to that way by anyone but her father. She concentrated on holding her temper, the one she just learned that Sam could arouse in her. "I needed a bread bowl," she said very properly.

"A bread bowl." He glared at her, and the vein in his forehead throbbed. A small spear of hair leaped from his neat part and quivered over his forehead. "Now that's a thing a man needs to pay good money for, isn't it?" Sam snapped.

"But it wasn't a *man* who bought the bowl, was it?" Emma startled herself. Usually people responded nicely to her nudges, and there was no need to be sharp. Sam required a firm hand.

Sam's slow intake of air expanded his chest, his eyes burning at her. "My assets are up, but I'm short of cash right now. But I want to see those books, so I know what I owe you."

The spear of hair quivered over his tanned forehead. She watched that spear and decided that she would not argue with him; instead she would be logical. She rose slowly and began clearing away the table. "I will get them. But I do not expect payment—and I needed the geese. I didn't have goose fat for rubbing on chests and helping winter colds. There are no feather ticks here, and the geese—"

Sam stood abruptly, looming over her, his hands on his hips. His words shot at her like bullets. *"Where are the books?"*

Emma stared at him and tightened her lips. "Sometimes I think you are not a nice man."

"Because you've got everyone hopping to do your bidding but me."

This time Emma put her hands on her hips. "It does not hurt to have good manners. But you are used to having women fawn over you and excuse your lack of them. I will not."

Mary's giggle slid into the room, and Emma began moving around the kitchen quickly, cleaning the dishes and putting away the food. She refused to be bullied by a man who— "Because you have not made that woman happy does not mean you can come into Harry's home and be mean. But you are my employer, and I suppose you deserve to see my books. You see, I am logical and you are not."

Sam looked at her blankly, and she noted a loose button on his shirt. She wanted peace with Sam Taggart and offered, "If you will take off your shirt, I'll tighten the loose button. Buttons are expensive, and if you lose one of the set—"

"The books," he said in a tight strained voice.

She noted the pulse quickening in his temple and hurried to soothe him. "It is only one book with a small list of bargains. I took another because I want my business to grow—"

Sam looked as if he were swallowing whole boiled eggs, the tiny vein throbbing in his temple.

Monty came to the open door and peered warily into the kitchen.

"I am fine," Emma stated, and wiped the table clean. She would not have food spots on her ledgers because

Sam was being nasty and impatient. Normally when she wrote, she folded a used paper, keeping her writing hand on it. She went to the shelf where she kept her new books and pen and ink. She removed her mother's doily from the top of the book and folded it with care.

Sam glared at her as she walked back to the table. "I suppose you traded for those, too—the new books, the pen and ink."

She placed the books precisely on the table in front of Sam's chair. She was now a businesswoman, and she would be treated with respect. "I mended a shirt, washed and pressed it for a very nice man who deals cards and is good enough to make a living at it. He taught me how to play cards while the shirt dried on the line. *He* liked my doughnuts. *They* were the wager, because *he* said they were *delicious*," Emma stated very carefully to remind Sam that he still had not complimented her on the food. "You are rude, Sam Taggart, and I cannot help that the woman did not like your advances."

"What woman?" Sam looked at her as if she'd grown horns.

Emma sat at the table. "I do not wish to know about your rutting practices. If you cannot . . . if the woman did not welcome your advances, you should not have pursued her. This, too, is manners."

Mary giggled frantically behind the closed door. Sam stalked to the door, jerked it open, glared at the girl, and ordered, "Out. Now."

"She's got you," Mary stated triumphantly. "It's your fault for bringing her here. You think it's been fun, living with someone who's cleaning and working all the time? You just get comfortable in your clothes, and off they come into her wash pot. You can't find a place to sit because she's asking you to move so she can clean—"

"Out," Sam repeated.

"My cat slept in her bread bowl, and you'd a thought that the Devil had come. She's strong as a horse, you know. If she'd a caught my cat, she'd a wrung poor Baby's neck like a chicken—" Mary stopped talking and moved quickly out the door when Sam leaned forward.

Emma pressed her hands together beneath the table and waited for Sam to study her books. She was a sturdy woman, not willowy like Greta, but made to last. . . . When she'd seen the cat in the bread bowl, licking its bottom, truly she could have punished the cat.

He retrieved his glasses from his coat, jammed them on, gripped the chair, jerked it back, and sprawled into it. "The button . . . your shirt," Emma reminded him softly after a time.

Sam undid the buttons with one hand and flipped through the pages of Emma's neat book with the other. Her throat dried; she'd forgotten to tell him that if he would change into another shirt, she could mend this one while he examined her sums. She parted her lips to tell him, and then her mind went blank as Sam slid away the shirt. She gaped at the smooth muscles flexing on his chest, the deep pattern of scars, the dancing of his small flat nipples as he ran his finger down her work. He wasn't hairy like her father. His shoulders were bare and gleaming and smoothly powerful, unlike her father's, which had hair.

Sam's stomach had muscular ridges!

Emma blinked and went dizzy; she ached to touch his

dark skin, to feel its warmth. Then she remembered she hadn't breathed since he'd removed his shirt. His skin gleamed in the filtered light from the windows, the cords of his arms flexed, his muscles bunching as his finger moved slowly down her sums. She wanted to kiss the scars on his chest, to soothe them with her lips—

Emma sat very still. Other women probably did not kiss men's chests, yet she longed to kiss Sam's. She gripped her hands together and knew that she was a berserker, just as her father had said. After a time Sam snapped the book shut and glared at her. "I can't pay you now."

From living with her father and Fritzi, she recognized the tone—she'd hurt his pride. "I have not asked for payment. You are my employer. It would be illogical for me to ask that of you, when you are already providing me with a home, food, and payment to my father. You sent the red cow, Frieda, and now Hilda—oh, I love her so already—why did you choose her?"

Sam scowled at her, the vein in his temple continuing to throb.

Monty came to the door again, peering in. "Uh . . . Sam. She makes good doughnuts, don't she?"

The gentle reminder that Sam needed to offer Emma a compliment for her food—a tradition in her family— didn't faze Sam, who was looking darkly at her. Her needle pricked her finger, and she sucked the blood from it. Sam continued to glare at her. "That's my last shirt. Don't bleed on it. And get anything you need from the store, not from passersby."

She studied the lines in Sam's face, the circles under his eyes, and the way his cheeks seemed too lean. He'd lost weight since she saw him last—probably chasing after the woman who didn't want him. "There are things not in stores," she murmured, unwilling to let him destroy her bargaining ability. "How long has it been since you slept?" she asked, shifting the conversation.

"Does it matter?" he rapped out.

From his glare she knew that he was preparing to order her not to bargain. Emma hurried to stop him. "Perhaps sleep would improve your temperament, Sam Taggart. There is a bedroom waiting for you with clean sheets."

"How much?"

"What?"

"The clean sheets. You bought them, too, didn't you?"

She'd hadn't had time to enter that bargain in her book. "The family needed good stockings rather than the sheets. They were headed to the mines, where the woman will cook for all the men without wives. I thought I would embroider flowers on the sheets and make them pretty. There was little patching to do, and I made pillowcases from one that was torn badly. I made Mary clean drawers and a shift. There was enough for drawers for Harry and Monty, too." Because it would be shameful to take all the credit, Emma added, "Harry sharpened my scissors."

Mary had refused the shift and rushed away each time Emma politely asked if she could offer advice for Mary's upper chest aches. She had ignored the way Mary tossed "bosom growing" at her to see her flush. Emma omitted that the traveling family needed foodstuffs and that Emma had allowed the bargaining to be in the poor family's favor. She'd given them salt and flour and the cornmeal she'd traded from a farmer who'd stopped to water his horse. The horse needed tending, a small wound, but the man was tired, and Emma had gladly applied flowers of sulfur and grease to the wound, wrapping the leg in clean rags. The man was taking cornmeal to his wife. The meal was ground at the miller's miles away, and he'd poured a small portion into Emma's bread bowl, thanking her for her doughnuts and his fine new pair of stockings.

Emma had felt quite independent that day, pleased that she had made a good bargain. She would not have Sam ruin it for her.

Sam took off his glasses, rubbed his eyes and shook his head. Despite his poor manners, she ached for him and pointed to the room next to hers. "I do not think my father will mind if you sleep in the house this night."

"Go to sleep, Sam Taggart. I am only taking your clothes to wash and mend." Emma's soft voice eased the violence within Sam. He'd awakened to her movements, her scents in the small dark room. He breathed slowly and forced his fingers to relax from the knife, beneath a fold of the blanket. He'd lived on the edge for too many years, usually sleeping on his bankroll. Noises usually meant trouble, blood, and bruises. Emma's fresh womanly scents were almost as threatening, especially since he was beholden to her.

Sam had never been beholden to anyone, but he was too drained to argue. He turned on his side from her, ignoring her sharp intake of breath, followed by tight silence. "There are dirty clothes in my saddlebags," he murmured even as he slid off to sleep, sniffing every last scent that clung to Emma. There was soap and bread and wood smoke and sunlight and wind and—

The second time Sam awoke, it was to moonlight shafting into the room. He hadn't noticed the room before—dropping his clothing on the floor as he passed to the bed—and now he did. His boots, the dirty laundry, and the saddlebags were gone. A woman's and child's fringed and beaded moccasins gleamed on a small rough wooden chest. Beside them was the small berry bucket his mother had used, filled with her awl, beads, and needles, and the small flower-beaded sheath of her hunting knife. A lacy doily ran beneath the bucket; the separate lives of two women blending in the night. A man's moccasins sat on the floor beside the chest.

On the wall was a framed tintype of his mother and father and Sam as a happy boy of eight. He closed his eyes, wanting to shed the memories and leave Harry's house. The moonlight outside told him it was eleven o'clock.

The house was spotless, just as he had wanted. Scents of baking and soap clung to every corner. He could walk away from Harry now that he was looking better. Looking better? Harry was blooming.

Sam found he'd been holding his breath and slowly released it. He hadn't forgotten the warm, soft feel of Emma beneath him that day, the shape of her breast, the way his body had lurched into sensual life.

Her hazel eyes were clear, seeing straight into him as if she saw all his devils, while he couldn't drag one out of her. Emma didn't have an evil mood in her, but she could be prodded into igniting. One eyebrow dragged higher than the other when her temper lurched, and soft color flowed up her cheeks like a flower blooming. The shape of her untutored lips, ripe with innocence and waiting to be kissed, caused his body to tighten. Just watching her eat, which she did very primly, everything neat and clean aroused him.

Sam stretched his cramped muscles, familiar enough with his body to know that it was time for a woman.

The desire for sex was ripe upon him right now, throbbing in the cold night air. Just thinking about Emma's mouth, her lips curving firmly, her teeth biting down on a doughnut, had caused him to lurch into sexual need. He remembered how she had gasped when he removed his shirt, her eyes widening and her flush blooming. He was weak now, drained physically and mentally, and she'd come sneaking up on him with her soft scents and her prim ways and good food.

She'd paid for that food, bartered for it with socks she would never give him.

Sam breathed slowly, methodically, leashing the irritation he never allowed himself. He didn't need her socks. He had good store-bought ones that cost a pretty penny and were just like those the "copper kings" wore.

Sam closed his eyes, forcing himself to calm. He didn't like owing Emma . . . owing anyone. If she wanted to raise his temper, maybe he'd set her off, too.

Tenkiller's snorting caused Sam to lurch to his feet, knife in hand. He slid into his pants and the moccasins and eased from the room noiselessly, only to see Harry already sliding off into the night. In the corral Tenkiller sidestepped, rearing, hooves flailing at air.

Emma's white petticoat hems flashed in the moonlight as she hurried across the field to a large man seated on a mule.

Sam noted Harry's path, arcing away from Emma, concealed by serviceberry bushes. He followed Harry and issued the call of an owl that Harry would recognize, then Sam eased into the shadows of the bushes with his father. In the moonlight, Harry's eyes were as Sam remembered—bright, deadly, flicking over the scene.

In a quick flurry of German, Emma argued with Gilbert, who towered over her. Beneath her bonnet she was furious, pacing in front of the big man. She pivoted on him, her shawl wrapped tightly around her taut shoulders. She spoke in precise English. "Shame, Gilbert. Shame on you. You should not be here. What would my father say if he knew? I think I will tell him."

"Then I will tell him that you lay with the half-blood in the bushes. That I saw you rutting with him."

Harry's scowl shot to Sam, who scowled back.

Emma jabbed her finger against Gilbert's broad chest. "I am a businesswoman, Gilbert. You will not interfere with me."

He snorted in disgust. "You are promised to me. It is unseemly that you live with two men. I think I will rut with you now and get you with child."

Emma faced him, her body taut, her hands on her waist. "*You* think so? I have nothing to say about this?"

Harry shook his head, then whispered, "I think I'll finish him off now."

Sam shook his head; he had seen Emma manipulate Gilbert. "She'll run him off."

"Bet?"

"Bet." Sam ignored the familiarity of the scenario he remembered from his boyhood.

"Your share of her cookies against mine," Harry offered, and Sam nodded curtly. Since meeting Emma, he'd been lowered to making deals that involved cookies.

Emma faced Gilbert with the air of a rapier duelist. "If you make trouble for me now, Gilbert . . . and the year and five months pass and you receive my dowry, I will never cook for you again—if you make trouble," Emma repeated very slowly, her voice humming with anger.

Gilbert towered over her, his voice filled with outrage. "A man's wife cooks for him—pies and bread and meat and dumplings. She makes cheeses and potato noodles and sauerkraut and pickles. Do you make *hasenpfeffer* and *fastnachts*—doughnuts—and *streuselkuchen* for these men?"

Emma crossed her arms over her chest. "Stop yelling. If you are bad, I will never make them for you. Or I will make them badly. There is a young sweet girl living in the house. Do you think her father would upset her by rutting with me? No. I will tell you why—because I am like his daughter, his sister. He needs me. So does Monty. They say nice things to me. Not 'fetch this, fetch that,' but 'thank you, honey.' 'Buttercup,' Harry calls me in a fatherly way. *They* help me with housework, and poor Harry misses his three wives. He tells me this, not keeping it to himself. He does not hoard his heart. I like these good men."

That was true enough, Sam thought, glancing at

Harry, who glared back. Harry had never hoarded his heart from a woman.

She stepped closer to Gilbert and shook her finger in front of his nose. "What would my father say if he knew you were using his mule and making him tired?"

Harry grinned and whispered, "He'll be lucky if she doesn't shame him. I've seen grown men stick their tails between their legs and almost crawl away when she shames them."

Gilbert sank his jowls down into his coat. After a long moment he mounted up, kicked the mule, and hurried away to the Rechts'.

Emma stood outlined in the moonlight, her hands resting on her hips. She muttered in German, then smoothed her clothing and straightened her back as though she had finished a task that needed doing. "So. There, I think that went nicely," she stated in perfect crisp English.

Harry smothered a chuckle and whispered, "She says that after she's done something to suit her—like the day she climbed up to nail down the shakes. That was the day you left. Hammered away like blue blazes, then came down, cool as a mountain spring, and said that same thing."

Tenkiller whinnied in the field, rearing and pawing air, and Emma hurried to his corral, her petticoat hems flashing. She paused, talking softly to Tenkiller, and stepped out of her petticoats. She wrapped them in a bundle and placed them on the ground. She bent, grabbed her skirt, and brought the back into the front waistband of her apron. In the next instant she was up and over the wooden corral boards, walking toward Tenkiller, who had gentled.

Sam and Harry didn't talk, realizing the danger of Emma, next to a horse who could kill. Both men eased silently through the bushes, so as not to startle Tenkiller. Emma's soft voice continued in a steady hum as she walked around the corral, the horse studying her. Then she walked toward him and stopped—

Sam realized his heart had stopped. He knew just how powerful Tenkiller was and how skittish the formerly mistreated horse was of anyone other than Sam.

At the edge of the barn Harry turned to Sam. "So you've had your eye on Emma—tried to lay with her in the bushes? Boy, that isn't the kind of a woman to play with. She's the marrying kind."

"Did you marry Feather?" Sam shot back. He ignored Harry's scowl and watched Tenkiller slowly walk to Emma. The horse sniffed her outstretched hands, then nibbled whatever she offered. He lipped her hair, and she laughed. The horse pranced backward, shaking his head. Then he moved close to her, allowing her to wrap her arms around his neck.

The sound of her voice gently crooning to the horse caused Sam's mouth to dry. She rocked against Tenkiller, who stood perfectly still as she hugged him. He followed her to the corral fence like a puppy, and when she stepped up, Tenkiller grabbed a mouthful of her skirt, tugging gently. She laughed again, a musical delighted sound, and the horse pranced off. Harry nodded and slid back to the house.

Emma swept up her petticoats and hurried to the birds' coops, checking on the pigeons and the chickens.

Satisfied that she wasn't going to scare him further by playing with Tenkiller, Sam loped back to the house and slid into bed . . . before he gave way to the anger riding him and followed Gilbert. The farm worker needed a few lessons in manners.

The next morning, kitchen sounds awoke Sam, and he realized he'd slept late. The bright sunlight outside said it was seven o'clock. Harry's clean clothing hung on wall pegs for Sam's use. He traced the margin of sunlight running along the ceiling and listened to the unfamiliar sounds of a woman hurrying to make breakfast, the clatter of stove lids and pots, and the whip of a wooden spoon against batter. Emma hummed softly as she worked, a lively polka that did not reflect her midnight hours.

Sam's body protested moving, aching from hours in the saddle and lack of sleep. He wanted to leave just as quickly as he could, yet the scent of cooking food—bacon and coffee—had his mouth watering. He realized he hadn't eaten anything for days but jerked meat and hardtack soaked in coffee—he'd been traveling hard, bargaining with miners and loggers and banks. His records were nothing but scraps of paper, deeds, agreements, and lists of contacts—he realized his system was inadequate for a businessman, especially after seeing Emma's neat ledger.

When Sam entered the large kitchen, Emma was flipping pancakes onto a platter. Thick slices of bacon were already on the table. Monty and Harry helped set the table and poured the coffee, while Mary sat coldly glaring at them as if they were deserters. "My bosom hurts," she tossed out at Sam, just to start the day in her favor.

"That's nice," he returned as Monty pulled out a chair and indicated that Sam sit.

"You're a sight thinner than your pa," Monty said to Sam, "but the clothes fit just the same. The moccasins, too."

"I'll have my own clothes back soon enough." Sam didn't want anything from Harry. He wanted to set his account straight with Emma, lay down the law about supporting his father, and be on his way.

It was hard to leave or to start laying down laws with a mouthwatering breakfast waiting for him. Sam almost melted at the sight of black currants swimming in the hot brown sugar syrup. He noted that Monty and Harry waited until Emma sat and said a brief German prayer. They shook out the ironed napkins beside their plates and tucked them into their collars before they began eating. Mary stared at them all contemptuously before she dived into her food. "Syrup dripped on my bosoms," she stated.

Monty and Harry looked squeamish while Emma smiled. "You might use your napkin," she suggested.

Sam stared at her. He wasn't finished with her yet, and he wanted her to know it. Emma avoided looking at him, serving breakfast. The small morning chatter flowed around Sam, and he continued to look at Emma. He didn't like the feeling that she could best him in an argument. "I *am* logical," he said finally, "and I have good manners."

"You are talented and inventive, a good businessman," she returned tightly, sidestepping his blunt statement.

After breakfast, Harry leaned back to sip his coffee. He was clearly wallowing in his new comfort and proud of Emma.

Emma smoothed her braids, wound tightly on top of her head. Tendrils curled and gleamed around her face and the back of her neck. "I am sorry. I overslept. Once we have a rooster, I am certain that I will awaken before dawn. We will need a rooster to get more chicks."

"You've been polishing Sam's boots and washing his clothes and doing his books until all hours," Harry stated roughly. "You're tired. You just sit still while me and Monty do the dishes, honey."

Harry was fairly crooning, and Sam resented his temper snapping. "Doing *my* books?"

He didn't share his life with anyone—or his finances. It burned him that Emma would see how he had invested everything and that he was stripped of ready cash. She flushed, her bonnet and gray dress looking clean and freshly pressed. "I wanted to help you. You seemed so tired."

"That's none of your concern. I hired you to—"

Harry's fist hit the table; dishes clattered. "Boy, that's enough. The girl wanted to help you. You could say thank you."

Sam ignored Harry. "Let me see my books."

Harry and Monty hurried to clean away the dishes while Emma retrieved his books from the shelf next to hers.

Sam flipped through the neat expense entries, the dated entries of his ownership in mines, and the orderly papers tucked into the back page. Emma had summed and organized, her numbers running down neat columns. According to her figures, he had invested everything he owned.

Sam frowned at her; it burned to have a woman sit across the table from him and know his business—that he didn't have the change to pay her back. He ran his finger down the list of new purchases, to the smallest gold mine. The neat assets column startled him; he hadn't seen all of his businesses listed, and the sight told him that he had the makings of the empire he wanted. He'd bought into Peterson's mine for the price of two good mules. By selling his share, he could pay Emma what was due her. He leveled a look at her. "You'll have your money."

Emma shook her head. "I learned from you that it is wise to take small chances. You make smart purchases, Sam Taggart. You are a good businessman, even if you don't sleep and eat right. It is important that your clothes are clean and you are well rested to bargain well. This is why I washed for you, not on a regular wash day."

He looked at his two dress shirts and his trousers hanging to dry on a line over the stove. His vest and two dress jackets were hung on another line. His polished boots gleamed against the wall. His black string tie lay across a softly folded padding, a small iron with a wooden handle next to it. His two pairs of store-bought stockings were neatly folded beside his two ironed handkerchiefs. He knew without looking that Emma had patched the holes in the toes.

"I've been traveling hard," he stated harshly in his

defense. She made him appear as though he couldn't tend his own business or his clothes. On the other hand, she was right—he needed to look like a businessman, and he needed rest. He looked at the tiny spots of batter on the apron covering her round breasts and his heartbeat lurched into a faster pace. He looked at Emma's soft mouth and gentle eyes, and something within him softened. Then he left the house quickly with a feeling that he was retreating from a battlefield.

Chapter Seven

This man, Sam Taggart, could he not say that my doughnuts are good and that he appreciates his clothing patched and cleaned? When his black eyes burn at me, I feel as if the fire has lighted in me, and I would like to hit him. Without his shirt Sam Taggart is even more beautiful, if poor mannered. Putting his papers in order was a joy. His assets are growing. I am proud of him, too. He is a man of the new world, but he is weary, and the past drags at him. I wonder of the woman who has scratched him. This morning, when he looked so dark at me, I could have dumped flour over him. I think he is used to women admiring him and obeying his wishes. I will not. I will only obey those commands he gives me as my employer. He is outside now, cleaning the barn, and that is good, because he took his dark temper with him. I do not like having this temper Sam Taggart can fire in me, and now I bake more bread. E.

From the barn Sam caught the glint of a rifle barrel. A lone rider came toward the Big T ranch house, and the rifle traced his path. The rider of the red bay was a big man, wearing fringed white gauntlets, woolly chaps, and a broad-brimmed Texas hat that gleamed white in the sun. From his spurs to his hat to his Bowie knife and double pearl-handled Colt revolvers, the man was pure Texas. A woman's big hat box was tied to the back of his saddle.

Emma ran from the house to meet the big Texan. She flapped her apron at him, as though she were shooing chickens away. "Harry still does not want to sell. Go away before he sees you."

The Texan leaped to the ground and locked his boots on the Big T. He hooked his thumbs in his belt and watched Sam walk toward him. Over Emma's head the tall men eyed each other. "Who are you?" the Texan asked.

Emma, clearly impatient with him, said, "I was about to introduce you to the man who hired me. This is Mr. Sam Taggart, son of Harry Taggart. Sam Taggart is a fine businessman with assets."

"Howdy. I'm Tex Murdock, and I own the New Alamo. I want to buy this place, so's I can have the Dancing Miranda run down to my spread on the other side of hill. I've offered a fair price to your pa, but he's not having none. If you sell to me, the whole kit and caboodle of you can live here and run a few chickens and such, and those she-cattle over there. Once I put my boots on dirt and like it, it's usually mine. I'm kin to the men who died at the mighty Alamo, fighting against Santa Anna, so's I'm not likely to give up."

Tex rocked back and forth on his boot heels, locking his cold blue eyes with Sam's narrowed ones. "I got your note, saying you were in the area. I'd say the old man was holding this worthless spread for his kid, and now that you're back, maybe you can make him see the sense of selling to me."

"It's Harry's land and his to do with what he wants," Sam stated, disliking the way Tex's eyes softened as they rested on Emma.

"The offer stands, and Harry can live here. You'd better move on. Old men are one thing, and you're another. Oh, hell, I'll get the land, and I want the girl, too. Can't carry on the fine blood of those who died at the Alamo without a fine breeding woman," Tex returned, whisking the big round hat box from the horse and bearing it to Emma proudly. "My mama had one like this, and I had one made up for you. It's even got the little feather bird up on top. Since this poor bunch can't dress you as a lady, I thought you'd like this for church going."

Emma was clearly frustrated, pushing away the box he offered to her. "Tex, you cannot keep trying to give me things that remind you of your mother. Please do not speak of breeding."

"Miss Emma, my dearly departed mama was a good woman. Just like you, everything clean and neat. It'd please me mightily—"

Sam had had enough of Tex salivating over "Miss Emma." "Is that your man up on the mountain?"

Tex pivoted, scanning the mountain, and then slapped his hat from his head, hitting his thigh with it. "That dirty sidewinder is my brother, Otis. He's all worked up because he can't stand Injuns or half-bloods. He got all roostered—skunk drunk—when he heard that Harry's grown pup came back. Otis is ornery as a blind rattler anyway and sneaky as a fox, and I'll whip his butt when I get my hands on him. I told him never to point that fancy shooter of his near Miss Emma."

"Harry isn't selling." Sam propped his boot on the corral and watched Tex take in the fancy leather tooling and the silver tips. Sam recognized the fighting glint in Tex's eyes. He didn't know why, but he didn't like the idea of Harry selling to the Texan. Maybe it was because Feather rested up on the knoll, or maybe it was because Sam didn't like the way the Texan looked at Emma.

"He'll sell. I've been sweet and easy until now. You put a different face on the bull." Tex spat in the dirt near Sam's polished boots and eyed him speculatively, one fighter gauging another. "Just how much grit do you have, fancy man? What do you say we settle this here and now—any way you like? I see you're carrying a good knife on your back—not as good as a good Jim Bowie, but I reckon it would do the work."

"Mr. Murdock!" Emma was indignant. "Sam is a businessman. He uses his knife for cutting cheese and the necessities a man has—"

Tex spat again, close to Sam's boots, and snickered. "Look at him, Miss Emma, he's all riled up with hardly no trouble at all. Oh, I'd say that he'd fight when put to it, all right."

Emma crossed her arms over her chest. "He is only amused because he is a businessman. There will be no fighting, Tex Murdock."

He grinned shyly. "She sure is like my mama. Everything neat and clean and smelling like soap. Heard her shame two buzzards once that mistreated a cayuse—now that was a sight to see. I bought that sad little cayuse because Emma made over it so. You should have seen those two galoots hunch down and look miserable when she shamed them. If she'd have been at the Alamo, she'd have set Santa Anna running with her broom."

No longer soft, Tex's gaze cut to Sam. "Some men hide behind women's skirts, and others take it like a man."

Sam had had enough; he didn't care for Tex sniffing and clearly enjoying the air over Emma's braids. "Get back in the house, Emma."

"Here, little honey. Take this hat and try it on your pretty little head while we men talk and settle the dust." Tex looked at Emma with adoration as he handed her the hat box.

She pushed it back again. "I cannot accept a gift from you. It wouldn't be proper—"

Tex began to guffaw, but stopped when he saw Sam moving toward him. "Now that's more like it, fancy man," Tex purred in a low dangerous tone.

"Mr. Tex Murdock, if you torment Sam Taggart, I will not be happy," Emma announced imperially and crossed her arms over her chest. She tapped her foot.

"Emma, step aside." Sam didn't intend to back down, least of all from a man bearing Emma a fancy hat. Not while he couldn't afford one for her. He wondered if Tex was wearing Emma's socks. Sam's temper rose, because she had promised never to give him a pair of her socks.

"Sell out, or there'll be hell to pay," Tex stated.

"Call this the Alamo, Tex. We're not selling, and if you want a fight, you can have it," Sam drawled quietly. "Take back the hat."

Tex whipped off his hat again and slapped his thigh. "That tears it. You sayin' that because I want this ranch that I'm kin to that skunk Santa Anna?"

Sam noted that Harry and Monty were standing on the porch. In the old days his father would have leaped into the fight easily. Maybe Sam had more of his father in him than he wanted, because Sam didn't intend to lose anything that was on Taggart land, including Emma. "I'm saying that if the Big T is missing more cattle and mustangs, I'll know where to go."

"Are you calling me a no-good rustler?" Tex asked too quietly, and placed his hands on his revolver butts.

Emma placed her hand on Tex's arm; her other hand pulled a ball of socks from her apron pocket. "Tex, if you will leave now and not hurt Sam, I will give you this pair of socks."

Because Sam had had enough of her interference and the big Texan wanting her, he said, "She's promised, Tex, to a man named Gilbert, who wants her grandmother's dowry."

Emma glared up at him, clearly not pleased.

Tex slapped his big hat against his thigh again. "Oh, hell, Miss Emma. What did you go and do that for? You know I'll just have to put a slug in him, too."

"He likes her apple dumplings." Sam couldn't resist prodding Emma. He didn't want to be the only one with a simmering temper.

Both men watched Emma as she struggled for control. After a long moment she lifted her chin, nodded curtly to Tex, and hurried back to the house.

Sam didn't like the way Tex admired the sway of Emma's skirts, or the way Tex tilted his head to see more of her petticoats and boots.

Emma hurried to the pigeon coop, carrying a bucket of fresh water and a pan of wheat kernels. It was midafternoon now, only a few hours since Tex had ridden off on his big red bay. Emma had kept to herself, though she was mad enough to repatch the roof and plow the garden again. After scrubbing down the kitchen, she was in control now and determined to avoid Sam. She smoothed her skirts. If Sam mentioned Gilbert's dumplings again, tormenting her, she would smile blandly and ignore him.

Recognizing their approaching mistress, the pigeons began cooing immediately. Mildred, a sleek bluish female and bred from the Volga German drummer dove, waited on the landing board, preening in the mid-June sunshine.

Five-week-old chicks were walking above the coop, learning the sights and sounds of their home. Mary's captive pigeons had been released to fly to their mates at the Rechts', but their chicks would fly above Taggart land. They were dragoons with red eyes and bred with the tumbler strain, an endurance breed.

While feeding them wheat, Emma saw that Sam was in the barn, polishing his saddle and tack until she thought he'd burn a hole through the beautifully tooled leather.

Their eyes locked in the morning sunlight, and her

heart started quivering so hard that she placed her hand over it. She was glad that her bonnet shielded her face, as a slow blush was rising in her cheeks. If only she hadn't found the tokens amid his dirty clothing. They looked like the coins Fritzi had described, which would buy favors from a saloon-upstairs town woman.

When Sam began to walk toward her, she thought he was the most beautiful man she'd ever seen; his shirt was unbuttoned to the slight wind, revealing his smooth tanned skin. The scratches on his cheek bothered her, and so did the thought that he'd held another woman in his arms.

Emma closed her eyes briefly and turned away. She was twenty-six and an untried woman. If she was to be given to Gilbert, she wished she could first be embraced by a man like Sam. He was gentle with animals, even with Tenkiller, who sometimes needed to be reminded who was the master. Sam smelled like clean pines and new life and the excitement of the Montana Territory. *He smelled like her new adventure.*

"Birds," Sam stated flatly as if the pigeons disgusted him.

"Pretty birds," she corrected, not allowing him to malign her four precious babies.

"I always liked pigeon pie," he drawled softly.

Emma whipped around to him, cuddling Hercules and Elena. Sam stood so close, she almost crushed the birds against her. The yearlings showed signs of stress, fluttering and cooing. "They aren't used to you. Aren't they a lovely shade of blue-gray?"

"That's a whole lot of pigeons," Sam remarked, tracing the yearlings circling the ranch yard. "And more on the way, from the way yours are setting on the nest. What's that about?"

She followed his look to a female hurrying away from the empty nest and a male chasing her. "He wants her to get back on the nest . . . to lay eggs."

"I've known a few men like that."

Emma sensed the dark clouds shifting within Sam. "Do you want children?"

He slashed a look at her. "You're always right there, aren't you? Nosing around in other people's lives. No, I don't want children."

"You are a man. How can you not want some small part of yourself to carry on your name? To leave your heritage to—"

"I'm not Tex, wanting to restock my own Alamo. A bastard half-blood has a hard life. Why would I want to give that to a child?"

Sam was different from any man Emma had ever known. The men that had been coming routinely to the Taggarts' spread had clearly indicated that they wanted wives and children. "When your wife gives you a child, you will love him, Sam Taggart. This I know."

"You do, do you? The woman I marry will think the same as me. I want a woman who is business savvy, knows how to hold up her end by socializing with people that matter. She'll be the perfect hostess—beautiful and in control of the elegant house I want to have—and she'll be pure ice on the inside, counting every penny. I've seen more than one empire built by a wife who knows how to set a table, serve dessert and coffee, and lead the conversation into business. Children don't enter into it. If she's not happy with the arrangement, I expect her to be discreet."

Emma understood arranged marriages, usually by the parents, who weighed the assets of the union. She did not want to think about Sam's perfect woman—the one that would share his bed. She lifted her head to watch the yearlings; she preferred to look anywhere, but at Sam's bare chest. Heat moved slowly up her body and flushed her cheeks—perhaps Sam would think it was the sun and the light wind. She lifted her hand to shade her eyes, following the yearlings. "They want to land to eat, but they won't, when you are standing here. They land only when the objects are familiar."

"I recognize the adult birds you brought here," he said. "You're keeping them in the cages. You released Mary's hostages, didn't you?"

"Don't tell her, please. She had taken good care of them, but it was time for them to go home to their mates. Fritzi will be glad to see them. He has been worried."

Sam stroked the heads of Hercules and Elena, cuddled tight against Emma's bosom. His knuckles brushed her breast, and she inhaled, easing back against the coop. Sam's black gaze slowly traveled across her flushed cheeks and down to the high button on her collar. "Mary wants me to take you with me. She thinks you're a plague."

Emma's throat tightened with the sensations of Sam standing so close. She knew how a kettle felt when it steamed. She didn't understand what was happening, but the sun seemed to stop in place as she looked into his eyes. Only the slight June breeze curled intimately around them, bringing his scent to her.

Sam leaned closer, his head only inches from hers. "How can you tell them apart—the females and the males?"

She bent her head, shielding her face with her bonnet, and handed him Elena. Elena—the tart—settled into Sam's big tanned hands as though she wanted to be with him always. Sam's thumb caressed Elena's feathered breast; while watching the motion, Emma's breast tingled, shocking her. "The females are softer, plumper. The males are hard, all muscle—"

The view of Sam's smooth chest stopped her. She forced herself to breathe, as she looked slowly upward to his beautiful mouth. "I think you are—kind," she whispered, glad that she hadn't called him beautiful.

She looked down to Elena and found Sam's long fingers stroking the bird. A tight quiver shot into Emma's body, awakening her soft places; her nipples nudged against her shift, evident in the plain cotton of her dress. She turned to place Hercules back in the coop and took Elena-the-tart from Sam. "I must go. I'm afraid that the rabbits will eat the new sunflower starts that the pigeons need for food."

"Walk with me up to my mother's grave."

Sam's soft tone raised the hair on the nape of her neck. She had chores to do— Instead she nodded. Sam was not a man to invite others to share his life; if she could offer him friendship to ease his loneliness, she would.

The wind swept across the hill, waves passing through the grass surrounding the tiny neat cemetery.

"You cleaned it," Sam noted, standing beside the big rock that marked Feather's grave. His open shirt caught the wind, sweeping away from his body. He looked alone, and Emma's heart went out to him; she had grown up protected in her family, while Sam had run away into a cold world.

"Harry loved your mother, Sam. He worshiped her."

"He didn't marry her," Sam's cold flat tone shot back at her.

She touched his arm, wanting to offer him her warmth. "He stopped roaming when he married her. They came here, to this small valley, because her people wouldn't fight here. It must have been difficult for him to settle down and break horses after a life of trapping and hunting. He did it for her. In his heart he was married to Feather."

The brackets beside Sam's mouth deepened. "Harry likes women."

"He loved his other wives, but not like his first love, your mother." The vein in Sam's head pulsed, standing out in relief, and Emma moved close to him, hoping to shield him from the cold sweeping wind as he grieved. "I think maybe he was looking for her when he took his other wives, though he loved them each in a different way."

"How the hell would you know?" Sam lashed out, grabbing her wrist and dragging her to him.

She refused to be bullied. "Harry told me how much he loved Feather and Evie and Juliet. I saw the truth in his eyes, so like yours, how he mourned their loss."

"He's probably looking at you for a replacement. Harry knows how to get to women."

"Sam. Shame. This is not so."

He searched her face as if digging at a lie he might find there. "You have no idea, do you?"

"About what?" She wished her heart wouldn't pound so violently when Sam looked at her, when his body heated hers. She prayed her nipples were not peaking against her dress.

Sam ran his finger slowly down her cheek, his touch featherlight. She trembled at what she saw in his eyes, the heat and storms. His thumb caressed her wrist, his fingertips settling over her racing pulse. "Afraid?"

"Of what?" She couldn't drag her gaze away from the warmth of his eyes, the amusement curling around her—and something else.

She wondered if he had Fritzi's "problem" in the mornings, his lower body hardening until it couldn't be disguised. There were so many things she wanted to know about Sam. She prayed she would not give way to her curiosity and look at his pants. She could be willful when she wanted something, and truly she did want to look at Sam.

"Are you afraid of me?" he asked softly, looking at her lips.

"I am not afraid of you, Sam Taggart," she answered slowly, turning her thoughts, because in all things she wanted to be honest. Yet she did not need to tell him that she was afraid of herself . . . of how she wanted to lay her open hand upon his chest, smooth the scars, and feel the beat of his heart. She watched the sunlight dance across his straight black lashes, tipping them in a blue sheen. *Sam Taggart would make beautiful children.*

"You are not a fighter or a hard man. You have been kind to your family."

The shutters in Sam's face began sliding closed, wariness replacing the heat and the storms. To keep him with her, Emma did the unforgivable for a nice woman—she placed her open hand upon his chest.

Instantly the heat and the storms lurched back into Sam's black eyes. "I need help in my business. You showed that to me when you straightened out my papers. You're neat and efficient, just what I need. You could assist me, and I'd pay you your worth. You could take messages and keep my papers straight. If some other woman took your place—working here for Harry and Monty—and I asked you to go with me, to help me in business, to travel with me, would you?"

I would follow you anywhere, Emma thought. Aloud she returned, "Yes. I would like that. Harry is much better now, and Monty and Mary. Perhaps we could find someone to help them as we travel. I can learn from you, I think. You know I am a businesswoman, too, but I am untried."

"Ah, yes. The almighty sock business."

"It is not like your assets of stores and mines and land, but I make very nice socks, thank you. I could have easily decided to sell my pies, but yarn and needles are much easier to manage. Since I have been here and all the miners passed through—so many kind, sweet men— I have decided to add a double layer of knitting to the toes in a special winter model. I notice that businessmen like to place special marks on their work, and I have decided to do so."

She took a breath, and since Sam was a shrewd businessman, she trusted him with her latest idea. "Because these men miss home, I have decided to embroider a tiny emblem like a house on some of my socks—to see how they interest men."

"Fine. You sell your socks," Sam stated in a quiet voice. "I've got no time for pampering a woman who can't hold her own camping or riding. You can't chatter about my business to anyone, because it would cost me. And no questions about how I run my business. . . . Will you come with me?" he asked again, as if giving her a chance to change her mind.

"I have said yes. But first we must ask my father. I will send one of Fritzi's birds home. I have already sent two yearlings to him by a passing cowboy—"

"For the price of your socks?" Sam sounded as if he were strangling, the vein pulsing in his temple.

"It was only a poor loaf of bread."

"You trust everyone, don't you, Emma?" Sam leaned closer, his mouth inches away from hers. "I think you might taste like an apple dumpling when you're kissed."

She loved the slow curve of his lips, as though he knew a secret she did not.

Oh, she wanted to stand on tiptoe and kiss Sam's mouth, to taste the taunting curve of it against her own. To lick the firm line like rich sweet cream. "No . . . it wouldn't be right. I could not permit kissing."

His breath stirred across her lips, and she wondered how she could release her hands to grab his ears and draw his mouth to hers—

"Will you speak to Harry, Sam Taggart?" she asked, wanting whatever stood between father and son to be put at rest.

Sam slowly straightened away from her, his expression hardening. "Get this straight. I like things between Harry and me like they are. I'll pay you back the money you spent. Thank you for straightening my records."

Then he flung away her wrist and left her alone in the sweet June wind.

I do not understand why Sam Taggart can light fire within me. His skin is like smooth dark steel, supple and warm beneath my fingers. He says he does not want children and that is a shame, for he would make beautiful smart children with good hearts. Sam Taggart has a good heart, or he would have not cared about Harry and the Big T. I saw today that he would defend his property, as he did with Tex. Sam Taggart is the first man that I have known who does not want children to bear his name. I think I am a woman who needs children in her life, and also I need challenge and business. I cannot see Sam Taggart with the cold woman he thinks he must have. He should be held and loved and petted. E.

"Here comes another one," Mary stated glumly the next day, as a good-looking Texas drover rode into the yard. The Texas cowmen drove stock up to Montana, and this one wore Mexican silver disks along his gunbelt. "Come to hang around Emma . . . come to help her do chores and eat her bread and make eyes at her . . . it's all enough to make a body—"

She eyed Sam, who had just finished dressing in his pressed, clean clothes and was sitting on the porch, going over Emma's neat notations. He heard Emma's hushed whispering to Harry, and in a few moments Harry stepped out onto the porch with two cups of coffee. He handed one to Sam, and Emma hurried out with a platter of freshly baked, dried currant cake, which she set on the table between them.

Harry looked at the cowboy as if he'd come to steal Emma. Mary jammed cake into her mouth and stated, "My bosom hurts. Sam is taking Emma away. She sent a pigeon home to her pa. He'll send one of the yearlings back—that's the way it works. The useless birds only fly one way."

Harry sent the cowboy on his way, then asked Sam, "What's this about taking Emma?"

Sam looked straight at his father. "I need an assistant."

"The hell you do. You're hot for her!"

"Aren't you?" Sam leveled a look at Harry, and the two men glared at each other. "She's not my type. She's good with records, and I need that right now. Record keeping has been taking a good bite out of my time," Sam said finally, because he wanted to protect Emma from leering minds.

"Just what is your type? Am I a grandpa and don't know it?"

"Leave it. You'll get no grandchildren out of me," Sam ordered, not wanting Harry to get to him.

"Someday I won't leave it, and then there'll be hell to pay between you and me. I never thought much of you running off like that. Emma tells me that I got to talk to you, and so I will. For her sake. But you're a cold one, Sam, not meant for a sweet, loving woman like Emma. There's drovers coming by, once they know we have a good-looking, hardworking woman hired on. . . . Damn." Harry squinted down the road and two more cowboys riding toward the ranchhouse. "All slickered up and—"

"I don't want Emma," Sam stated very clearly.

Harry's disbelieving gaze swung to Sam. "That so?"

"My bosom hurts," Mary whined, eyeing them.

"Let it hurt somewhere else," Sam ordered.

"Git, Mary," Harry ordered, glaring at Sam.

Mary moved closer to Harry. "Emma said I should rub my bosoms with goose grease, but I—"

Both men glared down at her, and Mary held her ground. "You know a woman's time can come on her about my age, and I'll probably die because nobody cares. Fritzi says—"

Sam and Harry turned to look at the cowboys and Emma, ignoring Mary. When Mary slammed her room door shut, Harry asked, "Just why don't you want Emma? She's pure all woman, through and through."

"You'd know, wouldn't you?" Sam didn't want anyone prying through his emotions. He hadn't felt anything unusually strong for a woman past the heat and the quick need; he doubted he ever would.

Harry's jaws clamped shut, a vein throbbing in his temple. "They were good women, my wives." His eyes locked with Sam's as Emma hurried between them to greet the two new cowboys. Then Sam followed Harry's gaze to where the two men were towering over Emma and making eyes at her. One took the bucket of water from her, while the other one drank from the dipper.

"Look at that," Harry said finally. "There's just not enough good women to go around. The drovers come here all the time, smiling and showing off for her. One galoot almost broke his neck doing trick riding to impress her. Another one tried to grab her between the clothesline sheets, and Monty nearly broke the boy's pecker off. By Jesus, I don't know how long I can take it, with that big farmhand out there on that mule almost every night, and a herd of them—all of them wanting to marry her—here by day."

Sam noted distantly that Harry spoke more now than he ever did while Sam was growing up. He stood, stretched, and then walked down to Emma and placed his hand on her shoulder. The two cowboys' friendly smiles turned cold.

Emma smiled warmly at Sam. "This is Elliot and X. Marsh. They have come for pairs of my fine socks, and my bread, and my—"

"I know what they came for," Sam said very quietly, his eyes locking with the men's.

"They wanted me to show them the barn."

Sam's hand shot out to grip Emma's upper arm. He knew why the cowboys wanted her in the barn. "Is that right?"

"I hear you make nice socks, ma'am," one of the drovers stated in a Texas drawl. "Sure gets cold in this country without good socks."

"Amen, brother," the other drover drawled.

Emma beamed up at them all, until she met Sam's dark look. "I will continue my sock business when I work for you," she stated quietly. "And bargaining. I will do my work for you and tend to my business, only when yours is finished."

"Yes," he returned, choking on the agreement. Because it galled him that everyone in Montana Territory would be wearing her socks before she gave him a pair. "Why don't you go along now and get your socks to show these boys?"

Relieved that Sam would not object to her selling her socks and bargaining, Emma smiled warmly at him and hurried to the house. He waited until she was out of hearing range, then leveled a look at the two drovers.

"You're half Injun. She won't want to hitch up with you," one of them drawled, his hand resting on his worn revolver.

"Call it," the other man stated, moving away from Sam.

"Maybe those boys would like to see the barn, boy," Harry called from the porch, then stepped in front of Emma, who was hurrying out the door with a basket of her stockings.

Harry hopped on his foot, let out a pained yowl, and sank into a chair on the porch. Emma immediately hurried to tend him. Sam nodded to the drovers and walked into the barn.

One flick of his whip curled around both men's boots and took them tumbling into the barn dirt. Another flick plucked the revolver out of the drover's hand, and the other man was smart enough to lie still. The whip coiled and gleamed and struck twice more, dusting off their hats. He slowly coiled the braided whip and slung it on his shoulder, looking down at the startled men. "Any questions?"

"Why you . . ." Both men were up, charging him. Sam tossed the whip away. If the men needed more of a taste, he was ready to give it to him. Their charge sent him reeling back against a stall, and one of the men picked up a pitchfork, running toward Sam with it—

Emma entered the barn in a swirl of her gray skirts, her sock basket in one hand. She wore a smile that died when one of the drovers slammed a fist into Sam's mouth. At the moment he was getting the worst of the fight, one man holding him from behind. She said one word, so quiet, it quivered loudly in the airy space of the barn—"Shame."

The men backed away from Sam, and Emma placed herself in front of him. He tried to push her away, but she pushed herself back, placing her sock basket between her and the men. "Shame on you. Two men against Sam, who isn't even a fighter. You see he wears no guns. He is a defenseless man. Shame on you, bad men. Go now. Shoo. Shame on you. Go away from here. You may not have one of my socks—"

"Emma, stand aside. I will handle this," Sam ordered, his pride nicked that he was being defended by a woman holding a sock basket.

"No. You bad men apologize to Sam. Do it . . . go on—apologize to Sam Taggart."

Interested in the brawl, the pigeons looked down from the hole in the barn roof. Droppings plummeted down to the drovers' heads, and they wiped furiously with huge red bandannas. "He started it," one of the men said, dusting off his dirty clothes and dodging another round of droppings as more pigeons landed.

"I told you. Sam is not a fighting man. He is a businessman with many interests in mines and logging and cattle. He owns stores. You are bullies, both of you. Apologize," she ordered in a regal, quiet, outraged tone, then softened it by adding, "Apologize, and I will give you cake to take with you."

"Emma—" Sam began, trying to hold his temper down. he'd fought his way through a war and a lifetime; he wasn't used to interference or a woman taking his part. He preferred— How could this one woman— *Why had the sight of them leering at Emma set him off?*

"Sorry," one of the drovers mumbled, stepping out of the droppings' path.

"Yeah," the other drover glared at Sam, then his mouth curled into a sneer that had Sam moving forward.

Emma pushed back against him, bracing her basket in front of her. "You men go to the house. I will stay here and tend poor Sam. Tell Monty that I said to give you cake. Be nice, please."

After they had gone, Emma placed her basket aside and stood near Sam. She stood on tiptoe to look at his bruised lip and took a lace-bordered handkerchief from her apron to pat it. "You are bleeding. Oh, those bad men—"

"You just traded my pride for cake." Sam had been pushed to his limit. He tried to ignore the dabbing at his lip, her soft, worried expression, her tsk-tsking and shaming, and the pounding of his temper—or was it something else? Her breasts nudged and bobbed and tortured his bare chest as she moved. He grabbed her wrist with one hand, placed his other hand behind her head to support it, and kissed her hard.

Her eyes were huge, staring up at him, her face pale. Her lips trembled, and Sam knew with a sinking feeling that he'd stepped over an invisible line. He'd never tasted a woman like Emma, who was certainly a virgin. The need to taste her again rose and bloomed within him. Her eyes remained opened as he closed his and slowly lowered his lips to hers.

"Put your arms around me," he whispered, needing her warmth and softness and the taste of her once more.

Her hands fluttered at his sides, then impatient with her slow untutored movements, Sam wrapped her arms around him and held her.

Hungry for her mouth, he bent his head and brushed his lips against hers, feeling the silky warmth enfold and heat him. The soft rush of her breath stopped, and her body fit snugly, like a dove settling softly against him. Sam almost groaned, surprising himself with his need to hold her tightly, letting her body flow against his. He slanted his mouth and kissed her slowly, softly, not wanting to frighten her. She sucked in air, and gentle thoughts stirred Sam's mind—she hadn't breathed, unfamiliar with kissing.

He opened his hands, smoothing her back, feeling the tension humming through her. Then slowly, slowly, he slid his hands beneath her arms and allowed his thumbs to brush her breasts. She shivered, but her arms tightened around him, and he gave himself to the soft untutored push of her lips against his. He ran his tongue across her lips, flicking at them, tasting as Emma held very still.

"Open for me, Emma," he whispered, desperate for more than a taste.

Emma's fingers gripped his shirt, her eyes squeezed

shut as the tip of his tongue slid into the tiny, sweet, hot opening of her lips.

Sam held very still, aware that her apron, skirt, and multiple petticoats were shielding the heavy thrust of his body. He teased her lips, opening the narrow margin to slide his tongue within—

She breathed unsteadily, her body taut against his, and Sam found her legs with his thigh, inserting it slowly, slowly, until she rested upon him. He nudged her gently, wanting more, and then Emma's tongue touched his. Her lips closed gently around his tongue, gloving him in her sweet heat.

Sam deepened the kiss, running one arm lower, his hand resting on her hip, pressing her close against him.

The sound came so softly, it startled him, a low husky sound that tightened his body. Her hips moved against him, her thighs riding his and her mouth slanted firmly up against him.

Sam dived into the warmth, the softness enveloping him. He gathered her closer, wanting her— In the next instant he picked her up, taking her leg around him, the petticoats bunched between them.

Emma pushed back from him, and seeing the wide fear in her eyes, he slowly lowered her to her feet. He stared at her, wanting her, resenting the rigid heat riding his body.

Emma smoothed her clothing. She flushed and looked away from him. "I understand, Sam Taggart. You have come from fear with those men and needed comfort . . . but perhaps . . . perhaps . . . I should be— You are forgiven. Please do not mention this again. I will

never speak of it. I must hurry . . . my bread is rising
. . . I should be—"

Every instinct in Sam knew exactly where she should
be—under him. When he took a step toward her, Emma
picked up her skirts and ran.

Chapter Eight

Sam Taggart has asked me to go with him to tend his business. I knew when I saw him that he would lead to more adventures, and now I am invited to ride with him, keeping his records. This is no small thing, an unmarried woman riding with a man, but now I will learn how he makes his bargains. I am excited and have sent a pigeon to ask Papa's permission, because while I start my life as a businesswoman tending Sam Taggart, I am also my father's daughter, and his blessings are important to me. The kiss Sam Taggart gave me was almost a present, it was so beautiful. Yet then the fire leaped in me and frightened me. He only needed comfort, and I took advantage of him. I try not to be selfish, but there are things I want, like being a businesswoman and being near Sam Taggart. He is exciting. E.

"Papa says I cannot go with you." Emma handed Sam the tiny paper, which had been attached to the pigeon.

She shielded her downcast expression from him, averting her head to whisper and cuddle the pigeon.

Sam locked his legs to the ground. "That was quick." He unrolled the paper. "It's in German. Read it to me."

"My father says that it would not be right for me, an unmarried woman, to travel with you. He demands that I come home before more foolish ideas are put into my head. He says women should not be in business." She swallowed and looked at Sam with a frustrated, helpless expression.

He would have fought ten men for her. The knowledge staggered him. He'd always been meticulous about minding his own business.

"I *am* going with you. You need help, Sam Taggart, if you are to build your business. Even your father says you need someone at your—ah—backside," she stated firmly, looking up at him with clear hazel eyes. "If we can find someone to take my place, I will go. But I would like my father's blessing."

Emma continued to look at him, and Sam went slightly dizzy. Her eyes reminded him of a clear stream, golden leaves skimming along the surface and secrets in the swirling depths. The tendrils escaping the tight confines of her braids glistened in the sun, the rich nut-brown touched with a ruby shade. From the prim set of her mouth, and the proud way she held her shoulders, Sam knew that Emma had a carefully shielded rebellious streak. Everything about her was neat, in control, and precise, presenting a real challenge to any man who liked games—Sam didn't, and he had no time for the fanciful thoughts that had just dropped into his head.

"Tell your father that I'll pay twice as much, and if

you're good at keeping my records, I'll add a good fresh bull, straight up from Texas, the next time I'm passing through." Sam wasn't losing a good asset.

She beamed up at him as if he'd handed her a bouquet of miracles. Her look unnerved him, and he went light-headed. He noted the spray of freckles across her nose and wondered how they'd taste. He wondered if her freckles ran down her body—

"Never hurts to sweeten the pot," Harry noted slowly, studying his son and Emma.

Sam turned toward Harry and met his gaze evenly. "She's good at what she does. This is business."

"Take her," Mary pleaded desperately. "She's ruining my life. She thinks I should learn how to read."

"People hereabouts won't like an unmarried sweet thing traveling with you, boy," Harry stated with a wide grin.

Sam turned slowly to look at his father, braced his weight on one leg, and hooked his thumbs in his belt. "What's wrong with me, Harry?"

The challenge from Sam hung in the air, a bastard son to his father. Harry stared back, his expression unreadable.

"Good. It's settled. I will make the offer." Emma hurried to her shelf where she kept precious clean paper and placed a folded piece of paper beneath her hand as she wrote. Sam admired the dip of her head and the slight frown of concentration. He wondered how the tender nape of her exposed neck would taste.

Emma worded Sam's offer very precisely, using her best writing skills. She wanted to go with Sam, to learn from him, and to make enough money to buy her way free of Gilbert. When put to the test, her father would settle for money. At times she wondered if he actually wanted Gilbert for a son-in-law.

Her mouth burned with Sam's kiss. It was difficult to concentrate with him watching her.

Their tongues had mated. His leg had gone between hers, nudging her in a rhythm that had made her melt. She had dampened her drawers with the heat flowing low in her body. . . .

Emma gasped as she made a mistake and began again. She'd wanted to move into Sam, to hold him closely and taste him. The dark heat in his eyes had stirred her, had caused her to tremble— Emma scratched through another mistake and began a third time. Sam was bothered only by being threatened by the men; she had seen people react strangely after great fear.

"What's wrong?" Harry asked intently.

"She never makes mistakes," Monty declared.

"It's her time," Mary declared wisely, and pushed her face into a taunting grimace. "My time will probably come, and I'll die, and no one will even care. You can bury me up there—"

"You hush," Sam ordered at the same time Harry did. Monty cleared his throat, his face a furious red as he hurried away.

"I will not go back, even if my father does not take Sam's offer," Emma stated quietly when she had finished. "I will just send this to Papa, and then I will clean the garden fence. There are lovely old flowers and garlic and winter onions there that need separating and cleaning."

She needed to be away from them. The old garden place had once been loved; now it was running wild with climbing roses and old plants left to fend for themselves. She needed to pit herself against a challenge that other women had touched, to drag her mind from Sam's delicious kiss.

Once in the old garden Emma raked furiously, careless of the sweat dampening her clothing and trailing down her temple.

Harry and Mary walked past her, each carrying a rifle and dressed in fringed buckskins. Harry touched his hat. "Mary is in a mood. I'm taking her up on the mountain to work out some of it. Don't you worry none. Everything will be just fine."

Monty began raking beside Emma. "He's mourning you already. Seems Harry's women don't stay for long, even the hired ones. He's aching, too, because Sam's a hard case, just like Harry taught him to be. Harry is carrying a load of grief each time he looks at Sam, but Sam ain't in a listening mood."

"Sam is a kind man. You should have seen those bad men picking on him. He is no fighter, you know. Harry should be proud of Sam."

Monty stared at her incredulously. "You think Sam can't fight?"

"He is a businessman and a thinker, not a fighter."

"Maybe. Sam's sharp, okay. But I don't reckon he'd back down if pushed."

"Sam does not have a gun. Already twice—" She closed her mouth, not wanting Monty to know that Sam had to be defended. She would protect Sam as they traveled.

She glanced up to see Sam, his shining boot placed on a log and his scowl leveled at her.

"It is much better to be a businessman-thinker than to be a fighter," she stated in his defense.

"Is that so?" Sam asked tightly, and strode away to the corral. Emma stared at his rigid back, thinking how beautiful he was, even when he was angry.

"He's mad," Monty said. "Good and mad. When old Harry looked like that, we used to get a fresh crop of mustangs every time. Broke 'em all to riding before he quit. It mellowed him out some."

Within an hour, another Taggart pigeon returned. Emma hurried to the pigeon's landing loft, cuddled the pigeon, and untied the message. She grinned, picked up her skirts, and ran to Sam, who was repairing a broken board in the corral fence. "I can go! I can go!"

She almost ran into Sam. He was still wearing a scowl. "We leave before daylight," he said. "We'll try a short trip first. I've got business at Swenson's logging outfit in the mountains. That will be overnight. We'll be back the next day. If you can't keep up this trip, the deal is off."

"Oh, yes, yes. I must hurry. There is supper to cook and getting ready—" She would pack her stockings and pen and ink and lunch. She prayed that she would not fail Sam. At least he would have her protection for this trip.

She stood in front of him, exhilarated, breathing quickly, her face flushed as she grinned up at him.

Sam's grim expression sent her reeling, then his hot

gaze dropped slowly down her body to brush her quickly rising and falling breasts. She realized suddenly that one of Sam's boots rested on the corral and that she stood between his legs.

"Before sunup," he stated, then slowly, firmly, removed his boot from the corral. He straightened, towering over her. "You make one wrong move—whine just once—and I'll bring you back pronto."

"I do not whine." Emma set her jaw. How like Sam to nettle her in a happy time!

Sam's mouth tightened. "I'm going into Deer Lodge City tonight, and I'll be back before morning. Make sure you take warm clothing. It's freezing up in the mountains, and I don't want to be slowed down by a sick woman."

She nodded solemnly and wondered why Sam would travel thirty miles tonight when he planned a business trip tomorrow. But as a businessman, Sam could not tell her everything. "I'll bring food and my papers and pen," she said.

And my sock basket, she added silently.

"Sam is gone." Mary seemed pleased with herself, even offering to help Emma with the early supper dishes.

Emma stopped stirring the antelope stew she had cooked for the Taggarts. She wanted them well fed while she was gone; she hurried to the potato bread that needed to be shaped into round loaves. One day she would have an outside oven like her mother's. Tomorrow she would place slices of the antelope roast with bread and— She stopped in midstep, the stew ladle in her hand, and turned slowly to Mary, who was smothering a grin and jingling coins in her pocket.

"What did you say?" Emma asked, uncertain that she had heard correctly.

"I can do all this, cook and tend my family. They ain't your family—they're mine. I was just seeing if you could set the place right before I stepped in." Mary eyed Harry, who was scowling at her, then turned and hurried back to her bedroom.

Emma swept into the room behind Mary and closed the door. Mary's expression said she knew something important. Emma skipped haggling and arguing and made her offer: "Two cats in your bedroom. Not in my bread bowl."

"Two cats in the *house*. Anywhere they want." Mary took out two large coins and studied them. Then she leveled a smirk at Emma. "He's gone to the whores. I bet he met Fritzi somewhere along the road. I hope Fritzi is alive when the ladies get done with him."

"Sam would not take my little brother to the—to the town ladies."

"I found these in his pocket, and I know that Fritzi has been trying to get some man to take him into town. Your pa is a hard case."

"That is true—my father would not like that." She studied Mary closely. "How do you know that Sam is going to . . . what he will do in town?"

"He had that look. I saw it before on a cowhand that stayed here once. Some of his fingers were missing 'cause he'd played with miners' blasting caps. . . . Men get all snarly and steamy looking, like they'll explode if they don't get to town pretty quick." Mary's tone rang with experience. "The cowboy came back wearing one big silly grin."

Emma closed her eyes and remembered Sam's taut steamy look as she stood between his legs . . . after their tongues had mated. . . . She quivered from head to toe, shaken by the idea that Sam had hurried to town to— She didn't want to think about Sam's mission. He should not involve Fritzi, despite how badly Fritzi wanted to see if his morning dreams could come true. Fritzi had tried incessantly to get Gilbert to take him to women, but Gilbert knew that one wrong move would cost him a potential bride, a fist hold on the Recht farm, and a dowry. "I must hurry to finish everything and pack for tomorrow," she stated, hurrying back to the kitchen.

As soon as the bread was baked and the pans scrubbed, Emma packed her paper and pen and ink and ledgers. She hurried back and forth to her room, packing and arranging a neat pile to take with her.

Mary, for once, agreed to take care of the chickens and keep her cats away from them. If Emma stayed longer than two days, Mary promised she would try reading.

When Emma had properly arranged everything for the early departure, she yawned hardily, as if she would fall immediately asleep, slipped into her room, and closed the door. She rummaged through the clothing she'd been patching, grabbed Monty's shirt and pants, and tugged them on. They were a bit snug at the bosom and hips, but with a jacket over them she looked like a boy. She plopped an old hat over her braids, pulled a small chest beneath the window, stood on it, and crawled out. In minutes she was riding Woden toward Deer Lodge City to rescue Fritzi from the town women.

Once she got Sam in her hands, she would not bake for him and never again offer him a pair of her fine socks. If Sam showed Fritzi the way to ruin . . . poor little Fritzi's legs— Emma bent low to her pony and begged him to fly through the night to rescue Fritzi.

Along the way to Deer Lodge City, she passed two men sharing a bottle between them and laughing as they rode. She tugged up her collar and nodded, and one of them yelled, "Hey, boy. Amanda's Place doesn't close to dawn. Until then the ladies are willing. Then they like to get some shut-eye."

"Sleeping during the day . . . shame on them," Emma muttered darkly, begging Woden to hurry faster. Though the territorial prison loomed on the outskirts, Deer Lodge City was a fine town, filled with large brick buildings and elaborate signs. She saw Tenkiller tied to a hitching post in front of a beer hall on the outskirts of town.

Just after midnight the sign for Amanda's Place swung as a bullet hit it—men were yelling challenges at each other and blasting away at the sign. Because they blocked the entrance to the well-lit, noisy beer hall, Emma decided to find an alternative route.

Within minutes she was sliding up the back stairway as several men staggered down, wearing happy expressions. Emma was shocked at the raw scents of the upstairs rooms, the cheap perfume and the other heavy musky odor. She pressed back against the wall as a blond woman passed, wearing white face powder and rouge. Emma gaped at the woman, whose nipples were

dark against the light camisole covering her breasts and
whose short pantaloons exposed her legs from knees to
ankles.

"What you doing here, honey?" The woman's eyes
were hard, glittering over the fragrant smoke of a dark
thin cheroot. "I'm free. You got tokens from the
barkeep?"

Emma slid back, and the woman eased closer, squinting through the smoke. "You look like a German kid I
know. He was in town with his pa, buying supplies for a
ranch. Nice kid. He told me I was pretty, and we talked.
He said he'd come see me and we'd just talk—"

"Has he come to you?" Emma knew that she was too
late; Fritzi would probably never recover now.

The girl pushed Emma into a room; she ripped off
Emma's hat to expose the tightly wound braids. She
lighted a lamp and placed her hands on her hips, staring
at Emma, all the time puffing on her small dark cigarette. "Thought so. You're a female. You came after
someone, didn't you, honey? To keep them on the right
path? You've got that righteous red look and the devil in
your eye. Who do you want?"

"Is the boy you know here? He is my little brother."
Emma noted the room, gaudy with color and fringes
and beads. A table with a mirror over it was filled with
fancy bottles. A beautiful shawl was draped over one
side of the broken mirror, and a tiny tintype was tucked
into the frame. A pitcher of fresh water stood in a por-
celain basin, a bar of soap placed on top of a neatly
folded towel. A sign on the door read, "Token. Wash.
Treat the ladies right. One hour."

She studied the woman, who had sunk to the bed. She

kicked off her pretty shoes with heels and rubbed her feet. She wore a tiny gold cross at her throat, and Emma immediately trusted her. The woman was no more than sixteen, looking old and hard beneath a high mass of ringlets that drifted down her back. "I know how it is to take care of younger brothers and sisters. I got into this because Ma died and Pa ran off, leaving me with Beth. My little sister is only four, and I'm only working to grubstake our way out of here. She's at a widow woman's now. I'm supporting us all."

The girl stood and jammed her feet into the shoes with the determination of a fighter donning a gun. She hitched up her lacy garter and said, "My working name is Let-go Lilly, but you can call me Lilly. The boys call me Let-go, because that's what I usually say. I make certain they know who's boss in this rodeo and that they handle me right. I made up my mind a long time ago that no man was calling my tune until I was ready. You'd do well to take that advice. . . . If your brother is here, I'll find him. You stay here. Make yourself at home. No one uses this room because they—well, the girls take care of me, mostly because of Beth, and they know I like things clean."

When the girl left the room, Emma sat on the bed, clasped her hands together, and listened to the strange sounds. The beer hall below was filled with one loud roaring sound, and the upstairs hallways with other harsh rhythmic sounds. Emma's knees were shaking from the ride, and from the fear of what might happen to Fritzi, and from her anger at Sam.

After an hour of listening to moaning and thumping and yelling and laughter, she decided to take off her boots and prop her feet up on the bed. She wanted to save all her energy for rescuing Fritzi and for teaching Sam a lesson.

Emma noted the heat from the room, took off her coat, and folded it on a chair.

Lilly jerked open the door and scanned the room, finding Emma instantly. "Don't you go anywhere, kid. I'll be tied up for another hour or so. Make yourself comfortable . . . uh—blow out the lamp, so people will think I'm in here. They know I don't like light when I work . . . uh—got to go. *Do not leave this room.* I'll be back as soon as I can. There's not a word of your brother, but I haven't checked all the girls."

"Thank you, Lilly." Emma blew out the lamp and sat on the bed. Once she got her hands on Fritzi . . . once she got her hands on Sam, she corrected. She would teach him not to lead poor young boys astray. Her head ached with tension, the long day's work settling into her body. Emma leaned close to the mirror and decided she had time to tidy her hair, some of which had begun to come free of her braids, curling down her nape. She released her braids, combed her fingers through her hair, and shook it, glorying in release from the braids' tight confinement. Her hair rippled and curled down to her waist, and she yawned. She had one whole hour to rest, and then she would be fresh to capture Fritzi and wrest him away from Sam's evil clutches.

Emma lay down on the bed and tugged one end of the quilt over her. How could Sam kiss her and then touch his tongue to another woman's?

He did not deserve her doughnuts, and she would never

give him socks, for he would stand in them and kiss another woman!

The door opened, light shafting into the room, and a man's body filled the dim light. He closed the door gently and braced one hand against it, resting for a moment. He peered at Emma through the dim light. "Here I am."

Emma lay very still. There was no mistaking Sam's deep drawl. He sauntered to the bed, lifted a strand of her hair, and smoothed it between his fingers as though he were thinking of something else. He tossed two coins onto the bed, then began to undress. "I don't like talk. There's this woman who talks about everything, and that's not what I'm wanting."

She closed her eyes, but then one lid opened, just enough to see Sam's entire dimly lit body, all hard angles and cords and shoulders and hips—

He moved to the table, and Emma's eyes widened as he began to cleanse himself, washing intimately.

She should have turned away. She should have told Sam how bad he was and asked where was Fritzi . . . but she couldn't move her lips, her tongue, and no sounds came. Emma shivered, heat racing through her. *He thought she was a paid woman.*

She could . . . she could touch him as she liked— Emma sucked in her breath as Sam turned to her. She should say something.

She wanted to touch him. To kiss him once more. She knew her berserking tendencies were running wild, and she didn't care.

This was her last chance before marriage to Gilbert.

The flush stirring in her lower belly rose slowly up to

her breasts, hardening them, and then crawled up to her cheeks.

Sam.

She wanted him upon her, in her.

She wanted to taste him again, to smell his clean scents.

Emma lay very still and shivered again as he sat down on the bed. It was true what her father said about her, that she was a berserker, ready to fling herself into danger. . . . She should . . . she should . . .

Sam shook his head. "The woman is like a burr that's— I just look at her, and I get hard. I'm not a man to get hard from one look. She's got this smell, like she's clean and new. None of it makes sense," he stated wearily, sinking down to the pillow beside hers. He moved his face into the swath of hair rippling across it. "You smell good."

His hand found her breast and cupped it, running his thumb across her nipple.

Emma fought to breathe as Sam chuckled, a rich deeply pleased sound. He unbuttoned her borrowed shirt and pants, stripping them from her as though he couldn't wait.

His hand grazed down across her stomach, his fingers curling over her intimately. He pressed gently, inserting one finger, and the melting heat came damp and free from Emma. She grabbed his arm to brace herself against the racing pleasure.

Sam's head bent to rest upon her breast, and she slowly lifted her hand to stroke his hair—his lovely crisp raven-black hair that would be so beautiful on his babies—

His lips sought her breast over her shift, and Emma's other hand grasped his shoulder, anchoring herself for the pleasure pounding at her with each gentle hot suckle of his lips.

Emma quivered from head to toe and locked her fingertips into Sam's skin. She held on to Sam and the pleasure racing through her when his lips rubbed against her skin and his hand gently kneaded her softness.

His fingers skimmed slowly down to her waist, setting on the shape of her, then locked to the flare of her hips.

In her lifetime, except for the times she'd deliberately taken thrilling chances, like swinging from the barn loft onto the mound of stacked hay, Emma had never been greedy. Now, she wanted all of her greed in one moment, locked on the squeaking bed with Sam sprawled next to her, holding her, his hands—

She heard the sound come up her throat, a low husky moan that quivered in the silence of the room. Sam's deep drawl seemed pleased, his lips moving up to her ear to whisper, "Be good now." He spoke to her so softly, with laughter in his voice. "Why don't you—"

Then he tugged at her shift, lifting it over her head, and began to unknot her drawers. She stopped him, her hand squeezing his. His fingers turned to lace with hers. "Yes or no, but don't play games. I've got to be going shortly."

She could lose her moment. Emma released his hand, and Sam pulled away her drawers. She lay very still, uncertain about what she should do, when Sam rose over her, placing his legs between hers, sliding his hands to her hips, then down to her thighs and lifting her legs over the back of his.

Emma held very still as Sam braced over her, her legs quivering around him. She should—

With a surge that tightened his body, he thrust into her, and she cried out, terrified by the pain and the quick violence of a man she'd trusted—

Above her, braced by his hands, Sam shook his head as though dazed. His face was angular, hard as she'd never seen it, a spear of hair crossing his forehead, quivering with the tension running through him. *"You're a virgin."*

His voice was deep with disgust. He was angry with her, about to leave her, and Emma bit her lip. She wanted him to finish as she had seen the farm animals finish, and within her Sam remained hard— She released the breath she'd been holding and gave him an excuse to stay. To linger with her past the first tearing.

Emma heard the sound come from her very soul, a ragged purring, as her body began to stretch to accommodate him.

Sam shook his head again, as though trying to clear it, and she knew that in another moment he'd be gone and she couldn't have that. She raised up, locked her arms around his neck, and took his hard mouth.

To insure her lock upon him, Emma thrust her tongue into his mouth and moved it as he had shown her just that day. She placed her hands along his cheeks and sucked him rhythmically. Her hips seemed to flow with the motion, moving against Sam.

Sam seemed to melt upon her, his weight wonderful and warm. "You should have told me you just started the business," he whispered against her ear, biting the lobe gently. "I'd have taken more time."

She held him tightly, shivering with the marvelous warm sensation that she had claimed him for her own. He felt marvelous—smooth power, muscles and cords, hard against her. He groaned unsteadily and rubbed his smooth chest against her, dragging his nipples against hers. His hand moved lower, lower between them, crossed her stomach, and she sucked in her breath as he touched between them.

Instantly the heat poured out of her, bubbled upward, and burst, and came again, time after time, throwing Emma upon a warm, sunlit perch filled with flowers and sunshine. She clung to the rippling pleasure, heard her exquisite cry, and then wilted into a warm flush that enfolded her from head to toe.

Sam's low chuckle delighted her. He bent to nuzzle her cheek, then placed his face against her throat. She stroked his back, the taut hard muscles ridging it, and realized that like male animals in season, he had not completed his business.

She waited for him to continue, her heart racing against her chest so wildly that she was certain he could feel it.

"Let's make this easy for you, little one," Sam murmured against her hot cheek, and began to move slowly within her until she was certain he couldn't go deeper. She feared he would leave her each time, yet he didn't. His movements grew faster, his breathing harsher, and Emma held tight, because she would not leave him to fight his demons alone. Sam needed her help—She lifted her hips and held him tight, and he cried out, pouring into her as if everything he was, he had given to her.

Sam had always been generous with his family and was generous with her now. Emma began to smile and then tensed as a second round of pleasure took her quickly, flinging her against him, until she was helpless but to hold him tightly and let the journey complete its full measure.

Sam's ragged groan said he had given his best, his body quivering upon her. She tried to lift her hands to comfort him, and they flopped boneless to her side.

Sam pushed free of her with what looked like a tremendous effort and patted her bottom, and soon, from the sound of his breathing, she knew that he was sleeping.

Emma lay very still, wrapped in her thoughts. She lifted her head slightly to peer down Sam's backside. It was true. He lay unclothed beside her, spent with his magnificent effort to mate with her. She was glad that he had not given himself to another woman.

Emma swallowed, her body cold without his. He would be shamed to find her here, to know that he had had her and that—worse—she liked the marriage act with him. Emma eased from the bed and found her clothing on the floor. She dressed quickly, and needing a reminder that Sam had given her a beautiful moment to remember, she scooped up the tokens. She would keep them forever.

She stepped into the hallway and bumped into Lilly, who grinned. "My, my. You're all hot looking."

She peeked into the dark room and quickly shut the

door. "You've done that fine young bronc in. He's sleeping like the dead. I couldn't find your little brother—"

Emma quickly placed her hands to her hot cheeks. She had forgotten about Fritzi. Sam would never have taken Fritzi into such a place; Emma was horrified that she had distrusted Sam, who had just made wonderful love to her. "Thank you, Lilly. Will you please watch for Fritzi? He is certain that with the help of a—of a woman, he can make his legs better. It is silly, I know, but my father has made him feel less than manly—"

"Shoo. You go on home now, honey, and I'll send your little brother home if he turns up. Don't you come back. While you liked this one, not all times are good. Know what I mean?"

Emma stared at her blankly. "No. He was wonderful. I felt so . . ."

"Like red-hot smoldering coals?" Lilly grinned as though she knew exactly how Emma had felt.

Emma blushed and hurried out the back door. Through the ride home, she relived every moment of Sam's body locking with hers, the furious pounding of his heart only for her, the gentleness of his hands, and his low husky laugh as the pleasure had taken her.

At least she had this night to remember.

I have to write quickly, for Sam and I leave early in the morning and there is barely time to sleep. After tonight it will be important to have a husband who can serve my needs. Wonderful needs too delicious to describe. A husband simply to fill the role of making babies and one who respects me is good, but now I know there is joy in the marriage act. I will look for

*such a husband as we travel. I felt as if I could fly
and burn in the sun. There are no words for my
delight. I am glad I pleased Sam. He pleased me. For
once, I was very selfish and was glad. E.*

Sam glanced at the passing deer sliding down the
mountain and then back to Emma, riding her pony behind him. He turned and settled back into the thunderous mood that had been riding him since he'd awakened
to find the woman gone. Before dawn he'd ridden to the
Big T with the scent of her tormenting him. Harry and
Monty scowled at Sam and hurried to help Emma.
Harry insisted that she take another pigeon; he reas-
sured her that if she needed—he glared pointedly at
Sam—help, Harry and Monty would be there. "And Tex
might like to come, too," Harry had added, letting Sam
know that there were men who wanted Emma and respected her like they did their own mothers.

Emma looked as though she were out for a grand
adventure, while Sam was faced with buying into a logging outfit without enough ready cash. On his way to
Swenson's mountain logging operation, there wouldn't
be any horse races for Tenkiller, or shell games, or
monte, or any other quick money. In his saddlebags he'd
purchased blank deeds for anyone wanting to sell to
him. All he had were deeds that he didn't want to sell.

All he had was an aching head from drink and a memory of taking a virgin—of sweet soft flushed skin, round
soft breasts, flaring hips, and the texture of her hair—
swirling around him.

At Amanda's he'd drunk heavily, planning to rid his
body of the taut need Emma had stirred within him.

Just seeing her fingers stroke Hercules was enough to make Sam's body harden.

The town woman had moved like warm silk beneath him, her cry of pleasure haunting him when he awoke to find her gone. Even now he could feel himself tearing through her virginity. The thought didn't help his conscience or his hangover. The second time he showed her how it could be, and tonight she'd be with someone else.

His scowl hurt as he shook his head. He'd certainly trimmed much of the need off him with that quick event. Right now he could have gone back for a second round. As a boy, he'd spent hours in bawdy houses, getting rid of his tension. As a man, he rarely indulged in sex or had a second time with a woman; he wanted his mind locked to business.

While he felt ragged and irritable, Emma had been too cheerful that morning, humming as she rode behind him on her little pony. Sam wondered what she'd think if she knew how badly he wanted to go back to town to find the agile, hungry, and strong little woman who had given him her first time.

He turned to look at Emma once more, half-hoping she'd be in trouble or her pony would be winded by the twisting tiny mountain train.

Hell. Even the two pigeons in the cage looked happy. The small pony was bred for hardships, carrying Emma and her small bundles. The sock basket swung from her saddle horn.

Her breasts rippled softly as the pony maneuvered across a small creek, and Sam's throat went dry. He remembered the woman's full breasts, quivering with her movements, soft against him and firm to his hand.

The texture of her nipples could drive a man insane. . . . The way she fit tight against him as though she were made for him, and the sounds she made—those sweet purring noises from deep inside her throat—

He jerked around, away from the sight. Just once he'd like to hold those round breasts in his hand, let the soft weight settle into his keeping, as the pigeon's had.

He needed a woman again. One ripe and hot enough to take the edge off his need, so he could get his mind back on business. After this trip he was going to find that little town woman, pay her for however long it took to get his mind cleared, and—He tensed at a noise moving up on a hill by a stand of lodgepole pine, and suddenly a giant logger stepped into view. Despite the cold temperature the logger had his shirtsleeves rolled back, and he stared at Emma.

Sam glanced back to find Emma waving at the man; Sam wrapped his hand around his whip handle. If the logger took one step toward her, he'd find himself on his backside. "Don't wave."

"But he is smiling." Emma's hand dropped as Sam continued to study her. Flushed with excitement, she looked as if she'd just tasted a wonderful dessert and wanted more. She looked at the logger too long; in another woman the look would be an open invitation, but as a virgin, Emma had no idea how that look could entice a man.

She looked at Sam, and a slow blush rose up her cheeks.

"Where's Swede Swenson?" Sam asked the logger, torn between business and wanting the town woman, and shaken by Emma's flushed, excited look.

He glanced back at her. She seemed different, softer, more womanly . . . hot. . . . Sam mentally shook his head; he was the one that was aching for more of the same—Emma had no idea about the intimate details of sex.

"In camp. Is that your woman?" the man asked in a heavy Swedish accent.

"She works for me." Sam knew instantly that the man would translate Emma's business relationship into a single bed. He remembered last night's gently creaking bed, his fingers sinking into the softness of the woman's hips, her legs strong around him. . . .

"Ya! Sure, she works for you." The logger's leer widened.

Sam pushed down the temper riding him. "Tell Swenson that I've got business with him."

In the mountains the sunlight died early, setting upon the loggers' tents and a small house of lodgepole pine. A Chinese cook stirred pots over a blazing fire and dug through the coals to extract three huge Dutch ovens filled with bread. Swenson invited Emma and Sam into the small single room that served as his office and as the cook shack for the men. Sam took Emma's upper arm and guided her into the room; too busy looking back at the group of smiling loggers, she had walked right into his back.

He nodded to Emma, who was standing on tiptoe to look out the crack of the door to the twenty loggers.

"Emma!" She hurried to spread Sam's business papers on the table, as he had instructed her. "Take off your coat, Emma," Sam ordered, his mind tracking through just what assets he could trade Swede, or how he would pay a promissory note. He noted Swede's interest, the seven-foot logger's gaze too intent upon Emma's bent head, her neat bonnet, and her vulnerable neck. "This is my clerk, Emma Recht."

Swede nodded, then lurched to his feet and jerked open the door. "Chinee. Bring food for the woman and her things in here."

Emma looked at Sam as if she adored him. "Is that what I am? Your clerk?" she whispered.

"Don't talk." Trying to appear relaxed, Sam gripped the table with fingers that ached. He felt as though he were all ragged edges, hung between a headache, and glued together with the promise that when he was finished building up his cash, he was headed back to the town woman in Deer Lodge City.

Emma beamed at him as if he'd just given her Christmas. "Yes, Sam. I am happy to be your clerk."

Chapter Nine

Today I met Swede, a wonderful big blond man who tells stories about Babe the blue ox and about Paul Bunyan. Sam has said that first he gets to know a business partner, and then the men play cards. I was too excited and put Swede's papers in order, for which he was very glad. Then I baked bread and cake in a tiny oven, and Swede has good manners, thanking me.

Tonight Sam and I are going to sleep in Swede's cabin, and Sam is angry at the men who come asking to talk with me. "Emma can't come play," he has said so darkly. Sometimes he just says no and slams the door shut.

Sam made a wonderful business deal with Swede, for lumber. He traded a small ring to Swede, who didn't know what he would do with it. I suggested it could be his dowry, as I had one that was important to me, and that a woman would like the ring.

Swede is a nice man, and I wrote down his stories

*of Paul Bunyan for him to add to his dowry. When I
have time, I will make a copy for Mary.*

*I got weak in the head and stomach, because I
have forgotten to eat. Sam was wonderful, hurrying
to feed me and even taking off my shoes. He seemed
so happy, tending me. He held me on his lap, like a
child. It is not for him to tend me. I always tend
others. I could not have him thinking that I was
weak, and protested. He became angry.*

*I wish tonight I could do what I did last night all
over again. The men here are lovely. E.*

Moonlight filtered through the lodgepole pines as
Sam sat down on a tree stump and began polishing his
boots. Swede came to join him, bearing a pottery jug of
whiskey. "How will the railroad help loggers?"

Sam spread his dream in front of Swede. "Settlers
need boards for barns and sheds and houses, for new
towns and schools here in Deer Lodge Valley. If this
works, then we'll expand and set up another base. They
need lumber up in Fort Benton country, more than the
steamboats can supply. There is talk of wheat, and
they'll need flour mills."

Swede talked for a time, impressed with the socks
Emma had given him.

"She gave them to you," Sam repeated hollowly, noting that the socks were Emma's new trademark model,
with the tiny house. He hefted the whiskey jug to brace
it on his shoulder. Emma gave socks to everyone but
him, and the thought irritated. *"Sam Taggart, I will never
give you one sock."*

Swede left, and Sam mulled his dark mood. It was bad

enough that he'd had to ruin a virgin last night—now he wanted to hold and cuddle Emma.

Hell. He was tired and ill at ease with a woman who knew how to keep his records. She was an asset to his business, nothing more.

Sam lurched to his feet and walked back to the cabin. He placed his hand on the latch and hesitated. He'd given Emma enough time to get into bed and shield her precious virgin body from his lustful eyes. His body told him that it would be a long night.

Sam entered the darkened cabin and found his bedroll neatly fashioned on the floor, waiting for him. Emma had placed his books nearby for his inspection, a clean, pressed handkerchief for the next day and his glasses over it. Sam stripped and slid into his bedroll, accustomed to sleeping in worse places. He folded his arms behind his head and listened for sounds on the other side of the blanket separating him from Emma.

Her small sleepy sigh tore across the room and jolted him wide awake. Sam forced himself to relax, to ignore the slight scent of Emma filling the room. He dozed, then found his hand on his knife even before he was fully awake.

Behind the blanket Emma shifted on the rope bed. Beneath the edge of the blanket, her slender feet slid to the floor, and her voluminous nightgown settled around her ankles. She stood upright, the blanket hem shielding her body.

Sam lay very still and watched as she slid the blanket aside and came into the square of moonlight shafting into the room. Emma stood beside him, an innocent dressed in a long nightgown. She circled the table, looked up into the moonlight coming through the window, and lifted her hands to her breasts, cupping them. They jutted out into the moonlight, peaking against the fine cloth. The look that crossed her face was like that of a woman making love.

Sam's throat went dry, his body riveted to the sight of Emma's hands floating, skimming sensuously down her body. Both small efficient hands slid to cup herself intimately. Her hips thrust against her hands, simulating sexual movements, and the sweet musky womanly scent wafted to Sam. He inhaled the elusive fragrance and began to sweat, his body hardening instantly.

Sam had seen sleepwalkers before. He frowned at her; no doubt she was responding in her sleep to all the leers of the loggers. She was an untried woman amid sex-hungry men. From what he'd heard of virgins, he knew that they were unreliable, emotionally insecure, and fragile.

It had felt so right to hold Emma on his lap.

In the moonlight her hands returned to her breasts, and her moonlit expression caused Sam's heart to stop. She looked so fresh, her braids still neatly upon her head, but her drowsy sensual expression was enough to start his heart racing. The moonlight touched her lips, pouted for a kiss. Slowly one finger rose to her mouth, where she suckled it in a slow delicious fashion that almost caused him to groan with longing. Her low uneven sigh curled right into his loins to devastate him.

Then she floated back to her bed, leaving him nothing but her soft sigh as she resettled into sleep.

Sam lay very still, shook his head, and knew that while he'd faced challenges before, traveling with an untried

virgin was at the top of the dangerous list. He vowed to
get back to Amanda's Place as soon as he could to finish
off the rest of his troubling excess lust. He flopped to his
stomach, shocked by the unfamiliar riveting ache he
hadn't known since a boy, and heard himself groan in
frustration.

"What do I dream about?" Emma echoed the question
as she hurried Woden. She tried to keep up with Tenkiller as he moved through the morning mist layering the
trail to Deer Lodge City—Sam had decided to make a
side trip to the town on urgent business. The last week
of June was warm, the mountain streams were filled
with rushing snow-water, and Emma had just sold ten
pairs of socks to the loggers. She hoped to sell more on
the ten-mile trip from Swenson's to Deer Lodge City.
She found the small leather bag of coins in her basket; it
contained the dented coin so precious to her—a me-
mento of the night Sam had entered her body, giving
himself magnificently to her care.

Sam had been acting strangely since he'd signed papers with Swede. This morning his back was very stiff,
his features hardened as he rode the big horse in front
of her. Sam had watched her as she cooked pancakes
for Swede, and now he had asked her the strangest
question.

She thought carefully before answering. "Sometimes I
dream I am knitting. Sometimes I am baking bread.
What do you dream about?"

He didn't answer. "You need a decent horse."

Emma placed her hand on Woden's mane. "Because
you are angry with my work, that I got tired yesterday,

please do not malign poor Woden. He is a wonderful strong pony."

Tenkiller reared as Sam drew him to a halt and waited for her to come even with him. "You know how this looks, for a businessman to be trotted after by a woman on a pony? It doesn't look good."

"You have just answered your own question, a sign that your temper is wearing. Perhaps you should have slept on the bed last night, and I should have slept on the floor," she returned, continuing on Woden past Sam, forcing him to follow her. She turned to look at Sam and found his gaze on her seat. He looked thunderous. "We will get used to one another. This is our first time," she said to placate him.

"First time," Sam repeated darkly, staring grimly into the distance.

They continued past a logging wagon stuck in mud, and Sam frowned as his polished boots sank into the mire. While Emma pulled Tenkiller's reins and he pulled with the other horses, Sam pushed behind the wagon. Sam was fastidious as he had removed his coat and hat and tied them neatly to his saddle, and then stooped to roll up his trousers. The whole process fascinated Emma, who was used to careless men in work clothing.

They passed miners on the way, and Emma sold two pairs of socks while Sam braced his boot on a log and talked with other men, all the time keeping an eye on her. When they mounted to continue to Deer Lodge City, Sam said very quietly, "You need different clothes. Lady clothes. So the men won't think they can come up and talk with you. . . . And stop smiling like that at them—all sweet and blushy and succulent. They'll get ideas, and the first thing you know, I'll ruin this suit holding up for you."

Emma found her temper wearing thin, as only Sam could make it. First he maligned Woden and now herself. "There is nothing wrong with my clothing. Gray is a practical color and does not show dirt badly, and it wears well."

"It's plain."

"I am a plain woman."

He stared at her, his gaze drifting down to her bosom. Sam looked at her in his direct way, as though he saw into her heart. "You sleepwalk, Emma. You can't do that while we're in logging camps and mining towns. You're an invitation to trouble."

Emma tilted her head so that he could not see beyond the brim of her bonnet. He pricked her temper by pointing out her weaknesses. She saw his thigh tighten as he nudged Tenkiller closer. He bent to peer under her bonnet. "Don't try that bonnet thing with me. You're in a temper, aren't you?"

"No. I have a well-tended temper."

"Uh-huh." The slow sound was not an agreement, it was a prod. His fingertip stroked her hot cheek, mocking her.

"I do not have a temper," she repeated a little louder, the sound ringing off the clear bright morning and striking the lodgepole pines along the road.

"That's right, Red. You do not have a temper," he repeated in her concise manner, and then he smiled evilly at her, and she knew that he had bested her. Sam removed his hat, dusting the dirt from it. He ran his tongue across his bottom lip in the way that he did when he had a winning hand.

Emma did not like him besting her. "I am glad that Swede took the woman's ring in payment for a partnership. I have a woman in mind that would suit Harry and Monty. She lives in Deer Lodge City and has a little sister to raise. She needs a nice home. I think she would do a wonderful job taking my vacant position. I am afraid to say this, Sam Taggart, but the part in your hair has come undone."

It is wonderful to travel with Sam and to see how he makes his holdings grow. He can be easy to bargain, or sometimes I think there is steel in his look. I do not like how women look at him, as if when he smiles at them, they turn to warm syrup on the inside. To me, he has bad manners. E.

Chapter Ten

At Deer Lodge City, Let-go Lilly didn't want to come with Emma and Sam. She said that Sam had the look of a man who was riding on a bad temper; Sam didn't like the looks of Lilly and said she'd cause trouble on the Taggart spread. He stood on the board sidewalk in front of Amanda's and scanned the women with interest. He seemed to be searching for someone.

Emma stood between Sam and Lilly and prayed one of them would weaken. "Sam, you know that I cannot come with you and work for you, if I have not filled my first obligation to Harry and Monty and Mary."

His expression remained set; Emma turned to Lilly. "Your sister needs clean air and good food and all of your attention. She will have a home and people who are kind to her. Harry is an excellent father to his daughter, and Mary is . . ."

She hesitated, catching the hope in Lilly's eyes; Emma

decided on one small lie. "Mary has always wanted a little sister."

She noticed that Sam was looking over her shoulder to the women inside Amanda's, dressed only in their shifts and drawers and loose Chinese robes. One of the women had not properly laced up her front, and her bosoms were spilling to Sam's view.

Emma crossed her arms. Her bosoms ached for the suckling of Sam's lips. She could almost feel an insistent rhythmic tug, matching the thrust of his powerful body and the cords heating and running straight down to her belly. A tiny clenching began in her lower region. . . . Her legs went weak, and she realized she had flushed once more.

Lilly studied Sam. "Didn't I see you the other night, visiting here?"

"I had a friend here. A new girl. Do you happen to know her name?"

Lilly's rouged lips parted, and she stared from Emma to Sam and back again. Emma folded her hands in front of her and prayed, then Lilly said clearly, "She's gone. Didn't like the business."

Emma relaxed, because Lilly had protected her.

Sam's expression hardened, as if he had taken a physical blow. "That's good. Where did she go?"

"She's just gone. GTT, I think. Gone to Texas," Lilly said with a grin. "I like Emma. Do you?"

"She's my assistant, and a good one." Sam's eyes ripped down her and then met her gaze. "She's good with records. A businessman needs a good clerk. Where's your sister?"

Lilly shook her head sadly. "The old woman who has

been keeping her died. Beth has been staying alone at the shack while I work."

Minutes later, they were standing at the door of a shack. Lilly knocked. "It's me, honey. Open up."

A thin, four-year-old blond girl slowly opened the door, her thumb in her mouth. "Honey, I told you not to suck your thumb when you get scared. No one is going to hurt you. We're moving to a—"

The girl backed away slightly as she saw Sam towering over Emma and Lilly. "Why does he have that big whip on his shoulder?" she asked.

Emma went down on her knees, instantly adoring the girl. "I think someone he likes gave it to him for a present. Don't worry, he is a nice man and he is not a fighter," she whispered. "You see? He wears no gun. He is a kind man."

Sam walked around the tiny cabin, and Emma noted how smoothly he moved, a lithe man used to movement. "Smells like soap, and it's neat. You're hired. Let's get back to the ranch, and then Emma and I have to go about our business."

Emma adored the way he shared his goal with her. She did not mind when he insisted that she ride behind him on Tenkiller and the little girl rode in front. Lilly followed on Woden with a few bundles of clothing. She waved at the other women as they rode out of town.

"Put your arms around me, Emma," Sam ordered quietly. "I don't want you falling off and breaking a wrist. You'd be no good to me that way."

Emma sat very straight and carefully eased her arms around Sam's hard waist. She felt the hard shape of the knife he always carried, and hesitated.

"I said hold on to me," Sam ordered, slanting her a dark look over his shoulder. He glanced at a fancy buggy. "Someday I'll have one of those, and you'll be safe enough. Until then, you'll have to make do."

She noticed that he followed the path of a wagon bearing a huge safe. "A Diebolt," he murmured, and she knew from his tone that he treasured the thought of one day owning a magnificent huge black and gilt safe.

"Yes, you will have what you want, Sam Taggart. You will have an office with a safe just like that. I am certain of it. But if I ride behind you, holding you tightly, the people will think—"

"People think anything. Get used to it," Sam stated harshly. "They know we're not a pair just by looking at us."

A man, crudely dressed, stepped out onto the muddy street. "Hey, half-breed. What are you doing with all these women? I heard from one of Swede's men that one of 'em sells socks. What's the matter, can't you keep up your women? What else do they do to make a living for you?"

Sam tightened Tenkiller's reins, and the horse butted the man out of the way. Sam's boot finished the job, sending him spinning into the mud. The man's curses followed them out of town.

Sam wondered how he'd ever allowed himself to be talked into more women as they rode from Deer Lodge City to the Big T. Chatting gaily away, the women ignored Sam's dark looks, meant to impose silence. The little girl sleeping in his arms would grow up to be just like them. He looked down at Beth's innocent face and wondered when women got devious.

He wondered about the virgin he'd ruined and if she was happy, and then when the sun began casting long afternoon shadows from the mountains, they passed the jackleg fence marker of the Big T.

"I said it before and I'll say it again, boy. You want Emma," Harry stated an hour later, as the sun began to set upon the mountains. "You went whoring the night before you left, I'll give you that—trying to trim off a bit of steam before you took a nice girl into places she shouldn't go." Harry's chin thrust out. Sam fought to keep his chin from reacting in the same manner.

"Why did you have to bring her back?" Mary whined as Emma, Lilly, and her little sister walked around the ranch yard. Clearly Lilly knew farming and ranching; she bent to study the earth, crumbling it between her fingers, and she clucked at the hens passing by her with their chicks. She took off her cloak and pulled the apron from the wash line, where Monty had hung it. She whipped on the apron, tied it, placed her hands on her waist, and planted her feet. Lilly gave every appearance of finding what she wanted; a home for her sister and a place to tend with righteous work.

Harry's eyes narrowed, following the women to the porch, where they sat to inspect Emma's precious scraps for quilts and rag rugs. "That's a sight I've missed— women talking about quilts and such. Now you collected another sweet thing and a baby besides. How do you find them?"

Mary folded her arms across her chest. "That kid isn't getting my room."

Sam avoided mentioning Lilly's previous occupation. "Lilly is going to take Emma's place. She needs a place to raise her baby sister, and Emma likes her. She won't come with me if Lilly can't work here."

"You can't have Emma," Harry stated again.

"Yes, you can. Just take her away." Mary's tone was hopeful.

"She stays with me," Sam shot back, aware that Emma was hurrying toward them, her petticoats flashing.

She ran right between them, forcing father and son to take a step apart. Emma shot a worried look at Harry and then up at Sam. "Lilly says her family used to have a dairy herd and that her mother taught her how to make cheese."

She stood on tiptoe to smooth Sam's hair part, and the soft brush of her body eased the hard tension within him.

"I never did know why a man wanted to draw a line down his head like that," Harry muttered. "Fool thing to do. Just tells a body where to scalp him."

"Sam is a businessman. He must look the role. I read in the newspaper that a man's hair part is the mark of a gentleman," Emma returned, looking up at Harry critically. She tilted her head. "You know, if your hair were shorter and a part just so"—she touched a spot on his hairline—"I think you'd look years younger. . . . Harry, I think you would look like the Fakir of Xanadu, the traveling one-man show. He is a handsome man. I saw his picture on an advertisement in the same newspaper where I read it was important for gentlemen to part their hair."

Sam watched his rugged father—the seasoned mountain man who had fought pumas and grizzlies and had taken scalps—turn to warm mush and glow. The look disgusted Sam because he knew that was just how he felt when Emma fluttered around him . . . and he remembered how Harry had looked at Evie all those years ago. Sam walked to Tenkiller, grabbed a handful of the ornery animal's mane, and leaped onto his back, leaving Harry and Emma.

"You're messing up your part, boy!" his father yelled, and guffawed.

They stayed only one night at Harry's, then Sam was ready to travel. After three days of traveling with Sam and his bad mood, they reached Lazy Dog, a small, thriving mining town. Emma was thrilled by the friendly faces of the men there. Sam went to Lazy Dog's tent saloon, leaving Emma to sit in the tent he'd rented for their use. She was to take messages for him while he did business in the saloon. She snipped and saved articles from the papers that Sam was always reading.

Meanwhile the miners had lined up outside her tent, waiting for their chance to buy her socks. When Emma had a free moment, she caressed the brass coin Sam had given her that night. Sam had given her something to remember, if she could not dislodge Gilbert and save her grandmother's dowry.

A black-haired, blue-eyed miner sat in front of her as she knitted. "You and that fancy half-blood doing it?"

Emma blinked and missed a stitch. She knew what

"it" was, reminded by the dented coin tucked into a handkerchief on her bosom.

"Are you married to him? Are you spoken for? Are you doing it?" the man pressed urgently. "I'd like it fine if you were to marry me—if you're not spoken for. We can get hitched soon as the traveling judge comes through. No one will ever have to know that you were living with a half-blood. I'll bash in any man's brains who says so."

Emma continued to knit, the pigeons' cooing sounds soothing her from the tenth marriage proposal. "Sam Taggart is a businessman. I am his clerk," she stated proudly.

She glanced at the young miner, who seemed nice despite his rudeness. Often these men lacked for manners, but their hearts were good, she decided. She noted the miner's neat, newly washed appearance. Most of the men bathed in the icy creek, and all of them seemed to do it before they came to look at her socks. Two of the men wore overpowering scents of Bay Rum, and one had apologized for his singed handlebar mustache, because he'd gotten too close to the fire, shaving and waxing the mustache for her.

With their gold nuggets in her sock-purse, she would be able to pay Gilbert back and save her grandmother's dowry.

"I don't care if you can't cook," the young miner pressed. "I'll do the cooking and the cleaning and everything you want done. Just marry me legal-like. I don't care that you've been a half-blood's woman—"

Sam entered the tent, his big whip on his shoulder, and the young miner lurched out of his chair. The two men looked at each other, and tension lay heavy on the cool air.

Sam's cool gaze shot at Emma. He batted a paper against his thigh, the paper from which she had just clipped articles. He thrust it at her. "I haven't read this yet. You know I make my living by reading the articles—What's going on here? There's a row of men outside longer than the street."

Emma was horrified that she had snipped Sam's paper before he'd read it. "I saw an article about using soda in foot-soaking water, and I—"

The young miner stood up, clearly ready to defend Emma. "She's measuring for socks. I want to marry her. I'll take good care of her, and she won't have to wear her fingers to the bone knitting every goddamn minute."

"I'm not her father," Sam rapped out. "You don't need my permission, and she doesn't have to knit."

"You should pay her more," the miner shot back hotly.

Emma didn't like the narrowed, dangerous look of Sam's eyes or the way his hand stroked the whip coiled around his shoulder. She worried that he would say the wrong thing and find himself in a fight from which she would have to rescue him. "You have two messages, Sam. Mr. Blue Hair Malone would like to sell you his mine on Fast Creek, and Mr. Fat Lip Smith says he's interested in hauling lumber to anywhere you want. He's an experienced freighter down from Canada, and—"

Sam snatched the messages from her hand without looking away from the young miner. "Get out."

"When the lady says so."

Sam took one step toward the miner, and Emma hurriedly said, "Please go. He is my employer, and I need this work."

When the miner reluctantly left, Sam tied the tent flap shut and placed one hand flat on the table. He slapped his roll of ruined and clipped newspapers on the table. "What's going on here?"

"I've been taking your messages and knitting. Some of the men just came in to watch me knit, and they said they missed their mothers. Sam, I really think there is a need for a bathhouse in Lazy Dog—a tonsorial parlor like the newspaper advertises. Every one of those poor men had to bathe in freezing water."

"Before they came to see you for their socks, right?" He glanced down at her basket of socks. "Is business good?" he asked in a tone she didn't trust. Sam had unknown edges around him, and she wasn't as certain of him as she would have liked.

"Very good. But I really think we could start a bathhouse here for the men. Lilly could provide soap, and with a few buckets and tubs, we could—"

Sam touched her ear, rubbing the lobe tenderly. "You like baths, don't you? Who's going to tend this bathhouse you want?"

"I could. While you are doing business and I am waiting, I could take their clothing and have it washed and ironed while they are bathing. I could cut their hair and mend their clothing and—"

"Fit them for socks? Fondle their bare feet with your hands?"

Emma did not like Sam's low tone. It reminded her of a wolf's warning growl.

"Let me remind you, Emma, that I am in business. That is the reason we are here—not to let naked men ogle you as you tend them. From now on maybe I'd better take you with me—"

A gunshot ruined the mountain's quiet morning, and then another gunshot. "Hey! We've been waiting in line for two hours and more. We want our socks and visit with the lady!" a man yelled outside the tent.

Emma stood very slowly, placing her knitting on the table. Sam's black gaze jerked down her body and locked on her hips. "What's that?"

She smoothed the material over her hips. She'd tucked the cloth into her boots and shined them to match Sam's. "Trousers. Pants. Men wear them, and they're comfortable for traveling. My petticoats are all muddy around the hems, and I thought— They only cost a pair of socks, for which you did not pay," she reminded him.

The fiery look Sam shot her sent her back into the chair. Without the padding of yards of petticoats and her skirt, her bottom sounded with a solid plop. The sound seemed to enrage Sam even more. "Your father is right. You are a little berserker. You take chances when you know better. You're wearing that damn plain bonnet and looking like an angel above the table, and like a—a woman beneath it. Don't you know that the sight of your—your round and elegant backside will cause these men to salivate?"

With his hand thrown out and his legs wide spread, Sam looked just like the stage poster she'd seen tacked to the dry goods store wall, right above the cracker barrel and the precious eggs resting in cool sand. He looked like the hero in the stage play *A Gentleman to the Rescue of Annabelle.* The willful spear of glossy black hair shot out of his part and trembled with his rage. Emma could see him rescuing poor Annabelle, tied to the railroad tracks, but Emma wanted her independence, determined to wrest her future and her grandmother's dowry away from Gilbert.

"It is proper that I wear my bonnet. You are acting like my father." Emma made the statement cautiously. She did not want to be like her mother, always acting as her father saw fit. Emma thought of herself as a modern businesswoman, dressing the part.

"Am I?" Sam moved closer, and Emma leaned back against the chair.

"The trousers are practical."

"Walk. Just walk around the tent, and *don't go outside,*" Sam directed with a flourish of his hand. He wrapped his hand around her nape as though she were a kitten and urged her to her feet.

"Was business good today?" she asked, hoping to change the topic.

"Bought into a brewery at Lobo. Walk."

Emma drew herself up to her full height, refusing to be intimidated. She wasn't certain that she wanted Sam to view her backside. "Anything else?"

"Bought Blue Hair Malone's mine. He came to see me in the saloon."

"Oh. Your assets are growing. Soon you will be a rich man."

"Walk."

Emma smoothed the tendrils from her nape up into her braids and then stiffly walked around the tent.

When she turned, Sam glowered at her. The desperation and frustration in his expression frightened her. More gunshots and shouting sounded outside the tent. "Put your skirts on, and let's get out of here," he said tightly, and turned his back on her.

She was used to his impatience and hurried to oblige. "Don't you like how I walk?" she couldn't resist asking as she slid her dress over her head.

"You don't just walk. You move," Sam stated obliquely, and stepped out of the tent. She packed his saddlebags with his business papers and ledgers and hurried after him, running right into his backside. He was looking down the long line of men as though he'd fight every one of them to keep her safe. He touched the whip at his shoulder as though he feared he might lose it.

"Ready?" Sam asked tightly as he took her elbow and guided her to the horses, which he always kept saddled and in waiting.

A man with a lovely tenor voice stepped out of the line and began to sing "Greensleeves." Sam turned to Emma and stated quietly, "If you wave, you're fired."

It is now the first week of July, and we visit so many interesting, small, busy towns. Tonight we are staying in Tadpole Springs. Sam speaks to me as if I were an intelligent businesswoman. He compliments my neat writing and how I keep his books. I love to write the letters he dictates to me. He is purchasing goods for his stores in Beartown, Garnet, and Coloma and giving farmwives seeds to make gardens. He will send a traveling tinker to them, in ex-

change for the fresh vegetables he will sell to the miners. I have a room to myself, and always Sam has a bath waiting for me. Sam traded two worn-out mines for two Percheron draft horses, a mare and a stallion. He got two Black Norman horses for Swede's logging sleds. I watched Tenkiller race and win. He is glorious and knows it. Sam is a brilliant trader—though his cash money is low, he is acquiring several small businesses. He has sold stud certificates for Tenkiller, and the mares will be brought to the Big T.

Today Tenkiller serviced a mare. The blond daughter of the rancher wanted Sam to do the same with her, to mount her. She wanted to marry him. I did not like her, and Sam called me Red again.

My body knows a new hunger. To watch the horses mate caused a certain heat within me. Sam is beautiful, more beautiful than the stallion. My heart races at the sight of him. But I did not like Sam to say that he might be seeing women as we travel, and that I should get used to it. This I did not like. E.

Chapter Eleven

$\mathcal{A}$s he stood on Tadpole Springs's busy street, Sam glanced up at Emma. She crossed her arms in front of her body and stared at him, clearly not happy at being told to "stay put." She would be safe in the upstairs room at the tavern, and he was going shopping for her dresses—in any colors but plain brown and gray.

While Tenkiller was breeding the mare, Sam had glanced at Emma and found her riveted to the savage sex, the stallion nipping at the mare, driving into her. A hard jolt of sheer sexual desire had slammed into him as Emma's eyes locked to his, her expression helpless, and now that desire rode him, making him restless.

"Sam! Why, you old—" Maybelle grinned up at him and launched herself into his arms. Glad to see an old friend, Sam picked her off the street and twirled her around.

She put her gloved hands on his face and gave him a big smack. "You're still one fine-looking man."

He grinned up at her. "You're a good-looking woman all decked out in satin and feathers."

Maybelle laughed. "Show some respect. The name is D'Arcy now. I'm a cattle queen from Wyoming, boy, up here to make a fat money deal with my herd. I married an old man as rich as a king, and now he's dead. I wore him out." When Sam laughed and placed her on her feet, Maybelle eyed him, drifting her gloved hand across his frilled shirt. "We're damn fine-looking now. Not two ragtag kids trying to survive in the war, are we, honey?"

Sam studied her fancy bronze dress with a huge hat of ostrich feathers. "I'd say we've done all right."

Maybelle leaned against him. "I miss you, Sam. There we were, you were fifteen and me sixteen, and you were determined to save me. We went all the way from war-torn Georgia to a new start in California. Scared as hell, we were. Remember?"

"Maybelle, you were having a good time, and you know it," Sam returned with a laugh.

She threw her arms around him again, laughing. "I was your first, Sam, and probably not your last. Who's that woman glaring down at us from the tavern's up-stairs room?"

"That's my—the woman working for me. She's a good clerk. Her name is Emma."

Maybelle twirled her bag. "There's more to it than that. You're frothing, all steamy-looking, at just the mention of her. You've got that dark closed-in look that says your feelings run deep. Are you taking me out to dinner and telling me everything?"

"Who's buying?" Sam glanced at the window of a

dressmaker's shop. "I'd sure as hell like to see her in something other than plain gray and brown."

Maybelle drew him into the shop. "You buy her dresses, and then I'll buy your dinner. Deal?"

While Maybelle surged into the shop like a general invading territory to be conquered, Sam studied the flurry of dresses and bonnets. He wanted Emma to have something feminine, a gift from him. He'd manage the money somehow, and he wanted to please Emma. He imagined the way she'd look, innocent and virginal. He touched a bonnet with yellow ribbons. "Something sweet . . . to go with her eyes. They're soft, like a stream in summer shade. When the sun is in her hair, it's a rich red color. . . . And she's got freckles, cute little ones across her nose."

Maybelle stared at him. "I've never heard you talk like that. Sam, you're in love, boy."

He scowled at her while the dressmaker hurried to him. "I'll need to know her measurements. How tall is she?"

"She's about so high." Sam held his hand at his chest level and floundered.

"I'll help. Is she bigger or smaller than me in the bosom?" Maybelle placed her hands on her hips and looked at Sam intently. "I want to know all about this girl, Sam."

He grinned. "She's curvy. Has a tiny waist I can put my two hands around."

The dressmaker whipped out her tape measure and noted the size of his hands. "Bosom?"

"About like this. . . ." Sam inhaled and adjusted his

hands, remembering the feel of Emma against him as they kissed.

Maybelle laughed until she held her sides, and tears streamed down her face. "Boy, you are horny. You ought to see that silly look on your face."

"Stay put," Sam Taggart said to me. I saw the woman hug Sam on the street, and he picked her up, smiling up at her like a boy. They went into a dress shop, and then the boy came with packages for me, dresses the fancy woman has chosen. I do not think I like this woman. First the blond one wanted to mount him, and now this one. I am a plain woman, I work hard, and I usually like people. I wish I were not in a hotel room but at Harry's making bread. Instead I will knit and not think of how the blond woman looked at Sam Taggart, or how gladly he smiled at the woman with the big feathered hat. E.

Sam hesitated in the hallway outside of Emma's room. She'd be sleeping now, her braids all tidy on top of her head.

He frowned down at the noisy tavern, filled with miners and drovers. Or maybe she'd be sleepwalking, strolling right down to the tavern with the men watching her, cupping her breasts and touching herself intimately. He could almost smell her sweet musky scent. He put his ear to the oak door and listened for sounds of her moving around.

The door jerked open, and a furious Emma stood in her huge nightgown, her braids neatly on top of her head and her arms crossed across her chest. Her eyes blazed up at him. "So! You're back from dinner with the fine lady, are you?"

Sam braced his shoulder against the door frame, admiring the length of her legs displayed by the lamplight behind her. "Maybelle D'Arcy and I are old acquaintances. She's up from Wyoming, selling cattle."

He looked past her, into the room. "Did you like those clothes I had delivered? Maybelle said they would look good on you. Buttercup yellow and a nice blue and a meadow green dress, all with matching bonnets."

"Maybelle." Emma spat the word. "I will not wear them." She drew herself up and tried to slam the door on him. He placed one hand flat on it and pushed it open easily. She braced both hands and pushed back.

Sam entered her room; Emma stumbled backward against the wall and glared at him. He closed the door and noted that the parcels of store-bought clothing had been neatly repackaged. His extra dress shirt and trousers had been washed and were neatly hung to dry beside Emma's plain brown dress. A small hand iron warmed on the tiny black stove. His ledgers were neatly stacked on the lamp table with a doily covering them, and she had meticulously straightened her sock basket.

Everything was neat, like Emma herself. The room smelled sweet and clean—like her. He had the odd, unsettling sensation that he had come home. He hadn't had a real home since he was twelve, and now he wasn't certain how he fitted into a homey picture.

One of Emma's socks hung over the bed's iron foot railing. The sock was unfinished and measured about two feet from the heel; with the knitting needles in place, it was still growing.

Sam ripped away his string tie and slipped it into his vest pocket. "What are you mad about?"

"One Maybelle D'Arcy," she shot back. "Today it was the blond woman at the pasture, eyeing you as though you were the stud and not Tenkiller."

He admired the way the lamplight passed through her nightgown to outline her curvaceous body. He stripped off his jacket and folded it neatly, following it with his vest. He placed them over the back of a chair, slipped the big knife out of its sheath, and tossed it to the chair. "I knew this was coming. We may as well have it out now. I told you there would be nights when I'd be busy."

Sam walked to a chair and sprawled upon it. He really enjoyed the sight of Emma bristling with temper. Suddenly he wasn't bone-tired anymore; Emma's flushed face and militant stance in the yards of old-fashioned nightgown looked enchanting and exciting, better than any game he'd ever played. "Maybelle and I are old friends. There's every reason we should have dinner together. Are you sore because you weren't invited?"

Emma glared at him, and Sam's senses leaped. She could be sweet and docile, but when she wasn't, she sent off sparks. Charged up, she ignited something in Sam that he hadn't known before with a woman.

Emma continued to glare at him. "You have been familiar with her. I saw that when she ran at you and leaped into your welcoming arms. You picked her up off the ground and swirled her around, and she . . . she kissed you. You liked it. You looked like a boy, grinning like a . . . Of course, one could hardly see you, buried so deeply in her hat of fluffy feathers. You were crushing her dress, and she messed the part in your hair. Your gentleman's part."

Sam twirled his hat on his finger and studied it. There was no business deal that compared to the excitement of igniting Emma. He enjoyed watching her eyes change to brown glowing heat and her hair seem to ignite into red flames. "I'm a grown boy, and I've been around. Remember that you're my clerk and not my keeper, Emma. If I kissed Maybelle—or if I did anything else with her—isn't your business."

He studied Emma's slender toes and remembered how her foot had felt in his hands. How her look of stark desire had set his body humming as Tenkiller mated the mare. Sam had wanted to vault over the corral and—

He decided to set terms for Emma. "I'll always see that you're safe, like now. There's a hired gun watching your room from downstairs. But there might be times when I'll want to stay with a lady, and while that's hard for a virgin to understand . . . it just could happen. A man has needs."

"Are you my father, to tell me this I know?" Emma paced in front of him, a sight he was beginning to enjoy too much. He admired the thrust of her thighs against the cloth, the firm lush shape of her backside—

She pivoted toward him, her face set and tense. For a full moment he enjoyed the full bloom of temper. "Do you have a problem with me, not as an employer, but as a man, Emma?"

She drew herself up, and Sam glanced at her breasts pushing up against the cloth over her crossed arms. She lifted her chin and looked down her nose at him. "I think you should know, Sam Taggart . . ."

Sam allowed himself a smirk. There wasn't anything he didn't know about Emma. "I know you are steaming."

For a moment Emma seemed to be deciding if she should speak. Then she slowly asked, *"Do you know that I am not a virgin, Sam Taggart?"*

The weight of her question took a full minute to slam into him. Then he lurched to his feet and grabbed her upper arm. He hadn't had experience with emotional women, and she was almost frightening him. "Emma, I know you've got a temper. But don't start saying things like that when you're hot—"

It was Emma's turn to smirk. "I got hot with him . . . when I decided to become a woman and experience the fullest measure. I knew the mechanics of rutting from my experience on the farm, but I did not expect to feel so like . . . so like a ripened tomato about to be harvested, to be juicy and ripe and to be suckled—"

Sam reeled with her verbal punch—the images of Emma hot and flushed and juicy unnerved him. Yet he did not let go. "Holy hell, Emma. I know you're mad, but don't start telling lies—"

She lifted her chin. "I tell you, Sam Taggart. . . . I am *not* a virgin."

He stared at her, uncertain of her mood or the anger beginning to rage within him. He needed to take time to dissect his emotions, or he would shake Emma until she was obedient. But Sam had never touched a woman while he was unnerved, which Emma had certainly managed to do. Playing for time to control his outrage, he flipped open the buttons of his shirt, leaving it open down to his waist. He slipped his gold cuff links from their moorings and tossed them to the table. "Clarify."

"You did not part your hair all evening. That is something you do when you are thinking business. It is not now parted. With *her*, the fancy woman from your past, you forgot you were a businessman," she tossed at him.

Sam placed his hands on his waist, fearing he would reach for her to shake sense into her. To buy himself calming time, he carefully took out his comb, parted his hair, then tucked the comb back into his pocket. He returned his hands to his waist. "It's parted now."

Emma braced her fists on her waist and glared up at him. "Do not threaten me with this male posture. I have lived with men all my life. Are you outraged because I had a marvelous, thrilling, heavenly experience with a tender man? Or are you incensed because I am not pure? Tell me why I see this rage in your face."

Sam towered over her. "You mean to tell me that you let a man touch you intimately?"

"If I am no longer a virgin, then he must have touched me intimately—and perhaps I touched him intimately, because I am a modern woman and not to be cowed. Perhaps I might . . . I might have touched his . . . his—"

Sam took a step closer, and Emma wondered if she had pushed him too hard. He bent to peer down into her face as though seeking her lie. "I don't believe you. You're as pure as fresh-fallen snow."

She saw no reason to spare him, as he had probably just arisen from the luscious cattle queen's bed. "At first it hurt. But then, when he lay deeply within me, I enjoyed him. He gave me the gift of his body and was tender later as he lay upon me—in my care. It was not as bad as my mother said. It was quite beautiful after the first spearing."

Sam paled. "Did this happen while you were in my care? Did someone . . ." He swallowed, visibly shaken. "Emma, were you raped?"

For a moment Emma allowed the tender scene to enfold her. She dived into it, remembering every sensual touch, the heat and the need. "No. I offered myself to him because he looked like an adventure too good to miss, a solid tree branch—I have always liked to leap from safety—like flying—onto tree branches, and that is what he looked like to me, then. The man who took me had not had a virgin before, but he was very tender. So gentle. So sweet. He kissed me as though he were supping honey—and yes, I was selfish, wanting him all for myself."

"God, Emma! No more." Sam sank onto the bed, holding his head in his hands. "You're no match for an experienced man. He probably came after you, and you were defenseless. I promised your father I'd take care of you."

She almost felt sorry for him. That sympathy shattered when she smelled Maybelle's French perfume, which refreshed her irritation with him. "He was a particularly lovely man. At his . . . height of passion, he reminded me of Tenkiller, a valiant stud. I thought of riding him, but he was quickly . . . ah . . . he was magnificent."

Magnificent seemed to suit Sam's lovemaking perfectly, and now, as a matter of pride, she did not want

Sam to think she had chosen a weak lover who had performed badly.

Sam's hands slowly lowered from his face, revealing a dark dangerous expression. Outrage trembled in his deep uneven tone. "You mean you actually looked at the . . . act of the horses and thought of that man? You tell me his name—the man who ruined you—and I'll kill him."

"You'll do no such thing. You know very well that you are not a fighting man. From now on I'm dedicating myself to business. I must repay Gilbert, or he will have my grandmother's dowry. I can't mate with him after the most thrilling experience in my life. When one isn't a virgin and has had one perfect moment, one sees things differently—"

Sam's hand wrapped around her wrist, and he tugged her over him as he lay down on the bed. "Just how differently does one see things?" he asked in a slow sensual drawl.

Emma sucked in her breath. Sprawled across Sam's great body, his big hands splayed on her hips, she wasn't certain what he wanted of her. He didn't seem happy with her, a fine tension humming in the air between them.

"Did you kiss him, Emma? Did you kiss him like you kissed me?" His fingers dug slightly into her hips, his eyes cutting at her as though he didn't believe her.

"I kissed him as he kissed me." It was important that Emma point out that she was an equal in the lovemaking. She would not be like her mother, taken at a man's desire and not her own. She had wanted Sam, and she had taken him as well. She smoothed Sam's taut cheek, running her fingertips over the high smooth ridge of his cheekbone and the tiny crescent-shaped scar she'd just discovered.

She touched the tiny hole in his ear. "Sam, you have punctured your earlobe."

"Earring." Sam's fingertip circled her ear, and Emma held her breath. She had discovered a Sam-secret and one she intended to hoard.

"A businessman does not wear an earring, Sam Taggart."

Her tease brought Sam's quick grin. "At the time I was in the business of living. The earring marked me to be one of the gang, and we protected each other."

She knew she shouldn't be lying upon him, but Sam locked her body to his. His hair gleamed in the lamplight, raven against the pristine white pillowcase. The tiny wild spears begged to be smoothed, like the tips of ruffled feathers. Only her nightgown separated her breasts from his gleaming hard chest.

Sam's gaze lowered to her lips, and she tried to stop them from trembling. Slowly his fingers relaxed, and his thumbs stroked the rising curve of her bottom. She shivered as his hands skimmed down her thighs, caressing them, and slowly, slowly lifted her nightgown.

"Always so neat, buttoned way up to your chin . . . smelling like soap and flowers and sunshine and all the time . . . ," Sam murmured as if to himself. "Since you're so experienced—able to match kisses—I guess you'd know what to expect if I put my mouth on you, wouldn't you? If I tasted you just there—"

His thumbs pressed gently on her nipples, and one eyebrow rose wickedly. "If I took you in my mouth—

maybe nibbled a bit here and there and licked just the tip . . . you'd know what to expect, wouldn't you? You'd know that we wouldn't stop unless you stopped me. You'd know that I'd want to . . ."

His lips brushed hers and then fastened to her bottom lip, tugging gently. "Amazing, with all your experience, that you are shaking. Why, Emma, I might even want to see you without a stitch of clothing on you . . . spread out all rosy and fresh and warm with those big hazel eyes looking at me as though you couldn't wait. Can you wait, Emma? Or are you one of those that likes it fast? Tell me, Emma—fast or slow. Would you want to play a bit first or dive right in and play later?"

The images he served Emma had her gasping, trembling for breath. She wanted to move away, and her breath caught in her lungs as Sam's gaze lowered to her throat and then to her gaping neckline.

"You're missing a button, sweetheart," he murmured, lifting her suddenly so that he could place his face within the material, searching for the rise of her breast, which he nuzzled with his lips, never kissing, always roaming, brushing lightly against her sensitive skin.

Emma melted, sizzled, and moved her breast against his lips, aching for the sweet tug she remembered. When Sam inhaled sharply, tugging away the material with his teeth and finding her nipple, she cried out, her fingers digging into his shoulders. "Is that what you want, Emma?" he asked shakily.

Sam's body thrust upward suddenly, his desire thrusting against her intimately. With one movement he jerked up her gown and flipped her beneath him. He shook violently as he stared down at her. "Damn you, Emma. This is no game. I want you."

She tried to speak but stared at his hard flat nipple. So different from hers, it fascinated her, and she wondered if he felt as deeply as she did when suckled. Emma lifted to place her lips on him.

Sam's tall hard body lurched against her, a ragged groan dragged from him, shocking her. To see if this first reaction had been an accident, Emma flicked her tongue across his other nipple. Sam's hard body bolted against her. "Where did you learn a thing like that?" he asked in hushed outrage.

Encouraged by his shocked look, Emma wallowed in her success. She needed to be honest with Sam. "If you challenge me, Sam Taggart, I fear I must retaliate. Today I thought you were beautiful . . . your skin gleamed in the sun, and the movements of your body . . . your bottom gets like two hard apples when you put your weight into controlling Tenkiller. There are tiny ladders of muscles on your stomach, and I wanted to place my hand on them, to feel them move."

She had stunned Sam, whose eyes widened momentarily. His low, uneven voice rang with male indignity. "You make me sound like a . . . Nice women don't just go . . . tasting men like that. Or talking about their backsides, like they were . . . studs at an auction. You can't just talk about me like I'm a peach you want to suck. Emma, you put your mouth on me like that again, and I'll—"

Sam's long body went taut, and he shivered as she took up his challenge. She placed the tip of her tongue exactly on his nipple and flicked it. She smiled at him and smoothed his hair, because he looked so shaken.

"At times, Sam Taggart, I am not nice but willful and determined. You should know that if you are to continue." She wanted him in her as before, throbbing mightily within her keeping. Emma sighed, lifting her thighs to accept him.

Sam jerked up, bracing himself above her, his face hard, all angles and shadows, his eyes brilliant beneath his narrowed lashes. The dim light danced across the straight black lengths, fascinating Emma, and she ran her fingertips across them, exploring another tiny scar at the end of his right eyebrow.

"Emma, I'm not certain I like every inch of me inspected like a prime— What do you want?" he grated out hoarsely.

The berserker within Emma lurched out of control, ignited by the questions tormenting her about Sam. She worried that she would not make him happy, though she had seemed to do quite well at Amanda's Place. She placed her hands on his cheeks and asked hurriedly, "Tell me how you have women. Have there been many? How many times can you act as stud in one night? I know stallions must rally, but a rooster flies from hen to hen—"

At first Sam looked blankly down at her, the spear of hair quivering across his forehead. Then the curve of his mouth softened, and his face gentled. "You'd better not push me. If you really had that one time, you're still close to being a virgin. If you push me now, I might do something that would shock your tight little idea of how it is with a man and a woman."

His tender look excited the berserker running wild within her. "Perhaps I have shocked you, Sam Taggart," she challenged him with a smile.

One black eyebrow lifted, and Sam bent to kiss her lips. "Why, Miss Recht. I believe you did. And perhaps your pigeons, too. They seem very interested in the proceedings." He glanced down their bodies, tangled on the bed, and when his gaze rose to meet Emma's, she fed upon the heat within him. "If I were to take you now, it would change things. I'd be wanting more."

More. The word sent Emma's arms around Sam's neck. Was it possible there could be more beauty than the first time?

"You're a warm woman, Emma," Sam whispered huskily after his hand stroked her thigh and her hips lifted against him. She moved slightly, making him aware of the slender muscles flexing beneath her soft skin. He looked at his fingers, lying dark against her milky skin, and allowed his fingertips to skim higher. "Are you really not a virgin?"

"Truly I am not." She shyly gave him her secret with a tender blush. "I know that I am not what you want as a wife, Sam Taggart. That I am plain and brown and unable to manage a fancy house with many forks at the table and oysters brought up from New Orleans in a barrel, and I—I have never—never hosted a ladies' tea party or organized a ball. I have never waltzed. I can only polka and schottische. I know that when you want a wife, you expect those things of her. I do not even know the proper language of the fan and—"

"How would you know about any of those things?"

Sam asked roughly, confused by the way Emma tossed everything he wanted at him.

"I learn from newspaper clippings. I save them, remember? I have hungered for you, Sam Taggart."

Sam had had women hunger for him, and he'd gone after knowing women, who knew the rules. He cupped her breast, considering the gentle weight, and ran a thumb over the peak of her nipple. "There are ways not to have babies, Emma. I'm not having children, and I know exactly what I want in a wife. If we do this, you'll have to let me go when it's time. A woman like you is meant for marriage, not a back room waiting for a married man. Then there is the moment when I might not have much will to stop, but I'll try, and then, Emma, you've got to free me."

The berserker within Emma quieted, saddened by the loss of Sam as a potential father. His past settled around him, and Emma ached for his pain. She wanted to give him beauty and hope, if only for a night, to give him the gift of herself. "Take me for this night, Sam Taggart. Fill me until we are one," she whispered urgently against his lips.

His hand rose to smooth her braids, a trembling caress that told her he cared for her, for the moment. Sam's mouth moved adoringly, sweetly upon hers, as though he realized the treasure she was about to give him. His fingers eased her nightgown higher, finding her intimately. The warmth within her bloomed damply, meeting his caress, and Sam's body tightened. "I'll be careful with you, Emma," he promised against her lips. "Very careful; and when the time comes, right at the

end, you can't hold on to me. Not when my seed comes.
. . . Let me go."

His hands trembled as they skimmed down her hips,
his long fingers locking into the soft flesh.

"I understand." She understood nothing but that she
needed Sam to touch her, that her heart would stop
beating if he did not kiss her once more.

As his lips nibbled at hers, his tongue played with
hers, Sam's fingers wooed her, slid into her, and caught
her with the rhythm. Then his manhood sprang against
her, heavy and hard and hot, and Emma trembled,
pressing her legs together to catch him. "Don't be
afraid, Emma," Sam whispered hoarsely as her hands
gripped his hair.

He bent to kiss her, to fuse his beautiful mouth upon
hers, and before he could, the first ripples caught her
unaware, tightening and tossing her over the crest. She
arched against him and cried out, flinging herself into
the pleasure. When the delight within her lessened,
Emma rested back against the pillow. With a mighty
effort she managed to look up at Sam, her lover.

"I haven't begun, sweetheart," he whispered softly. "I
just touched you. Put your mouth on me when you want
to cry out. I wouldn't mind a bite or two," he added
tenderly.

Emma closed her eyes and floated. She kept her fingers locked safely on Sam's shoulders, an anchor that
she hoped would draw her back again into the lovely
fragile mist. She heard Sam chuckle, his thumbs brushing her hot cheeks. She fought her way to the surface
and grinned up at him. "That was lovely, Sam Taggart.
Thank you."

With a devilish grin he returned, "I'll show you lovely. . . ." His kiss was hot, open, and demanding everything. His hands reached to cup her bottom, to lift and complete what they had begun— He began to enter and stretch her slowly.

"Sam?" Emma tried to find her breath, her heartbeat pounding in her ears. Or was it someone knocking at the door?

"I know you're in there, Emma," Greta called shrilly from the hallway. "A miner told Papa that Sam was racing here, and I made Papa let me come with the first transportation. I've spent two entire days and one night riding in a slow wagon filled with hides and a bad-smelling evil man. The buffalo-hide man wasn't happy when I had to tie him up—his attentions were not wanted. I've come all this way. This cage of pigeons is heavy. I'm dirty and tired, and you are cruel to play games with me. My hair needs washing."

Poised at the entrance of Emma's hot moist body, Sam groaned a protest.

Greta kicked the door. "Papa only let me come because I threatened to run away and secure the first drover I passed. I would—he knew I would, so he let me come. I'm tired of fetching and cleaning and Fritzi's devil-temper. You and Mama have spoiled him. His temper is almost as bad as yours. . . . Emma? Emma, let me in!"

Sam and Emma lay still, hearts pounding, looking at each other. Emma looked soft and drowsy and happy. She could be a bride, Sam thought, unnerved that they had almost made love. That he'd almost broken his promise to her father to keep her safe. That she deserved a man who would give her children and there were no children in Sam's future. Emma Recht was a sweet innocent, and he was a low-down, untrustworthy—

That beneath his taut hungry body, hers waited fragrant and moist and hot. . . . Her breasts were soft and round beneath his chest, quivering milk-white skin and a tender delicate flower for a nipple—the sweetest-tasting— After another furious round of knocking, Sam whispered roughly, "You're going to kill me, Emma."

"I would not do that, Sam Taggart," she whispered back.

Greta banged something against the door and yelled, "Mama sent a letter for you, Emma. I would think you would want it. Without you, she is changing."

Sam groaned slightly and placed his face within the curve of Emma's neck and shoulder, the only place that seemed safe. Full and hard, he entered her completely and held very still, his body trembling. Emma looked helplessly up at him and shuddered, the motion contracting her body around him. . . . She was tight and warm and strangely familiar.

"Emma!"

While Sam hovered between his immediate need and the knowledge that Greta could break down the door with her kicks, Emma held him tightly and stroked his hair. "Shh . . . Sam Taggart," she crooned to him, and began rocking gently side to side, as though he were a baby.

Sam could have stayed within her care for the rest of his lifetime. As it was, he suspected that Emma was shortening his lifetime. "I'm going to kill your sister," he muttered, and thrust himself back and free from her with an effort that he considered heroic.

Sam ached from head to toe, his heart pounding and his engorged manhood matching it with every beat. He fought for control, placing his arm across his face, and listened to Emma's hurried movements to arrange her clothing. At the moment, if he moved, it would be to grab Emma and reenter her sweet hot, moist, willing body.

He groaned again and shivered and jolted at the hurried, incompetent movements of Emma's fingers wrapped around his manhood. He started at her for a heartbeat, trying not to groan at her light inept efforts to stuff him into his pants. She was trying to fasten his buttons. She touched his erect member again, and Sam almost— "Good God, woman, what are you doing?" he demanded, catching her wrists with his hands.

"I was . . . Sam Taggart, you were—ah . . . protruding."

He glared at this woman who had just informed him that she wasn't the pristine virgin he had thought. Who he had spent nights aching for, and who had just ignited him. Who had just spun off into her own private heated universe with one touch of his hand. "Don't touch me. Just don't."

Without taking his hard stare from her, Sam stood and buttoned his pants, then his shirt, tucking it in. Emma quickly smoothed the bed, grabbed a huge shawl, wrapped it around her, and unlocked the door. She peered out into the hallway.

Sam pretended to study the street below as the intruder he wanted to murder entered the room.

"Well, is this how you greet your sister who has traveled all these miles to find you?" Greta demanded, lugging her bundles into the room. She dropped the pigeon cage on the floor beside the others, startling the birds, and a flurry of small feathers ballooned from the cages. She was dressed in her best blue dress with a matching bonnet decorated with seed pearls; a huge bow was meticulously tied beneath her chin. She dusted her skirts with perfectly matched gloves. "You could help me, Emma. You're wearing a shawl and the room is quite warm. Are you in a fever? Your face looks flushed, and your braids are untidy. What would Papa say?"

"Papa would say that it is rude not to let me know you were coming," Emma shot back. She glanced at Sam with a frustrated expression.

He glared back and tried to ignore the throbbing pain in his loins. He picked up the ledgers, pretending to study them. "Emma and I were just going over the books. Maybe you'd like to help us."

"Mama's letter," Greta announced imperially, and slapped a folded handkerchief with embroidered edging into Emma's hand.

Emma carefully unfolded the handkerchief and the note, reading it. Tears came to her eyes, and she dabbed at them with the handkerchief. "Mama is proud of me. She misses me, but she wishes she could have been a businesswoman when she was young. Mama thinks Harry is handsome and a gentleman. She wonders if he polkaed with me, because he looks like a dancer. Mama wonders if I have been to festivals—she used to love them when she was a girl . . . before she married Papa. She says that he is well. Fritzi wants Maximilian to be delivered to Lilly."

Greta flung off her shawl and handed it to Emma with the cage of cooing, red-eyed pigeons. They all looked accusingly at Sam. Greta nudged aside his knife, and it fell to the floor as she sat. "I have no time to play with you. I came to find a rich husband. Fritzi says you are traveling to mines and logging camps and ranches, sometimes two a day. Surely I can find a rich husband while traveling with you. If he is rich enough, Papa will be happy. Gilbert is worried you will find a way not to marry him. He says you can be devious when you set upon something you want. If you would just marry Gilbert, this would all be so much simpler," Greta accused Emma indignantly.

"Maximilian! You brought Fritzi's favorite tumbler pigeon!" Emma made kisses at the bird with feathered claws. "Pretty boy, pretty boy. . . . Greta, why has Fritzi let you have Maximilian?"

The sight of Emma's kiss-swollen lips forming kisses at the pigeon caused Sam to slam the ledger closed.

Greta looked at him and then lifted her chin. "He wants Maximilian to be delivered to a girl named Let-go Lilly in Deer Lodge City. Gilbert went into a rage when he discovered that you were traveling with this Sam Taggart."

Sam had had enough. The safest action now seemed to leave the women at once. "I think," Sam began very carefully, "that you two have a lot to talk—"

"I can't go back to Papa," Greta wailed dramatically. "I'll wither into a crone if I do. I must find my prince."

"She can't go back to Papa," Emma repeated, wringing her hands and looking at Sam helplessly.

Sam shook his head. Someday he'd learn to avoid looking at Emma's greenish-hazel eyes with their soft gold speckles. It seemed, when she looked at him like that, that his intentions and his spine turned to mush. The years of protective walls tumbled, and whatever sense he'd acquired as a man went leaping into her small capable hands. He thought about those busy hands trying to stuff him into his pants and groaned. He slapped his hat on his head, scooped up his belongings, and shook his head again.

"You can stay," Emma whispered to Greta, and began untying her bonnet. "Sam is a kind man. He just acts in pain sometimes because—"

Sam leveled a dark look at Emma-the-nonvirgin. The object of his problems knew very well why he was in pain; he wasn't certain he could walk at the moment. He wanted a good knuckle-busting, knife-slicing brawl, but he wouldn't . . . because he was a businessman, who didn't fight. He snorted at Emma's image of him. "Greta, nothing would make me happier than you traveling with us. Let go one of those birds in the morning to let your family know the whole goddamn lot of us are happy and husband hunting."

Emma placed her hand over her mouth, her expression shocked at his language. Sam smiled evilly at her. "You two brides just stay here, why don't you? Catch up on gossip and pick husbands. I'll be happy to help any way I can. As a matter of fact, I'd like to get you both married and out of my hair. But right now I'm going to—"

"The cattle queen with the feathered hat and tonnage on her bow," Emma breathed in a tone of hushed outrage.

Sam swept his hat gallantly in front of him. "Evidently you've been conversing with the pegleg whaler at the livery. I've had enough of female company for the evening. I'm going to my relatives. Red-skinned relatives, Greta. I'm a half-blood, you know. They're in the area, and I thought I'd socialize a bit. You're invited to dinner, of course—roots, berries, and perhaps if you're lucky, a delicious buffalo tongue and roast hump meat."

Greta gasped and placed her hand over her bosom, the picture of a shocked woman.

"He is emotional, but a kind man," Emma whispered to her shocked sister as he slammed the door behind him.

Chapter Twelve

This morning Greta wanted to sleep, and I discovered that Sam had already gone to Many Horses's camp, away from his friend, that Maybelle D'Arcy woman. I met a wonderful woman, May Flower, who lives in a tent and wears a silk robe with a dragon embroidered on it. She is a liberated woman, smokes cigars, and was the perfect choice to help me, as men seem to like her very much. Because I am no longer a virgin and Sam does not want children, I asked her instruction. May Flower and I had a very nice talk. She provided me with a supply of lemons and instructions, in trade for my socks.

Pegleg, a wonderful man at the livery, informed me that Sam had gone to visit his relatives, taking with him four fine Texas Longhorn steers. I hurried to catch up with him and met his wonderful uncle, Many Horses.

When I arrived, Sam was engaged in breaking wild

mustangs. He was magnificent, dressed in a breech-cloth and fringed leggings and moccasins.

However, and I am not happy about this, when I ran to save him from injury, he dismounted, ran for me, and tossed me over his shoulder. I barely rescued the lemons in my sock basket. A beautiful maiden was looking at him so intently that I felt obliged to share a lemon with her. It is afternoon now, and Sam has stopped on the way back to town. He is bathing in the stream and scowling at me. He is in a fine temper. E.

The woman was driving him to the edge.

Sam ached in every muscle. Today, the tough little mustangs suited Sam's mood, although he would have preferred fighting a wounded bear.

His encounter with Emma had left him in pain and sleepless and in an uncertain emotional quandary. A man who always knew his course—to succeed in business—Sam didn't like the clutter of emotion in his life. He hadn't been prepared for the uncertainty Emma had presented to him—whether he could draw back before his seed shot into her moist heated body.

The thought had shaken Sam; he'd always been in control.

He scrubbed the soap roughly over his chest. No other woman had taken him to the edge. No other woman had tormented him and played with him and excited him like Emma Recht, in her plain bonnets and prim ways. One look at the warriors eyeing her, and he knew that he didn't want another man touching her.

The thought had shocked him.

Sam sluiced the cold water over him; he shot Emma a dark forbidding stare that served to warn people away from him. There she was, in her neat brown dress and her brown bonnet. She'd already folded his breechcloth and leggings and placed his beaded moccasins over them as if they were his business clothes. She was writing in her journal.

Sam snorted in disgust. She hadn't been neat last night, with her nightgown up to her waist and the buttons undone. She'd been so soft and sweet and fragrant, and he'd just begun to enter her—

He sucked in air, fought the jolt of desire, and dived beneath the surface of the icy stream. All he had to do was define the rules and hold to them, he thought as he quickly dried and jerked on his pants. "Emma, we have to talk."

"I think you are beautiful," she said simply as he stopped in front of her. "Magnificent," she corrected with a timid smile. "You looked just like your uncle, Many Horses, when you were telling me how to write the bill of sale. So manly. I think you could command a country if you wanted. You are a kind man, Sam Taggart. You saw that your relatives needed food, and you took it to them, protecting them from harm with your business knowledge. Now there are two families who are lucky to have you, Sam Taggart—Harry's and Many Horses's."

She looked innocent and trusting and believing in him. Nothing could have been more effective to silence the lecture Sam had prepared. He'd led a lifetime of hardships, of surviving at the lowest level, of hating his mixed blood and the father who had spawned him.

Emma looked at him with her clear hazel eyes and dancing golden specks, and the pain gentled within him.

He simply reached for her and dragged her up to him, wrapping his arms around her.

Emma clung to him, wrapping her arms around his neck and burying her face against his throat. He lifted her, held her there in the dappled sunlight, and let her clean scents engulf him.

Her hand stroked his cheek, and for the moment Sam allowed the gentle trespass. She felt good in his arms, fitted tightly to him, soft and warm and— He remembered her handing a lemon to Cold Dove. "Where did you get the lemons?"

She stiffened slightly. "Lemons?"

Sam leaned back to look at her. He enjoyed the flush moving up her cheek and the quick shifting away of her eyes. He tugged at the bow beneath her chin. "They aren't easily found in these parts. If you've found a supplier, I'd like to know."

"I will speak to . . . her," Emma returned, pushing free of him and bending to straighten the slices of bread.

"Emma . . . ?"

She pivoted to him, clearly on the defense. "I have things that are private to me. Things I do not wish you to know. Am I not allowed these things?"

"I'd say I found out something last night, wouldn't you?" Sam fully intended to pry away Emma's lemon secret, but now he was more interested in how she felt about him. "Are you sorry?"

Her eyes were clear, dark as a lush meadow after a night rain. "I am not."

* * *

"Good, you found lemons. Make me some lemonade," Greta ordered as Emma entered the hotel room in Tadpole Springs. "Save some to lighten my hair."

Sam's hand reached past Emma to push open the door. Seated in front of the mirror, Greta lifted an imperial eyebrow at him. The woman was as welcome as drought and twice as nasty. Their gazes locked over Emma's neat bonnet. Sam took in the messy room; Emma was already folding Greta's clothes and smoothing the bed. Sam didn't want Emma fetching for Greta; he forced a smile. "If you're going to stay with us for a short time, Greta, you'd better remember that Emma is my employee. She needs her energy to take care of my business."

Greta snorted delicately. "Papa says that Emma is probably enjoying herself, working for you. He has a high opinion of you. . . . I don't."

"Greta! You will not speak that way to Sam Taggart."

Greta turned slowly from the mirror and folded her hands in her lap, regarding Emma steadily. "Just what are all these men doing, knocking on your door, Emma Recht?"

"What men?" Sam asked, entering the room and closing the door. He tossed the whip on his shoulder to the bed and sailed his hat to a bedpost. Emma looked at him quickly, then ducked her head, shielding her blush.

Greta pointed her finger at Emma, who was drawing off her shawl and bonnet. "They want to marry *her*! They say she's good wife material, when everyone knows that I am the most beautiful daughter and Papa only let Emma keep the dowry because she is so—"

She stopped when Sam looked at her. He wondered how the two women could have the same parents. "If the three of us are going to get along, Greta, be careful what you say about Emma."

"I have always known that I am plain. And Greta is tired." Emma moved to Greta's side and began stroking her hair. "Would you like me to wash your hair, Greta? I'll use a lemon in the rinse."

Emma glanced at Sam and blushed again. He ran his hand through his hair and didn't care if his part was mussed. The bed he wanted to toss Emma upon and finish what he'd begun, mocked him; the men waiting downstairs for a glimpse of Emma made him want to— "Greta, did the men leave any messages? For me?"

She waved her hand at the table and a stack of paper scraps. Sam jerked his glasses from his pocket and jammed them on, riffling through the notes. The first one began, "Marry me. Moses Drake, Esq." The second was a flourish of elegance and signed by Benjamin MacTavish, lately of Scotland. Another scrap was merely the catalog picture of a plain gold band signed by another X. Peter Olafson's neat printing asked Emma to marry him. He owned a small farm and had a herd of dairy cattle. He also had a brewery and a ready-made family of five grown unmarried sons. He promised Emma a hired woman and an elegant bedroom.

Sam crumbled the bedroom offer and stuffed it into his pocket. He didn't want to think of Emma in bed with any of them, much less Gilbert. Because he was feeling nasty at the moment, Sam spoke to Greta: "Looks like you got left out in the marriage department."

She glared at him as an angry flush rose up her creamy cheeks. "They are all blind and dumb."

Emma patted Greta's shoulder. "They're lonely men, Greta. It is only that they saw me first and women are scarce in Montana Territory. They're probably reconsidering their offers right now."

Greta preened and smirked at Sam. He jerked open the door at the first knock. "What?"

A tall good-looking drover held his big hat in his hands, his hair damp and neatly combed. He leaned to one side, trying to see around Sam into the room. "Is she here? Emma? The woman who cares if a man's feet are warm in the winter? I want to marry her. I'm just up from Texas, and I've got me a little spread, and I'm needing a wife. . . ."

"I am Emma," said Greta, rising elegantly to walk toward the handsome drover. She hurried to grab a shawl, tossed it around her, and hurried out the door.

Emma hurried after her. "Gret—ah . . . Emma, where are the pigeons?"

"In their cages. I attached a rope to the bedpost and ran it out the window." Greta smiled benignly as she looped her arm through the drover's. "They needed fresh air and sunshine."

Emma ran back to the room and tugged at the window, which wouldn't open. Sam reached past her to open it easily, and Emma reeled in her pigeons, soothing them. When she flattened his new paper on the floor and placed the pigeons upon it, they immediately dirtied the paper. Sam shook his head. "Either you're cutting holes in the best articles, or it's pigeons."

"I will buy you another paper." She tried a smile and

found Sam's dark scowl. Emma petted the pigeons, soothing them.

Sam's hand shot out to claim her wrist, jerking her up against him. "You treat those birds as if they were . . . lovers," he threw at her with disgust.

Whatever bothered Sam, it was something he didn't trust. His gaze jerked down to Emma's bottom lip, the one she had just dampened with her tongue. Suddenly the moment changed, and his thumb caressed her wrist, and he leaned closer to whisper in her ear, "Tell me about the lemons, Emma."

"I cannot. I . . ."

Sam's lips prowled around her ear and nipped her lobe. When his tongue flicked at her inner ear and his cheek nuzzled hers, Emma's legs began to weaken. The dark hungry look in Sam's eyes told her that he wanted her. That he wanted to lie upon her and—

She lifted her mouth to his, a small kiss to soothe him. Sam's mouth slanted and fused hungrily upon hers. He placed his hands beneath her bottom and lifted her higher against him. "Emma . . . ," he whispered against her mouth as the heat rose between them. His mouth lowered to her throat, and she shivered, needing his lips upon her breast, the delightful feeling. Her body clenched, her fingers digging into his taut shoulders.

Sam lowered her feet to the floor, keeping his hand on her bottom, while his fingers quickly unbuttoned her bodice and found her breast. When his big warm hand closed over her softness, Emma sighed, because that was what she had needed. His thumb gently rubbed her nipple, peaking it, and then she stood on tiptoe to meet his kiss. She wanted his body firmly against her, shaking with need, his manhood lodged deeply within her. "Sam Taggart, will you please undress?"

His lips curved slowly against hers, and he lifted his head, his eyes filled with humor. "Why, Emma. You have purely shocked me."

"I don't know about the undressing business. I have only experience with one time," she whispered back, frightened that she had failed to meet Sam's standards for a woman. When it came to a wife, he had a definite list of needs; Emma wasn't certain what he wanted from her. "What do women do?"

He grinned wickedly at her. "Usually they undress me. Or they are already waiting in bed."

"But I could never—" She glanced down Sam's tall body, and knew that she could manage to undress him, to unwrap him like a present especially made for her.

His lifted eyebrow challenged her, and Emma realized that she rarely dismissed challenges. At the moment her berserker tendencies wanted her to curl her fingers around him and watch the magic begin—Sam's body fascinated her.

"Let that little berserker in you run wild, Emma," Sam urged huskily.

"You will not mind?" Delighted with him, she stood on tiptoe and kissed him again.

Sam groaned and took her hands in his, kissing them. "I'm dying, Emma," he whispered rawly.

Greta's angry yell sailed into the room. Sam's hands locked to her breasts, and he groaned as if in pain. Emma saw that she had gripped his hair bringing his face close to hers, and it stuck out in peaks. His mouth was softer, swollen by the hungry kiss, and a dark red color ran beneath his tanned skin. His look at her accused as Greta swept into the room.

She slammed the door, stomped her feet, and plopped onto the bed, groaning dramatically. "That man only has two hundred acres. Two hundred acres is a pittance. He won't do."

Greta flopped the hand covering her face to her side and glared at Emma. "What have you done, Emma? What did you do to these men that makes them want to marry you? Papa said you have devious ways when you want something."

Emma sank to the bed and began stroking Greta's hair. "You'll feel better in the morning."

"I want a rich husband." Greta eyed Sam, who remained disgusted and silent, as though she expected him to provide for her needs at the moment.

Sam hadn't removed his stare from Emma. "I think I know of one for you, Greta. He has over seventy thousand acres."

Greta sat up, immediately interested. "Who?"

Sam continued to look at Emma. "Tex Murdock. He's wife hunting. You'll have to ask Emma about him."

Chapter Thirteen

After spending the night in a chair, protecting the women inside the rented room, Sam wasn't in a good mood. He rummaged through his papers, neatly organized by Emma, and stuffed them back into his saddlebags. The past few days hadn't let him concentrate on business, and he had to get Tenkiller back to the Big T before the mares started arriving. He wasn't certain how Harry would react to the horse-breeding business.

He sat at the downstairs breakfast table and brooded about his fortune. The mustangs had cost him a few bruises and aching muscles, but Many Horses's acceptance and approval had been worth it. The drovers, miners, and farmers looking for Emma had left more messages than he'd had in his entire business career. He wasn't happy at how Emma looked at the men, as if each one was a potential husband. He sipped his morning coffee, tried to read the *New Northwest* paper from

Deer Lodge City, and waited for Emma to arrive downstairs.

Sam looked over the top of his glasses. What had been a tavern by night was now a restaurant. The wood shavings filled with tobacco spit had been swept out. Behind the kitchen door Emma talked with the cook as was her custom, seeing that their food basket was filled with properly cooked food from clean utensils.

Sam pondered his new project. Arne Young, a New England lumber man, had designed a one-room building, simple to erect, that could be freighted in pieces. While some catalog cabins were shipped up the Missouri River by steamboat to Fort Benton, Arne had been certain that with ready lumber there was a profit in his design. Unfortunately, Arne had died in a gunfight, and the undertaker and preacher had provided Sam with the drawings because his name was printed on the bloodied sketches.

He unwrapped the cold cloth from his bruised, swollen knuckles. He hadn't expected an army of men to be interested in Emma—or his own violent need to protect her. Just past midnight a shadow had slid by on the hallway wall; Sam had stepped out onto the roof to follow the man, who stopped in front of the women's outside window. He was just in the process of using his knife to open the window when Sam asked, "Is there something you want?"

The man hadn't stopped prying his knife around the window and tugging at it. "Hell, yes. I'm getting one of those women and taking her back to my ranch. If I can get a baby in her belly before they find us—"

After Sam's fist hit him, he had rolled, almost elegantly, from the roof and plopped to the ground. As Sam had made his way back to the window, his bare foot had stepped on the fingers of the man who was crawling up from the porch posts. The man took one look at Sam's cold smile. He eased his hand from beneath Sam's foot, smiled warily, and eased down to the porch. He disappeared into the night.

All night, one look from Sam, leaning back on the two legs of the chair against the sleeping women's door, blocked men just wanting a peek. By dawn, Sam had managed to get an hour's sleep in the chair and only hurriedly returned to his room to change clothes.

Now, Sam glanced over his morning paper to Greta, who was coming into the barroom-restaurant. She glared back at him, and he knew that anytime he wanted to vent his raw nerves and unsteady temper, she was the right person to approach.

Greta smiled at a miner, who sat up, preening his hair, and spoke to her. Greta's face turned thunderous. "No, I am not Emma."

She swooshed into the chair opposite Sam. "I've got to find someone who knows all about the Alamo. If Tex Murdock has seventy thousand acres called the New Alamo and plans a bigger ranch, I'll become an expert on the Alamo. . . . I had a bad night. Emma took forever to wash and straighten my clothes and to wash my hair. Then we had to sleep together. She moans and squirms and—"

The image brought a sharp pain surging through Sam; he studied the ads for equipment sales and the new one for Tenkiller's stud services, and in his mind he saw the image of Emma lying warm and flushed beneath him. She could turn to fire in his hands—

Sam stretched slightly, uncomfortable with the tight restless need of his body. His fist crushed the newspaper. He'd find the man who had dishonored Emma. Whoever he was, Emma didn't regret making love to him, and the thought didn't set well with Sam.

He lowered his newspaper while Emma brought two heaping plates of fried ham and potatoes covered by a thick slice of bread from the kitchen, balancing them expertly. Greta began to eat the moment hers was on the table. Emma placed his plate on the table.

She paused and stood very still for a moment before hurrying back to the kitchen. Then she returned with a granite coffee pot, filled their cups, and sat.

Sam folded his paper slowly, carefully. "I don't want you waiting on tables," he said for the tenth time.

"Yes, Sam Taggart," Emma said, even as she stood, straightened the cloth serving as her apron, and hurried back to the kitchen.

"She's up to something," Greta stated around a mouthful of ham. "She's got that berserker look. Mama has started to get it, too."

"Excuse me." Sam wanted to define his rules for Emma; he followed her into the kitchen and closed the door. He disregarded the cook, who was either a man or a woman, a cigarette dangling from his/her lip.

Sam focused on Emma, fighting the need to take her into his arms. He resented being such easy prey for her pleading hazel eyes. "May Flower isn't coming with us. Lilly was one thing, because she had Beth and wanted her sister brought up right—"

Emma pivoted to him, tears in her eyes. "Sam, look at poor Shen-Yu. He is supposed to wait on tables and clean. There is no one to care for him. He's a doctor, and look what they've done to him."

"You can't have him," Sam repeated in his firmest tone.

Emma reached to touch his cheek; she frowned slightly. "You have developed a twitch, Sam Taggart. Perhaps you should rest more."

Emma had wanted to adopt the small Chinese doctor; Shen-Yu had been tarred and feathered by loggers who didn't like his needles. Sam took one look at Emma's pleading hazel eyes and his resistance fell to his boots. He agreed to her adoption of Shen-Yu.

Later that day, alone in his room, Sam removed his glasses, folded them, and tucked them into his pocket. He had had his bath and time to think. While Emma merrily adopted her unlikely crew, the guilt that he'd taken a virgin nagged him. The blood on the sheets of Amanda's Place had damned him; he'd continue to look for the virgin. According to Lilly, the virgin hadn't liked the business—and that statement labeled Sam as an inconsiderate brute. Sam tucked the virgin into a mental drawer; he would do what he could to find and help her.

Emma, on the other hand, wasn't a virgin. She seemed as practical about their lovemaking as she was about business. She'd been raised on a farm and understood male animals and their needs. He'd remind her about his rules and his desire not to have children. She already understood his need of an ideal socialite wife. An intimate, but not binding, arrangement could suit both of them, and he could definitely protect her better while installed in her bed every night. Emma was a logical woman and would agree with him. Perhaps if she changed her mind about being a modern businesswoman, he'd help her find a husband—

Sam realized his body had tensed, just as it did when something he wanted was wrested from him. He turned his mind back to tonight and Emma in his bed.

He'd gotten rid of everyone but Emma, and tonight he would make love to her.

In four days, July the fifteenth, Tenkiller would begin servicing mares at the Big T. Sam intended to be at the Big T when the mares arrived, but before he left on the journey, he wanted his time alone with Emma. The taste of her haunted him with every breath.

Sam remembered the erotic torture of lying very still within her and forcing himself to withdraw. The next time, he would only withdraw when—

Sam overlooked the darkened street and thought of any loose ends he might have left untied in his quest for Emma. Greta and Shen-Yu had gone on ahead, with the pigeons, and Tenkiller; they would reach the Big T just in time for the arrival of the mares. With Sam's money in her purse, Greta had insisted on making a side trip to a new emporium at Deer Lodge City to buy sewing goods for her husband-hunting venture. That would add an extra two days to the two-day trip from Tadpole Springs to the Big T.

Without Greta to care for, Emma would not be exhausted tonight. There would be no red-eyed pigeons vying for her attention, because only one would be left in Emma's room at the hotel, while Emma stayed with

Sam. Sam had managed to send all the others either to the Rechts' or to the Big T.

Greta knew how to bargain—and in the end she agreed to go to the Big T because she would not return to her father's clutches. Sam, in return, had promised to root out any potential wealthy bachelors and provide her with a written inventory of their assets. As a secondary plan, he had promised to secure a book of Alamo stories for her to study—at this point Tex Murdock was a likely candidate for Greta. Also Sam had to furnish her with money for proper husband-hunting clothes and accessories, like a corset.

Since he was sending Tenkiller on ahead with Greta and Shen-Yu, Sam had traded four mustangs for a mare to use as his traveling horse. Kloshe, whose name meant "fine" in the Chinook jargon, was a big and fast Appaloosa, which he traded from a Canadian métis who fondly remembered Harry. Batiste, a seasoned, jovial mixture of French and Blood Indian, happily agreed to protect Greta and Shen-Yu on their way to Deer Lodge and the Big T. Greta rode Batiste's gentle mule; Tenkiller was amazingly docile with Shen-Yu, and Batiste rode one of mustangs, using the others to pack goods to the Big T.

Emma had asked Sam for the remaining pigeon to send a note to Mary. After a staged minor objection, Sam had agreed. He smiled tightly and knew that he'd wrapped up every obstacle to having Emma.

Now, as he waited for her in his hotel room, Sam saw Emma's brown bonnet on the bed and brought it to his face. He inhaled her scent and wallowed in the evening alone with Emma. He ran a ribbon across his lips and coiled it around his finger. He'd never seen Emma with her hair down, and tonight he intended to spread it over his chest.

Sam glanced around the room he had just neatened. After her afternoon nap, which he'd insisted upon, Emma and he would enjoy a quiet meal together—the cook was preparing to serve it in Sam's room—and then Sam intended to wake up in her arms. He hurried to fold his vest, because he didn't want Emma distracted in an untidy room. He polished his boots and shaved and smiled at himself in the mirror. Emma would awaken from her nap, take a relaxing bath in the hot water he'd ordered, and then she'd come to him to take business notes.

Sometime during their session, Sam would turn the topic to the temporary sexual and business relationship he wanted from her, and the convenience of the arrangement. He would, of course, take care of her when their liaison was finished. Sam lowered the lamp wick and pulled the curtains closed. After a moment of listening to the drunken miners on the street, Sam pulled the window closed. He wanted no distractions.

He smiled, recognizing Emma's cautious knock at his door. "Come in."

She hurried through the door, looking just as tired as when he last saw her. She glanced at his shirt, opened and rolled back at the wrists and hanging free from his pants, then hurried to her bonnet on his bed. "There it is. I didn't know where I left it."

Sam glanced at Emma's Goodyear galoshes and the bits of mud clinging to her skirt; her eyes were tired, with bruised circles beneath them. He'd wanted her rested; Greta had had Emma washing her clothing and her hair until late last night. Emma was up before dawn, preparing food for Greta's trip. The hair on the nape of Sam's neck lifted as he sensed that not all had gone as he planned. A man who lived by his instincts, Sam surveyed his intended and asked cautiously, "Did you have a nice nap?"

She smiled gently. "I could not. Sleeping in the middle of the day—when there is so much to do—is not for me. When you don't need me, I must tend my own business."

"Emma . . ." Sam decided to approach her carefully. He realized suddenly that Emma could make him wary; she was often unpredictable. He hadn't cared enough to bother with volatile women, but tonight with Emma was worth trying logic. "I thought we agreed not to work this afternoon," he began.

"You explained to me that you had no need of me and that I could rest in my room. I had business to do."

"The sock business?" Sam watched teenage boys carry a small metal tub and buckets of water past his door. He stepped out into the hallway. "In here."

"Uh . . . must have got the orders wrong," one of the boys said as Sam dropped coins into their hands, then shut the door behind them and turned the key in the lock.

"Do not look so angry, Sam Taggart." Emma folded her bonnet. "You look so fierce now, just as you did when I came after you at Many Horses's camp. Thank you for agreeing that Shen-Yu should go to help Harry's foot. Thank you for using the lemon peels to rid Shen-

Yu of the tar and for providing the horsehair for his braid."

Sam dismissed how easily he gave in to Emma's idea to provide Shen-Yu with this honor. One look at her soft hazel eyes, and he'd grabbed his hat, on his way to lop a tail from one of the mustangs. "What are you going to do with that, mister?" the stable boy had asked with big eyes. "Make a horsehair lariat?"

"I'm a good man. The horse won't miss that tail," Sam stated flatly and without sincerity. His motives had nothing to do with "goods," he mocked himself. He and Batiste helped relieve Shen-Yu of his tar and feathers because Sam didn't want Emma's hands on the man. "What did you do this afternoon? Replenish your lemon supply?"

Emma looked around the room, clearly uneasy with Sam's open shirt and his frown. He realized that he'd never wanted or cared enough to shake a woman as he wanted to now; the thought distracted him more. He tried again forcing his tone to be pleasant. "Emma, it's almost eight o'clock. Tell me what you've been doing."

"Woden and I went for a ride. We visited two nice farms, all neat and with good gardens starting." She fingered her grandmother's brooch. "They had sheep."

Sam clenched the knob on the bedpost. Emma had ridden right into the army of men wanting to marry her. He remembered a wolfer's atrocities on a woman traveling from her farm to her daughter's. The man had been killing and skinning wolves and had brutally slaked himself upon the woman. An icy shroud enveloped Sam; he'd seen the wolfer's handiwork. "You went riding without me?"

"Only a little way. You were busy at the emporium. I saw you looking at bolts of cloth. Are you going into the cloth and dress business now, Sam Taggart?"

"The store master in Coloma wanted cloth for shirts. The next time the traveling seamstress comes, he wants to be ready." Sam didn't like the way Emma had put him on the defensive. He wasn't used to explaining himself. he had been looking at the fine muslin and lace and imagining Emma wearing only her underclothing . . . perhaps standing in the rain amid a field of wild flowers . . . with her hair loose about her shoulders. The vision had interfered with his bargaining for a shipment of cloth to be delivered to Coloma's store.

Emma smiled at him. "You were wonderful when the clerk accused the little boy of taking a jawbreaker from the jar. I saw the whole thing while I was passing on Woden. I saw you stop the clerk from striking the boy, and I thought, 'The boy will be fine. Sam Taggart will not let him be hurt.' "

The boy was part Arapaho, born of a white captive mother. Once freed, the woman chose to take her son with her and faced a harder life with him at her side. Sam had admired the woman's courage, and his appearance at her side, the purchase of the jawbreakers for the boy, and a meaningful look had instantly quieted the clerk.

Sam didn't want to waste energy or time on emotions, and the vision of Emma standing wet and luscious in a field had shaken him. He intended to have his evening with her, setting out the rules and beginning their relationship. Once his emotions and aroused body were under control, he could turn his mind to business.

"I suppose you're ready for a hot bath, aren't you?" Sam, fighting the need to grab Emma because he finally had her alone, pushed her to sit on the bed. He bent on one knee to pull off her galoshes and unlace her boots, kneeling at her feet. "You can tell me about the sock business while you bathe."

"It is not as important as your business, but I thank you for letting me sell socks in my free time." She gripped her bonnet in both hands and blinked at him.

Sam tugged off her boots and didn't give her a moment to protest. "You've seen me without a shirt and you've seen me just like this before, Emma. There is no need to be nervous. I believe we have passed the shy stage."

Emma glanced worriedly around the lighted room. "Sam Taggart. I cannot take a bath here—"

Sam placed his hands firmly around the two delicate ankles he had just revealed. Her feet were beautiful; he could almost feel them brace on the backs of his calves, lifting, deepening his intimate stroke. "I've seen almost every part of you, Emma. Now tell me about the sock business while I undress you."

He complimented himself on the diversion. Emma relished talking about her sock business. He slid her grandmother's brooch from her collar, and her hand clasped her bodice closed as he began to unbutton it.

"The sock business is good," she said, watching his hands. "I've been enlarging."

"Have you?" Sam's breath caught as he studied the high firm soft shape of her breasts. He bent to lick the tip of one, through the plain thin camisole, and then the other, the dark shape of her nipples clinging to the cloth. Finally . . . he had her alone. He forced himself to take his time, because tonight there would be no Greta and no red-eyed pigeons stopping him. He eased her skirt higher, enjoyed the sight of her knees beneath the dark skin of his fingers, and then slowly bent to kiss the inside of her thigh.

"Sam, stop." Emma pressed her skirt between her legs.

Sam kept his hands in place, easing back the skirt. "Tell me what you did today, and if you want me to stop, then I will."

Emma inhaled as he nuzzled her skin. She smelled like flowers and rain and . . .

She whispered raggedly, "Two farm women say they cannot knit enough socks for the bachelors alone, but they think that together we can make a profit. They want to help me in my sock business."

"Mmm. Do they?" Sam kissed her other thigh—this time nipping it gently and inhaling the scent of her, allowing himself to wallow in the success of his plans to have Emma alone. He eased her voluminous petticoats and skirts aside until he held her bottom in both his hands. He caressed her buttocks with his hands and rubbed his cheek against her breasts, enjoying the rippling soft weight.

When he lifted his head, he found her drowsy, steamy look—tonight nothing would stop them. He wanted to linger in the moment, to set the rules as they progressed for their new relationship.

She met his kiss as he stood, drawing her with him. He bared a creamy shoulder and bent to kiss it, then the other, drawing her bodice down to her waist. "You have beautiful breasts, Emma."

She blushed and looked away. "Please do not say such things. Vanity is harmful. I . . . I think I should go to my room—"

He slowly twirled a fingertip around her nipple. "Let me bathe you, Emma. I'm pleased that your sock business is doing so well."

"Are you?" She looked at him with wide eyes. "Papa said that men did not like women in business."

"He's old-fashioned, don't you think?"

She didn't answer but stared at her clothing, pooled at her feet. Sam bent to kiss her and lift her up in his arms. "I am too heavy. . . . You should not carry—"

"Do you like kissing me, Emma?" Sam flicked the tip of his tongue across her lips, reveling in the moment when she suckled him into the hot sweet interior. The purring noises she made in the back of her throat almost caused Sam to toss her upon the bed; he braced himself, cuddling her closer. He wanted her to understand this new relationship and the enjoyment they both could have and share. She was a logical woman; she would understand the convenience of their arrangement. *Control,* Sam repeated mentally to himself. First the business layout, and then— His body tightened painfully.

"I like kissing you." Her soft admission slid along his lips.

He gathered her closer. "Do you remember if you liked what we were doing before Greta arrived?"

"Yes. I liked that, too."

Sam decided not to ask if she liked it with her first

lover. For some reason it mattered very much that he bested her first encounter. Emma had been looking for potential lovers to follow her first experience, and he did not want her looking for his replacement soon.

When Emma was in the small tub, her shoulders and knees shining above the water, Sam stood to appreciate the sight of her lips, swollen with his kisses, and the desire shadowing her eyes. The steam had caused the tendrils at her nape and surrounding her face to curl; they caught the lamplight in a coppery glow. He enjoyed the swell of her breasts above the water, pressed high by her folded arms. There in the milky water was the dark triangular nest of curls, her thighs— Sam ripped off his shirt and paused. He remembered how Emma liked tidiness and carefully placed it on a chair. He picked up her petticoats, still warm from her body, and placed them beside his clothing on another chair. "This is where I want your clothes to be every night," Sam said softly. "We'll rent two rooms, but at night we'll be together, and—"

He picked up her dress and shook it. A small cloth sack fell from her pocket, and a lace-edged handkerchief floated from it. A coin escaped the handkerchief; it hit the rough plank flooring and rolled to Sam's bare foot. It twirled on its rim several times and then slowly wobbled in a circle.

At the same time Emma stepped out of the bath and hurried for Sam's discarded shirt. By the time the dented coin stopped fully, she had buttoned the shirt. Sam bent to pick up the coin. He held Emma's wrist as she reached for it. "What's this?"

Chapter Fourteen

Emma watched, horrified, as Sam traced the dented coin and the new hole with its black ribbon; she tied the ribbon to her neck each night. With the coin safely in her hand, she could dream of Sam's wonderful lovemaking. When Sam was at his worst—silent and hard—she would wear the coin beneath her dress. It helped her keep her patience, because if there ever was a man who could bring out her secret temper, it was Sam Taggart.

Sam fingered the marks in the ribbon where she had tied it. He put the ribbon through the hole in the coin; he looked at her and slowly tied the ribbon around her neck, matching the ribbon's markings. The coin warmed the skin between her breasts.

"I remember this coin. It's dented and has a scratch," Sam murmured thoughtfully.

Sam slowly parted the shirt she wore to reveal the coin, and fear shot through Emma. "I found it. Isn't it pretty?"

"You found it," he repeated slowly. As if exploring territory he remembered, Sam put his hands on her shoulders, lowering them slowly along her side to her hips. His big hands locked to her hips, his fingers digging slightly into the softness. He looked down at her face and then up to her hair.

In the next instant Sam sprawled upon the bed, taking her down with him. Emma scooted back, only to have him catch her ankle and draw her back slowly, firmly to him. He flipped to his back and drew her knees apart, easing her to straddle him. "Undo your hair, Emma."

"It wouldn't be seemly." Emma tried to squirm away, only to be locked in place by Sam's hands on her waist. A strange, wonderful feeling of being strong and wild shot through her. She looked at Sam's dark furious look and knew that she was truly a berserker . . . that she wanted him feverishly now . . . that she did not want to be as her mother had prescribed, a woman who lay still beneath a man.

Sam spoke too quietly, as he did when he was very angry. "Take down your hair, or I will."

She had always been taught that hair should be loosened only to be washed and dried. The new intimacy frightened Emma because it seemed as if she was truly giving Sam all of herself. She doubted that her father had ever seen her mother without her braids. Lying with Sam at Amanda's had been different. She had escaped into another heavenly world for one moment of her life . . . and the room was dark.

Sam's face was rigid with temper, the spear of hair crossing his forehead trembling as he began to unbutton the shirt, his eyes locked with hers. "Emma, I am asking you to take down your hair."

The request was too intimate, and she shivered.

Sam's hands smoothed her thighs, easing the quivering muscles, and slowly rose to ease aside the cloth, exposing her breasts. He drew her down to nuzzle and suckle her breast, flicking it with his tongue. "Do it, Emma. Or . . ."

She gasped as he drew more deeply upon her breast, finishing with a gentle nip. He lay beneath her, his hands cupping her breasts. She couldn't let him know that she had been at Amanda's, that he had been her first lover. . . .

Sam's mouth hardened. "Emma, we can do this the easy way or the hard way. I'm fully prepared to do either. I've been tormented about ruining a virgin, and I'm not happy to find out that that virgin was riding right beside me . . . and I didn't know it."

His last words shot at her like bullets. "You've had a good time, haven't you? Hoarding your secrets? Letting me know you've already had a lover and me worrying about breaking my promise to keep you safe. . . . *Emma, take down your hair.*"

"You won't use force with me, Sam Taggart." She had never seen Sam look so determined, even when he was facing Harry. Nor did she like the imperial way he demanded she reveal herself to him.

"Won't I? Like it or not, you're going to tell me everything, Emma." His hands smoothed her body gently, firmly, as though it were his to claim. One hand swept slowly down her body to the nest of curls. He massaged the mound beneath them and studied her. "You were at Amanda's, weren't you?"

"I . . ." The tips of his fingers slid to stroke her intimately, and Emma gripped his hands. "Sam . . . I cannot."

"You can tell me, Emma, and you will. Now take down your hair." Though Sam's tone was quiet, Emma recognized the steel sheathed within the deep velvet.

She lifted her hands to free her braids, carefully placing the tortoisetone hairpins upon Sam's chest. The braids fell past her breasts to rest upon his stomach, and Sam sucked in his breath. He slowly undid the bindings and began to comb his fingers through her hair, draping it around her breasts. He eased the shirt from her, until she wore only the coin and her hair. "It was you at Amanda's," he said finally, tracing the coin.

"I—I had need of you. I have always wanted to leap upon branches, and there you were— Please do not feel badly toward me."

With his hand curled around the nape of her neck, Sam drew her down to kiss her gently. "Why were you there?"

She told him about Fritzi, surprised at Sam's tender smile.

"I'd say that would strengthen a man's legs all right. You came to rescue Fritzi and let your berserker tendencies rule you. You wanted to experiment before—"

"Gilbert." Emma clearly dreaded Gilbert bedding her.

Sam almost shuddered at the thought. "Gilbert isn't getting you."

*   *   *

An hour later Emma dug her heels into the mud outside the traveling preacher's tent. "You cannot just dress me and drag me to my wedding, Sam Taggart."

Above her his jaw clenched. "Can't I? We're getting married, Red."

She eyed him and tried to tug her wrist away from his grasp. "I did not mean to throw that pitcher at you. You were laughing at me, chasing me around the room like a boy tormenting a girl. You delighted in tossing me over your knee and—"

She tried to wrench her wrist away again and failed. "Sam, to hold a woman in such a position . . . a woman without clothing . . . and to—to pet her backside, and telling her what you intend to do with her upon a bed, is not proper. Shame, Sam Taggart. Shame."

He glanced down at her, and the grim look fled, replaced by a boyish grin. "You like it, Red."

She lifted her chin. "I do not."

"Do. You like kissing, too. You purr like a kitten when I touch you and when we kiss. You're as volatile as miner's nitro, Red."

She refused to answer as the preacher opened the tent flap. "I do not want to marry this man," she stated firmly.

"Give us a minute, will you?" Sam asked, and the flap closed. "Now, Emma. Be reasonable. We'll talk more later . . . in bed. This all makes sense. We're good together, in business and in bed. The arrangement will be a good one. We can relive the whole night at Amanda's later, but right now we're getting married, and then we're going to bed."

She crossed her arms. "I am not your ideal wife."

Sam crossed his arms and looked down at her. "You'll do just fine. This is the best solution, Emma."

"You have your business future to protect. I am plain—not a woman who knows how to give fancy parties. However, I wish to compliment you on the way you have progressed . . . expressing more of your thoughts—"

"I intend to express more than that once we're married." Sam turned from her and stood, legs braced, hands behind his back. She noted that he had forgotten the ever-present whip and that he did not wear his hat. His perfectly polished boots were sunk into the mud, while hers were clean. He had carried her from the hotel down to the preacher's tent, despite her protests. He seemed to enjoy carrying her.

Emma covered her hot cheeks with her cold hands. "I cannot marry you, Sam Taggart. I am not the ideal wife."

Sam pivoted to her, his expression hard. "I've thought about it. We'll do fine. We've worked through difficult situations before, and we succeeded. We'll fashion a marriage to suit both our needs. I cannot have you use me like a toy and then toss me aside, Emma. It is a matter of honor."

Emma's hand went to cover her mouth. "You say that I have dishonored you?" she asked, horrified.

"No, not yet. But you have slaked your wild passions upon me, and therefore you should worry about my honor. Marriage would prevent the ruination of my sterling reputation."

Emma frowned. "It is true that I did take you."

"I was but a helpless leaf in the storm of your passion."

He walked slowly back to her, a tall lean man, alone in the moonlit night. She wanted to wrap her arms around him to keep him safe and warm. Her kind thoughts fled as he leaned down to whisper, "You see, fair Emma, you either marry me, or you are relieved of traveling with me. I suppose your sock business will thrive nicely at your father's ranch and when you are married to Gilbert. If you marry me, on the other hand, I will be more inclined to help you build your business."

Panic shot through Emma; she did not want to leave Sam.

With the tip of his finger, Sam lifted her chin. He bent to her. "I will be faithful to you, Emma. I will never intentionally hurt you. The question is, do you want me?"

The dark flicker behind his lashes told her that for just a heartbeat, Sam was uncertain if she would want him . . . to declare to all others that she belonged to him. She realized he was posing another question to her: *Do you want to marry a half-blood who doesn't want children? Do you want to marry a man who is driven by the past, haunted by old wrongs?*

Emma wanted Sam. She reached into his pocket and extracted his comb, tilting his head down so that she could straighten his part. Then she kissed his forehead to tell him that she understood. "I will be a good wife to you, Sam Taggart. But I cannot promise to become your ideal wife. I am a plain country woman."

Sam looked at her mouth, traced his finger across her lips, and murmured, "You'll do fine."

Emma shivered, heat skittering over her skin at his dark smoldering look. "You look at me as though I were an apple dumpling," she whispered.

"Mmm," Sam murmured in an appreciative hungry tone as his look skimmed down her body.

"I think with you, I could be a berserker, and you might not mind."

"Mmm," Sam returned with a grin that slid away. "I promise to be good to you, Emma. I'll try."

"But you already are." Emma smiled up at him and fought throwing herself into his arms. She wanted to grab him and hold him and take him as selfishly and greedily as she could. He would be hers, a delightful present to come into her life, a grand adventure, and she could look at him as she wanted, feel him in bed beside her at night and— Emma tried to swallow as the next thought buffetted her: She could mount him once again.

Minutes later, Sam paid the preacher, lifted Emma against his chest, and carried her out of the tent. He walked quickly down the muddy street and up the stairs to his room. He carried her into the room and said, "You're not getting away from me. Don't ask if you can go back to your room to change. There is a pigeon there, and you'll want to stop and pet him."

"Tomorrow I will send Attila to Harry. He should know that we are married—that I am now his daughter."

"You don't need to do anything." Sam placed her on her feet and sat to jerk off his muddy boots. He tore away his clothing in a manner Emma had never seen and stopped her when she hurried to fold it.

Sam stood in front of her, his hands cradling her hot cheeks. He eased her bonnet from her and tossed it aside. He unpinned her grandmother's brooch and placed it on her shawl for safekeeping. The gesture endeared him to her, taking care of what was precious to her.

"The lamp . . . please," Emma whispered as Sam began undressing her. He looked as if he could devour her, and she felt the same; she wanted to be close with him in the dark.

Sam blew out the lamp and opened the bed, easing her between the sheets. He followed her, and they lay side by side in the dark. Emma breathed quietly. She wanted him to hold her and to whisper to her in his soft velvety voice. "I am uncertain about lying without clothes, Sam Taggart. You have no nightshirt. I have no gown. I should go to my room and get one."

"No." Sam lay still, his hands behind his head, looking at the leaf patterns created by the moonlight. "We're married," he said finally.

"Yes." She knew by his tone that he was already regretting the impulsive ceremony. She had created the guilt in him. She turned to her side, away from her new husband. She was unwilling to let him see her tears. She felt so cold and afraid. Sam needed his ideal wife and had settled for her.

The bed creaked as Sam turned slowly to curve his tall body around hers. She eased away from his heat, fearing that she would turn to grab him in her fear. Sam nuzzled her hair, his big hand gliding around to cup her

breasts, his other arm easing carefully beneath her head.
He drew her back to him, and she started, his arousal
thrusting at her. "It is not right to sleep without clothing—without braids. My hair is everywhere."

"Mmm." Sam buried his face in the curling masses
and drew her tightly against him. "I'm sorry I was rough
with you that first time at Amanda's."

She asked the question plaguing her. "Did I stain the
sheets?"

"Yes. Do you have any idea how I felt when you told
me you were not a virgin? How I could have killed the
man who had you?" Sam's voice was deep, raw, and
uneven.

In the next heartbeat he turned her beneath him. "I
need you, Emma. I'll try to—"

She didn't want him to be gentle and slow; she latched
her arms and legs to him and inhaled with delight as he
joined their bodies and the bed began to creak.

Sam slipped into the room with the breakfast tray. He
didn't want interruptions this morning; the boy downstairs would tell his business contacts that he and Emma
were gone. The preacher's paper with both their names
was propped against one cup; Sam wanted Emma to
remember she was legally his. He eased the tray onto
the table beside the bed and undressed as he enjoyed
the sight of Emma, sleeping soundly in the bed they had
thoroughly mussed.

There she was waiting for him, his Emma, amid the
blankets and sheets. A long leg, bent at the knee, the
delicate shade of pearl, escaped the cloth. Sam sucked
in his breath as he discovered a sweet shadowy curve of

her breast, the dark rose color of her nipple enticing against the white sheet. She was his, his virgin and now his wife—a part of his future life and success.

Sam shook his head; he'd been alone for years, and the realization that Emma was now his, stunned him.

He hurriedly tossed aside his clothing and eased carefully into bed beside his new wife. The aroma of morning coffee mingled pleasantly with her flowery fragrance and the deeper, headier scent of their lovemaking.

Sam cherished the sight of Emma's rosy nipple, webbed by her wildly rippling hair, the way she slept on her stomach, remaining as he had found her this morning, sprawled delightfully over him, clinging to him as if he were her prisoner.

He smoothed the cloth over her bottom and remembered how she had dived into her sensuality, biting him to keep from crying out. When she snuggled closer, wrapping her arm around him and nuzzling his chest, he closed his eyes in delight. She was warm and soft and sweet.

He inhaled her fragrance and frowned, aware that he hadn't drawn away from her at the last moment, but that the thundering pleasure had ridden him, and he had poured himself into her. Emma's heat sheathing him had rippled unexpectedly, and he had been unable to withdraw. He smoothed her hair, drawing it across his bare chest. In lovemaking as in business, one could expect a few mishaps. As they adjusted to their new arrangement, she would develop more control, and he would not be as desperate.

Sam lay very still as Emma began to purr softly, her leg slipping between his, her foot rubbing his ankle. He smiled as she moved over him, pushing her hips gently downward to find him. He closed his eyes as her heated cove found him ready, enveloping him in the velvet, liquid tight depths.

The restless sounds she made against his neck told him she needed him. Sam positioned her gently above him and began to move slowly, tutoring her once again.

She gasped, her movement desperate, her hands tightening on his chest, her short nails digging in slightly. "Tell me, Sam Taggart," she whispered drowsily.

He smiled again, kissing her ear. Emma had tried not to show her delight when he whispered to her, telling her how to move and what delighted him. . . . This time he asked questions of her: "Emma, do you like me inside you?"

The inner walls of her body tightened instantly, reassuringly. Sam moved slowly, rhythmically, as he whispered to her, his hand finding her breast, treasuring it, "Do you like me to kiss you here?"

He ran his thumb across her nipple, and she moaned, jerking against him. He lifted her slightly, taking her in his mouth, and Emma cried out, gripping the railings beside him, her body rippling above his.

Patience, Sam reminded himself. Emma was not used to a man but gave herself entirely, all at once, an unrestrained medley of heat and motion and soft skin, her hair flowing around him, cloaking him in her scents. He found himself enveloped in a womanly storm, feasting upon him, stunning him with pleasure. He found his body tensing, building, tightening, pouring into her at the same time she cried out.

Heartbeats later, he lay beneath her limp body, her hand stroking his hair.

She'd had him, well and good. She'd moved over him, taking, giving, and he'd forgotten his restraints, his rules of a lifetime. He curled her fragrant hair around his fist and brought it to his face. With practice they would learn to harmonize his withdrawal.

Emma nuzzled his chest, finding his nipple with her lips. She nibbled on him lightly, and he inhaled, aware that his body hardened for her. At least they would have this and the home she would make for them in her neat practical way. He would buy her books on entertaining, on domestic social skills of the wealthy, of recipes for the expensive palate— He groaned as her hips began rotating sweetly, drawing him deeper within her until he was fully sheathed—

Emma awoke to Sam's bewildered shout, to her body flying through space and the dream becoming reality.

Her body clenched as his hard one rolled her over, taking command, his seed pouring into her.

They lay still, heartbeat raging against heartbeat, lungs racing for air, the waves of pleasure receding in the tight embrace.

"Sam Taggart?" Emma asked shakily, aware of his mouth moving gently, reverently across hers.

"Mmm?" His hands roamed luxuriously over her beneath the warm cove of the blanket.

He seemed ill, his heart racing wildly, and he breathed as though he'd run uphill. Unable to lift his head, he draped over her in a pleasant weight.

Sunlight skimmed into the room from the window, gleaming on his shoulders. She lifted her head to look down the length of his body, saw the twin rise of his buttocks, and fell back to the pillow. "It is morning."

He nibbled on her shoulder. The sound of a man who had feasted well in luxury steeped his tone. "We're married."

"Sam? Someone brought breakfast. They saw us—" Alarmed and shamed, she struggled to sit up, but her hair was caught beneath his arm.

"I brought it." He ran his fingers over the swath of her hair covering his chest and slowly wrapped it around his hand, drawing her closer. He looked at her with amused slumberous eyes. "Emma, my dear wife, you have ruined me."

She tugged the sheet higher to her breast and looked away from his bare back—then looked again, shocked by the red marks of her nails. "Sam . . . I have hurt you?"

"Ruined me," he corrected with a wicked, lazy grin. "It will take me a minute to recover."

Emma closed her eyes, regretting how she had given in to her berserker tendencies. Now he lay sprawled beside her, a magnificent man, forever ruined and grinning because he did not know it. He would discover his ruination and then be angry with Emma, because she had wanted to marry him. "I am sorry, Sam Taggart."

"You should be. I lost sleep over the virgin at Amanda's. Lilly gave me the impression that I'd ruined the girl for the business." Sam drew her closer and placed her head upon his shoulder. He stroked her hair lightly, experimentally. "You're mine now."

Emma kept the sheet firmly between them. Sam

seemed unaware of their lack of clothing. "And you are mine. The sharing is equal."

He nuzzled her hair. "It's different with a man. He has to provide."

Emma wished she hadn't grabbed Sam's offer of marriage. Now he resented his responsibility as her husband. She lay very still in his arms. After a time he began to ease upward, drawing her with him until they sat side by side against the headboard, braced by pillows and covered by the quilt. "Please pass me the breakfast tray, Mrs. Taggart," Sam asked very formally.

Emma held very still. It was the first time she had heard her new name. She carefully lifted the tray and Sam took it from her, propping it on his lap. "I've always wanted to do this, sit up in bed and eat breakfast. It's a bit cold now because of your . . ."

He winked at her and grinned. "Because of your need of me, Emma."

Emma held the sheet to her chin, her eyes wide. "We cannot sit in bed and eat."

Sam sighed heavily and tore a strip of bacon to place in her mouth. His eyes darkened as he watched her chew. "We can, just this once. We're married now."

"Did you marry me to save me from Gilbert?" she asked suddenly. Sam would protect the ones closest to him, and he also feared losing her as a clerk. To give himself—to ruin himself for all time on their marriage night—was too much of a sacrifice.

He devoured the eggs and stuffed a buttered bit of bread into her mouth. "Yes—and because you suit me."

"But I am not the ideal wife. Is this a temporary position?"

Sam's face hardened. "Emma, don't."

She sipped the cooled coffee. "Why are you looking at me this way?"

His gaze took in her wildly disheveled hair and the sheet drawn tightly up to her chin. "I'm beginning to see why Harry remarried."

"I am sorry I ruined you," she cried out, and threw her arms around him. The motion upended the tray and sent it to the floor, dishes rolling in all directions.

With a delighted shout he caught her in his arms and drew her across his lap. "Sit there, and we'll try to remedy my ruination."

Because Sam seemed so boyishly happy, Emma smiled back, keeping the sheet tucked high against her chin. Then his big hand smoothed her breasts, drawing the sheet away, and his eyes darkened. She held her breath as he drew a line from her hot cheek to her throat to her collarbone. "You're so soft, Emma."

For once he did not shield his expression, and she saw the old wounds tear at him, the lonely uncertain boy. "You are what I want," she said firmly.

We have been married two nights and one day and have not yet left Tadpole Springs. Sam seems not to worry about tending to business. My new husband is perfect and sometimes plays like a boy, picking me up and tossing me on the bed, and we laugh. I adore him. He is a wonderful businessman, always reading and jotting down notes and thinking of ways to build the empire I know he will someday have. I cannot wait until Sam asks for my dowry, as this is the tradition of our women to make a happy home. Sam

Taggart is important to me, but so are the ways of my family. I am merely a simple woman who respects my heritage. I would bring what is a part of me to my marriage. Sam has not yet asked for my father's permission to marry me, and this too is important. Though some ways are new to me, a marriage without children I understand. I am certain that Sam will understand my need for my dowry and the tradition of my heart. Tonight we will camp on our way to Harry's. I will tell him then. E.

"What do you mean, I have to go after the dowry, Emma?" Sam carefully folded the newspaper he had been reading and removed his glasses. He was lucky that the last two nights with her had left him with enough sight to read. Tonight, with the clear night sky above them, he intended to hear that wild feminine cry burst from her as her body tightened and rippled beneath his. He had chosen to leave town later in the day; he wanted to spend a glorious night in his bride's willing arms under the stars.

He inhaled the night air, the fragrance of sweetgrass floating on it, mixed with pine and fir. The campfire burned low; Sam let his gaze linger on the neat picture his wife made, sitting on the bedroll and waiting for him in her voluminous nightgown and shawl. Tonight he intended to replace the dented token with a tiny gold cross, more fitting for a bride. They would finish the matter of the dowry, and then— "Emma, I asked you why I have to go after the dowry."

She carefully put away her scissors, the articles she had been snipping neatly into her basket, and folded the massacred newspaper. "You have said we will visit my parents, Sam Taggart. But while we are there, you must ask Papa for the dowry. It is the custom of the husband of the eldest daughter. Papa will not give it to you unless you ask. I already informed Harry of our marriage and asked him to send a pigeon to my papa, informing him that we would be coming and that now that we are married, I want my dowry. I said you would come ask for my hand."

"You what?" Sam clamped down his outrage, the elemental anger that Emma could arouse in him. In his lifetime he had asked for little, and it nettled him that his wife wanted him to bend his pride.

He struggled for control. As a businessman, he cared little for tradition, considering it lost time. As a new husband, his pride was dented—he could support his wife without her family's help. "I'll pay back Gilbert for his time, and I'm certain that Greta would like to have the dowry. You don't need it."

Emma sat very straight, her hands folded neatly in her lap. Her lack of a ring irritated him; the store was out of her size, and instead he had purchased the delicate cross as a temporary substitute. He picked up his boots and began polishing them.

An owl hooted, and coyotes howled up on the mountains. The moon passed through the trees. Emma was too quiet, studying her folded hands. She toyed with the lace edging of her nightgown sleeve. "It is the custom that a man wishing to marry a woman would talk with her father and ask his permission to marry. The men would agree upon the dowry before marriage, and the husband-to-be would compliment the father on how rich the dowry is and promise to take care of it. But we did not follow tradition, and a part of me feels as if we are living in sin. With it in our home I will feel truly married. It is a part of me and what I am. I can accept that you do not want children, but you must accept this of me."

She looked at him across the campfire. He didn't trust the set of her jaw. "Is the dowry more important than me, your husband?" he asked tightly.

Emma's mouth tightened. "You are angry now that I have said what is in my mind and in my heart. You are like most men, certain that their way is right and that a woman's wishes do not matter. I would be less of a woman if I did not hold to what made me as I am. I will be no less, or I cannot be your wife."

"I will not let my wife dictate to me, custom or not. I do not have time to deal with such—fancies." Sam stood and stretched, easing the taut muscles of his body, already aching for his wife. The flickering flames had cast light upon the full shape of her breasts; he could almost taste the sweet cinnamony flavor. He ripped away his clothing, scattering it as he walked to the bedroll and slid into it, beside his wife, who remained seated on top of the blankets. Her eyes had widened at his arousal . . . before she closed them, blushing furiously.

"Come to bed, Mrs. Taggart," Sam whispered, leaning to nuzzle her nape, his hand on her thigh.

Soon her hands would be touching him, experimenting. . . . He turned her to him, seeking her mouth, hungry for her. . . .

Heartbeats later, Sam stopped kissing Emma's immobile mouth and leaned back to study her. He wasn't

letting her get the upper hand in their marriage; he'd
seen men ruined by women's demands.

"You'll feel better when you have a ring on your finger," he said finally. The dowry was just one hurdle in
their marriage and a small one, Sam decided as Emma
settled down beside him.

Emma's soft bottom backed against his thigh, and she
wiggled, getting comfortable. He eased his thigh away,
because in another moment, he'd— He wouldn't force
her; he had little respect for men who used force on
their wives.

He dozed, and his hand, searching for Emma's warm
curves, found cold dew upon the meadow grass. He
grabbed his knife as he leaped to his feet— If anything
happened to her . . .

In the dawn filtering through the pines and the layers
of fog swirling around her, Emma—fully dressed in her
brown bonnet, dress, and practical boots—walked to
him, bearing a large brown-paper-wrapped parcel. She
averted her eyes from him as he walked toward her.
"Mr. Taggart, you have forgotten your clothes."

"And you, Mrs. Taggart, are wearing too many." He
studied the picture she made, her face pale in the mist,
her eyes luminous and green now, as green as the lush
grass in the mountain meadow. His body lurched at the
sight of her mouth, rosy and damp.

He was about to reach for her, to pick her up in his
arms and kiss her sweet mouth, when she firmly thrust
the package between them. "A gift for you, husband.
Please do not make me wait to see you open it, husband."

He tried a smile and tasted an endearment he'd heard

other men use. "Come back to bed . . . sweetheart.
We have plenty of time. I'll open it later."

She held the gift higher, and he slowly took it. He
stared at it, realizing that this was his first gift from a
woman.

Emma watched him as he slowly opened the package.
"Do you like it?" she asked finally when he had unwrapped the leather satchel.

Sam ran his hands over the smooth reddish-brown
leather, the big ornate S and T cut into the flap closing
it. Emma reached to unfasten the brass opening, and
inside were separate compartments for papers. "A businessman should have this—the clerk at the emporium
said so."

"I think . . . I have never seen anything so fine," he
said honestly, startled that his throat had tightened with
emotion. He ran his fingers over the elegant tooled initials, shaken by the emotions surging through him, ones
that he had kept tightly wrapped for years.

Emma beamed up at him. She reached suddenly for
his face and tugged his lips down to hers. "I knew you
would like it, Sam Taggart."

Her lips brushed his, and he reached for her, crushing
the satchel between them. He found her mouth, fused
his to her, and lost himself in her sweet taste. She
wrapped her arms around his neck, and he swung her
high against him, the satchel on her lap. He was two
steps from the bedroll when Emma stopped kissing him
and asked, "Sam Taggart, what are you doing?"

The mist swirled about them, settling damply in the
tendrils around her face, making them cling to her

cheek. He'd stepped into one of the dappled areas of light and now saw Emma's face clearly without the layers of mountain mist. "You've been crying."

Sam lowered her to her feet; she looked away from his naked body. He had never allowed himself the luxury of a temper. But now it rose in him, and he gripped her wrist. "It's still there, isn't it? That damn high pride that demands you get your way."

"I have no less pride than you." She tugged at her wrist, and when Sam jerked her closer, intending to prove that she needed him, that once she was in his arms, nothing meant—

Emma swung the satchel upward. The corner of the leather case hit his eye. He'd had more painful blows, but none that damaged his pride as much. "Red, you'd better watch that temper of yours," he finally managed after a full minute.

He angled his head away from her soothing hand; Emma had clearly shocked herself.

"Poor Sam," she murmured sadly. She dropped the satchel as though it had caused her to hit him. "A fighter would have escaped the blow. I am sorry you will have a black eye."

Sam didn't trust himself to say anything, then he tried to keep his yell soft. "Bed. Now."

Emma crossed her arms over her chest. "I dislike your tone. I refused to be bullied. When my dowry is with me, I will feel like I am married. Until then I cannot sleep with you, Sam Taggart."

He stared at her, this creature he had married. The mist swirled around her as she looked at him, the damp tendrils clinging to her nape. "Do not wear that whore token again, Emma. You're my wife."

"Yes," she agreed too easily, but the hard set of her mouth and the fiery green and brown shade of her eyes told him that Emma had agreed to nothing more.

Chapter Fifteen

Why can my new husband not see how important custom is to me, to make me feel that I am a true wife and not a woman living in sin? He looks so dark at me, and I cannot bear that he cannot accept this part of me, which is somehow more important than my body. My heart aches at the sight of Sam Taggart, my husband, but I will not sleep with him because then I would only be giving a shell of myself. A marriage of paper is not a marriage of hearts and minds, and our minds are traveling different paths. I will not be as my mother and let my husband bully me. I pray that with time Sam Taggart will understand my heart in this small thing, which is my honor. E.

At Harry's ranch pasture breeding had its disadvantages. The sight of Tenkiller mounting a mare in the meadow didn't help Sam's dark mood. He'd been married five days—two nights without Emma in his bed. His delectable bride was avoiding him.

He'd planned to wait her out until she returned to their bed, but each night she slept upon the floor. Little but his pride kept Sam from scooping her up and tossing her into bed. He had no doubt that the gang beneath Harry's roof would come to her rescue. He looked at Emma in the garden, hoeing the squash with Lilly.

Tenkiller continued mounting the mare, and Sam scowled so deeply, his head ached. Three days without Emma's soft ecstatic cries had taken their toll. He couldn't concentrate on what investments he wanted to develop or to trade and sell. He wouldn't beg for her attention; she'd have to come to him. He hadn't set the dowry between them.

Emma had given him a satchel, but not socks. Almost every man in the territory was wearing her hand-knitted socks, except her husband. He was wearing a black eye and a nasty mood.

He hadn't been prepared for the pain that went deeper than his sexual need of her.

He'd thought nothing could hurt him again, that he'd had everything walled from him, and that nothing could get too deep enough to wound him.

Thirty-five pigeons of all sizes, colors, and sexes watched Sam curiously. Sam shrugged as Leon, a bluegray tumbler who liked Sam, came to perch on his shoulder. He shrugged again, and Leon went into his tumbling act, then soared up and joined the rest of the circling pigeons.

Sam ignored Mary, who was running behind him into

the barn, her favorite hiding place from Beth. He locked his polished boots to the Big T's ranch yard. Emma had chosen to place a wedge between them, and she would have to come to her senses.

Tenkiller, finished with servicing the Appaloosa mare, shivered and pranced. Sam remembered a bit of shivering himself; he methodically rolled back the cuffs that Emma had neatly turned. Once he had her installed in a new house, she would be too busy, learning about giving dinner parties and balls, to worry about her dowry.

Beth came hurling toward him—a mass of blond curls topping a white dress and blue pinafore. At four years old Beth sometimes couldn't determine which tall Taggart she wanted. Since she couldn't see their faces from her height, she didn't care if she'd captured Sam instead of Harry, who was delighted with her. Beth grinned and hurled herself at Sam.

To protect his clothing and because he enjoyed Beth treating him like her favorite climbing tree, he lifted her into his arms. "Harry?" she asked, smoothing his face.

"Sam." He playfully nipped at her chubby finger as it touched her cheek.

The first time Beth had come running at him, he'd been lying in bed, willing Emma to come to him. Beth had peeped into the room, glanced at Emma sleeping soundly on the floor, and leaped over her, sprawling on Sam with a hushed giggle. "Harry, take me up to the sisters on the hill," she whispered with a grin, bouncing on his chest. "I picked flowers last night to take to them."

"Can't. I'm not Harry." But in the end he'd held her hand on the way to the knoll. The little girl's hand in his softened the past; it seemed right that the wilted flowers rested on the dewy grass, something that Feather would have liked. Somehow Sam had finished the expedition by rocking Beth on the front porch and telling her Swede's Paul Bunyan stories. Beth told him that Lilly said most men were no good, and she didn't trust anybody but Harry and Monty.

Another time Beth had stood between Harry and Sam, looking up at the tall men curiously. They'd said a few curt necessary words about racing horses and breeding good stock and were ready to part. Beth had taken each man's hand and had skipped along beside them as they walked. "Two Harrys. My two Harrys," she had singsonged.

Beth grinned at him now as he stood near the corral, her blond curls bouncing. "You look like Harry. You talk like Harry."

"I'm not Harry."

Beth had ignored Sam's dress shirt and trousers and polished boots; Harry always wore patched clothing, well washed and pressed.

Beth wrapped her arms around Sam's neck and hugged him tightly. She kissed his cheek, and Sam blinked, startled by the sweet novelty. "Harry hugs. He picks me up and he hugs me. But every time I want to hug you, I have to climb up you. It's a long way up here. Why don't you hug and laugh like Harry? Why don't you like Emma's pigeons? She said you didn't, but I like them. Leon likes you. I kissed you. Why didn't you kiss me back? Where's Mary?"

"In the barn." Beth's quick list of questions had Sam off balance, and he settled for Mary, a safer subject.

Mary hadn't stopped glaring at Sam from the moment they arrived. She accused him of bringing her torturer back to the Big T. Lilly couldn't read and didn't present a problem, other than her pesky little sister. But Emma had given Mary a primer, and Harry had made her listen to Emma's teaching.

Sam found himself cuddling Beth. He wondered if all females grew up to be as determined as Emma. He braced himself and gave Beth a brief, experimental kiss on her cheek. She grinned at him, kissed him, and shrugged free of the hug that Sam was just beginning to enjoy; it was small comfort when his new wife avoided him. He lowered Beth to the ground and looked across the garden to where Emma stood, hoe in hand, watching him.

Their eyes locked in the late July sunlight. Sam placed his hands on his hips and waited for her to walk to him, to tell him that she had been irrational about claiming the dowry.

The pigeons swooped and circled the ranch yard, and Emma dropped the hoe and placed her hands on her waist, facing Sam.

Behind Sam, Monty chuckled. "You've picked a strong woman, son. You'd better back up fast and sweet."

"Not likely."

"You won't hurt her, will you? If this keeps up—her dodging you, and you glaring at her—one of you might get angry enough to take a swing. It better not be you. She says you're not a fighter, but she's mighty proud of you as a businessman anyway."

Sam snorted in disgust and refused to glance at

Tenkiller, who was preparing to mount another mare. Sam avoided the pigeon male chasing the female back to the nest; he tried to ignore the mass of tumbling feathers and the squawking of the rooster and hen at his feet.

"The Calhoun boys, all six brothers, are wanting wives. They came around here after you and Emma left, one at a time, trying to get a glimpse of her. Zeb said that he'd heard Emma was prime enough for him to make her a widow. That set Greta off, and poor Lilly-Belle had to clean up the mess Greta made, howling and turning things over like a Tasmanian devil. Lilly-Belle is an angel. I sure wish you hadn't a brought Greta here, Sam," Monty muttered. "There ain't a peckerwood with any sense that would take her. Beats me how Emma can be Greta's sister."

"I wouldn't mind meeting those Calhoun brothers," Sam stated softly.

Monty guffawed. "Or breaking a few mustangs? Harry used to do that same thing when he was all het about one of his women and she wasn't cowing down to him."

"I'm not Harry," Sam answered automatically, his mouth drying as Emma bent over to pluck a weed.

Tomorrow Sam says we will go to my father, and he will ask for my hand, as is the custom. My heart is filled, and I adore him more now than ever. He has thought the problem through like he thinks of his businesses—in a methodical way. He will do what is best for us. I pray my father is in a good mood, because Sam is taking this first step to make us one

family. I must have my family, and I must have my
husband. Though I did not lie with Sam in the mar-
riage bed, I could not stop myself from leaping upon
him and taking him down in the field. We came to-
gether like fire and then the softer time, with Sam
stroking my hair. While he has great businesses to
tend to, he takes time to make this visit and tend
what is important to me. E.

"You are not welcome here." Joseph Recht crossed
his arms over his chest and watched Sam and Emma
dismount.

The first of August lay hot on the fields, and Sam
hoped the visit would settle his wife. They were too uneasy with each other to camp and had ridden all night.
For Emma's sake, Sam intended to try to make peace
with her father. He wanted her to keep her pride, but he
had his own to keep, too.

Joseph wasn't ready to oblige; clearly his pride was
ruffled. "Magda, get back here," he ordered as Magda
rushed off the porch to hug Emma.

"Why can't you be like Harry?" Magda cried, embrac-
ing her daughter. "Soon we will not have any children."

One glance at Emma's rigid pale face, and the tears
shimmering in her eyes swept away Sam's dark mood. A
new husband, bringing his wife home to her parents for
the first time, should have held her in his arms the night
before. Then Emma leaned slightly against Sam, her
fingers lacing with his, and Sam stiffened—aware that
she needed him now and that he would not fail her.

Fritzi's pigeons circled the clear sky, and Gilbert lumbered from the field, leaving the plowing mules standing in harness.

"You look so pretty . . . blushing. How is Greta?" Magda whispered to Emma as she stroked her hair, her cheeks.

Emma's fingers tightened on Sam's. "She wouldn't come. . . . She's afraid Papa will keep her here."

"Yes, that is true. He would like to keep you, too. How is Harry? Is he a dancer?" Magda asked.

"Harry is wonderful."

Magda smiled dreamily. "Yes. Mary's notes to Fritzi are filled with how nice her papa is."

"Magda!" Joseph glared at his wife, and she hurried back to his side, muttering to him in German.

"What's she saying?" Sam asked Emma, surprised at Magda's sharp, scolding tone with Joseph.

"She said that he was never good at dancing the polka and that I am his daughter, no matter if I married without his permission . . . that he is not his father in the old country, and that we are in a new land." Emma looked up at Sam and the sunlight glittered on her damp lashes. "He says I cannot come home to visit. He is very angry that you did not ask his permission. I cannot have his blessing or the dowry."

"You don't need it." Because Emma looked as though she would break, Sam placed his arm around her, drawing her close to him. She eased away from him, but the proud look she shot him told him it mattered that he cared.

Sam locked his boots to the ranch yard, stunned by his immediate impulse to protect Emma and by her dismissal of him. She had no less pride than he, and he

admired her—she stood there, head up, her will clash-
ing with her father's. "I have chosen this man, Papa. I
ask that you respect my choice. Sam Taggart is a good
man, and he is all that I could want in a husband. Do
not make me choose between you and him, I ask of you.
You are dear to me, but Sam is my husband. He knows
how I love you, and we come here to be a family. I will
not ask for your blessing, because clearly you will not
give it."

Joseph crossed his arms over his chest, glowering at
her. "The man asks the blessings of the father," he reminded her.

"America is a new land with new customs. But that
does not mean the old ones are not dear to me. Sam
allows me to speak for myself—that is why I cherish him
as my husband. You know what he does, Papa? All day
he deals with business, to make good money, and yet he
is proud of me, of my mind, and of my sock business,
which is so small in comparison. He provides for his
family, and he listens to me. Look at me, Papa. I am a
businesswoman and a wife. Yet I am your daughter. I
honor you and the old ways, and that is why I want us to
be a family. Sam Taggart is a man who learns new ways.
Can you not learn, too?"

Sam swallowed the wadding of emotion tightening his
throat. He cared, despite the hollow aching pit inside
him. Emma had reached inside him to touch something
he'd discarded. He wasn't certain he liked the invasion.
He was certain that Joseph Recht wasn't in a listening
mood and that Emma's emotions could not tolerate
more pain. "Emma, I think we should go."

Gilbert loomed beside them. "Shame. I knew you

would be bad with Sam Taggart when I saw you laying with him in the bushes. Now the dowry is mine."

Emma turned white. She slowly rounded on the farmhand. "I was *not* bad!"

"We're married." Sam felt the snarl coming out of him and the raw anger. He took a step toward Gilbert, only to find Emma firmly placed between them. If Emma's hand had not been locked with his, he would have— He struggled to remember that he was civilized and not a violent man.

"Leave her alone!" Fritzi used his crutch to make his way to Emma.

"Shoo, pigeon boy," Gilbert ordered, and easily brushed Fritzi aside. The boy tumbled awkwardly to the ground. Magda ran to him; Joseph grimaced at the sight of his boy, unable to rise easily.

Gilbert glared at Joseph. "You do not see Sam Taggart defending Emma, though she has captured him. He has brought her home to leave her because she is a berserker. But first I will hurt him—"

Before Sam could move toward Gilbert, Emma grabbed the workman's shirt with one fist. With her other hand she reached into her pocket and extracted a handkerchief. Then, using it, she pulled the hair protruding from his nose. Gilbert let out a painful shout and hopped around the ranch yard, holding his injured nose; Emma calmly walked to the watering trough to wash her hands. She walked back to Sam, her head averted. She was close to crying, despite her pride. "There. I think that turned out nicely. I am ready to go home now, husband."

Sam nodded but kept his eyes locked with Joseph's furious ones. "I will be back."

"Berserker! Nose-hair puller!" Gilbert bellowed, mopping the tears from his eyes. "I would not want you for a wife! Neither does he. . . . That is why Sam Taggart brought you here—to see if Joseph would take you back."

Emma looked at Sam and paled. "Yes?" she whispered uncertainly.

"No. I'm keeping you." He grabbed her wrist and pulled her to him, wrapping his arm around her. No one was taking her away from him.

Sam had helped Fritzi to his feet, and Emma kissed her brother, hugging him despite his efforts to get away. "I am taking good care of your pigeons. You should see them—there are so many now. Sam will not mind if you sell them. He says we have too many, eating up his profit. You come to the Big T when you can and bring Mama. Harry is a nice man. Sam treats me well. I am happy."

Sam thought she didn't sound happy on the long ride back to the Big T. She was too quiet, her face pale. Her single sob tore through him like a steel-tipped arrow.

"I would like it if you would dance with my mother," she said finally that night as they camped. Her knitting needles flashed quickly in the firelight.

Unaccustomed to dealing with anyone's emotions but his own, Sam ached for her. He placed aside his boots and polishing rag. "Emma, we'll deal with this."

"My heart is breaking," she said simply, a tear gleaming in the firelight as it rolled down her cheek. She placed her needles aside and leaned back wearily against the saddle.

Sam's heart was tearing, and he realized that she was frightening him. He had to do something to comfort her. He eased down to the blanket she sat upon and lifted her onto his lap. "I'll polka with your mother the first chance I get. How's that?"

"You do not know how to polka, Sam. You have said you have no time to dance."

Sam decided not to tell Emma about high society parties, waltzing until dawn. When he was a teenager, there was a Scots-Irish girl, full bodied and strong, who loved to dance the Bonnie Dundee with him. Emma needed to give him something, and he decided it was wiser to take than to refuse. "You'll teach me. Maybe a schottische, too." He bent to look at the soft smile on her lips. "Just like you can teach me to knit."

Emma leaned back against him with a sigh. "You are like Papa. Good beneath and hard on top. Like bread that has been poorly baked."

The image of being a poorly baked loaf of bread haunted Sam as Emma folded his hands around the knitting needles and taught him how to knit. Only the soft movements of her hands and the scent of her hair kept him from laying her down and kissing her. After a time they gave up knitting, and Sam held her on his lap, their hands joined. "I would like it if you held me tonight, husband," Emma said quietly, and turned her soft mouth to his.

Sam gently returned her light kiss and knew that he would not press Emma tonight; she had lost too much. When she was lying spooned to his chest and lap, her bottom nestling against his hardness, he cursed his gallantry and listened to her worry about Fritzi's pride, her father's inability to understand emotions, her mother's desire to polka and hold quilting parties, and . . . "My mother is still a girl in many ways. She loves Papa, but she wants him to be romantic. She wants a valentine card from him before she dies, and I fear her wish is hopeless. Papa will never be romantic, Sam Taggart. He thinks it is foolish and a waste of time."

She wiggled slightly, settling deeper against Sam. He realized he'd begun to sweat, despite the cool summer night. "Lilly has such harsh ideas about men. She's worked too hard her entire life, a young girl raising a little sister. I would like to see her happy. And then Greta—"

Sam eased his hand to Emma's breast. If he had to listen to Greta's problems, he wanted the comfort of Emma's breast. He concentrated on the soft shape while Emma worried about how people misunderstood Greta.

When Emma was finally quiet, Sam leaned down to kiss her throat, his body aching for hers. "Emma? Do you think we could concentrate on us . . . ?"

With a sigh, she turned to him. He bent to kiss her and found her sleeping deeply.

My husband said he is keeping me. This should be all a wife needs. But I am selfish and greedy. I want for all of us to be a family. I respect Sam because he has tried. He is angry with me. I see it in his eyes. E.

While Sam hitched the wire around another X-support, Harry scanned the stream winding through the Big T. Sam pulled off his leather gloves. He looked at his father. "You've changed. Years ago, you would have gone after Tex for blasting the Dancing Miranda to change its course."

A shared look said they both remembered the day of Harry's revenge. Harry's expression hardened, and he looked off into the mountains. "You remind me of Feather, boy. Had eyes that said everything, and she didn't have to open her mouth. Reckon she wouldn't have liked what I did that day either."

"I don't want to talk about my mother or your wives—" Sam found Emma in the ranch yard below the knoll and inhaled the hot August wind, hoping to catch her scent.

"We didn't need a preacher to tell us we were married, boy . . . not me and Feather," Harry stated softly, taking a tiny leather-wrapped packet from his pocket. He opened it with reverence, until a small circle of gold gleamed in the Montana sun. "You might remember this. I saved it for your woman. From the tears in her eyes, she's needing it. You two have hit a rough spot, I'd say, and you've just found out that she's got a mulish streak, like all women do. Take it. Things like that—her dowry and such—mean a heap to womenfolk."

Harry sucked in air and shook his head. "Sometimes the old temper comes upon me, but you remind me of those days, the heat riding you and old wounds lodged deep."

Sam looked at Harry. The nightmare flashed in his mind: men begging for mercy . . . Harry's bloody knife flashing in the sun. Sam's lifetime promise was to stay away from violence, to choose a different path from his father. Sam fought only when his life was threatened, to survive. "I'm not anything like you."

"You are. I've seen the black fire in your eyes, the way a man looks when he's done things to live that shame most men. . . ." Harry cleared his throat. "I'm sorry about that, boy. That I didn't give you what you needed as a pup. But I promised Emma I'd tell you this, and by God, I will—poor little thing cried when I told her how it came to be between you and me—how it came to be that I gave Feather this ring and what it meant—"

Sam didn't want to hear about his mother and Harry; he swung up on Kloshe. "I'll have a talk with Murdock about blasting up high on the mountain and trying to change the course of the Dancing Miranda."

Harry's hand shot out to grip the mare's bridle. Tears shimmered in his eyes, skimming his craggy cheek to drip to his shirt.

Something kept Sam from jerking Kloshe away . . . maybe it was the tether to when he was a boy and loved big tough Harry Taggart. "Say it, and then don't talk about it again."

"You're a hard case, boy, carrying all those scars inside you." Harry's rough hand swept across his face; suddenly he looked old, burdened by the past. But Harry squared his shoulders and said, "Emma says you need to hear this . . . that you're special to me, and how I carry you and your mother in my heart. She's a good woman, your Emma—even when she's plenty riled, like now. You were what I did right, boy. Times were bad back then, too dangerous to take your mother out of this peaceful valley. The traveling preachers wouldn't marry us because of the wars, scalps, and lives taken on both sides. After you were born—"

Harry dropped Kloshe's reins and turned away, looking toward the knoll with the three women's graves. "I never told this to anyone but Emma. When she cried, somehow I felt she was mourning Feather, too, and maybe what's riding you. Feather and me . . . we made our own ceremony up on the mountain, under God's stars and moon and good as any written paper. You lay there between us on the blanket, nothing but a fat little nubbin with a mop of black hair . . . a part of her and a part of me. I put the ring on her finger, and we said our vows under the big round moon."

He turned suddenly and flipped the ring in a high shining arc to Sam. "Take it. Your woman should be wearing a ring. Tex and every other manjack in the countryside are out to get her. I'd hate to go on the warpath at my age, with this poor old foot and Mary nagging after me, but I would . . . for Emma."

Sam caught the gleaming band in his palm, and Harry turned his back slowly on his son, looking up at the mountains. He pivoted, the wind catching his neatly cut, curling hair. He braced his weight on the big staff at his side, his shoulders slumped with age. The wind carried his voice back to Sam— "If you're on your way to pow-wow with Murdock, you'll need to know that I've deeded this place to you. It's yours. When I saw Emma and you look at each other hungrylike, I thought Feather might like it fine if your little ones were brought up here where she could hear them and watch them play."

"I don't want the ranch, and I'm not having . . . little ones." The impact of his father's emotions slammed into Sam, sending his own churning bitterly.

Harry's steel gray eyes flashed with humor. "You picked the wrong woman then, boy. Because if ever I saw a woman who looked like a natural mama, it's Emma. There's nothing prettier than seeing your woman suckling your own baby-child."

For an instant the image stunned Sam, melting him.

Then Harry shrugged and turned back to watching the mountains; Sam recognized the way Harry acted when he was restless for the old ways.

Sam eased Kloshe closer to Harry and studied the hard set of his father's face. He had seen that look before, when an old mountain man had returned to the high country to die. The tight emotion in Sam's heart startled him; after years of hating his father, he wasn't prepared to lose him. "Harry, don't go to the mountains. Not while I'm gone."

Harry nodded but didn't turn away from the mountains. "Sometimes I think I hear them call me—the men I've known and buried. Sometimes I think I belong more to them than to this world—that men like me were dead before we were born, our time gone as a new dawn moves on. But I won't go just yet . . . because of the women. Monty and Shen-Yu wouldn't be much good in a fracas. You go do what you have to do. I'll stay here until you don't need me."

Today, after building a fence to keep Tenkiller and other ranchers' mares safe, Sam rode to visit Tex. He will not speak of what was said, but he has another bruise to match the one I gave him. I suspect that

Tenkiller may have bucked, causing Sam to fall. Oh, I am so sorry for hurting him. It is sundown now, and Sam is leaving on business before bedtime, and I want to cry, but I will not. He is not taking me, his wife and his clerk. He makes me so angry that he does not understand what is dear to me, my dowry and tradition, and I fear for him at the same time. It seems to me that life is a quilt, with many pieces to be fashioned together as a whole design. The pieces would be my family, Sam's family, and my husband and me. I thought this was so, but now I wonder. I am losing him. My heart hurts so. E.

Sam slammed the door behind him. His stare accused Emma, and she flushed, realizing that she had driven him from his home. She closed her journal and fought tears. He wore the black eye she had given him, when she swung the satchel at him, and a bruise along his jaw. His dark look at her stopped her from touching him.

Emma hurried after Sam and braced herself from him as he turned in their bedroom. She closed the door and placed her hands on his chest.

"I am leaving," he said too quietly. "Unless you give me a reason I should stay the night."

"But—"

His dark look stopped her. He caught her close to him with one arm and dropped the door latch closed with his other hand. Emma backed up against the wall, and he towered over her, his hands braced flat at her head. "It's been a long day, Mrs. Taggart. Are you coming to bed with me now, or not?"

"Sam Taggart—" She stopped as his fingers prowled

through the braids on her head and loosened them.
Thick and heavy, they uncoiled down her bodice. Sam's
black eyes followed his fingertip over the braid to the
crest of her breast.

"You're not good at this game, Emma." He unwound
the ribbons binding her braids and eased his hands
through her hair. "Look at you, Mrs. Taggart. One
touch, and you're ready for me . . . your eyes get all
soft like the mountain meadow, little gold flecks darkening . . . your breath is uneven as if it's a deer, running
too fast for you to catch it."

Emma squeezed her eyes closed, her heart racing at
the sight of Sam's dark expression, the scent of him
close to her. She shook when he removed her grandmother's brooch and began to unbutton her bodice,
bending to kiss the skin he had exposed.

"I am sorry I have hurt you, husband," she whispered
unevenly, nuzzling Sam's crisp black hair.

He stopped, his hard face resting against her throat.
"You want me, Emma. Don't deny it."

Sam took her trembling hand and placed a gold band
on her third finger. Sadness and regret flashed in his
expression as he studied the ring. "This was my
mother's. It will have to do, until—"

Emma glanced at the ring, tears welling in her eyes.
She knew what his mother meant to him and how deep
inside he mourned her still . . . how the terror of seeing Harry go mad with grief had shaped Sam's young
life . . . how the boy had resented Harry's new wife.
Emma wished she could make all that go away . . .
that Sam would talk to her, share his life from that mo-

ment on with her. She knew so little about the deep currents swirling through him.

She stood on tiptoe to brush a kiss on his chin. . . . He held very still, letting her rest against him. The tension in him quivered, his body shuddered, his muscles rigid around her. She hoped that she could ease his storms and keep him safe. She wrapped her arms around him, mooring him to her.

"Does this mean . . ." Sam's uneven, deep voice stirred the hair along her cheek. His hands opened on her breasts and caressed them. She gave herself to the gentleness within him, the reverence with which he touched her, until he asked, "Does this mean that you've come to your senses, Mrs. Taggart?"

"Sam Taggart . . . open this door! I want to talk with you about a husband for me and the ones on your list and how much money and holdings they have!" Greta's demanding voice and the knocking at the other side of the door caused Emma to jump away from Sam.

He hauled her back and tossed her on the bed, following her down. "She'll go away," he murmured, hurriedly drawing up Emma's skirt.

Sam was shaking, his face hot against her throat. She pushed his hand away, her drawers tearing. Sam moved violently, his body bearing down on her, and the bed crashed to the floor.

"What are you doing in there?" Greta demanded shrilly. "Are you bothering my sister again?"

Sam's groan came low and slow and uneven. "Let me have you, Emma," he whispered urgently against her lips, biting her bottom one.

"I cannot . . . ," she whispered back desperately as

Sam's hand found and began to caress her intimately, the warmth flooding through her. She gripped his arms, her body flowing, rippling beneath his against her control.

"Emma—" Sam's urgent whisper matched her desperation to hold him.

"Take me with you," she whispered, holding his face and, for once, not caring if she mussed his gentleman's hair part.

"Greta . . . I'll talk with you in the morning," Sam called after a quick kiss.

"No, now. You're leaving, and I want to know what you are doing about finding me a husband. I think we should have a party—my party, not Emma's—and invite all the bachelors in the Territory."

Harry and Monty's guffaws and Mary's hoots were loud enough that Sam and Emma could hear them. Lilly tried to shush them. Greta's voice rose, and glass broke.

"They are fighting. I have to go to her." Emma pushed slightly at Sam's chest and found his heated skin. She traced the smooth rippling of cords and the flat nipple dancing as he moved. She bent to lick it, and his tall body contracted and shuddered. He lay still for a heartbeat, then in the next minute lurched to his feet and began straightening his clothes.

His dark determined expression frightened Emma. She scrambled to her feet and buttoned her bodice. His icy look stopped her. "It's either those damn pigeons taking your time, or Greta needing something, or the rest of them— I've grown to hate those pigeons, Emma . . . the way you hold them, talk to them . . . a man can only stand so much. You make certain that you don't talk to the Calhoun boys or Tex or any of the men that come calling. I'm going to Deer Lodge—"

"Tell me about the women you've known." Emma slapped her hand over her mouth. She hadn't wanted to ask Sam, not the intimate details, because she didn't want to think of another woman's hands on Sam's lean powerful body.

Sam wrapped his money belt around his waist and buttoned his shirt, tucking it in. "I wondered when that would come about. . . . I've known women. I was engaged to a lady, Emma. She came from the best family, and her father hired me to rout out the skimmers working for him."

His gaze slid down to her boots and then back up to her wildly rippling hair, jarring her with its flashfire intensity. "But I married you, Red."

Chapter Sixteen

My husband is gone. It has only been hours, and I miss Sam horribly. He was so angry. I wonder if it is true, what has been told to me by my grandmother, that the dowry will make a happy true marriage. I cannot bear Sam Taggart's anger, and yet I cannot leave behind what is mine. My father's blessings are important to my heart, my soul. I ask that Sam know these things and that he give me things dear to his heart. I pray that as in business, our hearts will find a way to overcome this burden. I believe with all my heart that a healing time will ease our pain. I believe the quilt pieces of our families can be sewn together. E.

The next morning, Emma could not bear that any of the people she loved could think Sam had killed the pigeons littering the ground. She brushed the tears from her eyes and mourned the small pitiful bodies.

"Sam didn't kill those birds," Harry said, bending

painfully to study the tracks around the pigeons. "Whoever did it rode his boots to the outside and had fancy Mex spurs. See that? Where one foot goes deeper than the other? He was wearing a heavy sidearm. His knife was dull, tearing more than cutting. My boy keeps his blade sharp, and he doesn't pack a gun," Harry stated with pride. "Sam is like the oldsters, ones who like quiet."

Emma placed her hand to her throat. "Sam did not do this," she repeated.

Greta held a handkerchief over her nose. "This is a foul sight for a lady to see before breakfast. I don't know how I can eat. See what happens to men who marry Emma? She drives them to become insane butchers."

Monty looked at Harry. "Knife work," he said finally, then began to mutter about the sins of the fathers.

Harry's neck turned red. He glowered at Monty, then turned from the women. "Ah, hell, Monty. My boy didn't do it."

Like a feather floating through the blue Montana sky, a lone pigeon circled the ranch. The moment Lulu landed, Emma hurried to remove the message band and read it aloud. "Fritzi's entire coop was demolished last night, except for Lulu. He'd kept her in his room. He wants to know if I'll send him pairs to begin another flock."

"My boy couldn't be in two places at the same time," Harry stated firmly.

Emma crushed the note to her chest. Fritzi's loss was double, because there were no birds to send him.

Harry tracked the boot marks a distance away from

the coop. "He rode in close, traveling fast, and came up bold as you please. Left a path in the dew leading toward the New Alamo. Broke a path right through the sunflowers."

"If Dog would have been here, he'd would have set up a howl," Monty muttered.

"How many times do I have to tell you, Monty? Best forget about Dog. You find something good once, and you may not have it again." Harry wasn't talking about Dog, he was talking about his son. Emma touched his cheek and found it damp; she saw the pain in his gray eyes. "I'm a worn-out old man, or I'd track that son of a . . . I'd follow those tracks. . . . I'm not what I used to be, the old fight is gone—a shell of what I was. I'd make a mess of it now, if I were to tangle with the outlaws. I have promised never to draw my blade again in anger."

"Sam Taggart is not a bird killer. He is not even a fighter," Emma stated furiously. She didn't like how Harry looked at the mountains, as if little kept him to the Big T. "And Harry, you are not worn out. You are simply healing, a natural resting time. You'll be like yourself in no time at all."

Mary's jaw went out, reminding Emma of Sam's stubborn look. "You made Sam fiercesome mad, Emma. I never liked you anyway."

Emma swung to Mary. "I have always liked you. You are a berserker like me, ready to fight for what you believe. Sam could not do such a thing. He is a businessman."

Monty continued muttering, "Hell, he's just like Harry . . . same thing. . . ."

"Men" was all that Lilly said, as if the word explained all the wrong in the world. "Women take what they can, make do, and fashion a life. Men tear it down."

"Men are no damn good," Beth said, repeating what Lilly had often said.

Emma placed her finger on Beth's lips. "Shh. Harry is good, isn't he? Doesn't he make you toys and tell you stories?"

"Sam doesn't. He doesn't say much." Beth's lip went out stubbornly. "He just looks at me like he doesn't know what to do with me. Sometimes I think I scare him. It's always Harry who comes in my room and hunts under my bed for bears. Then he tells me a story about the old days."

Emma thought of what Sam could tell her and did not; he hoarded a part of himself, tucked safely away. "Sam is storing up his stories, and when he gets ready, he'll be just like Harry, telling the most wonderful stories you ever heard. He's just waiting because he hasn't decided which is his best story, and that's the one he wants to tell you first. It is an important matter, which story to tell first."

Lilly hesitated, then nodded. "Beth, you listen to Emma. Sometimes I get things messed up. I don't want you growing up with bad thoughts about every man. I don't know about Sam, but I like Harry. He's the best man I know," she added firmly, and turned to Harry. "I said it, and I mean it. I'd be comfortable with the idea of having you as my man. And Emma's right, Harry Taggart. You're just having a bad spell. You'll be fine, and when you're feeling up to it, I expect you to come courting me."

"You're nothing but a girl, a snot-nosed little girl," Harry finally managed to sputter.

"Honey, I am all woman and older than my years by a long shot," Lilly returned with a cheeky grin. "You just get to feeling better." She sent a meaningful look at Mary. "He's the best man I know. I'll treat him good."

Emma could not continue the day as if nothing had happened. She had to do something.

"I am going to find who killed the pigeons. It was not my Sam Taggart." Emma ran to the meadow, hitched up her skirts, and swung up on Woden's bare back. She urged him to follow the killer's path through the field's dew.

I pray that my husband is safe and that his business is going as he wishes. Today I went to find the pigeons' killer, and the trail led to the New Alamo. Tex is nice, but he doesn't want me to go home. I will clean his house instead, for I am a plain woman who cannot sit idle, and our neighbor does need a woman to take charge of his house. My husband, where are you? Please return to me, or I will have to show my wild side and come for you. This I would do, dress like a man and ride to find you. E.

A small starving puppy stood, all four legs braced, in the middle of the road leading to the Big T. Kloshe balked, and the puppy yipped wildly, clearly defending his territory.

Sam braced his forearm across the saddle and studied the puppy that barred his way to the Big T and Emma. In the three days he'd been gone, he had bought shares in more logging and mining operations, but he'd spent most of his time thinking about Emma. While the puppy barked, his bony sides heaving with each sharp rap, Sam thought about how he needed a respectable wife in a town home—away from the influences of Harry and his gang. Joseph Recht was going to make things easy in that respect. Still, arguing about Emma's feelings and wishes wasn't something that came easy to Sam; he hoped that time would soften Joseph's stance and that he'd be sensible about Emma wanting her family to be whole. "That's all I need, is to be adopted into the Rechts', like Emma wants."

Sam fingered Emma's small gold cross, tucked in his vest. It would look proper on a high lace collar . . . but not as appealing as the whore's token that she'd worn around her neck.

He tossed a slice of roast beef to the puppy, who quickly devoured it before starting to yap again. There was something oddly familiar about that puppy—prickly, and making certain that Sam knew he wasn't liked. Sam reached for his canteen and swung down from Kloshe. He poured water into his hand and watched the puppy waver, undecided about drinking from a human hand. When he finally gave way to thirst, Sam reached to pet the puppy's shaggy head and was met with a snarl. "You remind me of Mary," Sam said. "She's just as sweet."

The dog continued to yap as Sam mounted and tossed another meat scrap to the dirt. While the puppy devoured it, Sam eased Kloshe around him. He gave a little whistle, and the puppy's ears picked up. Sam tossed another scrap to the ground.

By the time Sam reached the Big T, he was out of scraps. The puppy was yapping angrily a short distance behind him.

The pigeons weren't flying overhead, and the little cow stood alone in the pasture. Strips of meat were hung over a rack, a slow smoke rising from the coals. Smoke plumed out of the smoke house, and a black soap kettle had recently been used. The red cow's hide was stretched on a drying rack, flies buzzing around a stack of hooves and bones a distance from the house.

Tenkiller was in the field, mounting a mare. The primitive sight gripped Sam's taut body, locking it in pain. Once he'd installed Emma in a house and in his bed, he'd be able to get his mind back on business. Sometime in the night Sam had decided that he wanted to make love to Emma more than he wanted to bargain for a new Diebolt extra-heavy, black and gilt safe.

In a rash moment, the first night without Emma, he'd decided to rid himself of his tension with a steamy welcoming blond widow. He'd wanted to prove that his need of Emma went no further than the ridding of his needs. It was then that he'd discovered Emma had unmanned him for any other woman.

Sam intended to reclaim his wife, his manhood, and his dream of an empire.

He heard the shot whistle by him and recognized the sound of the small-caliber rifle. "Mary!"

He swung from Kloshe and walked behind the mare, using her for protection. When he was within a few feet of the porch, he dodged the next shot and leaped onto the porch, pushing open the door with his shoulder.

Mary was innocently sitting on the floor with Beth,

playing with her kittens and glowering at him. Harry, Monty, and Lilly were playing cards, and Shen-Yu was meditating by his burning jasmine incense.

"Nice shot, Mary. How's the bosom-growing business?" Sam asked, advancing on her. He paused to grip her rifle, leaning against the wall; he smelled the barrel and found it still rank and smoking. He ripped off his coat and began to roll up his sleeves. "How do you want it? Because your backside is getting blistered this time for sure."

"I wouldn't put it past you to torture an innocent sweet girl. You're evil to the core, Sam, and a pigeon killer to boot. Emma said ladies always say their prayers, and they don't talk about bosom growing," Mary said, hugging Beth for protection as Sam came toward her. "What's that yapping outside?"

"Something that reminded me of you." Sam stopped in midstep when Harry, Monty, and Lilly stiffly ignored him. The hair on the back of his neck lifted slightly, as it did when trouble was nearby. Sam searched the shadows and found no sign of his wife. The senses he'd trusted all his life prickled with warning. He forced himself to breathe slowly as Mary ran out of the house. He inhaled the air and found Emma's scent weak, replaced by the smell of cooked beef. "Where's Emma?"

With a cry, Beth launched herself from the corner, ran to Sam, and bit his thigh.

Sam painfully extracted the little girl, who was usually sweet and loving. He held her up by the back of her dress and avoided her small pummeling fists. He looked at Greta, who was stirring a pot on the stove. Strangely, his sister-in-law offered the only hope of understanding what was amiss on the Big T. Whatever Greta's faults were, she never avoided telling the truth and she never softened it.

Sam released Beth slowly, warily. As he rubbed his injured thigh, he watched her to make certain she wouldn't bite him again. He pushed down the panic he'd begun to feel and strained to keep his tone calm. "Greta, where is Emma?"

Greta waved her hand airily. "Berserking. I'll be lucky if she doesn't ruin my chances with Tex."

"She's been gone to the Murdock place for the past three days," Harry said too softly. "I was giving you one more day, and then I was going after her. Murdock is soft on her. He won't hurt her."

"What I need is mountain oysters," Greta murmured thoughtfully as she stirred the chili. "All cowmen seem to like them, and Tex is a cowman. All I need are the gelded parts of a male animal. Since we don't have calves . . . I suppose any animal of the male persuasion would do."

Harry leveled a look at Sam. "That's another reason I didn't go after Emma. Tenkiller wouldn't be able to go about his business if that woman had her way."

Sam retraced the whole scene since his arrival and asked carefully, "What's this about pigeon killing?"

"The pigeons are dead, and so is the red cow. Everyone but Emma and me thought you might have killed them. She ran off to save your honor," Harry stated after a moment. "You'd better take Tenkiller with you," he suggested wearily.

*   *   *

The New Alamo spread out at the base of the same
mountains as the Big T. As Sam rode past the pile of
rocks that marked the Murdock ranch, he pushed down
the fear that Emma could be dead or misused and clung
to the thought that she was alive.

Sam realized from the creaking noises of his tooled
saddle horn that he had been gripping it with all of his
strength. If Tex had hurt Emma—touched her— The big
church bell in the top of an adobe brick tower rang a
warning; Sam knew that he'd been seen.

Sam angled Tenkiller down the rocky incline and
searched for Emma. She was in the back yard directing
six drovers. She wore a floppy straw bonnet to protect
her from the sun and heat and occasionally stopped
hanging clothes to hurry to the garden. The five drovers
hoeing corn watched her in dread. She took the hoe
from one, chopped around a plant, and handed it back
to him after the lesson. The sixth cowman stood impatiently at the clothesline, holding a big straw basket. All
of the men wore gun belts, bandolier-style. Despite the
heat the man holding the clothes basket wore fancy
woolly chaps, the height of cowman fashion. He shifted
his weight restlessly as he waited for her to return. An
arc of spit gleamed in the sun as he looked toward the
small herd of sheep pastured next to the house.

Two more men labored in the sun, digging a huge
hole. Emma hurried to them, pointing and marking off
a larger dimension in what might be a new root cellar.
From the brisk, competent way she moved, her skirts
flaring at her ankles, Sam realized that Emma had not
been hurt, and that gave him grim satisfaction.

Sam scanned the sprawling log-and-adobe-brick castle

that strangely reminded him of the Alamo. Sunlight glinted off the rifle barrels on the top walk of the house.

As Sam rode closer, a big man lurched out of the porch shadows and a huge chair made of Texas longhorns.

"You must be Otis," Sam said as he swung down from Tenkiller. The man looked like Tex, but with coarser features. He was wearing two blackened eyes, and beneath the stubble on his jaw, there was a swollen bruise.

Otis leisurely chewed the toothpick and moved it to the other side of his mouth. "You're Sam Taggart, half-blood son of old Harry. You couldn't keep your woman. . . . I'd say that's a mark against you, Nancy boy. Tex fancies her—"

Sam had learned long ago that name calling was a ploy to rile opponents. He couldn't afford to be impulsive—not with Emma in danger.

One of the men snorted, and Otis glared at him, then looked at Sam and sneered. "Tex and her have been real friendly. Most every night at the dinner table, he admires the fine picture she makes at his side. My brother won't cotton to you coming here, trying to end her visiting. He's in town, trying to find some fancy cloth for a tablecloth and napkins. He's set on making her happy, and she says that only heathens would eat off'n a table without a proper cloth. Reckon he'll buy her some pretty geegaws, too."

"Then I'll have to talk with you, won't I?" Sam saw his hand tremble as he placed his hat on his saddle horn. He fought the rage inside him, because he could endanger Emma.

Otis snickered. "Old Tex didn't expect you to turn up

after the great pigeon murder. Heard that you bedded a widow lady. You're a fancy man, all duded up with that suit and vest and those fancy boots. Wouldn't it be a shame if someone messed you up, maybe even ventilated you a bit here and there?"

While he spoke, Emma hurled out of the house and down the stairs, only to be hauled back by one of Otis's men. "I heard that. Sam, what does he mean by 'bedded a widow lady'?"

Otis grinned, revealing a gold tooth. "She owns a real friendly ranch up north. We do resale business with her sometimes, running horses to the Mounties—'course they were Mountie horses in the first place. She told one of the boys that your husband was real nice . . . but that he couldn't—ah—do the job."

Emma's eyes widened and shook her head. "That was not *my* Sam Taggart."

The object of male performance standards, Sam inhaled slowly and counted to ten. He managed a tight smile at her—to tell her with his eyes that she would soon be safe. "Are you all right?"

"I am having a nice visit," she returned in a proper tone, frowning at him. "Tex is our neighbor and needs my help. I was coming home soon."

The most important thing in Sam's life at the moment was that Emma believed in his innocence. "I didn't kill the pigeons or the cow, Emma."

"I did not think so." Emma kept frowning at him as if trying to understand him. Sam felt the color rise up his cheeks; she was wondering about the "widow woman." He dug his boots into the dirt and glared at her; she'd ruined him for other women.

His next question tore at his stomach, festered there, and despite his pride, crawled out of him—"Do you want to come home? With me?"

"I knew you would come," she whispered, her hazel eyes soft and warm as they met his. Her hand pressed flat at the base of her throat, where Sam knew she wore the dented coin. "Yes, I have had a nice visit, but I am ready to come home, husband."

His mother's ring gleamed against her lightly tanned skin, and the dark fear within Sam eased.

From the snarling bitter mass of his past and his emotions—rage and fear for Emma—Sam realized that a feeling like a tiny rosebud had begun to unfurl in him.

"She's a damned pain in the behind," one of the cowhands complained. "Cleaning and rearranging things that have been good enough that way for years. We never had to beat the dust out of no rugs before she came."

One of the hands moved closer to Otis and whispered coarsely, "I seen the look on Tex's face when she took down his champion bison head and his longhorn and some of the stuffed heads on his wall. I don't think he wants her much anymore. I think he went into town to do some real thinking about keeping her."

"I hear that this son of a buck is now the owner of the Big T." Otis chewed thoughtfully on his toothpick. "It would be real handy if we could get him to sign over the place before Tex came back."

Otis gestured to his men, and three of them moved toward Sam. Another held Emma firmly. "Tie her to the chair."

"I wouldn't do that." If they had hurt her . . . if Otis

had put his hands on her . . . Sam played for time, taking off his jacket and vest and placing them on Tenkiller's saddle. He didn't want Emma to see what he was, what Harry had taught him from a toddler, and what he'd learned in the war. He didn't want to unleash the darkness inside him, or the rage that these men had kept Emma.

He didn't want her to see what he was, at his deepest roots, when civilization was scraped away. He didn't want her to know why his captain had sent him alone on killing missions when he was only a boy. . . . There was hatred riding him then, more for himself than for the men he'd killed—

Otis's first punch didn't give Sam a choice. He decided to get Otis's attention, all of it, diverting it from Emma. Otis reeled back with Sam's first punch, his nose spurting blood. "You make another sneaky move like that, and George will hurt your woman bad. Get him, boys!"

Fearing that Otis would make good his threat, Sam let himself be taken. Otis moved in, fists swinging. "Hold him!"

Sam lost himself in the pain, giving himself to it . . . he'd keep their attention . . . playing for time . . . they wouldn't hurt Emma if they were beating him. He swore he'd come after them when she was safe. He thought he heard his rib crack and went down amid kicking boots, pain shooting red arrows inside his head.

In the distance Emma screamed in rage and in terror. They had stopped the worst of it, Sam realized dully as he lay sprawled in the dirt.

"Shame! Shame on you." Emma's voice cut through

his pain. He saw the men advance on Emma. Sam had to protect her—he sprang to his feet.

Tenkiller came at his whistle, and the whip, coiled around the saddle horn, seemed to leap into Sam's waiting hand. He brought down two of the men with one hissing strike. He leaped over them, the big knife gleaming in the hot August sun as he approached Otis. "Let's try this fandango again, shall we?"

"Sam Taggart—no! Do not—" Emma cried out, struggling against her bonds.

For an instant he regretted that she'd see what he was, that he knew how to kill and fight and survive. . . .

And he knew how Harry had felt that day, enraged that men had touched his wife, defiled her, and killed a part of him.

Sam smiled grimly, coldly, knowing that when he wanted to be, he was the best at fighting. It came naturally to him, by way of Harry; he despised it and yet knew that to save Emma, he'd give himself to hell. . . .

He threw the knife at Otis's raised arm, which was poised to strike Emma. The knife sank into flesh and then wood, pinning Otis as he shrieked and struggled free. Sam plucked the knife back to him with the whip and held it in his fist as he clipped another man on the jaw. Sam swept out a boot and raked the man's feet from under him. "You'll stay there, if you know what's good for you," he ordered as the two men on the ground leaped at him.

In quick efficient movements Sam ran his fist forward and back, taking down both men. With a wild yell Otis ran at him again, and they went down, the other men piling on top of them.

Sam leaped into his instincts to survive. In the storming crash of flesh and bone and blood, he disabled the four men quickly and leaped to his feet. He kicked away Otis's bloody hand, gripping his boot. The men groaned in pain, and Sam scanned their wounds. Something had kept him from killing them, some small tether on humanity. He retrieved the knife and flipped the handle into the waiting palm of his hand. He wiped the blade on Otis's shirt, slightly surprised that he had not used it. Then he trailed the knife tip down Otis's throat, drawing a tiny trail of blood. "I'll expect just payment for what was lost, the livestock and the pigeons. Understood?"

Otis's eyes widened. He shivered and nodded quickly.

Sam stood and slowly coiled the whip, placing it over his shoulder. He ran his tattered dirty sleeve across his face and sought what he needed most to see safe—Emma.

He saw more than he wanted—wide-eyed fear as he walked toward her. He hesitated, slammed by the grim realization that she would never look at him with those soft hazel-green eyes, that the gold flecks would be filled with fear. Now she knew that he was brutal, a potential killer, and she would hate him. He steeled himself against her cry, her abhorrence of having him near her. She watched his knife, still bloody, as he swept it through the rope holding her. She shivered at the sight, and Sam felt the rage die, coldness replacing it. He wiped the knife on the shirt of the man lying close and eased it back into its sheath. "This is what I am, Emma."

Her hand rose to her mouth and then to her throat.

Wearily, he took her wrist and tugged her to her feet. He couldn't bear her expression, the horror shadowing her face.

"Where is your grandmother's brooch?" he asked when her hand returned to her throat.

"I . . . Sam, you are hurt—" Her hand shook as it lifted to his face and came away bloody.

"I've been hurt before." He was furious with himself . . . he should have— "Where's the brooch?"

She'd had enough taken away from her that day, seeing him as he really was—he didn't want anything else taken from her. "I . . . it isn't important. Sam, you are bleeding. . . ."

He knew what Harry had felt, the rage, the need to kill— She'd seen him at his worst; he saw no reason to tread lightly now. "Where is the damn brooch?"

"The man took it before he ran away. It does not matter. Sam—let me tend you—you need needle and thread."

He didn't want her with him when he killed again—if the man who took her brooch forced the need. Already his stomach was churning, bitter in the aftermath of what he had done. He knew the feeling, the sickness because he'd had it many times before. . . . "Get Woden and leave."

"But you—" She touched his face, and Sam jerked back. He couldn't bear for her to touch him after what he'd done. He didn't want her soiled; it was bad enough that she knew his hell was never far from him. Killing had been bred into him, and it was buried bone deep; when his temper ignited, he was just like Harry. Sam felt every minute of his years, as weathered and ugly as cold mountain rock.

Emma belonged to laughter and sunshine.

"Now." Sam looked at the other New Alamo hands who had come to watch and knew that if one of them moved toward Emma—

She looked at the men and clung to his arm. "If I leave now, it will be with you. You'll come home, won't you?"

"Yes," Sam agreed, even as he planned to send her home alone. "But first I'll get the brooch."

Chapter Seventeen

It is one week since my husband has left me. How I feared for him, yet I knew that I would fight just the same for him. I think of him constantly, even as I travel between small towns and take care of his businesses in his absence. I am not a woman to sit still when there is work to be done. Tonight this roadhouse is the same as the others in our journey to do Sam's business. It has a big room for eating, and men drink there. Our room is clean. Fritzi and Greta are sleeping. I am thankful for their company. Greta is husband hunting, and Fritzi has run away from home. He will not return. At times I do not like my husband. I try not to think of how his glasses glint as he turns his head at a certain angle, or how black and sleek is his hair. And I try not to think of what he calls forth from me, with a touch, a look, a kiss. I am very angry with him. My grandmother's brooch is not so dear as his life. He should know this. E.

Emma closed her journal and turned the gold ring on her finger. How dare Sam frighten her like that, walking into Murdock's Alamo as if he didn't know the danger? While she was perfectly safe—except for Otis's attempt to lift her skirts—Sam was in danger.

Fritzi stirred, and Emma settled down with her thoughts. She hadn't slept the entire week since she'd last seen her husband. Now, when dusk crept into night and her body was tired, Emma picked up her embroidery hoop and selected a light pink skein for the wild roses she was embroidering on Sam's shirt.

Sam Taggart did not deserve a moment of her thoughts, much less a fine, old country festival shirt.

Emma closed her eyes and saw Sam wading through the five men, throwing his knife, using his whip and fists, and the look on his face—as if hell burned within him. He'd kept so many secrets from her, because he didn't want her in his life.

Where was Sam? Was he alive?

Emma dabbed an already-damp handkerchief across her eyes and tucked it back in her apron pocket. Sam was not worth one tear, running off without her.

She wished she could hit him. She would wait until he got back, and then she would punish him. There would be no doughnuts for him—

She wished she could hold him, tight against her, where his heart beat against hers, and where he was safe and she could take care of him. Emma gripped the shirt she had begun instantly upon Sam's dismissal of her— he had as much as told her that he didn't want her. He'd looked so fierce, so alone, so worn and bloody standing there and arguing with her. She'd wanted to hold him close, to protect him. But he didn't want her. . . .

She buried her face in the soft muslin and cried. "Oh, Sam Taggart, my husband, come home to me. . . ."

Sam glanced at his hand, toughened by leather, sun, and wind and freezing sleet and snow in the high country. Was it three weeks since he had shown Emma what he was? Or was it an eternity? Sam wondered as he rode down into the cool valley just miles from the Big T.

Soon September would bring the scent of winter, and Sam hated the thought of life without Emma. She wouldn't want him now, not when she had seen what he was.

He took off his hat, dusty with trail dirt; sweat rolled down from the damp bandanna tied around his head. He glanced at Many Horses, riding at his side. His uncle's head was high with pride; he led four fine Appaloosa mares with mottled rumps. Many Horses had insisted that Sam pay the bridal price as a matter of family pride. In Many Horse's parfleche bag, decorated with beaded blue and white flowers, were his ceremonial buckskins. Many Horses intended to wear them as he offered Sam's bridal price to her father, or to the male representing her family.

Emma wouldn't want him—not now. Sam reached into the small coop tied to the saddle and extracted a tiny soft pigeon chick. He cradled it close to him and dropped a crust of dried pigeon "milk" into its open waiting mouth. Sam fed the other chicks as he went, enjoying the soft feel of them against him and thinking of Emma.

Emma! The name sent pain shifting through him, tightening the fist wrapped around his heart.

For every minute of the past three weeks, Emma's terrified expression had haunted him. He'd left her crying, after she'd finally promised not to follow him. She'd damned him at first, shocking herself, her head high, and gold and green flashing in the hot brown of her eyes. She'd slipped the thong holding the dented coin from her neck and placed it on him. "You will wear this to remember who you belong to."

Helpless to say what was in his heart, he'd reached for her nape, lifting her lips to his. "You stay put, woman. I want to think of you in my bed."

"I say you are horny, and you are—" She'd begun when he fused his lips to hers.

Now Sam was past desire. He had slept only a few hours and, last night, rode by moonlight.

Dust rose around Sam, settling on him like the past as Tenkiller walked at a steady pace. The stallion, drained by the hard ride into geyser country and back, no longer had any interest in bullying. A bullet had sliced a path across his rump, leaving a scar, and he was thin, despite the lush grass along the way and the grain Sam kept in his saddlebags.

The thief was dead, and Emma's brooch, safely wrapped in the moccasins made by Many Horse's wife, was tucked in Sam's saddlebags. Sam glanced at his fringed leggings and worn moccasins. He ran a quick inventory—his dress shirt was tattered; his boots were gone, traded for pigeon chicks to replace the murdered ones. Emma's brooch and moccasins were in his saddlebags with the gold cross. When he held them, he thought about the way she made him feel clean and young again . . . as if the world still held dreams.

A slight hot wind riffled his hair, longer now and waving deeply at the nape of his neck. He'd always known what he was—Harry's half-blood bastard, little more than a savage beneath all his fine manners. He'd replaced the earring, the golden hoop that reminded him of what he was, a survivor without dreams.

Sam glanced at the field where Flathead and Kutenai Indians came to dig bitterroot in the spring. The hunt for the brooch had cost everything he'd had, including the watch, chain, and fob given to him by his ex-fiancée's father. His custom-made saddle was gone, traded for food and information, replaced by a worn drover's model.

Sam glanced at the white-tailed deer grazing on the meadows and inhaled the scent of the sweetgrass. An eon ago, he'd had a dream about laying Emma down in the sweetgrass—

Sam threaded the dry, untended leather of the reins through his fingers and pushed that thought away. He'd give Emma back her brooch and arrange for a legal dismissal of their marriage. He'd do his best to mend the break between Joseph and Emma, and then he'd set up a bank account for her use. By selling everything, Sam could deposit a comfortable amount—unless, in the three weeks he'd been on the trail, his investments had been ruined. In this raw, new country, a man's fortune, his empire, could evaporate in his fists, upon a whim of nature or man.

His plans didn't matter; nothing mattered. He knew how to survive; he'd do what he had to do. He'd promised Emma he would return, and he would. The time with her was just a dream, smoke scattered by the wind.

A jackrabbit ran in front of Tenkiller, zigzagging into the sumac. The horse was too tired to do his usual fancy sidestepping.

Many Horses nodded toward the new jackleg fences on either side of the dirt road. Braced by two big stacks of rock, the short three-legged fences marked the beginning of Big T land. Sam followed his uncle's gaze—

Emma, riding Woden, topped the slight rise in front of the Big T. She kicked her skirts, hurrying the pony toward Sam. Dust whirled from the pony's hooves as Emma descended the slight hill.

Tenkiller's head jerked up; he immediately went into his fancy sidestepping routine at her flashing petticoats and big white apron. Beneath her brown bonnet Emma was beaming and crying at the same time. She gripped a cloth sack and the saddle horn with one hand and Woden's reins with the other.

Sam sat very still, trying to decide whether he'd had a taste of locoweed or if the sun had gotten to him. Many Horses herded the mares back to safety.

Woden ran smoothly toward Sam, and Emma's joyful cry echoed in the layers of sunlight between them, "Oh, Sam—Sam Taggart, how I have missed you!"

Tenkiller began to rear, and Sam used all his strength to control the stallion as Emma—petticoats flashing— leaped into his arms.

The impact caught him off-balance, sending them hurling off Tenkiller and into the sweetgrass. Sam just had time to twist his body, to protect Emma as she landed on top of him. He lay on his back, winded amid the sweetgrass, as Emma snuggled on top of him. Her bonnet had come undone, and a fiery halo covered her braids as she leaned over him, grinning. "Welcome home, husband."

Sam looked at her and blinked, certain that he had gotten a heavier dose of locoweed than he'd at first thought.

She laughed—a rippling, joyous sound that stunned him—and placed her hands on his cheeks to gave him a quick kiss. While Sam tried to focus and catch his breath, she gave him another. In seconds Sam lay almost swooning beneath a torrent of kisses across his jaw, his chin, his nose and eyebrows, and trailing across his lips. He knew he wore a silly grin and didn't care. He kept his hands spread on her full wiggling hips, because if this was a dream, he wanted to remember the feel of it. For a moment he wallowed in the taste and the feel of his wife, then groaned and wrapped his arms around her, rolling her beneath him. He fused his mouth to hers, giving himself to the fantasy of her scent, her body lifting beneath his, the taste of her—

Tenkiller's hairy lips weren't welcome in the kiss, nor was Many Horses' crouching beside them. The chieftain skimmed the flat of his hand over Emma's coronet of braids, toying with the tendrils that gleamed like liquid copper in the sun. "I think the fire-woman has captured you," he said very seriously though his black eyes lit with laughter. "This is the time for the woman. . . . I will take the horses to the ranch."

Emma held Sam tightly, burying her face against his throat as he ran, carrying her—leaping over fallen logs

and brush and flying into the sumac and lodgepole pines
and Douglas fir. White-tailed deer, resting in the shade
from the heat of the day, leaped to their feet, tails held
high, and bounded into the thicket.

Tenkiller answered Sam's whistle, moving into the tiny
clearing and drinking from the small rippling stream
that flowed from a rock ledge.

"Emma . . . I'm dirty," Sam protested as she kissed
his neck. He was hallucinating—yet her scent curled
around him.

"Sam . . . ?" Her eyes swallowed him, devoured
him, and he fell into the soft hazel depths. She dropped
the sack she'd been carrying throughout his run and
began to unbutton her blouse.

"No." He shook his head as her trembling fingers
searched his features, stroking the new scar at his ear.
He let her slide down his body, reluctant to release her.
Then before her feet touched the ground, he clasped
her to him and forced himself not to—

Emma's legs swung suddenly as he braced her above
the ground, her heels connecting, not painfully, with the
backs of his knees. Unprepared for the wrestling tactic,
Sam's knees buckled and he went down, laughing, amid
the sunflowers and daisies and sweetgrass of the glade.
Emma straddled him, grinning down at him. "You came
back to me."

He ran his hand up under her skirts and found the
solid, slender length of her thigh as he admired her
perched on top of him. "I did."

She gripped the dented token in her fist and jerked it
lightly. "Have you mated with another woman since we
have been wed, husband?"

"I have not," he answered slowly, inching his fingers higher to the soft sweet mound of her femininity. *"Emma!"*

She eased the sweaty bandanna from his head and ran her fingers through his hair, studying him. Her gaze moved slowly over his face, to his throat, and she opened her hands on his chest, covering each nipple. The sultry look she shot him startled him, but there was no denying her husky sensual tone, "You will obey me, husband, and do as I wish . . . for I have truly longed for you."

Emma hitched up her skirts as she sat upon him, and in a fluid competent movement she unbuttoned his pants.

He sprang hard and heavy into her moist, tight keeping, groaning as she resettled her hips upon him. She rocked slightly as she lifted her arms to loosen her hair. The coppery mass tumbled down in waves to her throat and spilled around the milky breasts she had just uncovered.

Sam gritted his teeth, willing himself not to move, not to release the painful desire punishing him. "Emma!"

She began to rock slowly, and in the next heartbeat the soft constrictions within Emma caused Sam to forget that he wanted to be clean before he touched her, before he made love to her. Through a red haze of passion he saw her frown, concentrating on their fluid movements.

Sam strained for control, strained to be gentle, and failing, he gave himself to the pounding rhythm, the poignant calling of everything he was, churning, pulsing from him. Before the last he saw Emma's face leaning over him, her eyes half closed with passion, her face flushed.

She was too intimate, too close, a part of him, seeing into him, into his desire. Her breasts dragged against his chest, and in the distance he heard cloth tearing as he sought her softness, needing the taste of her skin.

What he was, what he had been and would be, tore from him and became hers, and despite his will Sam hung suspended in the pleasure rippling through him, the sense that he had never been home, but now that he was. . . .

With a cry Emma tensed, her body shuddering and taut before she collapsed upon him.

Sam lay beneath her softness, his shredded shirt telling him that Emma had torn away cloth, too. She panted delicately against his throat, shivering as he stroked her thighs and began to untie her boots. "Do you say that you are mine, Sam Taggart?" she whispered unevenly as he found her breasts, caressing them. "Do you say that you missed me?"

"I do," he whispered, curling his hand around her nape to draw her down to his kiss. With a smile on his lips Sam murmured, "Not every man has a berserker for a wife."

She looked at him and began to grin. "You are so pretty, Sam Taggart. With your hair long and waving and your crooked smile, you look like a boy. I will think of you like this when you wear your glasses and look so coldly and properly over them to me. I will remember you like this and how you smile at me—"

Her finger traced his mouth, and he nibbled it delicately, unused to close inspection when he had always held others at a distance. "You're shy of me, Sam Taggart. Tell me why."

"Tell me about your lemons. I've never seen a woman so concerned with lemons." Sam didn't want to think about the past or how tired he was, or anything but laying Emma down in the sweetgrass. He wrapped her hair around his fist and tugged lightly. "Come kiss me, and we'll trade secrets—"

Emma moved slightly, removing her boots. She eased from him and sat, adjusting her skirts, looping her arms around one knee and resting her chin on it. She looked at him steadily. "I want to admire my trophy. It was not so difficult to bring him to the ground."

She hadn't asked about what he'd done or where he'd been— Sam managed enough strength to curl his hand around her ankle, caressing it. "I missed you," he said, meaning it.

"That is not evident now," Emma returned with a cheeky grin as she looked down his sated body.

"You watched me." Sam was uneasy with the image of her leaning over him, devouring him with her soft brown-green eyes, his reflection one of passion. He knew now that in making love to Emma, he gave her something he'd given no other woman—trust. He'd given himself into her safekeeping.

"Yes, I watched because you are magnificent, beautiful, and now you are blushing, Sam Taggart . . . and then there was no time to watch, for I had visions of my own." Her smile died, and she took his hand. "Oh, Sam Taggart, do not tell me to go away from you now . . . only let us have this moment—"

"Come here," he whispered finally, filled with emo-

tion that this wonderful woman would want him, treasure him. That Emma would welcome him into her arms
after she knew what he was—

She settled softly against him, her head on his shoulder and her arms around him, one thigh resting between
his legs.

Sam drifted in her softness, the scent of their lovemaking, and the sweetgrass. Emma held him tightly,
snuggling against him, and as he dozed, he realized that
Emma was sleeping softly.

When he awoke, Sam eased from her. He stood
watching her sleep, curled upon their clothing, her body
dappled with leaf shadows. Her hair billowed around
her, waves of reddish brown lying upon the tatters of his
shirt; the bruised marks beneath her eyes told him that
she had not slept well. Sam crouched by her side,
smoothing her hair.

He was unprepared for the jarring gentleness within
him.

He wasn't certain he liked the feeling . . . that part
of him belonged to her keeping, that his shell—his walls
had been breached. In his lifetime he'd allowed nothing
to tether him, and yet she fascinated him, each move
changing, surprising, delighting him.

Emma was the only woman who'd made him forget to
withdraw. The only woman to watch him—

Drawn to her breasts, lying soft and full in the shadows, Sam frowned when he saw his marks upon her, the
tiny patches of his stubble. He regretted the marks, that
he had not shaved before she saw him.

Her skirt twisted above one knee, and Sam found a
bruise upon her thigh. She'd made him forget to hold

himself, and he'd given everything— He stood suddenly and briskly unsaddled Tenkiller, leaving him to graze.

Sam washed in the stream, lathering with the soap he'd saved for his homecoming. He shaved, using the stream as a mirror. Emma had given him no time to prepare, to tell her how he planned to establish an account for her, to dissolve their marriage. The afternoon heat dried his skin quickly, and Sam decided that he would settle the matter between them before returning to the ranch.

When he had opened his bedroll, Sam gently moved Emma onto it. He couldn't resist running his fingertip down the curve of her breast, lingering on the sight she made, sleeping deeply near him. Sam leaned back against the saddle, stretching his legs in front of him. He drew the tatters of his shirt across his hips and sat studying her, his fingers playing with her hair. "Emma, wake up."

She sat up quickly, blinking at him. "You are here," she stated firmly as if reassuring herself. "You came back."

The dappled sunlight lit her hair, streaming around her face. Sam knew he would always remember her this way, sleepy, just awakening, a soft pleased smile upon her lips, still swollen from his kisses. He had to make it easy for her to tell him that she didn't want to be touched by him—

Sam frowned, struck by the way Emma had run toward him, her expression one of joy. He didn't trust his memory. She might not have wanted to love him, and he had taken her too quickly. . . . He'd wanted her

. . . she was probably trying to be obedient, as she had been raised.

Obedient? Emma? Sam decided it was safer not to pick through the meaning of the last hour. He wanted to make the end of their marriage easy for her. Now that she knew what he was, who he was at his very bones, she would be eager to find someone else—*to knit someone else the socks she'd never knitted him.*

What right did he have to want her to knit for him the damn socks that every miner, logger, and cowman in the country was wearing? Yet he didn't like the tiny wave of anger passing through him as he thought of another man holding Emma. She began to move gently, softly, her hips imitating the lovemaking they had just shared. Little tethered Sam from supplying—he jerked himself back from the fantasy even as she began making the noises that pulled his body taut— He shook her shoulder and tried not to look at the full breast that spilled out of her bodice into the dappled sunlight. "Emma, I want to talk with you—"

She yawned and sat up slowly, holding her bodice closed. "I know. You are concerned about your businesses. I have the papers in order, and I have been traveling, checking on your interests—with Greta, of course. And Fritzi. He has come to visit us. Mama and Papa have made him uncomfortable. They are quiet and angry with one another. Behind the bedroom doors they yell. . . . Gilbert is still working for Papa, but he is in a bad mood and eating mountains of onions. Mary is reading the Swede's Paul Bunyan stories. She's an amazing student. She also likes to read the catalog and dime novels. I see no reason why she should have to learn from primers, do you?"

Sam shook his head. He wasn't certain he wanted an itemized list, bringing him up to date. He was prepared to be gentle, to deal with her emotions and to contain his own. He wasn't prepared for business as usual—or for his wife running over the countryside tending his businesses.

"Sam, I know how you think Harry is a womanizer and a wife getter. But Lilly has decided she wants him, and she has had many men to judge Harry against. She says that he is what she wants. He is fighting her, because he cares what you think, my husband."

Emma pushed back a heavy swath of hair and dabbed the trickle of sweat between her breasts with her skirt. "You look so stunned. At first I thought she might see him as a father, but then I saw her looking at him in a special way—as I enjoy looking at you."

After fastening her loosened buttons, she crossed her legs and covered her toes with her skirt. She placed her hands in her lap, sitting very straight, as though preparing for a business conference with her employer. Sam didn't know whether to yell or to kiss her. "Let me understand what you've been up to—You and Greta and Fritzi made the rounds and checked on my holdings?"

She nodded. "I kept records. I think you will find that you have made good investments. The brewery is doing nicely. The Welsh miners prefer a darker ale that reminds them of home. I think you should look at Gottlieb's land—it is perfect for grapes and hops. He is not a good businessman and knows it. Yet he has a feel for the soil. You would make good partners. You need a good barrel maker. With the railroad coming the barrels could be sent everywhere." She clapped her hands and grinned. "You could put a big S.T. Beers brand on them."

Sam crossed his arms across his chest and looked at her. She did not seem the sensual woman who had taken him. She had not raised the question about his darker side, about what he was, a savage. "Do you have anything else to say to me?" he asked grimly.

Her face lit, and she squirmed as if unable to hold her thoughts one minute longer.

Sam waited for Emma to tell him that she wished she'd never seen him, married him. She would be happier without him—

Emma reached to touch his leg and accidentally brushed him intimately. He fought groaning and lifted away her hand. He braced himself; he didn't want her to soften this final scene with a touch . . . an intimate touch at that.

"Sam Taggart, you are scowling at me. You are the best scowler I know. . . . I have a wonderful idea for your business. With old mines and caves in the mountains, there is no reason we can't store cheese and beer in them. What do you think?"

Sam thought they should get on with dissolving their marriage—with the logical discussion he had planned. While he was circling that idea and how to ease into the topic, Emma rummaged through the cloth bag and pulled a shirt free. She knelt to hold it up to his shoulders. "There. I think that turned out nicely."

"Emma—" Sam glanced down at the fiesta of embroidered flowers flowing down the front of the fine muslin shirt.

"For you, husband. I made it while I thought of you. Harry helped me with the design—there is sweetgrass and willow and milkweed and lilies." Her fingers traced the intricately woven design of leaves, grass, flowers, and berries flowing around the narrow stand-up collar and down the front. "Harry told me how your mother gathered bitterroot, and there are chokecherries—he said when you were a baby, you loved chokecherry cakes with bees' honey."

Emma arranged a full sleeve on his arm, checking the length and width. "It is not the fashion, but a shirt like men wear to weddings in the old country. Mama said Papa wore lederhosen and a shirt like this, but fashioning the leather for the short trousers will take more time. Then you will need to wear suspenders, embroidered with flowers to match this poor shirt. For you, husband," she repeated softly, and kissed him before he could move.

While Sam tried to think, Emma touched his cheek. "You have bathed and shaved. Always so clean and straight and proud—you are shocked, husband. You do not have to wear the shirt, but I did not feel like knitting more socks to keep busy. I wanted to make something for you—"

Sam managed a swallow, his throat tightening. No one had ever given him anything like this, especially for him, without requiring payment. Emma had given unselfishly, even after seeing what he really was. "I . . ."

Emma looked down at her hands and shielded her face from him. When he tipped her face up, she tried a wobbly smile. "You do not need to blow the fluegelhorn as Papa did for Mama at their wedding. It was over seven feet long, and he—"

Sam realized she was trying to tease him, to ease a tense situation, and she was uncertain of the outcome. His hand shot out, grabbing her arm, and she tumbled into his arms. The shirt was crushed between them as he took her mouth, devoured it.

He was home, wallowing in the flavor of Emma, in her scent, in the softness of her arms and the tenderness of her eyes. . . . He slanted his mouth across hers, savoring the fit and the way her lips lifted to answer his. He traced her lips with his tongue, and her tongue darted to play.

Emma gripped his shoulders and braced away, panting and laughing at the same time. Sam blinked and tried to do something other than grin as Emma sat astride him. She tugged the shirt over his head and adjusted the embroidered front upon his chest, smoothing it. "So. There, I think that turned out nicely."

Then Emma leaped to her feet and ran toward the stream, leaving a trail of petticoats and her dress. She waded into the stream, bathing herself.

With his hands spread across the fiesta of Montana's grasses, flowers, and berries, Sam savored the picture of Emma, her hair rippling around her, catching fire in the sun, her body pale and rounded and full. He understood in that moment why Harry said there was nothing like a woman, a wife to fill a man's heart, to ease him.

Chapter Eighteen

S am awoke to the cool shadows slanting across him, and from their angles he knew that two hours had passed while Emma and he slept; it was now six o'clock. Deer had moved from the cool woods, grazing nearby in the meadow's shadows and watering at the stream. In the mountains, the August night was cool.

A skein of Emma's hair fluttered beneath Sam's jaw, tickling him. She held him tightly, tethering him with arms and legs as if fearing he would leave. When she shivered, curling to him for warmth, Sam dragged his new shirt over her naked back. He paused, flattening his hand over the sweep of her back and tracing the shape. He wasn't one to linger, to caress, and the novelty of touching Emma with tenderness and not desire pleased him. Sam gently placed his open hand on her shoulder, testing the fit and shape and strength of her smooth body against his roughened hand.

Emma's fingers smoothed his chest, and he watched them, fascinated by the neat short nails, the capable fingers, and the absolute sensation of being treasured. He had seen women run to their husbands, joyful tears filling their eyes, but he never expected that same look would only be for him.

Sam smiled softly into the tendrils flowing around his mouth. Untutored and sweet, Emma's abandonment had been energetic. His hand eased to her backside, his fingers pressing gently into the lush contour. He had never lingered in the past, but now the image of slow thorough lovemaking with Emma surged through him, his body responding instantly.

Drawn to a bit of color, he picked up the embroidered flowers to study the fine needlework. He traced his fingertip over the tiny stitches that formed a serviceberry; the design was Montana country, rich with larch and camas and thistle. No one had ever made him anything so fine.

Emma stirred and whispered drowsily against his chest, "When the shirt was done, I was coming after you. I had one more wild rose and a stalk of sweetgrass. I hurried as I traveled to check on your investments—to Beartown, Garnet, Coloma, and the others—some of the stitching is not as neat as it should be."

She stretched luxuriously in his arms. "I am an impatient woman and was not that happy when we parted. I'm afraid I cut the first shirt too quickly and ruined good cloth—but that was because I was angry with you for hurting me."

He stroked her hair, gathering the rich texture into his fist. "You shouldn't have left the Big T. Anything could have happened to you."

"You weren't there to stop me, and as your wife, it

was my place to watch over your investments. You were expected to make your rounds. With Lilly at the ranch I saw no reason not to go. I used your satchel, but I left it very neat and was careful to replace the forms I used."

When Sam had restored a measure of his restraint, he laid out rules that Emma badly needed to understand. "I don't think you traveling across the country without protection was wise."

"Wasn't it?"

Her challenging tone caused a prickle of uneasiness to skitter up the back of his neck. He chose a safer subject at the moment; he reached into his saddlebags for the packet containing the brooch and the gold necklace. "Here is your brooch."

Emma instantly pushed from him, sweeping her petticoat to her breasts for protection as she stood. Sam rose slowly, gripping the brooch and the gold cross. He braced himself, uncertain what to do as she paced through the small area of dappled shadowy light.

Her hair rippled and flowed and surged like a fiery storm around her head, catching the dim light. She held her petticoats to her chest, and they moved like a flag in her wake, exposing a curved backside and a slender thigh. Sam admired the sight while she muttered in German, threw out one hand in an angry gesture and caught the cloth she had just released, drawing it up to her chest again.

Her legs gleamed in the shadows, and Tenkiller sidestepped warily. Finally she turned to Sam, regally drawing herself to her full height. "You! You would leave me for something so worthless as one piece of jewelry. You would make me worry for you . . . cry for you. You would stand there grinning, your hands on your hips and waving your—"

"You do that to me," Sam answered dryly. Another time, when her temper did not rule her, Emma would have blushed.

She dismissed him with a wave of her hand and a flood of German. Then she turned to him, strode to him, and held out her hand. "Give it."

Sam didn't trust her anything-can-happen look. "Red, you're not—"

"It is mine. You charged off without a care of how I felt about recovering it. Now you are thin and worn, and now I wish that I had not told you how much it meant to me. You risked everything to get it for me. Give it. I demand it." Emma's eyes burned at him, green catching gold from the sunlight.

"I think I'll wait until you've cooled down—" Sam reeled backward as Emma's hand flew to his cheek. The slap echoed in the silence that followed. He tensed—braced for the moment in which she told him how he disgusted her—

Instantly her eyes widened, her hand over her mouth. He realized slowly that she had shocked herself more than him. She began to cry. "I have never hit anyone like that—*how could you leave me?*"

Sam steeled himself; she would tell him now how much she despised him and that she wished they'd never met. She would tell him how much he disgusted her, how—

Emma hurled herself into his arms, the mass of petticoats between them as she locked her arms around his neck. Sam stood still as her tiny kisses quickly covered every inch of his face. He wasn't certain if the dampness on his cheeks was from her tears or his.

"I am sorry I hurt you," he began unevenly, only to be stopped by her grabbing his ears. The quick movement stopped his thoughts while Emma kissed him hard on the mouth, then released his ears.

He floundered; words that dealt with his heart, tightened in his throat. "Emma—"

"Give me the brooch. I will throw it away. I could never look at it again without thinking of how you left me . . . how I feared for you . . . how you look now, as though you had been dragged through the mountains."

Sam looked into her tear-filled eyes and felt himself go weak. He cleared his throat, certain that he was misunderstanding her. "You saw me fight, Emma. You know what I am."

She tightened her arms around his neck. "Yes. I think you are the most noble man I have ever met. But stupid, when the danger is to yourself."

Sam grabbed her arms and pushed them down. "Emma. You don't know—"

"I know that when you are faced with a job, you do it. You worried for me, fearing the men would have their way . . . you see? Your face changes so. . . ." Her fingertip traced his brows. "One eyebrow lifts and quivers. . . . Such a scowl. But I do not fear you, Sam Taggart, and I did not like your pride later. I do not know how you have lived this long without me to do your thinking for you."

Sam tried to balance his emotions. He tried again to

show her what he was. "I killed in the war, Emma . . . with my knife . . . with my bare hands."

"It is no small thing to take a life. You have said so in your sleep. Someday you will give up your secrets to me, husband. In the war you were too young for the job that they made you do, but you did it. You shivered in the cold and took beatings and befriended a black man who died under a careless surgeon's saw."

"I . . . talk . . . in my sleep?" Sam waded through his sleepless nights with Emma soothing him, and realized with disgust that he was a real talker. Because he had to make her understand, Sam added firmly, "I cut men's throats, Emma, so there would be no noise for the soldiers who came after me. I learned quickly, and I did it well. Sometimes I wondered if I enjoyed it. I knew that I was Harry's son then, bred for killing."

Emma stroked his cheek. "It is only a moment that you talk, when you sleep. But the terror of a boy is there, and the conscience of a man. Sometimes you cry out so quietly as if you were holding all the evil in the world within you, terrified that it will escape your command. Husband . . . then you tear my heart. You have a brave soul, but it is wounded, and so I ask that you share your pain with me."

Sam reeled with the knowledge that she knew more about him than he intended. He tried to pick through his thoughts and decided that for the moment, he'd take the easiest route out.

"Here," he said curtly, lifting her hair to fasten the gold cross around her throat. Emma held the petticoats to her and examined the cross. It was a small gift, worth much less than the brooch, and Sam tensed. "It isn't much."

When she was silent so long, he walked back to the bedroll they had shared, sat, and stared back at her. He decided he would wait until he had dissected each problem and knew how to approach her. At the moment she was an unstable commodity. *Or was he?* He wasn't used to the assault of tenderness and uncertainty.

Sam reached for his glasses because he decided, in a mass of confusion, they might help him work his way through his Emma problem. He looked over them at Emma and crossed his arms, studying her.

With the petticoats held against her, Emma continued to admire the cross. The shadows swept across her, and the gentle breeze spread her hair out and away from her.

Her capable fingers smoothed the tiny cross in her hand, the chain glittered against her throat, catching the last of the light.

Uncertain of his emotions, Sam swung back into the safety of anger. Emma had taken her clan on a merry business trip while he was gone. . . . He dug into the anger, clung to it, because he understood frustration and rage and not wild roses embroidered by a woman who had probably cried for him.

Sam locked the muscles of his jaw and scowled at her, this woman who irritated him down to his boots.

But he didn't have handmade expensive boots any longer; he had traded them for pigeon chicks.

Pigeons, he repeated darkly, and shook his head.

He inhaled slowly, trying to find the balance in his dreams and his life and the woman he had married.

Then Emma began to walk slowly toward him. Her hair flowed out and around her like a storm, framing her pale face; it tumbled around her shoulders and fell upon the petticoats she held over her breasts. The gold cross gleamed, swaying between her breasts as she bent to take away his glasses. "You won't be needing those. . . . Thank you, husband, for this wonderful present. It is the most beautiful I have ever seen, and I will treasure it," she whispered against his lips. "Please never yell at me again like you did that day at the New Alamo. . . . I was only trying to protect your honor—to make Otis admit he killed the birds and the red cow. He boasted of it to me, and I prayed for his soul."

She knelt at his side, easing her fingers through his hair, toying with it. "Please never call me an 'empty-headed, irritating, delectable female gnat who is driving you to lose your manhood,' I think we have just proven that is not true, and you know that those words call forth the berserker in me. And I have never seen you wave your arms around like that—pacing and shouting and snorting."

"You ever go off like that again, and you'll pay. And I'm not crazy about your raid on me earlier. You could have been hurt when you jumped from your pony." Sam eased her into his arms, comforting himself that she hadn't been hurt.

"But I wasn't hurt. Woden is used to me jumping from him. We used to practice, and I would leap from him to a branch. Today you were that branch." Emma grinned up at him and settled into his arms, placing his hand upon her breast and covering it with her own. Her other hand caught the dented token at his throat and slowly drew him to her kiss. "The delectable part was rather nice—mmmf!" she exclaimed as he tenderly assaulted her mouth and dragged her, petticoats and all, beneath him.

As Tenkiller carried them through the dusk toward the Big T, Sam cradled Emma on his lap. He wanted her in his arms, because at any minute he'd wake up to find that the entire afternoon and evening had been a dream. Now he knew how other men felt, why they spoke of home and wife and family as though they'd bleed to death before leaving. . . .

He'd found he had a soul and gentle dreams, and the knowledge terrified him.

He didn't understand how she could give herself so readily to him, hungry for his touch. He didn't understand the tears burning his lids, his need to bend and kiss her, to bury his face in her hair and take the sweet scent into his head, washing away the past.

She stirred against him, smoothing the embroidered shirt, and lifted to kiss his chin. "Welcome home, husband," she whispered, her hand lying upon his cheek.

Sam floundered, struck by the tenderness in her face and the softness of her voice.

A nighthawk soared suddenly, and the hair on the back of his neck lifted. Sam listened to the owls and the sounds of the night and knew they weren't alone. He'd been lost in his thoughts and not focused on the danger. A quick glance at the moonlight filtering through the lodgepole pines, and he found the men.

Tex Murdock's big white hat caught the moonlight as he stepped onto the road. He pushed Otis in front of him, and the six Calhoun brothers moved from the shadows, blocking the road.

Emma sat upright and quickly smoothed her hair that Sam had insisted remain loose, drifting around him. He damned himself now, for Emma was an appealing picture. She drew her shawl around her, hiding the torn buttons of her dress. "Good evening, Tex. Wonderful night, isn't it?"

"Miss Emma." Tex took off his hat. "You are looking right pleasant."

When Emma's fingers remained locked with Sam's, he tried to pull away. If he needed to fight, she'd be in danger. Emma had that set look to her face as though she'd pit herself against anyone to protect him. She dug her fingers deep, and to remove her hand, he would have to hurt her—

"Been out doing it with the bastard, your half-blood, huh?" Otis leered at Emma.

The back of Tex's white glove hit Otis, and blood spurted from his nose. "My brother apologizes, ma'am. He's going to South America and wants to pay his respects. I'm hoping he's learned his lesson and that he treats the South American ladies better than he has you."

Tex shoved Otis into one of the Calhouns' keeping and stood beside Tenkiller. "No need to dismount, Mr. Taggart, or to lift your fur, which I hear that you do right nice when you're het up about your family. Your bride is safe, and she will remain safe whenever she comes to the New Alamo and wherever my men can protect her. I have sworn by my honor, and by the men who died at the Alamo, that no harm will come to her or your kin.

I'm hoping you'll come to my ranch, too, because you're the breed—sorry, ma'am, no offense—you're the breed of new man we need in these parts, especially with the railroad coming. Miss Emma has said how rightly smart you are, and she's not a one to tell a windy."

Sam nodded, tensing for one move that could bring harm to Emma. He heard a bird call and knew that Many Horses waited in the night, ready to help.

Sam reached past Emma to grip Tenkiller's mane; the horse stood still, waiting for Sam's command.

The Calhoun brothers, tall and dangerous and wearing their Colts tied low to their sides, came closer. "We're sorry," all six men said in unison.

"Why would you be sorry?" Emma asked worriedly, and looked up at Sam. He preferred not to tell her about his conversation with them.

Tex shifted restlessly. "Well, ma'am, reckon all of us run a little wild when a pretty filly comes close. And we're sorry for interrupting you and your husband while you're courting. But Otis here—"

He pushed Otis closer. "Otis wants to pay his respects. I'll send over a cow and his wages to boot . . . to pay for the pigeons. He won't be inheriting the New Alamo, because I ain't dyin' to oblige him. I made up my mind long ago that Otis didn't rightly understand the grand high honor of the men who fought at the Alamo. That's why I was so fierce about woman hunting—I got a notion to make a boy-child of my own."

Tex placed his hat on his head and reached to shake Sam's hand. His straight, meaningful stare locked with Sam's. "I wanted to say this man-to-man and in front of

Miss Emma. Sorry for the wild hare idea about marrying you, Miss Emma, and I'd appreciate it, Mr. Taggart, if you don't have any bad feelings."

Sam gripped his hand, and Emma's hand settled softly
over the men's. "We will come visiting soon. I will bring
your favorite bread and pies. Please take good care of
the sheep—they are going to make fine wool—and
please come visit us."

A staunch cowman, Tex nodded after a moment in
which he obviously debated the value of sheep. "Some
things have to be said and some don't. Your sister has
been sending her fixins' over to my place by every passing cowpoke. She can't cook a bean, but I hear that
she's mighty interested in the New Alamo. Pass in
friendship, pilgrim."

Tex ran his hand across his face and looked at Emma
sheepishly. "No offense, ma'am. But I've had enough of
any woman acting like my dear departed mama. I'm a
man who likes to ramrod his own spread and rule his
own house. I didn't like moving my chair every time you
came at me with a broom. And sometimes a man likes
to put his boots on the table with the boys and spit."

Tex grinned at Sam. "She speaks mighty highly of her
husband. A regular man would have a hard time living
up to a Paul Bunyan of a man. When you have time,
come see me. We'll palaver about business, and you can
hide out from the broom sweeping and washing."

"Wasn't that nice of them, Sam?" Emma asked as
they continued and Many Horses came to ride beside
them. "Oh, hello, Many Horses. Isn't it a lovely night
for a ride?"

I have to hurry. My husband is coming to bed soon. Sam rode so slowly, so tired, his wonderful dress shirt in rags. My heart flew when I saw him, my beautiful husband, with his hair waving and long. From his touch I know he missed me. It is no small thing, a man missing a woman, and my anger eased. I have a small idea that he is frightened of me, and I don't know why. When we arrived home, Many Horses offered four mares to Fritzi, as he was the eldest male of my family nearby. The mares were a bridal offering and came from my husband's family. Sam said I was worth more, and I could not stop from kissing him, even though the rest saw me. My heart is full with the beauty of the gift and its meaning. I was so foolish to hold my heart apart for the dowry. I must go now. My husband is leaving the others and coming to me. My heart is so full. E.

Emma yawned and stretched and knew she was sinful by lying with her husband when the sun was almost up. She played at sleep as Sam eased from her; in the three days since he'd come home, he had risen early, restless with his thoughts. Harry would be waiting with cups of coffee and stolen gooseberry strudel.

Sam dressed quietly in the shadows, and Emma couldn't resist watching the muscles ripple along his back, the taut curve of his rump. He turned suddenly as though sensing she looked at him, and desire leaped instantly between them. It would be night before they came together, because even now the rest of the house was stirring.

His hand reached to smooth the embroidered shirt,

hanging on the wall. He slowly, lightly traced the flowers and serviceberries, woven into the waving stalks of sweetgrass. Emma smiled in the shadows, because her gift had obviously pleased Sam.

Sam found her watching him and took a step toward her, desire flashing between them. . . . Emma promised herself that she would not cry out when he touched her, that when the flames leaped and tossed her into pleasure, she would not bite him.

Her fists gripped the pillow as Sam stood over her, his gaze following the path of his finger, easing away her nightgown from her breast. He touched her nipple, already peaked and aching—

Greta knocked on the other side of the bedroom wall. "Sam, are you absolutely certain that there were four thousand men led by Santa Anna at the Alamo? And only 188 men in the mission?"

"Yes, Greta." He groaned wearily and covered Emma's breast.

"Stay," she whispered, catching his hand and drawing it to her mouth. Holding his eyes, she kissed the pad of his thumb and then drew his fingers, one by one, into her mouth to suckle. Then because her berserker mood was upon her and Sam looked so desperate, Emma turned his palm and slowly stroked it with her tongue.

"You'd better stop, little girl." Sam's voice was deep and uneven as if he were strangling.

Because he had challenged her, Emma bit his thumb and took it to her nipple, arching to the touch. The leaping heat between them pleased her; Sam's eyes narrowed instantly. "You look as if you would like to pounce upon me, my husband," she whispered.

"I'd like a nibble, that's for sure," he agreed, inhaling sharply.

"Perhaps I would like to nibble, too." Emma grinned up at him. "You are blushing."

"Sam! Eleven days in the siege right?" Greta called shrilly.

"Emma, we need our own place." Sam shook his head and with a reluctant last glance at her, left their room.

It is September now, and Harry and Sam talk more. I pray for a mending of their hearts. They have bought two old racing carts and discuss business. My father is still angry because we married without his permission. I trust Sam, who says that my father will "cool off in time." I am old-fashioned, and a part of me still wants the dowry, though I have placed our wedding paper on the wall. I wish to be as my mother and grandmother before me, to know that I am a truly married woman and that our marriage is blessed by custom. Though my husband is my heart, I cannot help this need that I have known since birth. A part of me, of the piece of the quilt of our lives that I wish for, is missing. E.

Chapter Nineteen

"Sam, Beth checks under the cabbages every day for a baby. Pretty soon Emma will cut all of them for kraut, and there goes the baby crop until next year," Mary called as she sat on the corral board, holding her pregnant cat and smoothing its stomach. She knew Sam heard her, even though he ignored her. The back of Sam's neck always tensed in a certain way and he stopped whatever he was doing when Mary threw a baby hint at him. She thought it was better than the bosom-growing ones.

Of course Mary knew how babies were made, but she wasn't certain that Sam knew how to perform as well as Tenkiller.

She eyed her half-brother. Once he loosened up, Sam wasn't that bad, and he'd stopped looking so grim. Yep, she thought, bosom-growing talk wouldn't get to him, but baby talk would, and he'd look poleaxed.

Things were fine, Mary mused, inhaling the crisp September air and scanning the color changing on the mountains.

After his pause Sam braced his shoulder against Tenkiller and pushed him back into the light harness of the racing cart.

Harry moved quickly to adjust the leather harness around Tenkiller and held the newly repaired spokes of the cart.

Mary lightly kicked Fritzi, who stood leaning against the corral, his crutches nearby. While he preferred to ignore her, she liked to torment him—because when his pants finally caught up with his brain, she'd be old enough and established in the bosom-growing business, and he'd start looking at her. Because Fritzi had no right to look so grown up and distant, she stated, "I heard you moaning and groaning again this morning."

"Go suck eggs," he returned, glaring at her.

"I'm marrying you when I grow up." Mary felt it was decent of her to serve notice.

"Go suck eggs," he repeated.

Mary petted her cat. Things weren't so bad. With Paul Bunyan stories to read, and newspapers and catalogs, learning was fun. She liked the house filled with life and people stirring in the morning and good food on the table. She didn't even mind the chores because everything made sense now, like a pattern—a family pattern. Shen-Yu had almost cured her father's foot, and evenings were the best, when they all sat outside on the porch and the talking was low and soft.

Mary knew the changes were because of Emma, because she knew how to make a family.

Fritzi taught her about pigeons; he was patient and

gentle, and Mary watched him change day by day. He stood more erect now, not leaning on his crutches as much, and she noted a proud tilt to his head. Harry told him to watch Sam, because Sam was a "cross-over," a man bridging the distance between the old rough ways and the new civilized ones. Harry acted just as proud of Fritzi. At the Rechts' Fritzi had had to help with "woman work," but at the Big T Harry took time with him, showing him how to braid a horsehair lariat and how to throw hatchets and knives. Sam had him working on the old carts, softening and repairing the leather and whittling new spokes from wild cherrywood. Harry and Sam spoke to him as they would any other man— and not to a boy.

Mary realized that before Emma had come to contaminate them, everything had been scary. "Things aren't so bad here," she told Fritzi. "Lilly isn't as much on fancy cooking, strudels and such, or cleaning, like Emma is, or doing fine needlework and making socks, but she sure can garden and raise chickens and make cheese. I like all the pigs and sheep and babies growing everywhere. Sam got those pigeons—"

"They aren't tumblers," Fritzi interrupted stubbornly. "The only tumblers I have left are those that Monty took to the Lost Dutchman's mine when he left a week ago, the one that flew in from Swede's . . . and Lulu."

But Mary caught Fritzi's pleased smile.

Mary glanced down at Fritzi's legs. She'd tormented him into letting Shen-Yu treat him. With Harry's healed foot as a recommendation, Fritzi tolerated the needles and painful massage of oils into his skin. Though he didn't know it, his legs had started to move.

Sam had dark quiet moods that Mary did not understand. Still . . . he was the only chance that the Big T would get what she wanted it to have—a baby.

Emma was a good bet to get him to do it. She had Tenkiller running after her and affectionately lipping her hair. If Emma could tame Tenkiller, she could manage Sam.

At that moment Mary decided not to torment Sam about her bosom-growing problem anymore. He looked as if he'd had about all the torment one human could bear—until he looked at Emma. Then something leaped in him, as if his life mattered, as if he wanted something other than land and holdings and bankroll.

"I'd really like him to make a baby with Emma," Mary told Fritzi. "You think their baby would have black hair or that wild curly stuff like Pa's and Emma's?" she whispered, thinking how many mares Tenkiller had bred and how Sam looked only at Emma, as if he wanted to hug and kiss her all the time. Yet sometimes he just frowned, as if he wondered when it would all end.

Sam never looked at another woman like he looked at Emma . . . as if she somehow scared him and as if he wouldn't have it any other way.

"Why do you think Sam traded for those carts? They don't hold much and can't take much weight," Fritzi asked, and Mary smiled . . . she knew.

At separate times Harry and Sam had each told her about how popular horse racing was in Montana and that Tenkiller was the best trotter anywhere. He could train other horses, some of them his offspring, and cart racing at the Big T would be a good business—in addition to the breeding and training stables. She would be helping with foaling and training. Fritzi had a real knack for training and horses; he was light enough to be a good cart-man.

"Get over here." Harry and Sam both looked at Fritzi, their hands on their hips, and said the same thing in the same playful way.

Mary fought giggling. Sam was just like their father, yet neither man seemed to realize how much they were alike. Except maybe Harry, who sometimes looked at Sam as if he'd bust with pride, and then there was the other, too, the sorrowful look, as if his heart was bleeding. Once Mary had seen Harry reach out to Sam, when his back was turned, as if Harry wanted to touch him . . . maybe hold him.

Sam wasn't a holding man. He rarely touched anyone, unless it was to hold Beth, who crawled her way up him as she did Harry. But when Emma took Sam's hand in the quiet hours on the front porch, he let her, and Mary noticed how he seemed to ease at the touch, his thumb caressing the back of Emma's hand.

Emma and Lilly and Beth came to stand on the corral boards beside Mary as Sam called to Fritzi, "Get over here and drive this rig."

"Me?" Fritzi almost fell. But then he swallowed, held his head high, squared his shoulders, and walked awkwardly to the cart—without his crutches.

"I wish Papa could see this," Emma whispered.

Mary crossed her arms as Harry and Sam lifted Fritzi into the rig and began to instruct him. In harness, Tenkiller stood still, as if waiting for the moment to show off.

"I'll need to learn how to use that other cart," Greta stated thoughtfully. "It will make me look more ladylike when I go calling on Tex."

Mary traced the flowers Emma had embroidered on her shirt. She really wanted that Sam-Emma baby.

When Fritzi lifted the reins, Tenkiller started his fancy trotting. Sam and Harry stood, two tall men, side by side, hands on hips, watching the cart move in the circular path they had designed for a racetrack. Emma came to stand beside Sam, and he put his arm around her. Harry jumped when Lilly slid her arm through his, but this time he didn't move away.

Mary liked what she saw, all of them standing together in the September sunlight, with the three women resting up on the knoll. She hopped down from the corral board and walked to stand between Sam and Harry. They looked down at her, and Mary looped her arms between theirs, liking the feel of having a family. "I'm going to learn how to do what Emma does," she stated. "I'm going to learn how to make a family from bits and pieces and make them all come together and like one another. She knows how to fill the aching places of people's hearts with sunshine. The way I see it, Emma's got talent."

"I bought it," Sam said a week later, when Emma had finished walking through the empty house. She'd been delighted with the huge kitchen, the spacious parlor, and the wide front porch. She'd exclaimed about the bedrooms, each with a big wardrobe closet. Sam tried to stop the excitement racing through him—he could see Emma dressed perfectly and entertaining his business colleagues. The house in Deer Lodge City was exactly what he wanted, and it was already furnished; it was located on a shady street with other elegant houses, and he could walk to his office on Main Street. The big table in the dining room with matching chairs and serving sideboard were perfect. A freighter had delivered them from Fort Benton. He could see Emma seated at one end of the table and himself at the other.

And the businessmen and wives sitting between them would not question his mixed blood heritage or that he was a bastard.

Deer Lodge City would be close to the railroad, when it came, linking Wyoming and Montana Territory to the east and west. With the help of the railroad Sam could build up his small store businesses and develop his brewery, shipping bottled beer or kegs. Within thirty miles of the Big T, the town was close enough to keep up on the horse-breeding and -racing business. There would be social balls and church committees for Emma, and the parlor would be perfect for tea parties.

Sam looked around the high ceilings and the elegant woodwork. This was what he wanted, a gentleman's home and not a half-blood bastard's.

September's leaves washed against the windows. He glanced at Emma, who was staring at him blankly. After a week of traveling with him and staying in hotel rooms, she looked tidy in her brown dress and bonnet.

She'd be happy to have her own home. Sam inhaled slowly, waiting for the moment when Emma would throw her arms around him and tell him how happy she was. He felt himself growing hard at the thought of the big bed upstairs. There would be a dressing table for

Emma, where she could brush her hair before coming to him. Sam visualized her in the steamy bathing room with a water closet. He saw her with a baby at her breast, and for a moment the floor seemed to rock beneath his feet.

He glanced outside the window to a young mother pushing a wicker baby carriage. He could see Emma with a baby, her bodice loosened after nursing. His stomach contracted as it did when he thought about their lovemaking, which was anything but controlled. He hadn't been able to spill his seed away from Emma's keeping, and he wasn't certain he wanted to. The way they were making love, a baby was certain. Emma needed to adjust to one thing at a time, he told himself.

She turned to him, her hand gripping the cherrywood banister. "What is that you say?"

Sam grinned, waiting for her surprise to turn to pleasure. He hooked his thumbs in his belt and braced himself for her leap at him. "I bought this house."

Emma's hand went to her throat, covering her grandmother's brooch. "When?"

In just a moment she'd realize that this house was hers, a gift from him. "Less than two weeks ago. I had to come to Deer Lodge on business, and the house was a good price. The owner hates Montana Territory and wants to move back East. I don't want you traveling like we did this past week. It's the middle of September now, and we need to be settling in a house, and I'll have an office on Main Street."

His plans were all coming together, everything exactly as he wanted. "I'm going to concentrate on timber and a brewery and on horse breeding and racing. Marcus Daly needs competition. I think there will be a nice profit in marketing Swede's lumber and Arne's quick house idea—all I have to do is find a good carpenter to ramrod it. I'd like to start a furniture business, too."

Sam cupped her face in his hands. He didn't like what he saw in Emma's eyes, the darkening of green until her eyes were shadowed. He realized that he was asking her to trust him—that at any moment a turn of fortune would send him scrambling. "We'll be fine, Emma. Trust me. . . ."

"I have trusted you from the moment I saw you," she returned softly.

Sam ignored her frown; he'd waited for this moment. "Now, Emma, don't skimp on anything. We'll have everything you need shipped from St. Louis to Fort Benton and freighted here. It's important that everything be in place for a party just as soon as possible. If Lilly can't come to help you—temporarily—we'll hire someone. . . . I do not want Greta here—yet. When Lilly can help, she and Beth can stay in the servants' room, next to the kitchen, and later on, we'll hire someone to come in days and watch the place when we're gone. Deer Lodge City will be a good place to live."

Sam raced on with his vision; he didn't want his house infested by any of his extended family. He wanted Emma alone . . . to make love to her and listen to her unmuffled wild cries—he could almost hear them echoing in the bedroom. . . . He thought of the study with the walnut paneling and the elegant massive desk where he intended to build an empire. From the moment he ran his hand across the fine cherry surface, he imagined Emma lying upon it—

Because she looked so pale and helpless, he took her hand and kissed her forehead. "Don't worry, Emma."

Emma slid her hand from his and went to lock both fists on the handle of her sock basket. Sam frowned slightly; he didn't like to see her frightened. She looked as though she were clinging to the basket, tethered to her old life and not to him. He pushed away the fear nagging at him that something was deeply wrong and that it could change the course of his life.

Sam thought back to the times after the drover had stopped by with a message from Rechts'. Emma had turned stark white while listening to the man and had run to the small cemetery of women. She'd been crying when he found her and wouldn't tell him why. Emma could be immovable, and whatever troubled her now went deeply to the heart of her. He moved to her and wrapped his arms around her from the back. "You'll do fine, Emma."

"I am not what you want, Sam Taggart," she whispered, her head bent. "I am a selfish woman, especially for you."

He kissed the side of her cheek, enjoying the familiar scent and taste of her smooth warm flesh. He smoothed her body, bringing her close to him and settling her lush bottom against his hardening body. "Oh, you're what I want."

"I am not your ideal wife. I am a plain country woman with old-fashioned ideas."

She remained stiff, but Sam knew that was because she was frightened . . . because he was asking her to begin a life with him, alone and without the infestation of family. He rocked her in his arms. "You are my wife."

She was too still, and Sam turned her slowly. Tears fell from her cheeks, and he tipped her chin up to him. "Emma?"

"I cannot live here with you, Sam Taggart." Emma closed her eyes, and her lips trembled. "I do not belong here."

"Explain." Sam's senses told him that something was very wrong. He wanted to understand the exact problem, dissect it, and fix it. He stepped back and placed his glasses on his nose and crossed his arms over his chest. "Tell me exactly why you can't live here with me."

Emma swallowed, her eyes pleading with him to understand. "I do not belong here," she whispered simply.

"You belong with me in our own home. Not in a makeshift tent, or in a farmer's backroom, or in a room over a bar. You belong here, Emma, as my wife." But he understood only too well. "It's the dowry, isn't it? I told you—in time your father will see what's right, but right now he's too stubborn. It won't do any good for me to approach him now about our marriage. In fact, it could slow things down."

She picked up her sock basket and clutched it to her, her head bent. "I cannot live here with you."

Sam jerked the basket away from her, spilling the balls of socks. He picked her up in his arms and carried her up the curved stairway to the biggest bedroom and dumped her on the bed. He ripped off his jacket and his necktie and flipped the knife from his back into a high arc that landed with its point in the carpet and its handle quivering. He sat down to jerk off his boots. "We're going to lie in that bed now, and you're going to toss any fool notions out of your head. You are my wife, and you belong with me."

He fought the rage that she held—a barrier between them that meant more to her than he did. He fought the crawling fear that none of what had happened between them was true. His hands trembled as he pulled off one suspender.

"It is morning, husband," Emma whispered too quietly.

Sam pulled off the other suspender and began to unbutton his pants. "It is morning, and we're in our house and in our bedroom."

Emma sat on the bed, propped up against the massive carved headboard, her skirts neatly covering her legs and her boots neatly placed together. She primly folded her hands on her lap. "You are angry."

"Damn angry. . . . I thought you knew that I could provide for you, that we didn't need the dowry, or anything from anyone. I'll take care of you, Emma. You have to trust me." Sam had never asked anyone to trust him before, and now the words hurt his pride.

Emma took a handkerchief from her pocket and dabbed at her eyes. "I trust you. But I am not the wife that you want. I see that now. I want you to have what you need. This house is so grand—"

"Emma!" Sam found himself yelling and fought to keep his voice down.

"I think you should get another wife, one who suits you. I do not know how to entertain businessmen and cook elegant dinners and wear fine dresses," she continued, and worried the tatted edge of the handkerchief with her fingers. "I am a plain woman."

With the desperate feeling that everything he wanted was sliding away from him, Sam ripped off his shirt. He threw his shirt over a chair and followed it with his pants. Emma's tears were still sliding down her cheeks, despite her efforts to stop them. Somehow he knew that if he could hold Emma, kiss her, the nightmare would shred. He lay down on the bed beside her, his legs stretched out in front of him. He folded his arms behind his head. All he had to do was to use logic. Emma was a logical woman, and she would come to understand—

"You're muttering, Sam Taggart." She did not look at him.

He eased his arm around her and drew her close. The feel of her body against him settled it as it always did. He decided for another approach. "Emma, I think we need a house for the baby we've probably already started."

She stiffened slightly. "But you do not want children."

Sam gently tugged at her bonnet ties. "Since I seem unable to control the situation, and you're a wild woman, all fiery and sweet at the same time, I think I'd better modify my plans."

"Lemons," she muttered.

"What?"

"There is a lemon shortage now, and you have been eating raw oysters."

Sam mentally shook his thoughts and tried to get back logic. "Emma, tell me—"

She slid from the bed and hurried out the door. Sam ran behind her, dressed only in his stocking-covered feet. He caught her quickly gathering her socks in the basket and spun her to him. "You are living here with me, Emma. This is our home."

Emma's mouth firmed. "I do not wish it. You cannot bully me, Sam Taggart."

He felt evil and mean and capable of anything. He'd planned for this, waited to see her joy, and now she flung it back in his face. "I thought you gave yourself into my keeping a month ago, when I got back with your brooch. If I want to bully you, I will," he said, realizing how stupid the statement was immediately.

"Bully," she accused him again.

"If you were a real modern businesswoman, you would see that it is important to live in a house like this and mix with the right people—"

Her finger shot up. "Ah! You see? I am not what you want, for I care not what the suit looks like but for the man beneath it."

"Emma!" Sam realized he shouted again.

Only the tears in her eyes kept him from reaching for her.

The house is so grand, and I see that while Sam belongs in it, I do not. I am a plain country woman. My husband does not understand. I would have all my family and my husband, too. E.

Emma cried and kneaded the bread with enough force to flatten the yeast starter. At midnight, she was very careful not to awaken anyone, but she couldn't sleep in the bed Sam had shared with her. Two days and nights without him had proven her point—Sam needed an ideal woman and was probably looking for one in Deer Lodge City.

Her tears dripped into the bread, and though it was far past time to stop kneading it, she continued.

When he had shown her the house, he had looked so happy, like a little boy bursting with a secret.

She wasn't as modern as she thought, or the idea of living in a grand house wouldn't have frightened her. There were so many fine things, and Sam, in his meticulous business suit, looked as if he belonged in that world of elegant people.

Emma rubbed the back of her flour-coated hand across her face. She was a simple country woman, who had dreams of entering the sock business. She was successful as a businesswoman but not as the ideal wife Sam needed to fill his home.

Her dowry haunted her. She longed to have it in her keeping; it lay deep in the heart of her, given to her by the women, handed down from one generation to another. Because she did not think Sam wanted children, the dowry would comfort her, and someday, adding the cross he had given her, she would give it to Mary. Always the dowry was in her, though Sam had taken his portion of her heart.

She did not fit into Sam's new world. There were words to say—meaningless small words that filled air and not hearts. She did not know how to curl her hair into high ringlets or wear fine clothes—the clothes that Sam had bought her stuffed the closet. Some of the fancy clothes were never washed, merely aired, and Emma did not think she could wear dirty clothes.

Emma dashed her hand across her tears again and

sniffed. He did not want a simple country woman as his wife.

She slammed her fist into the dough, and it whooshed, flattening. How could he trade and buy that house with those fine things? Did he want to show her how she did not fit into the world he wanted? How could he not know how important the dowry was to her? Or that she would have her family *and* him?

Emma punched the dough again. The things of her mother and grandmother were in Gilbert's sausagelike fingers. Her father, angered that Sam had not asked for her properly, as was the custom, had given Gilbert the dowry for payment.

Men. Always fighting, swaggering, or acting like little boys pleased with themselves—especially when presenting fine gifts to unsuspecting women.

He should have told her, prepared her.

Emma picked up the hem of her apron and dabbed her eyes, fighting a sob. Sam belonged to another woman, who didn't need her dowry . . . a brave, modern woman who knew how to tend his fine home.

She fought the wail moving up and out of her. . . . She wanted his children, wanted to carry a part of him in her, to nourish their baby at her breast, and to know that a fine man had created him just for her. She closed her eyes and hugged herself, rocking in place as the tears dripped down her cheeks.

A heavy warm hand on her shoulder told her that Harry stood beside her. She swung into his arms, burrowing against him and wishing for Sam. "Your son is a stubborn mule," she stated between sobs. "And I am an old-fashioned silly woman."

Harry's hand smoothed her long braid. "He lacks a thing or two when it comes to women."

"He is evil, making me worry for him, and then when I am happy enough, settling for what can be with us, he buys the house . . . such a house . . . for another woman, it is. Not for a plain woman like me, who does not have town ways."

"Well, honey, I'd say you're making him think plenty about his evil ways," Harry murmured.

"I do not want Sam Taggart. He can go find his ideal wife and place her in the house. She will know how to make fine dinners and empty talk and place the right forks around the plates, and water glasses so, and wine glasses so, and—" Emma was horrified when she wailed aloud. "He knows me so well. I have my pride, my honor as a woman, a wife. What wife would not see that her husband is fed and clothed? He knows that I cannot leave him in that big house with no one to see that he eats right, or that his shirts are pressed and the cuffs turned. I am not a woman to be forced into making a life we will both regret."

"Did you ever give him a pair of socks?" Harry asked gently over her head.

Emma sniffed. "He has fine store socks, fine black ones. He would not want my poor socks."

"Wouldn't he? Emma, I'm not saying Sam isn't thick-headed, but have you thought about his pride? It goes down hard on a man when his wife won't live with him."

Emma pushed away from Harry and sat down, pulling up her apron to cry into it. "I am frightened. I am a plain country woman. . . . I cannot forget what was my mother's and her mother's before her. It is the blessings, more than the wealth of the dowry. A part of me wants to live with Sam, to learn new ways and do as he wishes. Yet a part of me knows that I am plain and old-fashioned and that it would be an untruth to try to be other than what I am. I am selfish. I want my husband to have all of me, because I want all of him—his darkness, too."

Harry washed his hands and began to softly knead the abused dough, working in more flour. Emma watched, fascinated while Harry shaped the bread into mounds to rise, oiled the tops, and covered them with a damp cloth. He dipped water from the stove's hot water reservoir and made tea in the pot, placing a cloth around it while it steeped.

"You see, honey," Harry began as he poured tea into two cups, "Sam is a prideful man—always was. He's probably licking his wounds right now, and he's made you mad, hasn't he?"

Emma rummaged through her emotions. "He should not call me Red. I fight my berserker moods, but he pushes me into them."

"I'd say it's a standoff then, you on one side and my boy on the other."

"He wants an ideal wife. He told me so. I am not ideal. I am selfish because I would have everything in this life of ours. I want the old and the new." Emma fought the bitterness in her tone and the tears crawling up, burning, to her lids. "I am frightened that I will shame him."

"You won't shame him." Harry leaned back, watching her closely. "Poor old Sam. He's probably wandering around that big old house, hungry for good food, and his clothes probably have a hole or two by now."

Emma sat straighter. "I will go to town to clean Sam's house. I will not have anyone say that my husband is not well tended. He cannot become ill, for his businesses need him. Will you come with me, to see your son?" Emma asked hopefully. With Harry at her side, Sam would not try to kiss her . . . because if he did, she would melt and be untrue to what was born into her. "The house in town puts you and Sam apart. It shouldn't be."

"Can't come with you," Harry said after sipping his tea. "Got things to do. You're alone in this one, honey."

Emma stared at him. "With Sam I am selfish. I do not trust myself if another woman touches him. I can be . . . not nice. At times I feel like throwing things at him. Especially when he grins and calls me Red. I have never wanted to fly at a man before, and—" Emma flushed and looked away as Harry began to chuckle.

her. The black lettering of *S.T. Beers, Sam Taggart, Proprietor,* was scrawled across the gold label.

Sam sat in the dark kitchen in the drawers that Emma had made him during their happy month at Harry's. The drawers were embroidered with his initials. He smoothed the shirt she had embroidered for him and studied the black businessman's store-bought socks on his feet. He wiggled his toes against Emma's neat patching; he wanted *her* socks. He sniffed the scents in the kitchen; the clean soap smell mingled with scents of the supper she had cooked for him—cabbage rolls and mashed potatoes. Every meal that Emma had cooked in the last week reminded Sam that she wouldn't let go of her heritage—the damn dowry—to be with him. It was as if she were saying that she was a simple country woman not meeting his ideal-wife standards.

Sam placed a doughnut on his third finger, left hand, and remembered his mother's ring on Emma's finger.

They were married, damn it. She should be with him, upstairs in their big bed right now—Mrs. Sam Taggart should be in her husband's arms. When he could manage to sleep, he dreamed of his wife, but his body awakened ripe and ready to an empty bed and pillows in his arms. He dreamed of life and holding a child that Emma would give him.

He'd changed from wanting a cold society wife to wanting Emma and babies. He didn't want his lonely uncluttered life anymore. He wanted what Emma had brought to him—a family and dreams. He considered the thought: with Emma as a mother, his child would have those softer edges and a loving heart.

Sam glanced out into the night and caught a glimpse

of a shadow sliding through the trees. There was something familiar about the man's movements. As Sam sat still, a knife slid quietly along the window, and two big familiar hands shoved it upward.

Harry, dressed in buckskin and fringes, eased through the open window. He stood in the middle of the room, letting his eyes adjust to the dim light. Mary slid in the window behind him.

"Rather late for a stroll, isn't it, Harry?" Sam asked, not removing his feet from the table.

"Well, hell, boy," Harry stated after a moment. He whipped off his beaver hat and plopped into a chair. "You almost scared me spitless. What's this?" he asked, picking up a bottle.

"That's the first of S.T. Beers. Why are you here?"

Mary eased around Harry, looking curiously at the dark shadows of the house. Sam sighed wearily. "Go ahead. Check out the lay of the land," and Mary moved silently into the shadows. "There's a bedroom upstairs. Crawl into bed if you want," he added, thinking that someone should be sleeping in his house, if not him. He hadn't been able to sleep without Emma.

Harry took his time and, at Sam's nod, opened the bottle. He sniffed it appreciatively. He got up to check the food cabinet, covered by a cloth, and extracted a large loaf of round potato bread.

"Try the warming oven. Emma comes every other day and leaves my meals in the stove," Sam suggested. Harry padded over to retrieve warm cabbage rolls, mashed potatoes, corn, and green beans. He dipped them onto a plate and came back to the table. He opened a small covered pot and scooped a dollop of

Emma's new green tomato relish onto his plate. He lit the lamp and began to eat.

"I'm going to bed," Mary called from upstairs. "I never saw anything so fine—all pink and ruffled."

"Make yourself at home, Mary . . . Harry," Sam said dryly, and opened another bottle of the sample beer. He tasted it; Emma was right about the tasty brew.

He was right about a wife living under the same roof as her husband. He hadn't planned for whatever he felt for Emma; he hadn't set out to want and need her as he did now, but he did.

Harry dug into the food. "Emma is wearing herself down to her bones worrying over you."

"Is she?" Sam sat very still.

Harry ate, then pushed back the plate and pulled off his moccasins. He placed his feet on the table with Sam's and sipped the beer. Then he eyed Sam. "You're stubborn, you two, and making a mess of a good thing. She's got her pride, and you got yours. Two knotheads butting against each other and looking like hell. She's scared, Sam. And when a woman is scared, you don't bully her into doing something that scares her."

"I didn't ask you for advice or for her to come here, cleaning for me."

"You wouldn't. Emma is a neat woman, and she can't stand the thought of you living without good care. That's because she's got her pride and because you're her world."

"Am I?" Sam refused to give in to the leap of hope.

"She hurt you by not moving in here—" Harry scanned the elegant kitchen. "But what you've got to know is that she comes from an old line of people—

women and daughters—for generations. As men, we hand down other things, but women are close to their mothers and grandmothers, and that little box of things means a heap to Emma."

"She'd rather have that damn dowry than me, her husband." Sam fought the bitterness in his tone. "I don't need help providing for my wife."

"Nope. That's not it at all. But a woman makes a home and brings with her what makes her a woman. She's scared, and if she had that little box of things with her, she'd feel better."

"You'd know, wouldn't you, Harry?" Sam shot back.

"I would," Harry returned, unbothered by the taunt. He looked into the shadows. "You see, boy, women are peculiar creatures, filled with little bitty soft worries, and it's up to us men to pet and hug and make them feel safe."

He eyed Sam. "You're sitting there in that fancy shirt she embroidered for you, wearing drawers with itty-bitty flowers on them, wearing no righteous pants, and looking at your socks as if you hate them. Now tell me, boy, that you aren't nettled and peculiar. And you won't admit it, but you're hurt inside. You thought she'd just jump for joy when you showed her this house, didn't you? You thought this house would make everything right, didn't you? Well, you've got the house, and it's empty, without a good wife. Emma isn't the kind to be bought."

Sam slammed his empty bottle on the table and opened another one, drinking deeply. "What's your point, Harry?"

"Emma is your wife, so says the paper she looks at in

her room and cries over. She's accepted you as you are, and wants you to accept her the same. But she's scared, too, and wants what's familiar to her, what she grew up with—woman things—"

"Recht isn't ready to listen to reason, or I'd already have that damn box here for her. Ah, hell, Harry—look around, this kitchen has everything brand new. . . . The whole house is grand, and upstairs are Emma's dresses, especially made for her, by the best seamstress in town."

"Emma is a good woman, and it seems to me, boy, that she's done all the running. With her help you've got what you wanted, a nice little empire started. Wouldn't hurt you to bend a bit, would it?"

Sam glared at Harry, who was grinning. "Why don't you just make it easy on all of us— By Jesus, I hate it when Emma puts salt into pies instead of sugar . . . all that flaky crust and looking good and nothing but salt. . . . Emma would walk through fire for you, and you know it. Old man Recht is hopping mad and gave that dowry to Gilbert. Seems Mr. and Mrs. Recht are at odds over that, and their marriage is in trouble. I'd say, to make things easier— Jesus almighty, I hate it when Emma cries—such a woeful little soft cry, as if she doesn't want anyone to know how bad she aches. To make things better, and to take a step to please her, you might soothe Recht's ruffled feathers and get the dowry."

Harry opened another beer and eyed Sam. "By the way, did I tell you that Gilbert has planted himself not far from the Big T, up in that old trapper's cabin on the north quarter mountains? He's let Emma know at every chance that her father gave him the dowry. Rode down on his mule and told her himself. Emma won't go back on what her father had done, or let me get it for her. It's up to you to get it for her."

"Did she send you?" Sam hoped that Emma was softening and that she'd sent Harry as a peacemaker.

Harry looked straight at Sam. "No, she didn't send me. After you went loco about that brooch, she was afraid you'd get hurt recovering that dowry, so she didn't tell you that Recht gave it to Gilbert. I came because I care about you, boy, and I want you to be happy. Because back when your ma died, I was ashamed of what I did—of taking you with me. I was ashamed every time I looked at you, and then there was the other . . . the way you reminded me of your ma."

Harry swallowed deeply, his eyes dimming with tears. "I should have told you then how much I loved you and that a man grieving for his wife can sometimes go sour. I should have said the words, but they just dried on my tongue and I couldn't. Every day it got deeper, you looking at me, all gangly and hollow-eyed, waiting. . . . I flat didn't know how to do the things Feather did, the holding and kissing and saying words. But here they are, and they are true from my heart. . . . I've always loved you, boy. You're the best part of me. Emma has made a change in you, in all of us, for the best."

When Deer Lodge City began to stir to life the next morning, and the convict wagon rolled out of town with the chain gangs, Sam paused to listen to Harry snore in the other bedroom with Mary curled beside him. Then

Sam eased quietly from the house; he saddled Kloshe and headed toward Gilbert's cabin.

Harry was right. Sam had had enough of the dowry. He would get it for Emma, and he would try to please Joseph Recht, and then he would court Emma as she should have been.

Emma urged Woden over the crest of the foothill on her way to Gilbert's shack. She had packed his favorite lunchtime favorite, *hasenpfeffer* rabbit and apple dumplings with extra syrup. The midday meal of Gilbert's favorites would put him in a better mood to listen.

Her father had been angry when he'd given Gilbert the dowry. Gilbert had come to the Big T to taunt her, carrying the small box in his hands. He could sell it off, all her grandmother's things, and then it would be lost. Emma had to retrieve it.

As she came out of the woods, she saw the shack and two men pounding at each other in front of it. One was heavily built without a neck; that was Gilbert. The other was lean and quicker—Sam! She kicked Woden, and the pony hurried down the slight incline to the old cabin.

Beer bottles were lined up from one side of the house to the other. She dismounted, hurrying to the fight, and noted that while they were standing—and Sam's fine business clothing was dirty and torn—they were drunk, the blows missing each other. From the blood on their faces, with swelling eyes and lips, she realized they had once fought in earnest.

Emma hurried between them, only to be shoved away by Sam as though she were a gnat. "Sam! Gilbert! Stop this now!"

The grunts and swearing and dust flying around the men didn't stop Emma from hurrying back. Gilbert placed his hand over his nose. "Go away, nose-hair puller!"

"Mrs. Taggart, remove yourself from the premises," Sam ordered in his high-handed dramatic way. "I have come to retrieve your dowry, and I will not have you interfere. Do not harm this fine gentleman, as he is only testing the waters, so to speak—"

"Sam Taggart! You are—"

"Yes—" His hand flung out grandly. "I have partaken of libations, madam, the quality of which brew has no match—the S.T. Beers, now available in bottles or kegs. This good gentleman"—he hooked a friendly arm around Gilbert's shoulders and Gilbert returned the gesture—"this gentleman is accommodating and thinks that the quality is quite fine."

"Make her go away, Sam Taggart, and I will talk about the dowry," Gilbert managed around his swollen lip.

"Sam Taggart is not a fighter," Emma began, then remembered instantly how he had dealt with Otis's gang. She amended her statement. "He is too much of a gentleman to fight, unless provoked."

"That is why, my dear wife, this fine gentleman has obliged me in a drinking contest. First we raced, and then we boxed a bit." Smelling of his "libations," Sam leered down at her. "She's mad, Gilbert, old friend of mine. I call her Red when she gets that steamy look. Isn't she pretty as the dew on the daisies?"

"Shame—" Emma began just as Sam swung Gilbert away and the men sat down to another beer, ignoring her.

Sam propped his boots up on a stump and leaned back against the cabin. "Now this dowry thing is an important matter to Red. I can offer a lifetime supply of S.T. Beers, plus an amount of coin and—"

Emma hurried to dab a damp cloth on Sam's split lip. He nodded and gave her his comb. She parted his hair as he expected. He blew her a kiss, then as an afterthought grabbed her hand and placed another kiss in her palm. He folded her hand carefully over the kiss. "Go away, sweet Emma."

She placed her hands on her hips. "You will fight no more?"

Sam nodded and waved her away. "So say I."

Men, Emma thought darkly, and began to clean the porch around them, listening intently to them as she worked.

"Now, Gilbert, my friend, just what do you need to replace the dowry?" Sam began in a slurred business tone.

"I cannot work for Joseph Recht now. I did not like farm work anyway. . . . I am a carpenter."

"Aha!" Sam said. He looked at Emma over his shoulder and winked. "We are making progress. Soon you will have your dowry, and the world will be aright once more."

She glared at him. "Sam, I think you have seen too many plays. But . . . I think Gilbert would be an excellent partner, building the small houses to be shipped— the ones that Arnie planned. Gilbert is also a good furniture maker." While she was angry with Sam, she still cared about building his business.

Sam explained the plan of houses already built and

ready to be erected to Gilbert, who nodded. "I would like to be your partner in the houses. I build fine rocking chairs and dinner tables for big families. I am lucky to escape Emma. I will find myself a good woman and not one who is always taking chances and fighting with me. I am sorry you are unlucky, Sam Taggart, so as to have this berserker as a wife. I will get the dowry for you."

My dowry is on the mantel in Harry's house. Sam, my husband, is acting like a stage hero, or a knight on a mission. He is going to my father's without me to make things "aright." I tried not to laugh at how grandly he spoke, because his heart is good and apparently the quality of S.T. Beers is also good. E.

Sam lay by the cold running stream and placed his abused face in the water. It was only dusk, but he felt as though he had lived a hard week. After tidying Gilbert and himself, Emma had her dowry, and after much persuasion she was headed to the Big T. After he made peace with Joseph Recht, Sam intended to ask her to return to the Deer Lodge house—with her dowry.

He flopped back in the grass and let the cold October night wind circle him. S.T. Beers were potent and reliable, he thought, latching his arm around his saddle and drawing it close to him as he would have liked to hold Emma. He awoke at dawn and found that he had just kissed the saddle horn.

In two hours, after properly shaving and changing clothes, Sam sat across the Recht breakfast table from Joseph. Clearly the Rechts' long marriage was in trou-

ble, because Magda had refused to cook. She did make
a pot of coffee for Sam and kissed his forehead, patting
his arm. "I like you for a son," she said simply, and went
back to her room.

Joseph poured coffee into his empty cup and glared at
Sam's full one, poured by Magda. "Soon you will have
my whole family. I don't know why."

Sam inhaled and placed an elegant gilt scrolled box
on the table between them. He opened it and held out a
curved and carved thick pipe to Joseph. "I wish to ask
your permission to marry your daughter," he stated
carefully.

Joseph snorted, though he took the pipe and cherished it with his hands, setting aside his clay pipe. "The
cart comes too late. The horse is gone."

"Your blessing is important to Emma. I'm asking that
you put aside your anger toward me and let our marriage begin."

Magda hurried into the room, her eyes bright with
tears. She kissed Sam's head again and hugged him.
"We could have a wedding festival and invite all the
neighbors—"

She frowned at Joseph, who was now puffing the pipe
and squinting through the smoke at Sam. Then she hit
Joseph on top of the head with a potholder and hurried
back to her room.

Sam inhaled and continued his peacemaking. "I'll
tend your business as I would tend my own. I will honor
your name. If you need a good bull, I will find one. If
you need help, I will help," Sam offered, surprising himself.

"I know you will keep the little berserker safe. You are a strong, good man though you have much to learn— Magda doesn't like me," Joseph muttered.

"She's upset," Sam offered, surprised that he would counsel the older man. "Her children are gone."

Joseph took a long time putting more tobacco in the pipe and lighting it. He puffed it slowly, his expression thoughtful. "I could not bear to look at Fritzi, this boy who risked his life in the barn fire, to save our stock. I could not bear to think of his screams and how I should have stopped him, but then . . . I was too worried about the stock and was trying to save them, too. Then the rafters fell, trapping Fritzi. I did not want him to work or to worry after that."

"He's got a good mind, and his body is getting stronger every day. He's getting treatment." Sam thought of what Harry had said about the guilt of the father for harm to the son.

Joseph nodded. "I didn't know how to tell him how badly I felt in my heart." He glanced at Magda's closed bedroom door. "She loves you already, like a son. What can I do?"

Sam fought running out the door. He'd come from a solitary life into a complex family situation. But Emma wanted peace in her family, and he respected that. "Women are peculiar creatures," he began in a knowing tone.

"Emma knows how to make things right," Joseph stated.

"We'll have to learn more about making them happy," Sam stated. "Let me tell you what I think—"

Six days ago my dear husband made peace with my father and arranged our wedding in the old ways. The dowry is safe and in our room. I have all I need, a wonderful husband who knows that what I believe is important. We are staying at the Big T now, together. I have been too busy to write and too happy, for Sam seems so pleased with himself, so happy. Monty has been gone too long, and my dear husband went into the mountains after him, for the wedding. Sam was only gone one day, and Otis sent a note by pigeon. Now Otis has Monty and Sam. Otis wanted me to bring him all of Harry's money and Sam's and any deeds. He sent a map with directions up to a cabin in the mountains. I will have my husband back in my arms and safe. I fear for him, this man of my heart, and I prepare to go to him with the ransom. If Sam is hurt, I will not be nice to Otis. E.

Chapter Twenty-one

"*G*ive him water," Sam rasped, his throat dry. Tied to the outside of the cabin five miles up into the torturous moutain path behind the Big T, his arms lashed above him with rawhide thongs, Sam ached from Otis's fists. After shooting Monty in the leg and using him as a shield, Otis had taken Sam captive easily. Worn by lack of food and care, and with a bullet festering in his leg, Monty barely clung to life.

Otis glanced at Monty, who lay on the dirty pallet on the trapper's porch. "It would be a waste of good water. He's almost dead anyway and out of his misery."

"There's a lake full of water just yards from here," Sam stated, realizing that after two days of Otis's treatment, his own strength was failing. The middle of October lay on the mountains, cold at nights, and Monty had only a dirty blanket to keep him alive. At midday, the mountain wind was cold, the wind whipping leaves against Sam and tumbling over Monty, who shivered violently and groaned.

Otis picked his teeth with a dirty fingernail. "Yeah, there's a lake there, okay. And a whole lot of water is going down the Dancing Miranda when I blow that beaver dam. There could be enough water to jump that ridge behind Harry's place and wash out the house, maybe kill a few folks who should have been nicer to old Otis. Meanwhile, that lake will make a nice place to send you and the old man . . . down to the fishes. When I set the blast, I'll send you home in pieces."

Sam prayed Emma would not come, that Harry would stop her. He sank into unconsciousness, hanging by his wrists until a cold wash of water hit his face. Otis tossed the bucket aside. "I like you clean, nice, and wet. You're not so frisky now, are you? All it took was a shot in the old man's leg to stop you getting ideas."

Sam pushed his head up. "Give him water and something to eat."

Otis looked down into the ravine leading up to the cabin. "Well, howdy. We've got visitors, half-blood. A pretty little thing in a brown dress standing just where I told her to stand. Mmm, and she's got her sister with her, too. Mrs. Sam Taggart has a satchel held tight to her, probably the deeds and the money. I want you to watch this, half-blood, what I do to your woman and that juicy blonde when they fight me."

Sam strained at his bonds, aware that one of them was loosening, stretching with the blood at his wrists. He needed time, and he needed to distract Otis. "You've already made arrangements to sell my property, and you'll have money. Let them go. I'll make regular payments—"

Otis stuffed a rag into Sam's mouth and whipped another around his head to hold it in place. Sam, frantic to protect Emma, pushed away from the log wall and lifted his tied legs high, kicking and sending Otis sprawling backward.

Otis struggled to his feet, his expression filled with rage. "You hadn't ought to do that to your betters, half-blood." His revolver butt slammed down on Sam's head—

Sam forced himself back to consciousness. Otis's back was to Sam as he watched the women picking their way up the rocky incline to him. With Otis nearby, Sam couldn't afford to jerk free of the loosened bond. Otis was fast enough with a gun to kill Monty—and Emma and Greta.

An owl hooted, too early in the day, and Sam allowed himself to take a long slow breath. Otis seemed unaware of the noises around him— Tethered to a tree, his hide red from the whipping Otis had given him, Tenkiller had been moving restlessly and nickering steadily. Horse hooves, not wind, broke the branches behind the cabin in the forest. The day turned dark, cloudy, and the wind began to hurl the waves against the rocky shore, only yards from the cabin.

Otis put the barrel of his revolver against Sam's head, nudging him roughly for the women to see. Emma's eyes filled with tears, her face white as she hugged Sam's satchel to her. Greta looked bored, holding her skirt away from Otis's trash as she passed it.

With his eyes, Sam tried to tell Emma that he loved her, because he expected Otis to shoot at any heartbeat. It would be the man's style, killing the husband in front of the woman.

Sam loved her. He'd come through pain and a war and thought there was nothing for him but a cold, powerful, and rich empire. He was wrong—there was Emma . . . light and happy and filling his heart. She'd shown him that he had a heart, and he'd already given it to her from the first moment—he'd been fighting what he knew was real . . . that Emma was his love, his life, his sunshine, and his reason for living . . . or for dying. He promised to keep that thought close to him as he died, because in one more jerk of the rawhide, he would protect her.

Glancing at Sam's struggles, Emma straightened and held out the satchel to Otis. Otis grabbed it and jerked it open to peer inside. "Good, you knew that old Otis meant what he said."

He jerked out the sack of Emma's money and another sack, opening it. "That is my dowry. The jewelry alone is a treasure, and the old coins are another treasure," Emma stated quietly.

She looked at Sam, her dark hazel eyes soft with tears. "My husband is my treasure. He means more to me than anything else. I would have him safe. You are welcome to take everything, but please—please don't hurt my husband anymore. I know that you want me, and I will go with you, but you will not hurt him again."

She fell to her knees and held her joined hands up, begging Otis, who laughed evilly and pointed his revolver at Sam. Greta still looked bored, studying her nails. Then Otis pushed Emma away and stepped onto the porch, where Monty lay. "This one first."

Everything happened at once, as quick as the rustle of dried leaves in the wash of the October wind.

"I did not say that I came alone," Emma stated too quietly, her eyes locked with Sam's as she stood, drawing a Colt revolver from her apron. She pointed it at Otis. "I am an excellent shot, though I do not like guns. Harry has taught me. Do not test me. For I would rather die than let you harm my family, any of them."

Dressed in black from head to toe, Shen-Yu slid around the house like a shadow, flattening to it. A chop of his hand sent Otis into the cabin, then Shen-Yu sliced the thongs at Sam's wrist. Many Horses slid his arms around Sam, because he was weakened and his legs had failed him, and dragged him from the cabin. Harry bent to pull Monty's pallet from the porch and a safe distance away.

Joseph knelt to tend Monty, giving him water. Shen-Yu hurried to open his case of ointments and herbs and began to tend Monty's wounded leg.

Sam jerked the gag from his mouth and reached for his whip, discarded by Otis after beating Tenkiller. "Get back, Emma. Now!"

Otis crashed open the cabin door, firing his gun. Sam flicked the whip, and before he could put his weight into it, curling the tip around Otis's wrist, the cabin began to shake and move and slide over the muddy earth toward the lake. Otis grabbed a porch post, unable to leap aside because he would be ground beneath the cabin.

Sam slowly, methodically-coiled the whip and tossed it aside. He glanced at Tex, dressed in his woolly chaps, leveling both his pearl-handled revolvers at Otis. From his deadly expression, Sam knew that Tex would fire at Otis if needed.

Sam grasped Emma's upper arm, holding her. He

wasn't certain what she would do, once she was set on revenge. Emma shook him off and started marching toward the cabin, her petticoats flashing beneath her skirts.

"Emma! Return to the embrace of your husband! Your place is at his side!" Sam heard himself command imperially in the theatrical manner that only Emma could drag out of him.

She stopped in midstride, turned, and stared at him blankly.

He looked at her, his wife, standing there in her plain brown dress, her glorious hair covered by the brown bonnet, with her practical boots and black plain coat.

She was everything he wanted, his wife, his heart.

Four mules, backing against the cabin and guided by Fritzi on one side and Gilbert on the other, continued pushing it, and with a solid splash the cabin floated out into the lake. With a horrified expression, Otis grabbed onto the porch and crawled up on top of the cabin as it slowly sank to roof level.

Emma hurled herself at Sam, holding and kissing him, and Sam held her as he fell into a cushion of brush, breaking the fall and kissing her desperately at the same time. She pushed free of him, ran for the water bucket on a stump, and hurried back as he struggled out of the bushes.

Sam grinned, feeling light-headed as Emma soothed and worried and kissed him and shamed Otis into the next century. "Oh, my poor Sam, my poor husband."

Sam inhaled her scent happily.

Many Horses grinned, and Harry's eyes misted as Emma nestled in Sam's arms. He wallowed in the feel of her, crooning and rocking him and kissing him and daintily giving him water from the dipper. She dabbed her handkerchief, edged in delicate tatting, into water and gently cleaned his face. The mixture was sweeter than honey to Sam, who got light-headed again and wondered if he was dreaming.

He locked his hands on the indentation of her waist to keep himself from floating into heaven.

Emma held Sam's face in her hands and kissed him, tears streaming down her cheeks. "You mean more to me than gold, more to me than the blessings of my father and the dowry of my grandmother. You are my life, my heart, my love . . . my husband."

He gathered Emma to him, then instantly pushed her away. "I'm dirty."

"Oh, my poor husband," she cried, launching herself against him, locking her arms around his neck and beginning a new flurry of kisses. "I will take you home and tend you until you are healthy and magnificent and beautiful. I will make you doughnuts and bread and cook soups for you and—"

Emma stopped talking and leveled a hot steamy look at Sam that told him other ways she would care for him.

Sam grinned and wondered if his feet had left the ground.

Greta's yell brought him back to the present. "You throw that satchel back here right now, Otis Murdock! I will not have good money sink to the bottom of the lake."

"I can't let go to throw the satchel—I'll slide off the roof. I can't swim!" Otis clung to the rock chimney and let go of it when a piece topped into the lake. He crawled along the rooftop, clinging by his fingertips.

"You diabolical worthless little eel. Throw that money to shore. I will not have it wasted," Greta yelled, stripping off her petticoats. When she began to unbutton her dress, Harry handed her his big shirt. "Thank you, Harry. You are always a gentleman."

"We should help her," Tex stated.

Emma smiled. "Do not help her. Greta has always liked moments like this, when she is left the responsibility. Watch. When she has her mind set, nothing can stop her."

"Just like my mama," Tex murmured, though he was looking at Greta's long legs.

Recognizing the stubborn similarity between the sisters, Sam bent to kiss Emma's cheek.

Fritzi moved close to Sam. He stood straighter, his body stronger. "My pigeons brought everyone together. I think we could make money raising them. What do you think?"

Sam reached out to shake his hand. "It's a deal. You're a good businessman, Fritzi."

Joseph came to stand beside his son. He rocked back and forth on his heels, his hands behind his back. Then in an awkward motion he thrust out his arm and placed it around Fritzi's shoulders. "You are a man of strength and honor. You have saved Sam and Monty and therefore, all who love them. Come home. I need my son. Your mother misses you. I will hug her, too."

Disbelieving, Fritzi stared at Joseph. "I like to race trotters," he said warily. "Harry and Sam are developing a racetrack and stables, and I am learning to train trotters."

"Yah. So do I like racing. Maybe we should give Sam and Harry competition, eh? You can work at the stables and the track, and then you can see that Recht horses make a good showing . . . though I expect you are already a businessman with Sam and too busy to be my partner, yah?"

Fritzi straightened. He carefully placed his arm around Joseph, and the two men stood there, side by side, looking at Greta by the lake. "Yah," he said softly. "I think we can work something out. The first thing we need to do is get a Recht mare in the pasture with Tenkiller."

"Otis, you miserable little worm," Greta muttered, gingerly picking her way across the rocky shoreline to the lake. She sat on a rock and began to unhook her good shoes.

"I'll drown . . . I know I will." Flattened on the sinking roof, Otis clung to it by his fingertips.

"Nonsense. I don't know how to swim either, other than the few times Emma pushed me in the lake, but cold water or not, I am coming after that satchel, Otis Murdock." Then dressed only in Harry's shirt, her camisole, and long drawers, Greta leaped into the lake and began swimming toward the cabin. Tex sighed dreamily.

"That is a good woman. She is moving too fast to notice the cold water," Many Horses murmured appreciatively as Greta splashed and kicked and made her way to where Otis had left the satchel on the sinking porch roof.

Greta retrieved it and checked to see that the latch

was locked. Holding it high in one hand, she made her way back to shore. Harry wrapped a blanket around her, and while Fritzi and Joseph held a blanket high, Greta began to strip. Emma hurried to help her change into Shen-Yu's clean clothes. Greta emerged, dressed in a tight black garment that clung to her long legs; she swung the blanket around her like a cape. She wrapped her long wet hair in a turban and secured it with a brooch. "Someone pick up my dress. There is a fortune sewn in the hem—just in case Emma didn't have enough money to distract Otis, I wanted to help. . . . Sam isn't too bad, once you get to know him. I may need him for a contact if—" She glanced warily at Tex and announced, "I want to go home now."

Then she paused and leveled a menacing look at her family, Sam, Harry, Monty—who was now sitting up— and Shen-Yu. "I will scalp the person who mentions this to anyone. I fear that I share berserker tendencies with my sister."

Emma laughed outright. "I know. Now it is good that you know, too."

"I suppose we'll have to rescue Otis," Harry murmured thoughtfully.

"No, he hurt my poor Sam," Emma stated hotly. Then after Sam leaned close and rocked her, assuring her, Emma ducked her head. "I have always been a little berserker. Yes, the man should live and go to jail."

Gilbert and Fritzi lined up the mules, and Harry threw the lasso, catching on the chimney stub. They hauled the house back to shore, and Otis scampered from the roof to kiss solid earth. A man with a purpose,

Fritzi made his way to Otis, drew the revolver from his belt, and waited while Gilbert tied the criminal's wrists.

"So there, I think that turned out nicely," Emma murmured, her arms tight around Sam, and then she fainted.

While Sam caught her in his arms and eased gently down to sit with her, Emma struggled to consciousness, her eyelashes fluttering. Sam knew that instant, that if Emma died, his life would be empty.

She placed her hand on his cheek, smoothing his beard, her eyes soft upon him. "I love you, my husband," and then she fainted again.

"Poor little nubbin," Monty murmured.

"Oh, good grief. Do I have to do everything?" Greta demanded. "She hasn't slept one wink, worrying about Sam. She's almost driven the rest of us into insanity. You are her Alamo, Sam, and she was relentless in the details, planning how to save you. I knew that none of us would have a moment's peace until she had you back."

Greta dampened a cloth to dab on Emma's face. "Sam loves you, too, Emma. So I guess we'll have to keep him," she stated in a bored tone. "Kiss her, Sam . . . tell her you love her and all that mush—and then she'll say the same, and then we can go home, and I can wash my hair."

Sam began to grin. "If you say so, Greta." He looked down at Emma, resting in his arms, her hand stroking his face. He tested the words in his mind and in his heart, and then he slowly formed them on his lips. "I love you, Mrs. Taggart."

* * *

"I love you, my dearest husband." Emma wasn't certain how Sam would react to the baby she was carrying. Lilly had noted her retching every morning, and once Emma traced her rhythms, she knew that Sam's baby nestled within her.

Would Sam want a child? He had once been certain that he never wanted to pass on his legacy. She touched Sam's cheek and whispered, "Harry loves you, Sam. It is time to make peace. Will you do that now, my husband?"

The mountain's chill crept within Emma's heart. Sam's expression had hardened, both men looking equally grim. She stroked Sam's abused cheek and kissed the wounds. "Tell him that you care and that you know he cares for you."

Sam looked warily at her, and she saw the uncertain boy, hurt so long ago. "Make peace with your father, my husband."

Sam inhaled, and Emma feared he would turn away from Harry. But instead he faced his father, both men equally tall. "It's time we finished this fandango, Harry," Sam stated firmly.

"I was wrong," Harry returned just as firmly.

Emma placed her hand on each man's arm, looking up at them. They were her loved ones, and she knew how difficult the past was, tearing at them. She allowed the tears to flow down her cheeks, because she wanted the moment so badly.

Each man was taut, unmoving.

Then Sam shot out his hand in a formal handshake.

Emma held her breath as Harry's eyes misted. Sam, her wonderful husband, was willing to try—

Harry's hand met Sam's open one, and the two men stood unmoving, tears flowing freely down Harry's cheeks. He nodded curtly, then eased out a hand to lay it upon Sam's broad shoulder. Sam stood rigidly, and Emma watched his head go up with pride, the hard swallow of emotion and the vein throbbing in his forehead.

Then in an awkward motion Harry leaned forward and hugged Sam quickly before he stepped back. Sam slowly smiled, his arm sliding around Emma. "She's pregnant," he told Harry. "You're going to be a grandfather."

"That's good," Harry said unevenly. "You'll let me see the tyke now and then?"

"Hell, yes. We're counting on you to baby-sit while Emma and I travel—not that much, and only when we have to see to business. If Emma wants, we're building a new house, close to the Big T. I'll get a clerk to stay at the office in town, and we'll use pigeons to do business. How does that sound?"

Then Sam looped his arm around Emma and took the damp handkerchief from her hand. He dabbed her eyes and kissed her lids. "I want our baby. I want to hold him and tell him how I feel about his mother and about him. I will do my best as a husband and a father, and Emma . . . I love my wife and everything about her. You are my ideal wife, my heart and my breath, and the woman of my dreams. I think of you each morning before I awake and every moment of the day, and I will cherish you all the days of my life. I will hold your hopes and dreams as my own, and I will keep close the treasure of your dowry for our child . . . our children," he corrected as she hurled herself into his arms.

After a long, promising, and satisfying kiss, Sam placed his wife aside. "There is more, my little berserker, but I think that can wait for the privacy of our bedroom."

Sam moved to Joseph and held out his hand. Joseph lifted his head high, looked at Emma, and reached to pull Sam into a big bear hug. He kissed Sam on both cheeks and stepped back.

Struggling with his emotion and the bear hug, Sam looked at Fritzi. The boy looked embarrassed and Sam winked at Emma, then said to Fritzi, "You might as well get used to this. Emma likes hugs and kisses."

Then Sam hugged Fritzi, and with the astonished boy in his arms, Sam kissed Fritzi on both cheeks.

Emma clasped her hands to her chest. This was her husband, the father of her baby, the heartbeat of her body . . . Sam Taggart, a man of new times and keeping the old close and unforgotten.

"I am courting your mother, Emma and Greta and Fritzi," Joseph announced grandly. "So say I."

Tex accepted Sam's handshake, and Greta crossed her arms when Sam moved to her. He bent to kiss her cheek, and she glared up at him. "Thank you for telling Emma that I love her, Greta," Sam stated formally.

Gilbert began bawling. He rushed up to Sam and grabbed him in his arms, lifting him above the ground. Sam looked at Emma and then at the sky as if wishing the moment were over. "And you, Gilbert. You are a good man and my friend," he stated.

"Yah!" Gilbert buried his face in Sam's neck, and Sam stepped firmly away.

Sam looked at Emma as if asking her help. She understood instantly—he had made his amends, but Gilbert's emotions were too much. She moved between the men, her arms around Sam. Many Horses smiled at them and dodged Gilbert's hug.

Sam swung her up in his arms. His whisper was sincere. "Thank you."

"Hey!" Monty called. "My leg hurts. Let's all go home."

Emma placed her hand on Sam's chest, stilling him. "I am happy to have your child within me, Sam Taggart, husband," she murmured, snuggling close to him. "But how did you know?"

"I'll tell you when we're alone, sweetheart. You have made me an extremely happy man."

Emma smiled and nuzzled his throat. "So there. I think that turned out nicely," she murmured, and they all began to laugh.

"I love you, Mrs. Taggart," Sam murmured one week later as they rested from the night's lovemaking. He kissed her soft fragrant breast and managed to lift his head from it to look down at her. He was reluctant to leave the warmth of her body, their limbs intertwined.

In their new soon-to-be-sold home, in the lush soft warm nest of their mussed featherbed, Emma stirred luxuriously and smoothed his cheek with her hand. "Husband, I am so glad you are safe. I was so foolish as to place the dowry above—"

His fingertip sealed her well-kissed lips. "No, that was

not foolish. The foolish part came when you did not trust me to escape Otis and when you endangered yourself."

Emma frowned and stirred restlessly, and Sam eased from her body. He drew her close and safe and listened to the late October winds outside their bedroom. Next week they would be married according to the Rechts' custom, and for the moment the rest of the gang was happy.

Emma's dowry sat beneath a doily on the new house's mantel, and she was in his arms. Sam drew her closer and sat up, allowing her to kiss the tiny bite marks she'd placed on his shoulders. He treasured each of those marks and the tiny scratches. Someday, when they were sitting side by side in rockers, he'd remind her gently of her fever for him—just to watch her blush.

"Mmm, Sam Taggart . . . husband." Emma nuzzled his neck and eased over to straddle him as he sat up.

Sam adjusted the hand-stitched quilt of her grandmother's around Emma's hips and back and looked down to appreciate her full breasts pressed against his chest. He tried to concentrate on getting control of his wife's berserking, especially when it led to dangerous situations. "We're going to talk about this. You cannot distract me, Emma. You could have gotten hurt in that raid, and you should have trusted me to escape," he repeated, the words coming out in a groan as she began trailing light kisses downward.

Emma surged upward suddenly, bumping his chin with her head. She immediately hurried to kiss it. She resettled, straddling him, this time capturing him fully.

Sam just had time to enjoy her sensual expression, her

hazel eyes softening, darkening, and then he reveled in the tight, warm, moist clasp of her body; his hands found her hips, capturing them as she gently undulated on his lap. "I am glad you are safe, Sam Taggart," she whispered, smoothing his hair. "I am sorry I hurt your pride. But you were so masterful. 'Emma,' you said in your round elegant tones, 'return to your husband. You belong at his side'."

Sam suspected that his tendency to be theatrical might be exposed more times in the years ahead with Emma. "You terrify me sometimes, Emma. There you were begging for my life. . . . Do you have any idea what Otis would have done to you—or Greta?"

She ran the tip of her tongue across his bottom lip. "I knew that you were loosening your bonds, ready to spring at Otis. You would have protected me, I knew. But Greta does so enjoy being put upon. Could we not move to the business of the hour?"

She made a purr in the back of her throat that caught him unaware. She pressed down with her hips, capturing him fully, and Sam watched as she circled her hips, concentrating on her pleasure. "I never lingered in love-making with any woman, Emma—"

Her eyes flew open. "This is not the standard fare? To keep warm in bed and play in the night? To make love in each and every room and on any surface?"

"It was not my regular menu, until marrying you." Sam locked his hands in her magnificent tumbled mane and brought her mouth to his. "Because this means more . . . because you are the other part of my heart and my body, because you are my life."

Epilogue

*S*am did not mind wearing the lederhosen and the matching suspenders, because Emma's fine socks were pulled high on his legs. He studied the happy little house she had embroidered on the socks, her trademark.

Only two hours ago she'd been a beautiful bride, standing with him on the knoll where the women were buried. They'd taken their vows with the November wind tugging at Emma's festival dress and chilling Sam's bare legs.

They hadn't needed flowers; beneath her heavy coat Emma's dress was richly embroidered to match his shirt, a gift from Magda and Greta. The ribbons tied to Emma's coronet of braids had lifted in the wind. Love swirled over the sunlit knoll, and Sam felt the beginning of his new life surge in him as he took his wife's hand. Together they would make a new life, a blend of the old and the new, soothing the hearts of all they loved.

Harry had stood beside Sam, proud and tall, the emotions storming his gray eyes making them warm.

Emma. His wife, his heart his love . . .

In the barn, a shelter from the cold wind, Sam watched her work with her mother and the other women to clean off the table before the festival. He talked with the men and then gave Mary a package, a gift from her brother. He told her to go to her room before she opened it.

Mary stepped out onto the front porch, dressed in a red satin jockey's outfit. She braced her legs apart, her hands on her hips and grinned at Sam. "Pants," she said. "You're not an old-fashioned geezer after all, Sam. You don't mind a woman entering the horse-racing business, do you?"

"I'm counting on you," Sam returned, lifting his bottle of S.T. Beer in a toast to his little sister. "What about you, Dad?"

Harry sputtered for a moment, surprised by the name. He glanced at Mary once, then took a long look. Lilly moved to his side, holding his hand as he said, "Jesus. Mary will be grown and gone before you know it."

Mary pivoted prettily in her sleek red outfit with pants. "Nah. I like it here too much, since Emma's made us all a family. Sam isn't so bad."

Monty began to weep openly, and Magda handed him a package, which he opened to reveal a lacy handkerchief. "It is time you found a woman," she whispered, and beamed at Joseph. "Treat her well, as my Joseph does."

Joseph lifted the long fluegelhorn to his lips and blew, the eerie sound signaling the beginning of the festival.

Sam frowned, looking for his wife. He'd begun to have that wary sensation at the back of his neck—the one that told him Emma was about to—

She appeared with Greta, standing in the center of the open barn door. Both women wore festival shirts, suspenders, and lederhosen. Greta wore shoes, while Emma wore the moccasins that Many Horses had given her.

Joseph picked up a clarinet and began playing a lively folk tune. The sisters placed their arms around each other, and with ribbons flying from their hair, they began to dance to the center of the festival, with Magda and Fritzi clapping their hands.

Her head high and her smile beaming at Sam, Emma bobbed and dipped in rhythm with Greta, who was obviously not pleased to be included in the dance—until she began to enjoy it.

The sisters twirled around and around, one arm around each other's waist and the other lifted high.

Each time she turned, Emma found Sam, her face lighting with pleasure.

He scowled back at her. "She's carrying my child and out there dancing as if—"

Harry shook his head and placed his hand on Sam's shoulder. He took a swig of S.T. Beer and grinned. "If the baby is a girl, I'd say you'd better get used to surprises and wild women."

Sam considered the thought and began to laugh. He handed Harry his beer and walked to the women, stepping between them. They showed him the steps, and he bent to kiss Emma at every dip. Then they all moved together, lifting their feet and bobbing with the music.

Magda came to join them, then Fritzi, then Lilly and Harry. He looped an arm around Many Horses, dragging him into the dance. They all danced away from Gilbert, who had been eating onions steadily and now had a big one in his hand, munching on it as he followed them.

"I'm giving up my sock business because now I know that I can be successful as a businesswoman, and you will be my business now," Emma announced as they danced. "Greta says that Tex is slow and that she wants to stimulate his interest in her by meeting other bachelors. But I will always see that you have my socks to wear, husband."

When the dances were finished, Sam lifted Emma high in his arms, laughed, and kissed her stomach. "So there, I think that turned out nicely," he said, grinning at her.

May swept across the three women's little sunlit knoll, the Big T's fields stirring to life after the hard winter.

Sam and Emma had stayed with Harry during the winter, but now the new house a short distance away from Harry's old one was almost finished.

After being summoned, Harry entered his son's bedroom to find Emma glowing, sitting up in bed after the short hard labor. Sam sat beside her, holding her hand. With a sob, Magda hurried out of the room, closing the door behind her.

Emma motioned Harry to come closer, to sit in the chair beside her. "Sam?"

Sam carefully, painstakingly eased the new baby girl from Emma's arms. Wrapped in an embroidered soft blanket, the black hair of the baby was thick and damp and wild. Sam held the baby, wondering at the miracle of her birth, at her perfect features, and at the way her tiny hand grasped his finger. Unable to speak, he looked at Emma. Her eyes were tired but filled with love. She nodded, and Sam eased the baby into Harry's arms. Sam watched his father's expression fill with pleasure as the baby settled close to him to sleep.

"So there. I think that turned out nicely," Emma whispered as Sam bent to kiss her.

He told her with his eyes, because he could not speak . . . he told her of his love that would grow each day.

She touched his tears with her fingertips, drawing him near to kiss him. "So it shall be, my husband. I love you."

I am happy. Every day with my beloved husband is better than the last. He is still the only person who can bring out the berserker in me. He laughs then, and I see that the quilt of our lives is a beautiful pattern and complete. E.